THE MUSIC OF THE SPHERES

The Music of the Spheres

Elizabeth Redfern

*It matters little whether the disasters
which have arisen are to be ascribed to
the weaknesses of Generals, the intrigues
of camps or the jealousies of Cabinets: the
fact is that they exist, and that we must
anew commence the salvation of Europe.*

William Pitt, 1795

CENTURY · LONDON

Published by Century in 2001

1 3 5 7 9 10 8 6 4 2

First published in the United Kingdom in 2001 by Century
The Random House Group Ltd
20 Vauxhall Bridge Road, London SW1V 2SA

Random House Australia (Pty) Limited
20 Alfred Street, Milsons Point, Sydney
New South Wales 2061, Australia

Random House New Zealand Limited
18 Poland Road, Glenfield
Auckland 10, New Zealand

Random House (Pty) Limited
Endulini, 5a Jubilee Road, Parktown 2193, South Africa

The Random House Group Ltd Reg. No. 954009

www.randomhouse.co.uk

A CIP catalogue record for this book is available
from the British Library

Papers used by Random House are natural, recyclable
products made from wood grown in sustainable forests.
The manufacturing processes conform to the environmental
regulations of the country of origin

ISBN 0 7126 84301
(Airport) 0 7126 74918

Typeset in Caslon by Palimpsest Book Production Limited
Polmont, Stirlingshire
Printed and bound in Great Britain
by Clays Ltd, St Ives plc

ACKNOWLEDGEMENTS

With thanks to my agent David Grossman and
my editor Oliver Johnson

Part One

8 June - 12 June 1795

I

lgol is the name of the winking demon star, Medusa of the skies; fair but deadly to look on, even for one who is already dying. Ah, the bright stars of the night. Almost they obliterate the clear white pain. A thousand stars shining in the ether; but no dazzling newcomer. And so little time left, so little time . . .

Yet still two-faced Medusa laughs from behind the clouds, demanding homage. Homage, Medusa, or a sword, a blade sharper than death itself.

The wind stirs. Night clouds obscure the universe. A lower music now, a different kind of death.

No stars tonight, my love.

No Selene.

It was past eleven of the clock on a rain-washed June evening when Auguste de Montpellier rose from her bed and realised that her brother Guy had gone from the house. Because he was not always responsible for his actions, and because he was, like her, a stranger in an alien land, she felt the beginnings of fear: a close, familiar fear that touched her skin with cold fingers.

'Guy,' she called. 'Guy.'

High in their attic bedrooms, the servants slept on. Only her own voice whispered back to her mockingly from the distant passageways and sparsely furnished rooms of this big house, which stood so still, so quiet amidst the fields and woods far to the west of the slumbering city.

'Guy. Oh, Guy.' Auguste ran up and down the wide staircases that twisted through the rambling mansion; though once she stopped, with a different kind of cry, because she thought she saw someone, a ghost, gazing back at her from the shadows of a forgotten room. But she realised quickly that the ghost was herself, captured by a looking-glass on the wall, her face small and pale beneath her close-cropped red hair. She stared, distracted, and saw how her silk robe was slipping from her shoulders. Pulling it more tightly across her breasts, she shivered and hurried on.

'Guy – where are you?' The servants, wakened at last by her footsteps and her cries, were starting now to stumble one by one from their attic beds, candlesticks in hands. Catching her fear like a contagion, they ran too, hither and thither, their nightgowns fluttering, knowing that the master was not well and that at such times he needed help, like a child. But Auguste had left them far behind; for now she was up on the roof of the house, where a wide balcony lay open to the cool summer night. Here, when the skies were clear, the heavens spread out to infinity, and the stars wheeled overhead. Here, night-long, Guy would search with his telescope for the lost star he called Selene. But not tonight. Tonight the stars were obscured by rain-clouds, and the precious telescopes had been dismantled and laid carefully to rest below, where the night air would not harm them.

Auguste laid her hands on the stone parapet and looked down at the old trees in the rambling garden, imagining she heard them whispering in the stirring of the breeze. When her eyes had adjusted to the darkness, she lifted her shorn head and gazed westwards towards Kensington village, to the deserted palace that was shrouded in wooded parkland; then north, to the lonely fields stretching up to hilly Hampstead. And finally she looked to the east, following the winding desolation of the rough turnpike road, night-time haunt of thieves and robbers, as it led through sombre heath and furzy woodland to the Knightsbridge turnpike and thence to far-off London.

No stars tonight.

She ran back down into the house, her satin shoes pattering as she went, her silk wrap billowing behind her. She hurried to her dressing room, and looked for the little lacquered box that she kept in her writing desk. She opened it with frantic fingers and saw that her gold had gone.

She closed it and put it away, staring into nothingness.

There were footsteps in the passageway outside. She turned and saw her maid Emilie, fluttering distractedly, murmuring fragments of prayers under her breath. 'Madame,' Emilie was saying, 'madame, we cannot find him, and the carriage is gone . . .'

Auguste bowed her head, in acknowledgement and despair. 'Is the doctor still here?'

'No, madame. He set off for the city some time ago; he will have reached his lodgings by now . . .'

And then someone else was with them, standing silently in the doorway; William Carline, the Englishman, dressed ready to go out in a long riding coat of olive green, with his hat clasped between his hands. His dark blue eyes burned with unspoken questions.

'Guy has gone to the city,' whispered Auguste. 'Please find him.'

Carline's beautiful face expressed no emotion. For a moment he stood so still that the candlelight burnished his long fair hair as if it were spun gold. Then he bowed his head and turned to go.

Auguste waited with her hands clasped to her breast for the sound of his footsteps on the stairs. She gazed out of the window into the night, until the muffled beat of his horse's hooves on the driveway had faded at last.

After that there was silence again.

One by one the candles in the big house were extinguished. Outside the trees whispered anew, their branches stirred by a soft breeze that bore with it a promise of more rain.

Once more Guy de Montpellier had gone to London to look for Selene, his lady of songs, and flowers, and stars. And each night he went, a woman died.

II

I wander thro' each charter'd street,
Near where the charter'd Thames does flow,
And mark in every face I meet
Marks of weakness, marks of woe.

William Blake, 'London' (1794)

'**W**ell, now,' thought Priss. 'Well, now.'
When Priss first saw the man, that night in the tavern, she guessed he was taking something, because of his eyes. Opium, most like. She'd seen it before. Gave them darker thoughts than gin.

Priss was a barmaid at the Blue Bell, a former coaching inn that lay in the warren of courts north of the Strand. No great travelling coaches drew up before the inn doors now, but the customers still came, finding their way to the Blue Bell from the over-ripe pleasures of Covent Garden and bringing its market smells with them too, of pulpy fruit and rotting flowers, like some fetid body in the heat.

The inn's customers were mostly lowly folk: grooms and stablemen, soldiers on leave, or street porters and vendors from the market. But sometimes it happened that a few of the younger gentry, though they might start their evening in more customary fashion with a visit to the theatre in Drury Lane and a meal at some chop house in the Piazza, would resolve, by way of a challenge perhaps to their jaded palates, to patronise Joshua Whitcomb's Blue Bell rather than their more usual haunts in Mayfair and St James. And by the time they'd found their way to Joshua's place, after calling in at other low hostelries in Henrietta Street on the way, they seemed not so different from his more regular customers, in spite of their silks and satins and fine lace; for their fine buckled shoes and stockings were coated with mire, their expensive wigs well askew, and their eyes hazed with drink.

Whatever their state, whatever the hour, paying customers always received a warm welcome from the Blue Bell's landlord. Though the walls were stained with tobacco smoke, and the candles that guttered on the window ledges were of cheapest tallow and stank like the tannery in Long Lane, at least the beer was sound, the barmaids were pretty, and Josh's rule was firm but fair. Soldiers on leave were welcome as long as they came here to eat and drink, not to brawl over lost battles; faro could be had in the back room at five shillings a time (providing the Watch weren't on the prowl, since Josh's establishment had no gaming licence) while upstairs, the former attic rooms intended for servants of travellers in the old coaching days were available for a different kind of voyaging, with obliging female companions, for those who had no objection to old truckle beds and the odd flea in the mattress.

Normally it was the soldiers and the market-men who were keenest to avail themselves of this kind of hospitality, while those clients with more money in their pockets moved westward to patronise the whores of the Haymarket and St James. It wasn't entirely unknown, however, for Josh's richer customers, suitably primed with drink, to take advantage of the more earthy pleasures available in Josh's attic rooms. Josh would charge them double, of course, for the novelty.

Priss had come to London from the West Country when she was fourteen, and was picked almost straight off the coach by Betsey, Josh's wife, who'd sold Priss's maidenhead for a guinea, several times. The customers liked Priss's red hair. And Priss found that she liked London, especially its crowded streets, and the noise and the bustle of people, and the shops on the Strand, whose windows were candlelit by night to show off all the finery within. Priss lived in hope that better things were in store for her very soon, because when she wasn't too busy serving customers, Josh sometimes sneaked her up to his own private bedchamber, and whispered to her beneath the heavy bed hangings that some day soon he'd send his wife away to the country, because she was getting fat and lazy. Then, he said, he'd make Priss mistress of the Blue Bell, and buy her all the finery, all the lace-trimmed gowns and silk shawls and feathered bonnets that she could desire. 'You've many talents, sweet Priscilla,' he'd say. He was the only person who ever called her by her proper name.

Priss was eighteen now, too old to sell her maidenhead any more, but still pert and pretty enough with her tumbling red curls and her shapely figure. When she wore her favourite gown of rose-patterned damask, the customers in the tap room would turn to stare, because it had a full, beribboned skirt of the old-fashioned kind that rustled as she walked, and a tight-fitting bodice cut low to display her lightly freckled breasts. She enjoyed the way the men's eyes fastened hungrily on her as she passed them their pots of ale.

Normally she kept the customers at a safe distance while she worked; she wasn't one of Josh's whores who regularly trod the creaking staircase to the attic rooms. But just sometimes, a group of the young gentry might catch her attention as they came in, fresh from the delights of the theatre or the opera house and determined to sample the fortifying ale in Josh Whitcomb's tavern before heading back to the more regular meeting places of the well-to-do. Then Priss would lift her pretty chin a little higher as she served them their drink, and her eyes would sparkle as she made a jest of their flattery; and indeed, occasionally, if one of these gallants took her fancy, if he looked clean and free of the tell-tale signs of the pox, then Priss might agree to go with him round the back of the tavern, into one of the dark little alleys lying between Maiden Lane and Henrietta Street. She always got a good coin or two in return, and afterwards she'd saunter back satisfied into the Blue Bell, to continue serving ale under Josh's watchful eye.

Josh had a pretty good idea of what she got up to. Sometimes he made out that he didn't like it. Sometimes he told her that the whores did their business upstairs, and she wasn't one of them. But on other occasions, if trade wasn't too busy and Betsey was out of the way somewhere visiting one of her friends, Josh would take Priss up to his room, and get her to show him exactly what had happened, out there with her latest gentleman. Josh enjoyed that. He said it was better than getting a share of the profits, like he did from the other girls.

Such, then, was Priss's life at the Blue Bell.

It was a quiet time of night when the man came in, only a little past eleven; and the Blue Bell hadn't yet filled up with the late-night revellers who brought its main custom. So Priss marked him out straight away, especially as he was on his own.

He was dressed in clothes that had once been of good quality, though his black, square-cut frock coat was now shiny with brushing, and she noted that the lace at his cuffs and throat was frayed in places. His dark hair was unpowdered, and drawn back to the nape of his neck with a narrow ribbon. He was young, not more than twenty-four or twenty-five, she guessed, and he had a thin, vivid face, and dark eyes that seemed haunted; in fact it was his eyes that Priss noticed most of all. She happened to be standing closest to the table where he settled himself, and so it was she who brought him the bottle of claret he ordered. After that she had other customers to see to.

The tavern was growing busier. But she kept looking over her shoulder to where he sat, and she noted that he seemed ill at ease. He had poured himself a glass of the wine, but he hardly seemed to touch it. Instead he sat there silent and alone while the thick tobacco smoke and raucous laughter of the other customers swirled around him. From time to time she saw that he brushed his hand across his eyes, as if the light from the tallow candles disturbed him.

When he'd ordered the wine, Priss noticed his voice straight away. He spoke English, but with a strange accent, and she felt sure that he was one of those Frenchmen Josh so detested. There were certainly enough of them in London just now; you couldn't move in the streets without hearing their talk. Priss felt sorry for them, driven from their homeland because they were rich, or of noble birth; it was terrible, all the killing that was going on over the water.

Only the other night a travelling man had come into the tavern carrying a big wooden box that would give them just a taste of the horrors of Paris, or so he told Priss and the others in spine-chilling tones as they gathered round him in eager anticipation; and indeed, his box opened up to reveal a sinister, gallows-shaped frame about two feet in height, at the top of which was suspended a heavy metal blade.

With a showman-like flourish, the man drew a slim wax taper from his pocket. He laid it across the base of the frame, at right angles to it; then he released a little catch at the side of the contraption. The blade, which was weighted with lead, dropped with a crash: the taper was sliced cleanly in two, and Priss and the others cried out and clapped their hands in mingled delight and horror. The man performed the same trick again, this time with a piece of cheese left on somebody's plate. The man grinned. 'Made by a prisoner of war on board a hulk in the Thames,' he declared proudly. 'A model of the guillotine, ladies and gentlemen. As seen by the prisoner's very own eyes, him being a Parisian born and bred. He told me that he saw the French king lose his head beneath that terrible instrument. It makes for a quick death, he told me, ladies and gentlemen, but the blood, oh, the blood . . .' And there he had to stop, because just then Josh Whitcomb came over and sent the man packing, guillotine and all.

Priss had learnt from Josh that there were two kinds of Frenchmen, each as bad as the other. One kind were the Republican devils, killers of their king and leaders of the fearsome Paris mob, who now raged across Europe in ragged armies, destroying their enemies, it was rumoured, with their bare hands and teeth if no weapon came to hand. The other kind, he told her, were the Royalists, once rich and powerful, but now forced to scurry to England with nothing but the clothes on their backs – a dire plight, thought Priss, but Josh Whitcomb clearly felt no pity for them. He said that all the Frenchmen skulking in London should be back in their homeland fighting the red-capped monsters who'd killed their king and queen, and not expecting others to do their dirty work for them.

Priss knew, of course, that the Frenchmen congregated in other taverns whose landlords were glad to take any kind of money: in the alehouses of Piccadilly like the White Bear, or the drinking places over at Moorfields, where the French *émigré* army paraded. Though now, it seemed, one solitary Frenchman had found his way here. She made her way over to the man's table again.

At first he didn't look up. She started to pour more wine into his glass, which was still half full. At least Josh hadn't noticed him, or he'd be out on his ear by now. She put one hand on her hip, knowing that the flickering light from the candle close by would be gleaming enticingly on her half-bare bosom.

'Well, now. All on your own tonight, sir?' she said. Her voice was still tinged with a soft country burr. 'Will you be wanting anything else? My name,' she added, 'is Priss.'

She thought he hadn't heard her, but then he suddenly lifted his head, and his restless eyes fastened on her red hair, as if he'd never seen anything like it. She felt a little shiver run down her spine. Sweet Jesus, but he was a strange one, and no mistake, with the looks of a dark angel.

He pushed the glass abruptly to one side, spilling some drops of the brimming liquid. She saw that his hand was shaking. Then he said,

'Yes. There is something else I want. Do you know where we can go?'

He was standing up now, scraping back his chair. Priss, hesitating, looked round quickly to see if Josh had his eye on her, but he'd gone through to the back room, to set up a game of faro. She turned back to the Frenchman. 'We'd best go outside,' she said hurriedly. 'Five shillings. That's my price. Have you got the money?'

His eyes searched her face; he looked agitated. 'Of course.'

Something about his gaze made her uneasy, made her hesitate again. Then she saw Josh's familiar frame filling the doorway to the card room; he had his back to her, but in a few moments he would turn and see her, and it would be too late to steal outside, too late for her five shillings. 'Follow me,' she said swiftly to the Frenchman. 'We'd better hurry, if we're going.'

Priss led the way quickly from the smoky tap room of the Blue Bell, out to where the courtyards and twisting tenements pressed down on them in shadows of dark sepia, blocking out the sky. A faint, foul miasma rose through the warm night air from the direction of the river. Rubbish, piled in damp corners, sent out sweetly rotting vapours; rats scuttled in the darkness. There were figures moving in the shadows; prostitutes, pickpockets, waiting for the unwary. A carriage rattled along nearby Bedford Street, its iron wheels jarring on the cobbles; from somewhere close by came a sharp, muffled laugh.

She took the man to a narrow lane she knew, close by a stable yard, where the high walls on either side gave them a kind of privacy, and the lamp that still burned over the stable's hanging sign gave them enough dim light to see by. Fumbling in the dark was something Priss loathed; it was what people did when their ugliness drove them to it, when they were old or pitted with scars.

She stopped close by the wall and looked at him expectantly. The man gazed round, then ran his hand through his black hair. 'Dear God,' he said, 'this place must be hell itself.'

Priss was worried that she was going to lose him. She said quickly,

'It gets crowded in the Blue Bell at this time of night. I thought you wanted to come out here. It might not be quite what you're used to, but it's private enough, and there's no questions asked. No one to see what we're up to.'

'No one?' He gripped her suddenly by her shoulders, and she saw that his face was almost white with fatigue. 'Not even the stars?'

Priss laughed. 'Jesus, mister. You don't see the stars in London most of the time, what with the clouds, and the smoke from all those chimneys.'

He was still staring at her, but somehow she felt that he couldn't see her. 'Sometimes she watches me,' he whispered. 'Selene, Selene. She is jealous, she wants only me . . .'

Priss pulled herself away. *Selene?* Dear God, he was rambling. If it wasn't for the five shillings he'd promised, she'd have left him standing there, muttering to himself. It had to be opium. The skin of his face was stretched taut across his jutting cheekbones, and the pupils of his eyes were pinpricks. She'd had a friend once who grew too fond of laudanum. She sold herself to anyone who would have her, and got the pox; then she took to street thievery and was hanged at Newgate.

She said sharply, 'There's no Selene here. I told you, my name's Priss. If you've changed your mind, we can go back to the tavern. No harm done, now, is there?'

He lifted his hands shakily to touch her long red hair where it tumbled from its pins. He said, seemingly with an effort, 'For a moment you reminded me of her. Forgive me.'

Priss watched him suspiciously. 'You'll give me five shillings, like we said?'

'Yes.'

Priss shrugged and began to unbutton her bodice, eager to earn her money and get back inside. The night air was cold against her skin, making her shiver. Surely to God the man was either out of his mind or Bedlam-bound; but then, he was a foreigner and Josh said all foreigners spoke of strange things.

At least now the Frenchman had stopped talking, and was getting on with what they had come out for. He tugged at the lace edging of her bodice and fumbled for her breasts; Priss, catching some of his urgency, began to deal with the fastening of his breeches, cursing her own brief awkwardness. 'Jesu,' she muttered, as he pulled her skirts up almost frantically around her waist, 'Take it easy, mister—'

He was well-primed, indeed, this Frenchman; she'd half expected him to be too full of whatever he'd been taking to be ready for action, but she was wrong. He was starting to hurt her now, and she cried out in protest; but he smothered her cries with his kisses, and took his pleasure swiftly and sharply. Afterwards, when his grip slackened, she stumbled and reached out blindly to steady herself against the wall, thinking, Josh was right, they were always trouble, the solitary ones like him. 'My money, if you please,' she demanded, pulling her bodice across her breasts.

He was fastening his coat slowly, his head bowed, as if he was suddenly very tired. She could see the perspiration sheening his forehead.

'Yes,' he said, lifting his head to gaze at her. 'Of course. You want money.' Already he was reaching into the pocket of his coat and Priss let out a little sigh of relief; she'd learnt early on that you were always safe if they paid up willingly. She held out her hand as the man pushed his closed fist towards her.

'Here it is,' he said. 'Take it.'

And the coins dropped into Priss's outstretched palm one by one, heavy and cold and glittering in the feeble lamplight.

Gold coins. Foreign coins. Sweet Christ, thought Priss, and they said most of these sad Frenchmen had nothing but the clothes they stood up in. She looked at the money in disbelief.

'No,' she breathed, 'no, you've made a mistake . . .' But she doubted if he even heard her, for already he was slipping away into the murky darkness, looking this way and that as he went, as if he was frightened someone was following him.

Priss looked down at her handful of gold coins again and shook her head in bewilderment. Suddenly she wondered if he was afflicted by more than opium; if perhaps he had some illness that made his eyes burn so in the whiteness of his face as he muttered about the stars and someone called Selene. She felt a flicker of renewed fear, because she didn't want to die, or suffer some dreadful disfigurement, like her friend with the pox who'd ended up hanged at Newgate because no one could bear to look at her face.

Priss stared down the street to where he'd disappeared into the blackness. The gold gleamed softly in her hand.

A rustling noise from the shadows nearby made her jump. Probably just a cat scouring the rubbish, Priss told herself quickly, or rats; but her heart was still beating fast. In the distance a band of soldiers, no doubt home from the Low Countries where they had all been soundly drubbed, were roaming drunkenly along Thatched House Alley, singing one of their filthy songs.

It was starting to rain now. Priss pulled herself together and made her way quickly back towards the noise and candlelight that spilt out so welcomingly from the grimy windows of the Blue Bell.

Once she thought she heard footsteps behind her in the darkness, and she quickened her pace. Then she looked at her gold, and laughed aloud.

III

The motive of change is always some Uneasiness: nothing sets us upon the change of a State or upon any new Action but some Uneasiness. This is the great motive that works on the Mind to put it upon Action.

John Locke, *An Essay Concerning Human Understanding* (1690)

Between the hours of ten and twelve that same evening Jonathan Absey, weary agent of the Home Office, found himself sitting in a flea-infested drinking and gaming lair known inappropriately as the Angel. He'd been told there might be French spies lurking here; and so he'd found his way to this den, in Kemp's Court, just off Piccadilly, and settled himself down with a bottle of wine and a game of cards, to watch for them. And indeed, there were Frenchmen here, of the poorest kind, drinking rough wine and growing maudlin as they lamented their exile and uttered curses against the Republicans in Paris; but Jonathan Absey heard no revolutionary songs, no talk of conspiracy. Instead they paid an out-of-tune fiddler to scrape out some old country airs of their homeland; to which some of them tried, clumsily, to dance and sing.

> 'Avril, le parfum des Dieux,
> Qui des cieux
> Sentent l'odeur de la plain . . .'

He felt mingled pity and irritation. Certainly, in their sallow, sentimental faces he saw no sign at all of revolutionary plots. He continued to play out his greasy cards in the company of a group of dour-looking English gamblers who looked and smelled as if they worked at the cattle market; then he started on another bottle of wine, and lost more money; and all the while he tried to keep his youthful assistant

Abraham Lucket, whom he'd posted over by the door to keep watch, well within his sights. Lucket, scarcely nineteen and recommended to him by the Hanover Street Watch, was supposed to have sharper eyes than forty-year-old Jonathan Absey, and sharper ears, to assist his master in pursuing what the Home Office paid Absey to pursue: spies, French spies, and all enemies of the state; but from what Jonathan could see – and it was easy enough to spot him, with his distinctive sandy hair sticking up like a brush's bristles – his young acolyte was chiefly occupied in ogling any pretty young woman who came into view.

Jonathan released a sigh of exasperation. As fresh clouds of filthy pipe smoke assailed his nostrils, and as yet more of his money disappeared into the big fists of his card-playing neighbours, he reflected that perhaps this kind of work was not his strongest point. Normally he looked for spies not in lowly taverns, but in his office room in Whitehall; officially he was just a clerk, known by the obscure title of Assistant Collector and Transmitter of State Papers, but unofficially his job was the gathering of vital intelligence, and to his desk, daily, came sheaves of letters from around the country that were suspected of being the work of enemy spies. To his desk, also daily, came complaints that too many secret letters, of the kind he and his colleagues were supposed to intercept, were getting through.

It was generally acknowledged, in the cold early spring and early summer of 1795 which saw England reeling from defeat in the Low Countries against the French enemy, that master spies were everywhere – especially here in London. The Secretary of State for the Home Office faced criticism from all sides in the Cabinet for the failure of his Department to stem the leaking of intelligence; the blame was passed down to his Under-Secretary, who in turn rebuked the Chief Clerk. The harassed Chief Clerk harangued the senior clerks, and the senior clerks the juniors; in a word, all Home Office staff were being urged, in a surge of ministerial desperation, to get out on the streets and do something.

'They are saying now that French spies are meeting secretly in the taverns around Piccadilly,' the Chief Clerk had mused distractedly to Jonathan earlier that same day as he came upon him folding letters into dispatch bags in the lobby of the Home Office. 'Tell me, do you know any of these places, Absey?'

Jonathan had looked up quickly from his letters. William Pollock was a diligent, dedicated official in his mid-fifties who had been Chief Clerk for thirteen years; Jonathan liked him and respected him. 'I've heard some mentioned, sir,' he said. 'The White Bear, for one. But aren't such places being watched already?'

'Not as well as they might be.' Pollock scratched his grizzled head and held up to the light of the window a copy of a letter that Jonathan had earlier suspected of being in cipher but that had turned out to be merely a sheet of livestock prices being sent from one market town to another. 'The magistrates say they have these places under surveillance; but it seems to me that too many refugees of most dubious allegiance are congregating in some of these inns. They lament their exile, and their state of poverty; but my guess is that some of them are not what they seem – they're primed with good French gold, gold of the kind that the wretched people of their own country never see: coins that fly as if by some witchery across the sea, from the secret vaults of Paris to London itself. Gold to buy secrets. I guarantee, Absey – find yourself a quantity of those golden coins, these *louis d'or* of the Republic, and you will have found a spy. These refugees are sending back vital knowledge of our military plans in God knows what diabolical ways, straight to their heathen masters in Paris; and we look at letters. Always we are told to look at letters. Now, tell me. Are these cunning spies going to send their treacherous missives through the public post? Are they?'

And William Pollock shook one of Jonathan's dispatch bags hard, and tied the loop at its neck as fiercely as if he were choking the life out of a traitorous Frenchman.

Jonathan said, 'They have sent messages in cipher through the public mail before now, sir, and we've stopped them.'

'But how many letters have got through, Absey? How many have been sent by secret messengers, down lonely roads to some deserted part of the coast, to travel on their way by fishing boat? We need to stop the scoundrels in their tracks, here in London, where all their intelligence is gathered, before their damnable letters are ever written. These traitors gather in public places with complete impunity. Only this morning I heard reports of a place called the Angel in Piccadilly. It used to be notorious chiefly for its whores, but now Frenchmen gather there as well, and the other night they were heard singing revolutionary songs and drinking toasts to the traitor Thomas Paine.

It is nothing short of treason, and the Under-Secretary tells us we must put a stop to such iniquities, even if it means going out on the streets ourselves!'

Pollock, growing more and more agitated, was forced to pause for breath; at which point Jonathan said quickly, 'I will go, sir.'

Pollock looked at him in surprise. 'But it isn't your job, Jonathan.'

'You've just said we must all do what we can. The Angel, you said? In Kemp's Court? I will go tonight.'

A messenger came in, to summon Pollock to the Under-Secretary's office; but Jonathan wasn't alone for long, because Pollock's footsteps had scarcely died away when another of the Home Office clerks, Richard Crawford, came into the lobby. Crawford was a self-important little man who suffered from dyspepsia and was always losing his spectacles; his precise lowland Scots meannesses and his neat, priest-sombre clothes irritated Jonathan beyond measure.

Crawford glanced after the departing Pollock, then turned back to Jonathan and raised his brows. 'So, my friend,' he pronounced. 'We're in a sorry state. The Frenchmen run rings round us, and nowhere can we find a spy.'

'So it seems,' muttered Jonathan, busying himself with some papers and wishing Crawford far from here.

But Crawford had drawn closer. 'Are you going, then, to this tavern, this Angel?'

He'd evidently heard more of the conversation with Pollock than Jonathan had bargained for. Jonathan, his head still bowed over his papers, said reluctantly, 'Yes.'

'It might be dangerous to go alone,' persisted Crawford. His breath was sour with indigestion. 'I'll come too.'

'I'll be fine,' Jonathan replied rather too sharply, drawing his papers together, 'I've got Lucket to help me. There's no point in us all going.'

For the briefest second, the look of fawning ingratiation that had been on Crawford's face vanished, to be replaced by an involuntary flush of hurt pride, almost of anger. Jonathan sighed inwardly; he was used to soothing the feelings of the touchy little Scotsman.

'But we'll dine together soon, shan't we, Richard?' he said hurriedly. 'I've heard of a new place near the Strand. Perhaps you'll be my guest one evening?'

Crawford sniffed again, and merely said, 'Sometimes I think it's not spies you're looking for, my friend. And if so it will do you no good to keep going back to these places. No good at all.' He turned on his heel and left; and Jonathan, with a sinking heart, was able to guess exactly what he was thinking.

Three years ago Jonathan's fifteen-year-old daughter Ellie had run away from home. She'd dreamed of becoming an actress, but like so many others she'd merely disappeared without trace into the dark streets of the metropolis. Night after night Jonathan had scoured the theatres, and the taverns close by, looking for her.

A year ago her body was found. She had been strangled in an alleyway near the Haymarket, and Jonathan was told that she had been living as a prostitute.

Perhaps it was then that Jonathan's life had changed completely. Since the shattering reality of Ellie's death, he had become withdrawn, obsessive; an insomniac who haunted drinking dens and inns near the site of his daughter's murder. His grim determination to bring Ellie's killer to justice had devoured his energy and his spare time. And his bitterness had grown as he slowly realised that the legal system had neither time nor resources to follow up a crime to which there were no leads, no witnesses; especially when the victim was a prostitute. Nevertheless Jonathan struggled on. As soon as his long day at work was finished, he would tramp the streets, asking questions. He hired private thief-takers, pouring out what little money he had on them; but gradually, with the failure of one avenue of enquiry after another, and with the slow extinguishing, not of his grief, but of any hope that the murder might be avenged, the oblivion of the wine bottle, and not conversation with colleagues was what he sought of an evening. The circle of friends he once possessed had slowly ebbed away.

It was Crawford alone out of all his former acquaintances at the Home Office who kept up an attachment, of sorts; the two of them had spent many an evening in various taverns with Jonathan barely uttering a word as bottle after bottle of claret was consumed and the demons ran loose about his mind. Just occasionally, if Jonathan stopped to wonder about Crawford's concern for him, he assumed it was because Crawford had demons of his own to deal with.

Crawford's work was lowly. And yet he had once worked for Evan Nepean, Under-Secretary to Henry Dundas in the days when Dundas was in charge of the Home Office. Jonathan used to see Crawford in the distance then, a busy scribe, hurrying to and fro importantly for his masters, copying and filing assiduously. But when last summer Henry Dundas was appointed to the newly-created War Office, taking with him his most able assistants, Nepean and Huskisson, Crawford, to everyone's surprise including clearly his own, did not go with them. He was left, puzzled and somewhat bereft, to take his place at the bottom of the heap under the new Home Office chief, the Duke of Portland; and his job now seemed to consist of the copying out of warrants that gave the nearby Ordnance Department its instructions regarding the issue of arms and equipment to the militia and the colonies. Humble work indeed.

Possibly Crawford felt a kind of kinship with Jonathan, whose career prospects had likewise diminished. Jonathan could only assume that was what drew the Scotsman to him. Yet even now, even after the many evenings in his company, Jonathan would not claim Crawford as a close friend; in fact in his own self-loathing he found himself treating Crawford as someone of even a lower order than himself, for being foolish enough to seek out his friendship. And he resented more and more the intrusive solicitude – to Jonathan feigned and over-unctuous – that was always writ large on the little Scotsman's unhealthily pale face.

Crawford no doubt thought that Jonathan had volunteered to visit the Angel, a haunt of prostitutes, because he still hoped to find a clue to his daughter's killer. Perhaps Crawford was right. One thing was for sure: wherever he went, at whatever hour, for whatever reason, Jonathan still found himself searching everywhere for his daughter's bright smile and her curling red hair.

At the Angel that night, though there might not be any French spies, there were certainly whores, most of them poorly clad and young, though their eyes seemed old enough as they searched the crowded tavern for custom. As eleven o'clock came and went, the place seemed fuller than ever: of prostitutes, of miserable French refugees, of surly Englishmen: Jonathan, losing yet another game, was almost on the point of getting up to tell Lucket that they were abandoning their task and leaving, when something happened to attract his attention.

To the rear of the room was an alcove, which was concealed by dingy curtains drawn across from wall to wall. Just before half past eleven, Jonathan became aware that some of the French *émigrés* were starting to organise themselves into a line before this curtain. He noticed too that they seemed to represent the most wretched of the exiles; there were several old men, at least one of them with a hacking cough; a youth with a fiery skin ailment; an aged crone whose limbs were gnarled with rheumatism, and a pale-faced mother whose baby grizzled fretfully at her breast.

After some time, the curtain was twitched back briefly and the first of these unfortunates disappeared behind it into the alcove. Jonathan turned to one of his fellow card players. 'What's happening through there? Do you know?'

The man, busy scrutinising his hand, scarcely lifted his head to reply. 'In there? Nothing much. It'll be that French doctor again – he comes to attend his sick countrymen once a week or so. Most of the foreigners can't afford to visit an apothecary, so they wait here to see him.'

'So late?'

The man shrugged. Clearly the subject held no interest for him. 'This won't be the only place he visits. There's sick and dying Frenchmen all over London, damn them. Your play.'

Jonathan played, and continued to lose money; he also continued to watch that curtained, secretive recess, and the pathetic supplicants who entered silently one by one; and he wondered what kind of doctor would choose to tend his patients in such a place, and at such a time.

Shortly before midnight, the door of the tavern opened, letting in a gust of night air laden with raindrops, and a newcomer. There was nothing unusual in that, for the tavern was thronged, and people were forever coming and going. But this newcomer, who was dressed in a loose coat of olive green with the collar turned up against the rain and a wide-brimmed hat pulled low over his face, seemed purposeful, single-minded in his quest. Without hesitation, he strode across the crowded room to the alcove where the doctor was. Pushing aside the queue and ignoring the muttered protests of those waiting their turn, he pulled back the curtains.

Jonathan craned his head eagerly to see what the draperies had hitherto concealed. There, in the candlelit alcove, was the doctor, with his shirt-sleeves rolled up, and his paraphernalia of ointments and phials and powders laid out beside him on a table, together with his physician's bag. Jonathan could see that this doctor was a big, raw-boned Frenchman, perhaps in his mid-thirties, with long dark hair and a heavy-featured, sombre face. He was in the midst of cupping a stout Frenchwoman; a silk ligature had been pulled tightly round her upper arm, and several leeches clung to her flesh, sating themselves.

The newcomer who'd interrupted all this didn't even look at the woman, but went straight up to the doctor and handed him a note. The doctor read the letter swiftly, then with extreme haste began to pull the leeches from the woman's skin. The woman cried out in pain; the punctures bled copiously. The doctor snatched some bandages and bound her arms briskly. Then he gathered the blood-engorged leeches and forced them into a jar, and with his medical apparatus dangling out of his half-open leather bag, he muttered his excuses to the queue of patients and followed the messenger out of the tavern. The heavy door of the Angel slammed shut after them; the tallow candles smoked and flickered in the draught. The curtained alcove was left empty, and those who had waited to see the doctor dispersed, grumbling.

Now letters of all kinds were, of course, Jonathan Absey's business. He had observed with acute interest how, as the French physician read the letter, his gaunt face had become riven with anxiety. And so Jonathan, who had just clumsily thrown away an ace and with it some of his last coins, turned in his chair and jerked his head sharply at Lucket. 'Follow them,' he mouthed. Straight away he could see Lucket frowning, no doubt wondering why; but Lucket was obedient, in his own way, and he went, slipping from his perch and hurrying out into the night. Then it was Jonathan's turn to wonder why he had sent him after them. A French doctor who proffered potions and leeched his patients covertly in a crowded, seedy tavern; a messenger with a letter: was it really enough reason to send Lucket hastening out in pursuit?

The most obvious explanation was that the messenger had come to tell the doctor that someone was sick. But Jonathan could not forget the agitation with which the Frenchman had gathered his things together and set off into the night; or the sight of his big hands, still smeared with blood from dealing so hastily with the leeches.

Jonathan realised the card-players were watching him impatiently; it was his turn again to play. He laid out a few of his remaining shillings, and won a little back. But he extricated himself from the game as soon as he could and stood up, looking around the crowded room, wondering restlessly how far Lucket had got in his pursuit of the doctor, and how long it would be before he returned.

One of the card players, a big man with arms like a blacksmith's and broken teeth that were stained with tobacco, leaned forward in his chair and tugged at the skirt of Jonathan's coat. 'You'll stay for another game?' It was more a statement than a question; the man, though he showed his teeth, wasn't smiling.

'I cannot. I have an appointment,' said Jonathan. He started to push his way towards the bar, conscious of the eyes of the surly card players following him.

'There was a French doctor in here,' he said to the landlord when he finally caught his attention. 'Can you give me his name?'

'His name? No idea.' The landlord turned abruptly to serve someone; his other customers were clamouring for ale.

'But he was in that room.' Jonathan pointed. 'You must know something about him.'

The landlord leaned his elbows heavily on the bar and glared at Jonathan. 'Look, mister. He paid me a few shillings for the room. That's all I care about. If he's a quack, if he's swindled someone, if the law's after him, it's nothing to do with me; nothing at all. Understand? Excuse me, I've got people to serve.'

Jonathan set off wearily towards the door. On his way he passed a pot boy, bustling by with a fistful of empty tankards. Jonathan caught his arm and said, 'There was a doctor, in the back room. Do you know his name?' He held out sixpence. The pot boy, who had a squint, reached for it eagerly with his free hand, but Jonathan held the coin just out of his reach. 'Well?'

'Can't remember,' mumbled the boy. 'I've heard it a few times, but I can't make sense of these foreign names.'

'A few times? Then he's been in here before?'

The pot boy was eyeing the sixpence warily, as if at any moment it might disappear. 'Once or twice, yes.'

'Do you know where he lives?' Impatiently Jonathan waved the coin before the lad's crooked gaze.

The pot boy tried hard, fixing both his roving eyes on the money. 'I think he's got lodgings somewhere in town. But they say he's out in the country whenever the weather is clear, because he watches the stars. He's an ast . . . an—'

'An astronomer?'

'Yes. That's it.' The lad snatched the coin with satisfaction. 'Knows a lot about the stars, he does. Thanks, mister.' He pocketed the coin with a grin and hurried off with his pots towards the bar. Jonathan stood there. An astronomer.

An innocent enough occupation, indeed, and yet it was one which for Jonathan held unwelcome associations. He happened to have a half-brother, called Alexander Wilmot, who loved to watch the stars. But Alexander had other, less acceptable preoccupations, and all in all he had brought Jonathan nothing but trouble.

Auriga, Capella, Spica . . . Jonathan had a sudden, unwanted recollection of his plump half-brother, when they were boys, lovingly reciting those names to himself as he pored over his star books. Jonathan was surprised and ill-pleased by the persistence of the memory.

Holding up his hand to fend off an ageing whore who importuned him, he pushed his way out of the crowded tavern and stepped into the narrow alley from which the stench of urine had not yet been washed by the steady downpour of rain.

No stars here. The cracked lanthorn that hung over the tavern's door gave off a dingy brown light that did little to illuminate these insalubrious surroundings. He looked this way and that as the rain poured down, wondering where Lucket was, wondering if it was worth his while even to bother waiting for him, for he had surely sent the lad off on a quite pointless errand, simply, perhaps, for the sake of seeming to do something. A brewery dray rumbled by in the distance, laden with barrels; he heard its iron-rimmed wheels scraping the dank cobbles.

At the end of the alley he saw a gang of soldiers pass by noisily: some of General Moira's new recruits, perhaps, up on leave from

Southampton barracks. There were soldiers everywhere in London, both French Royalists and English, all of them kicked out of Flanders by the Republicans and waiting for new orders. Jonathan had heard rumours from a colleague in the Admiralty that the fleet in the Solent was being readied to take these troops somewhere, but their actual destination was a secret, if indeed it had yet been decided on. Corsica, perhaps, or the West Indies, where the war was being waged in the French colonies.

Jonathan had even heard whispered talk that the emigrant Royalist regiments were being prepared for a joint assault on the coast of France itself. But the Republicans had little to fear, he reflected, from the English, even if such a venture went ahead; for the young soldiers he could see here, in their drenched and ragged clothing, exemplified only too well the poor quality of recruits dredged up by the crimping men and pressed into unwilling service in this seemingly hopeless war.

Jonathan was getting wet. He was standing under the overhang of the tavern's roof for shelter, but the rain was beginning to trickle down his collar and the damp was seeping through his coat. He cursed Lucket, and wondered again where he could have got to. His lanky assistant was all too easily distracted, especially by women; his lust bubbled up as swiftly as his pimples, and Jonathan reflected bitterly that he had probably been ensnared by one of the whores hereabouts, and might even now be engaging in action, all thoughts of his errand forgotten. Jonathan looked at his watch, undecided whether to hunt for him, or give up and go home. Almost midnight; and what had he achieved? A few shillings won at cards, and no doubt an aching head in the morning from the bottles of cheap wine he had consumed.

It was then that he saw Lucket hurrying towards him from the direction of Piccadilly, with his three-cornered hat of which he was so proud set foolishly askew over his stubborn hair, and the big pewter buttons on his second-hand coat gleaming in the dingy street light. For a moment his speed fooled Jonathan into some sort of hope.

'Well?' Jonathan gripped his arms and almost shook him.

'They got away, sir.' Lucket spoke with the surliness of defeat. 'I did my best. Indeed I did. They had two horses waiting, down the road. I kept them in sight for a while, because they had to go slowly at first as the street was crowded; but then they gathered speed as they headed eastward to Leicester Fields, and so I lost them.'

'You lost them?' repeated Jonathan, grabbing Lucket by the shoulders.

'Like I said, they had horses waiting, sir,' said Lucket sulkily. 'How can I be expected to keep up with horses?'

Jonathan released a sigh of exasperation and let him go. What had he expected to discover from Lucket's pursuit? For a moment, indeed, the way that the French doctor had reacted so strongly to the message had stirred his senses, and so he had acted on impulse, as he had often acted before, and with success. Such instinctive action was what had marked him out for advancement, when he was a junior clerk, scarcely older than Lucket was now.

But lately things had started to go wrong for him. They were going wrong for everyone, he knew, in the sense that the war was failing. But he felt his own inadequacy more than most; this was more than the usual self-doubt. Perhaps the decline had begun when his daughter disappeared; certainly it was accentuated two years ago, while he was still searching for her, and still hoping he might find her; for it was then that Jonathan had made the grave mistake of trying to help his half-brother Alexander the astronomer, who was in trouble of his own making.

Alexander was a homosexual. He had become involved in an illegal coterie, and prosecution of those associated with it was imminent. The punishment for sodomy was death by hanging; the sentence was rarely carried out these days, but the threat existed, and Alexander, in a frenzy of fear, had come to his brother pleading for help. Jonathan had succeeded in secretly gaining access to the Home Office evidence that betrayed his brother's name, and he destroyed it. But his deception was in part discovered, if not entirely understood, and this time people did not whisper about him, as they did when he searched for his missing daughter; they talked aloud.

At that stage in his career Jonathan could have expected further advancement, a reward for loyal service, for information steadily garnered and made sense of over the years. But, after the business of helping Alexander, the anticipated promotion did not come. He was still held in high regard by Pollock and others; was still told that he would have many more chances to prove himself, but Jonathan felt that his chance had gone. In the matter of his brother he had shown himself culpable in trying to protect him; Jonathan had thought he could do this without harm to anyone, but he was wrong, he had harmed himself. It was the first time, he felt, that his senses, which had once been so keen, so sharp, were failing him.

Sometimes, now, the job he was doing, this searching for an enemy he could not see, almost overwhelmed him. So far the mood of helplessness had always passed, but the sense of inadequacy was here with him again now, and the original purpose of the task he had set himself tonight seemed a phantasm, washing away in the steady rain that seeped through his coat and his boots. For a moment he could hardly remember the chain of events that had brought him here. As the rain poured down he found, suddenly, that he was thinking of his daughter.

'If I'd had a horse,' Lucket was muttering as loudly as he dared, 'now, if you'd given me money for a horse, I wouldn't have lost them. Sir.'

Jonathan ran his hand tiredly through his hair. 'It's late,' he said. 'Time to go home. Go and find a link-boy, to get me a chair.'

He saw the quick flash of knowingness in the lad's face as Lucket realised that his master had drunk too much cheap wine to manage the walk back to his lodgings.

'A chair, I said. On your way,' Jonathan repeated sharply.

And Lucket was on his way, pulling down his hat against the rain, turning up the collar of his coat. Jonathan, weary at heart, leaned against the wall of the Angel tavern, in the shadows. Jesus Christ, I am too old for this time-wasting, he thought. Past forty, and hunting spies in the dark. There must, there must be something else.

And then, rather surprisingly, there was. He heard several pairs of heavy footsteps coming purposefully towards him from the doorway of the tavern, and found himself surrounded by some of the English gamesters he'd played cards with earlier. They gazed at him challengingly and Jonathan felt the hairs at the nape of his neck prickle.

'Well, now,' said one of the men thoughtfully. It was the one with the arms of a blacksmith. Jonathan's heart sank. 'You turned down our offer of another game. Why was that, I wonder? You're a stranger here. Could it be that you were cheating us, and you were afraid that if you stayed longer we'd spot your tricks?'

'No,' said Jonathan tersely. 'I don't cheat. I have never cheated.'

They looked at each other. 'Now, how are a bunch of honest men like us supposed to know that? I'll tell you how we see it, mister. You've never been in the Angel before. Have you? You come in. You play cards with us. You win our money. You leave without giving us the chance to win it back.'

Jonathan was aware of more exchanged glances and his heart sank still further. 'I had other business.'

The man pressed closer, his tobacco-stained teeth malodorous. 'Ah. But we think you were cheating us. And if you won't come back in for more play, to prove us wrong, why, then, we'll have to relieve you of the money you stole off us in some other way, now won't we?'

'I stole nothing, damn you – *shite* . . .' The heavy thump between his ribs made him double up. He spewed bile and sour wine into the gutter. Another blow from another fist caught the side of his face, jarring his cheekbone so hard he thought it broken. His mouth tasted of warm blood where he had bitten the inside of his cheek. He slid groaning to the ground, and then they were all around him, giving him hearty kicks for good measure. He was aware of his watch going and his wallet being emptied, before they heaved him unceremoniously round the corner and dumped him in the darkness of the filthy passageway at the side of the tavern. One final kick thudded into his ribs, before the sound of their boots retreating swiftly down the lane told him they had gone.

He laid his aching head against the wet cobbles and retched into the silence.

Jesu. What a fool he was. No wonder his wife despaired of him.

Less than a mile away from the scene of Jonathan's humiliation in Kemp's Court, red-haired Priss bustled about in the crowded tap room of the Blue Bell, feeling somewhat mazed still by the weight of the gold coins in her pocket. Josh had looked at her questioningly when she came back in after the business with the young Frenchman, but she'd merely patted down her hair and set off to fetch a tray of empty pots from a nearby table, as if she'd been busy in here all the time serving customers. Josh let her get on with her work, because the place was busy and there were a lot of people to serve. But shortly after midnight things quietened down for a moment or two and Josh, seizing his chance, caught at her arm and said,

'You shouldn't go out on your own with foreigners, girl. You know they can be dangerous. How many times do I have to tell you?'

Someone, one of the other serving maids perhaps, must have spotted her going out and told on her. Priss frowned in annoyance, but Josh patted her arm soothingly.

'You're back now, at any rate,' he said. 'Did he pay you handsomely?'

Priss relaxed again. He was mellow tonight. Perhaps he'd have her up to his room later to tell him all about it. 'He gave me enough,' she said.

Josh laughed dismissively. 'I'll wager he gave you nothing. They've naught but the clothes they stand up in, these Frenchmen.'

Stung to defiance, Priss pulled one of the coins from her pocket. 'Look at this, then. Look. What would you say if I told you he gave me a whole purseful of these?'

Josh fingered the coin and grinned again. 'A purseful? I'd say you were dreaming, girl. And even for one of these, you still shouldn't risk yourself with foreigners.'

But Priss noticed there was a suitable respect now in his voice. He gave her back the coin, and she kissed it with fondness before putting it away. 'I know what I'm doing,' she said.

Josh nodded. 'Well, he took a fancy to you, clearly. Do you think he'll be back?'

Priss guessed he was thinking of the gold finding its way to his gaming tables. 'I don't know. He seemed confused.'

'Taken something, had he? Something stronger than ale?'

'Probably.' Priss frowned. 'He seemed to be seeing things. He kept talking about someone else – someone with a strange-sounding name . . .'

'Oh?' Josh cocked his head, still good-humoured. 'What name was that, then?'

'Selene!' She remembered it with triumph. She rather liked the sound of it. 'Selene, that was it. And he muttered something about the stars, even though the sky was as black as pitch and there wasn't a star to be seen.'

Some nearby drinkers were calling for more ale. Josh gathered several pint pots in his big fists. 'Sounds like a damned religious cove to me, who let his lust get the better of his ranting soul. Go out to the back yard, now, Priss, there's a good girl, and fetch us a couple of logs for the fire, will you?'

Priss hurried outside, round to the top of the cellar steps where the wood for the fire was kept. The rain was coming down steadily now, but she hardly noticed. Her mind was filled with the thought of the gold coins in her pocket, and what they would buy her.

It was then that she heard purposeful footsteps coming quickly towards her along the alley that crossed the back of the Blue Bell's yard. Her arms full of wood, she made for the light of the tavern doorway, eager to be back inside. Could be pickpockets, or the Watch. Trouble of some kind, at any rate, she guessed.

But she was too late. Even as she reached for the familiar side door, with its peeling blue paint and its squeaking latch, she cried out and dropped the wood, as some kind of cord was pulled tightly round her neck from behind.

She tore at the ligature with scrabbling fingers, but whoever held it was strong, and already her own flailing limbs were growing weak. Priss stumbled to her knees. She didn't want to die. She tried to say a prayer, but her swollen tongue was starting to fill her mouth, and anyway, she couldn't remember any words. Her eyes stared sightlessly into the dark; and as the catastrophe of dying embraced her body, she heard a voice behind her murmur, *'A dead body revenges not injuries . . .'*

And then, blackness.

Silently, a hand reached into her pocket for the gold.

IV

And when night
Darkens the streets, then wander forth the sons
Of Belial, flown with insolence and wine.

John Milton, *Paradise Lost*, (1667) Book I

By the time Lucket returned to pick his master from the filthy mud round the side of the tavern into which his assailants had launched him, Jonathan was fully conscious, but gasping with the pain of his bruises. As Lucket pulled him up, Jonathan saw that his eyes were wide with something that was almost respect.

'Sir,' Lucket observed. 'You've been in a fight.'

It was over-generous, reflected Jonathan sourly, to say that he had been fighting. He hadn't even had the chance to raise his fists. He started to brush himself down, but found he was achieving little by way of improving his dishevelled appearance.

'Was it French spies, sir?' Lucket went on eagerly, his face pink with excitement against his pale, bristly hair. 'Curse their impudence. Let me go after them—'

'No. Damn you, no.' Jonathan leaned hard against the wall of the tavern. There was a dull throbbing at his ribs, a pounding bruise at the side of his face, and a sick heaving at his gut; but nothing, it appeared, was broken, and for that he knew he should consider himself grateful. 'It was a bunch of ruffians from the tavern – no point in pursuit. They'll be well hidden in some stinking den in Seven Dials by now. You found me a chair?'

Lucket shrugged, starting to lose interest in his master's ordeal. After all, ruffians in this kind of place were common enough. 'None to be had,' he said. 'This foul weather means they're all taken, every one.'

'*All?*'

Lucket coloured a little. 'Well, there was one, yes. But he wanted a shilling first, to follow me here, and I found, you see, that I had no coins at all, for it seems my purse too has been picked, no doubt while I was in that cursed tavern.'

Jonathan touched his bruised face, tasting the warm blood inside his cheek. Mentally he cursed in turn all foreigners, all French wars and all light-fingered thieves. Then because Lucket was watching him, waiting to see what he would do next, he drew himself up with an effort, breathed in carefully because his ribs hurt, and pronounced grimly to Lucket's expectant face, 'In that case we shall both of us have to walk home. Shan't we?'

Lucket had lodgings with an elderly relative, not far from Brewer Street, which was where Jonathan lived. Lucket nodded. 'Very well, sir.' He glanced again covertly at Jonathan's bruised cheek and disarrayed clothes. 'Fancy you being caught out by ruffians like them, sir. And they've got clean away.'

Jonathan gritted his teeth. Just at that moment, Lucket's wide-eyed, feigned innocence was almost more than he could take. 'Yes. Fancy it. All right, then. Since you're so indignant about my misfortune, you can come with me to the Hanover Street Watch House, to report our bad luck and give the constables something to do.' He had a grudge against the Hanover Street men; they had recommended Lucket to him.

'But sir . . .'

'Hanover Street,' said Jonathan sternly.

Hanover Street meant a detour, and an even longer walk home. No wonder Lucket's face had fallen. Indeed, it wasn't long before Jonathan himself began to regret his decision to visit the Watch House; but there was no going back on it now, for Lucket, though rolling up his eyes in silent protest, was preparing to follow behind. So Jonathan, clenching his teeth against the pain of his bruises, forced himself to limp along the alleys filled with drinking dens that bordered Piccadilly, past the whores of Swallow Street, whom Lucket eyed longingly, and past the gaming houses clustered at the corner of Burlington Street, where men won on the throw of one die more than he earned in a year, as his wife always used to remind him.

By the time they reached Hanover Street, it was almost one o'clock and the rain had stopped at last. Just outside the Watch House, where a dim lamp hung over the faded sign and barred window, Jonathan saw one of the officers preparing to set off home with his lanthorn.

He struggled to recall the man's name. Bentham, Bentham, that was it: a thin, shifty constable, with a permanent trail of spittle at the corner of his mouth; one of the many he had spoken with this last year, during his search for Ellie's murderer.

'Master Jonathan Absey,' Bentham said. He bowed his head in some attempt at the servility due from a part-time constable to an agent of the Home Office, and one moreover who had suffered the loss of his daughter at the hands of a murderer; but his deference was clearly tempered by Jonathan's battered appearance. 'Now, what can bring you here at this time of the night?' He rubbed his bristled chin thoughtfully. 'You'll have heard, I think, of the young doxy that's just been murdered over by Maiden Lane. Am I right?'

Jonathan felt his senses start to swim again: it was beginning to seem to him as if fate had saved all her ill favours for this single, rain-drenched evening. He steadied himself against the wall of the Watch House and heard Lucket saying to the constable, puzzled, 'No. We've come about some ruffians at the Angel in Kemp's Court, who set on Mister Absey and—'

Jonathan gripped Lucket's arm to silence him, so hard that Lucket yelped, and Jonathan said to Bentham, his jaw aching with bruises, 'Tell me. Tell me about the murder.'

Bentham was already settling himself back against the wall of the Watch House, preparing to enjoy his role as the bearer of baleful news. 'The girl's name,' he began, 'was Priss. Priscilla. She was a barmaid at the Blue Bell tavern. I was called over there a little less than an hour ago to interview her landlord, straight after the magistrate was told. Her body was found round the back of the tavern.' Bentham shook his head. 'She'd gone outside, you see, with a customer. Stupid thing to do in a neighbourhood like that; all sorts of people, all sorts of men. He was a foreigner, a Frenchman.'

And there were enough of them in the lowly taverns of the city tonight, as Jonathan well knew. Bentham was watching him, waiting for his reaction; Jonathan put one hand to the side of his face, where the flesh was swollen, and said, with an effort, 'Did anyone see them leaving the tavern? Did anyone see them outside in the streets?'

'No,' said Bentham, leaning closer, 'this is the strange part. The Frenchman did what he wanted with her, took his pleasure of her. Then let her go back inside.'

'Let her go back inside?' Jonathan, as he spoke, was all too aware of Lucket looking eagerly from one to the other, bright-eyed with curiosity.

'Yes,' nodded Bentham. 'That's what I was interviewing the land-lord about. This Frenchman must be either very stupid or very confident, because of course once the girl was back in the tavern she talked about him. And when she slipped out the back a little after midnight for some firewood, he must have been there waiting to kill her.'

'How? How did she die?'

Bentham scratched the side of his head. 'She was strangled. An ugly business, as ever. I saw her body. She must have been a pretty wench. Freckled white skin, and red hair.'

Red hair, like Ellie . . . Jonathan started forward, jarring his bruised ribs. 'How old was she?'

'Only young.' Bentham shrugged. 'Eighteen, nineteen or so. Her nails were all broken,' he went on with relish. 'She must have struggled hard, trying to pull at the cord, or whatever it was round her neck; no, not rope, Master Absey, but something smooth. I particularly noticed it because it only bruised the skin, didn't tear at it like hemp does, you know?'

He nodded slowly and touched his wet lips with the tip of his tongue; and for a moment Jonathan had to lean against the cold brick wall of the Watch House to steady himself. The cord that Ellie's killer had used had been smooth too; one of the constables had pointed it out to him, though at the time Jonathan had hardly registered it, because all he'd seen was his daughter's face.

Ellie would have been eighteen this summer.

Bentham was watching him with a mixture of sympathy and prurient interest. 'Red hair,' he was repeating thoughtfully, 'red hair. Strange, that. And now I come to think of it, did you know there was another young redhead strangled not so long ago?'

'*No.* No, I didn't . . .'

'Well, someone was talking about it, I can't remember who. I think it might have been Dowson at the Bow Street office. In spring, it was, Master Absey; March, April, perhaps, though I can't be exactly sure. I only heard the news second-hand. But you'd find out at one of the other watch houses, if you asked around.'

Jonathan clenched his fists. He shouldn't have to ask around. He should have been told. He remembered how he'd trudged alone from watch house to magistrate's court, day after day, night after night after Ellie's death, asking about missing women, women found dead; but nobody had told him about this one who was killed in spring: another one who was young, with red hair . . .

There should be records kept of all violent deaths, no matter how lowly the victims were. And one thing was for sure. He would find out more if it meant covering all of London again.

Bentham was looking at his pocket watch and reaching for his lanthorn. Jonathan stepped forward, barring his way.

'Can you remember anything else? Anything else at all about the murder tonight?'

Bentham shrugged. 'I got nothing much from the landlord, I'll tell you that now. He said the place was busy, always is; no one else apart from Priss even noticed this Frenchman.'

'So no one knows what he looked like? Or how he was dressed? Or anything about the way he spoke?'

Bentham was shaking his head, frowning, then his face suddenly brightened. 'There was one thing. It might be something or nothing. But apparently this Frenchman went on about the stars.'

'The stars,' Jonathan repeated. He had gone quite still. 'You're sure?'

'Yes!' Bentham tapped his forehead meaningfully. 'That's what the girl told the landlord. Muttering about the stars, he was, even though there wasn't a single one to be seen. Moon-crazed, without a doubt. Or under the influence of something a little stronger than tavern ale.' He smothered a yawn. 'Well, it's time I was on my way, Master Absey. Let me know if there's anything I can help with, anything at all.' He couldn't resist letting his face twist once more into a leer of sympathy. 'I know how you worry about those girls on the streets.' He picked up his lanthorn and set off along Hanover Street. Jonathan stared after him until he could see him no more and the sound of his footsteps on the wet cobbles had died away into silence.

How many Frenchmen could there be, in this great cesspit of a city, where girls were brutally killed and men spoke of it with lust in their eyes; how many Frenchmen who were interested in the stars?

There was the doctor in the Angel. An astronomer, the pot boy had said. The doctor in the Angel carried ligatures of silk with him in his medical bag, with which to bind his patients' arms during leeching. Strong yet smooth, the long strips of fabric would leave no abrasions on the skin . . .

Had Jonathan been watching, earlier, a man who was a killer?

He turned abruptly to Abraham Lucket, who stood yawning in the shadows, bored now that Bentham had gone. 'The doctor you tried to follow, from the Angel. Which direction did you say he went in?'

Lucket jerked to attention. 'Leicester Fields, sir,' he said.

From Leicester Fields, it was but a short distance to the vicinity of the Blue Bell. The doctor had left the Angel with time enough to get there.

Jonathan gazed up at the sky. Above the murk of London's smoking chimney stacks, the crescent moon gleamed wanly between parted clouds. These men who studied the stars talked to each other. That much he knew from Alexander. They were forever comparing notes on such things as brightnesses, and eclipses, and transits, in a language all of their own.

Alexander might be able to tell Jonathan something more about the French astronomer doctor who had hastened out into the London night shortly before yet another helpless girl was killed. Alexander would not be happy to see him. But Alexander was in Jonathan's debt, and always would be.

He noticed suddenly that Lucket was drooping with tiredness. The lad had propped himself up against the damp wall of the Watch House, but his eyes kept closing. 'Go home,' Jonathan said to him. 'There's no more to be done tonight.'

Lucket nodded. 'Yes, sir. Goodnight, sir.' He went slowly off into the darkness, as if in a dream. Jonathan watched him go. Then, realising that he'd failed to report either the attack outside the Angel or Lucket's lost purse, he pulled himself together likewise and limped wearily home. He thought, every step of the way, about the redheaded girl who had died that night; and she had his daughter's face.

V

If Comets be burnt, consumed and wasted in the Starrie Heavens, it seemeth that there is no great difference between them and things here below.

J. Swan, *Speculum Mundi, or A Glass Representing the Face of the World* (1635)

'I thought I'd found her,' muttered Guy de Montpellier, struggling to emerge from a dark world of dreams as he lay on his sickbed. 'Her long red hair, and her pale skin; the way she kissed me . . . I thought she was Selene, and we were in Paris again.'

Auguste smoothed her brother's sweat-soaked dark hair back from his forehead. He was burning with fever, and she was afraid for him.

'Guy,' she whispered, 'Guy, it's me, Auguste. You must not talk of Paris.'

But she knew that he couldn't hear her, couldn't see her. When Raultier had brought her brother home an hour after midnight, Guy had been exhausted, almost prostrate, though now he was struggling to raise himself, and his eyes were wild. '*Selene!*' he cried out.

'Hush. Hush,' Auguste whispered, holding him to her.

The candle flames danced around the dark-panelled walls. The air in the room smelled sharply of sweat and illness; and Auguste, as she tried with trembling fingers to sponge her younger brother's dearly familiar face, was assailed by a terrible, wrenching sense of homesickness. She hated this house, hated this sunless, damp country, hated this time of exile, which had already lasted so much longer than they had been promised. Guy would be well if they were home. Not Paris, oh, no, Paris could never be home to them again, for the memory of death would always stalk its grey streets. The place she longed for was the place where they were born: Clermont-l'Hérault, in the tender climate of the Midi, where Guy would be succoured by the sun, by the clear, thyme-scented air, by the rich wines of the south. And there, they would be safe from their enemies.

She went to the door and called for Emilie, who as she entered glanced with barely concealed fear at the sick man on the bed.

'Madame?' Emilie whispered.

'Where is Doctor Raultier, Emilie?'

'Downstairs, in the parlour, madame, writing.'

'Then go to him. Tell him that my brother needs more medicine.'

Emilie curtsied and hurried away. Auguste saw that her brother was stirring again, so she went to sit by him, and bathed his forehead, and tried to soothe him with low words.

'You must not leave us again, Guy. You must not, my love.'

He knew her now; and he gazed around the high, bare room with a look of such sorrow in his face that it was as if he had hoped, in his dreams, for release. 'No more medicine,' he whispered. 'Do you hear me, Auguste? I don't want to dream again.'

She captured his fine hands, twining them with her own, trying to warm them. 'But you must sleep. And tomorrow night, who knows? If the skies are clear, then you and I can go out and watch the stars.'

His dark eyes blazed again. 'If I could find the one I seek, then I think I would sleep for ever.'

'Yes. Hush now, my darling.' And she kissed his fingers one by one.

Guy lay back on the pillows, his features as riven by exhaustion as they had been on that last, desperate journey from Paris to Calais when they travelled by coach through the rain and mud of autumn, armed with the papers Raultier had somehow obtained, the vital passports without which no one could leave France. The surly soldiers with their cockaded red bonnets and primed muskets had needed but one look at the signatures of Danton, Minister of Justice, and of Hébert and Fréron, the two powerful and vituperative journalists who had so fervently advocated death for all enemies of the Revolution: those chilling names had been enough to secure the travellers' swift passage through every barrier to freedom. But sometimes Auguste wished that they had not escaped, and that the mob had taken them. Then, for Guy at least, the suffering would be over.

The door opened. Auguste went swiftly across the sickness-scented room to the man who stood there, big, dark-haired, gaunt-faced, with his heavy doctor's bag in his hand. She took his other hand and pressed it against her cheek.

'Pierre, I need you,' she said quietly. 'Guy is so ill, so exhausted.

Give him some more of your medicine, I beg you.'

Pierre Raultier put down his bag and bent over her sick brother. Then he turned back to her. 'I cannot give him more datura,' he replied. 'There is already a weakening, a decline in the vital spirits. Can you not see it?'

She shook her head in agitation. 'Not datura. I meant the other, the medicine to help him sleep . . .'

She was clinging to his arm now; he looked away. 'Laudanum will do him no good. It could even be dangerous.'

'Give him just enough, Pierre. Please. I cannot bear to see him like this.'

'Nor I,' said Raultier even more quietly. 'Nor I.'

Auguste let her hands fall to her sides. For a few moments her emotions seemed to consume her. At last she lifted her face to the doctor's again. 'Tell me the truth, Pierre,' she whispered. 'Will we ever be able to go back to our home?'

'Soon,' he said hoarsely, 'very soon. But I still have obligations here that I must fulfil . . .'

'*Obligations?*' Her voice rose in disbelief. 'You promised us. You promised us, Pierre, that you would take us home. Sometimes I think my brother will die here, in this hateful place . . .'

Raultier appeared to be riven by a suffering almost as great as Guy's. Then the door behind them opened and he whirled round.

William Carline stood in the doorway: impassive, silent. Ignoring Raultier, he beckoned to Auguste with an almost imperceptible movement of his head. He said nothing, now or at any time, because a physical affliction of which Raultier had tried vainly to cure him had rendered him mute.

Auguste held the Englishman's gaze. She walked over to the bed, to kiss her brother's forehead one last time. He was sleeping now, without the aid of laudanum, but his breathing was shallow and uneven. Gently she smoothed his pillow; then she went to join Carline. Taking his arm, she left the room with him.

Raultier gazed after them, his gaunt features expressing all his yearning, all his despair.

In his youth, Pierre Raultier had never had any ambition to do anything other than tend the sick. Though from an undistinguished, almost impoverished family of peasant origin, his natural intelligence had led him as a boy to excel at the college near Auray that was run by the Benedictines; and, his desire to become a doctor already strongly implanted, he went on to become a medical student at the military academy in Beaumont. On completing his studies he turned down the offer of a place as an army surgeon, and travelled instead to Paris, where he obtained a surgeon's post at the Hôtel Dieu, the hospital that served the poorest in the city. There he had found fulfilment, of a kind.

Then came revolution, and exile; a time of danger. For a short time Auguste had regarded Raultier as her saviour. They had spent one night together, as lovers, and like a fool he'd imagined that the impulse of gratitude which prompted her brief bestowal of favour sprang from a passion just as deep-rooted as his own. His mistake. But to see her with Carline was almost more than he could endure.

He went over to Guy's bedside and checked his pulse, then moistened his parched lips gently with water before smoothing down the crumpled bedsheets. Those big hands that Auguste told him betrayed his peasant blood were still as strong, as sensitive as ever in tending those who suffered. He summoned a servant to bring fresh water and clean towels, then he pushed back the curtains and opened the windows, finding brief solace in the cool air of this fresh June night. Extinguishing all the candles except one, he settled himself in the chair by the sick man's bed and prepared himself for a long vigil; while Guy de Montpellier slept on, and dreamed his dark dreams of Selene, and Paris.

VI

Watchman, what of the night? Watchman, what of the night?
The watchman said, The morning cometh, and also the night.

Isaiah 21: 11–12

Dawn was breaking coldly over the fields and woodlands by the time Pierre Raultier left the Montpelliers' house and rode back to London along the deserted turnpike road. As he reached the outskirts of the city, the sun was piercing the barred clouds to turn church spires to the palest gold, and the streets were starting to wake to the cries of the coalmen and the rattle of the market-men's drays.

After traversing the narrow lanes of St Giles, where beggars slept in every doorway, Raultier came at last to Holborn, where his lodgings were. Darkness still clung to these mean streets, for the high tenements blocked out the dawn. But as he passed the apothecary's shop on the corner of Dean Street he thought he saw candlelight gleaming behind the shutters, so he stopped, on impulse, and dismounted.

Even at this early hour a ragged urchin was watching him from the shadows. Raultier gave the child a penny to hold his horse, and went to knock at the door. He heard the bolts being drawn back; and then the apothecary was standing there, candlestick in hand, blinking up at him.

'Well, Doctor Raultier,' he said. 'It is early indeed.'

'I was passing,' said Raultier, 'and I saw the light. If my visit is inconvenient, I can call back later.'

'Not at all, not at all.' The apothecary beckoned him in. 'I was up some time ago. We are forever on call, people like you and me.' He closed the door behind Raultier and started to light more candles. 'Now, what do you require?'

Raultier ordered tinctures of datura, and of laudanum; and the apothecary, after peering shortsightedly along his crowded shelves, measured the first of the two into a small glass phial, then stoppered it and began to inscribe the label.

Datura was a drug now fallen out of fashion, for it had once had a reputation for misuse, like belladonna or mandragora, and in earlier ages had been employed by deviants as a means of stimulating the carnal senses. But some doctors used it still in the treatment of convulsions and acute melancholy even though there were, inevitably, less welcome side effects in the form of hallucination, dehydration, and often a distressing fear of the light. A small dose of the narcotic would excite the heartbeat and the nervous system, thus leading to its reputation as a sexual stimulant; but in large doses it could paralyse all the muscles of the body.

Datura stramonium. The apothecary finished his writing and handed Raultier the bottle. 'It pleases me,' he said, 'when physicians use the older drugs rather than the newfangled medicines. May I enquire, doctor, for what sickness you prescribe it?'

'A sad case,' Raultier replied quietly. 'I use it to treat a young man who is sick of a tumour at the base of the skull.'

'Dear me.' The apothecary shook his head. As he began to measure out the laudanum, he proceeded to talk about the war and its futility; and how the French heathens, who were already rampaging across all of Europe, would no doubt soon be setting barges side-by-side and front-to-back all across the Channel, so they could make their way over to England's shores and start butchering all her honest yeomen, just as they had done their own.

'Begging your pardon, sir, you being French,' he said, as Raultier paid him and waited for his change, 'but you're not one of those Jacobins, are you? Of course not, or you wouldn't be here. Tell me, is it true that some of your countrymen piled their prisoners into boats, women and children too, and sank them in the river, because the guillotine took too long to do its work?'

Raultier picked up his phials. 'It is true,' he said quietly. 'Those in power in Paris are pitiless.'

He went outside to reclaim his horse. Fitful sunlight was brightening the streets as he led the mare to the nearby stables at the back of the White Boar Inn, where he paid for livery. Then he walked along Eagle Street and climbed the stairs to his lodgings.

Raultier had two rooms, a bedchamber, and a parlour which he had made into a study. Its walls were lined with bookshelves and medicine cabinets. In the corner was a desk; and it was to the desk that he went now, after removing his hat and his coat.

Spread out already on its surface were some star charts, exquisitely copied on to vellum. He moved them carefully to one side, then unlocked a drawer set into the desk top and drew out a small book. Its black leather binding was so worn and faded that the gilt letters on its spine – Lefèvre's *Mythologie* – were scarcely legible. The book was a simple guide to the deities and fabled figures of the ancient world; the kind of volume that might once have been a schoolboy's treasured companion.

He put the book on the desk, and opened it at a place marked by a lock of curling red hair tied by a blue ribbon.

Picking up the lock of hair, he held it to his lips, and it seemed to him, just for a moment, as if the trace of some sweet perfume lingered there; the perfume, perhaps, of Provençal flowers, that had once been to him like the scent of Paradise itself.

But for a man of science he had always, he reflected, been too fond of deluding himself; and besides, all he could smell now, as he placed the lock of hair back on his desk, was the odour of camphor from his medicine bottles.

Slowly he read the page where the book lay open.

Selene. In Greek mythology, goddess of the moon, and sister of the sun. When Endymion, her lover, lay sunk in eternal sleep in a cave on Mount Latmos, he was visited nightly by Selene, who sang to him and strewed his body with flowers. In art she is often represented as a beautiful woman with red hair, and a coronet . . .

Reaching wearily for pen and a sheet of paper, Raultier began to write.

The sun rose slowly behind ragged clouds and one by one the stars were obscured. Across the continent of Europe, wars raged and nations crumbled. The brave new Republic of France, led by its warlike convention, was in inner turmoil; its citizens starved and crops lay ungathered in the fields. And yet Holland and Prussia had already bowed their heads to the fervent might of the Republic's armies; Spain was in retreat, and Austria pleaded for English gold to maintain her borders. A ruined English army had been driven in a shambles from Bremen, and French forces were now ranged all along the coast of the Low Countries, preparing for a new, a different destination: the rainwashed shores of England.

The English king's chief ministers had not slept that night. Instead they argued behind secure doors and scratched their powdered, bewigged heads over the proposal that the army of exiled French Royalists, which was already formed into regiments here under the command of General Puisaye, should be granted English ships and arms in order to make a secret landing on the shores of France. Some ministers prevaricated. Others frowned and were silent, calculating. As great men talked, and as pieces of paper passed to and fro between the secret offices of Whitehall, the young boy-king Louis, known to his gaolers as Capet, was dying slowly in a wretched Paris prison, his bones wasted with sickness.

Overhead, far beyond the clouds and the blazing sun, the stars clustered inauspiciously, waiting for the night to come.

VII

*No man is so utterly dull and obtuse, with head so
bent on earth, as never to lift himself up and rise
with all his soul to the contemplation of the starry
heavens, especially when some fresh wonder shows
like a beacon light in the sky. By my honour, no-one
could embark on a more exalted study.*

Seneca, *Quaestiones naturales,*
VII, *De Cometis* (circa AD 62-65)

Alexander Frederick Wilmot, choirmaster, church organist, amateur astronomer, and also half-brother to Jonathan Absey, adjusted his vision to the darkness that enveloped the rooftop of his little house in Clerkenwell and prepared to gaze through his precious telescope with an expression that came very close to rapture illuminating his face. It had taken him many evenings of careful work, of polishing, and adjusting, and measuring, to perfect his modest two-foot reflector, but at long last the instrument was ready; and the night sky, cloudless and moon-free, was in a state of perfection also. The celestial dome awaited his exploration like some distant, unfathomed ocean.

The stars were Alexander Wilmot's passion. He was never happier than on a clear night such as this when, having clambered with some awkwardness out on to the walled rooftop of his small terraced house just off St John's Square, he was free to turn his back on the smoke and grime of the city to the south, and likewise on the darkened fields that sloped towards Islington in the north; free to lift his gaze and look instead upon the radiant canopy of the midnight sky. He spent many hours up here, with his telescope close at hand, a comfortable wooden chair for the ease of his plump, rather short body, and a warm rug to protect his knees against the chill. Alexander had once been a navigator, on ships that sailed the southern oceans; and many a night had he spent sleeping on the open deck, with the great star clusters of the Magellanic clouds wheeling above the masts like silver veils across the deep indigo of the sky. Though he cherished the memory of their beauty, he also carried another, less fortunate reminder of his time at sea, for the bitter winds of the Atlantic winters had left him with an aching stiffness in his joints which only the tender ministrations of Daniel, his young servant and his dear companion, could ease. He had also all but lost the sight of his right eye, the fate of many navigators who had spent too long calculating the position of the midday sun.

But if the weather was too harsh for stargazing, or the skies unclear, Alexander still continued his astronomical studies indoors. For he was a more than able mathematician, and that skill, together with his star knowledge, had brought him a certain mild renown amongst those who shared his interests. On settling in Clerkenwell eight years ago Alexander had made a study of the theories of the Alsatian scientist Johann Heinrich Lambert, who had succeeded in representing the motions of Jupiter and Saturn in mathematical terms shortly before his death. Alexander did some innovative work of his own on the orbits of the giant planets and the perturbations that affected them; and this work brought his name slowly to the attention of other, more famous astronomers.

The most renowned astronomer of all, in England and the whole world, was William Herschel, the great Hanoverian observer and telescope-maker who together with his sister and assistant Caroline had made England his home. Fourteen years ago, Herschel had discovered a celestial body which he named the Georgian planet, in honour of his king; and since then astronomers throughout Europe had sought to plot its unusual course through the heavens. Alexander had contributed his own theories on its orbit to scientific publications; and to his astonishment and quiet delight, he became involved in a correspondence with the great Herschel himself. Herschel acknowledged the usefulness of Alexander's suggestions in a published paper, and this in turn led to Alexander being drawn into an exchange of ideas with the famous French scientist Laplace: illustrious correspondents indeed for the humble ex-navigator.

And yet, in spite of his mathematical expertise, the actual watching of the stars continued to remain Alexander's chief love; and every time he assembled his telescope, and turned it with gentle fingers to the skies, he had a secret dream, one that he scarcely dared acknowledge to himself, let alone to anyone else, that he might some day be known as the discoverer of a new planet, just like Herschel.

He was far from alone in his hope. All across Europe, ever since Herschel's discovery, astronomers had been searching the skies for another planet, united in the belief that if an undiscovered heavenly body did exist, then it had to lie in the disproportionately large gap between Mars and Jupiter. Early in the seventeenth century Kepler had commented on the great distance between these planets; and less than thirty years ago a professor of mathematics at the University of Wittenberg, Johann Titius, had added to the speculation by producing a chart showing that the mean distances of the planets from the Sun formed a remarkable numerical sequence, with one number in that sequence conspicuously missing in the gap between Mars and Jupiter.

If the Earth's distance from the Sun is taken as 10, then the distances from the Sun of the other planets – from the innermost, Mercury, to Saturn, the outermost – are roughly proportional to the following numbers.

4 – Mercury	7 – Venus	10 – Earth
16 – Mars	52 – Jupiter	100 – Saturn

If the number 4 is taken from each, it will be seen that this results in the sequence 0, 3, 6, 12, 48 and 96 – a remarkable yet simple pattern (apart from the first) of doubling, all the more so for the extraordinary gap where the number 24 should be; this surely must represent the position of the lost planet between Mars and Jupiter . . .

Thus wrote Titius; and Johann Elert Bode, appointed director of the Berlin Observatory in 1772, did much to draw attention to Titius's figures. '*Can one believe,*' he asked, '*that the Creator of the Universe has left the position between Mars and Jupiter empty? Certainly not!*'

And then came Herschel's discovery. If one planet could be found, the first to be discovered since the days of antiquity, why not another? What was more, Herschel's Georgian planet, orbiting beyond Saturn, fitted the Titius–Bode law with a precision that was breathtaking. It was found to orbit at 19.6 times the earth's distance from the sun, a figure which, if multiplied by 10 and reduced by four, equalled 192 – the very next number in Titius's arithmetical sequence.

So sky-watchers everywhere renewed their search of the Mars–Jupiter gap, dreaming of claiming some new celestial object for themselves. Alexander dreamed too, and in greater certainty than most, because a little under two years ago, on two nights in succession, he believed he had seen it.

At first he thought that it was a dim star of the eighth magnitude, shining low in Pisces one clear October night. But he was puzzled, because it was not a star that he had seen before. He checked his catalogues, but still could not identify it. Carefully he noted its position, and watched again for it the next night. And he saw that it had moved. No star, then; and he had recognised instantly that its edges were too sharp, too clearly defined, for it to be a comet.

He tried to remain calm; but Herschel's renowned jottings on first seeing the Georgian star came inevitably into his mind:

'In the Quartile near Zeta Tauri, the lowest of two, is a curious either Nebulous Star or perhaps a Comet . . .'

Eagerly Alexander had waited for the next night, to track the object's path. But then disappointment overwhelmed him, for the sky was overcast, and remained so for several consecutive nights, until the waxing moon robbed him of his prey. And so, by the time the heavens had cleared again, he had lost track of the mysterious object's zodiacal path.

He had never forgotten, though, that intense moment of elation, when he thought he had discovered the lost planet. And he continued to dream that some day he would find it again.

Tonight, he intended to watch the sky with more modest ambitions. He was hoping that the moonless darkness would allow him to make a study of Cygnus, to him the richest constellation of the early summer skies, crowned by the bright jewel of Deneb; and so a night of quiet pleasure lay in store for Alexander, who planned to stay out here till Jupiter rose in the south-east two hours after midnight. The skies promised to remain clear, and even the cool night breeze was for once in the right direction, bringing him the verdant smells of the countryside to the north rather than the stink of the smoking brick kilns of Holloway. But his peace was short-lived.

When he heard the sound of Daniel's footsteps hurrying up the narrow iron staircase that led to the roof, he looked round in some surprise, for Daniel was not in the habit of interrupting him once his telescope was aligned.

'You have a visitor,' said the boy, clinging to the iron handrail and peering uncertainly into the darkness of the rooftop.

'Who?'

'I don't know . . .'

Daniel looked afraid. Alexander felt fear too, because he'd had night-time visitors before. He rose stiffly from his chair. It was past eleven. Who would call on him at this hour?

He covered the mirror of his telescope with a heavy heart, aware that his hands were shaking a little as he worked. He tried to calm himself. 'Ah, Deneb,' he breathed, 'Algol, demon star, and beautiful Capella; wait for me.' Then he checked automatically that his wig was not askew, and that there were no stains of wine or gravy from his supper down the lapels of his shabby frock coat, for to Alexander Wilmot the essence of sartorial elegance did not come easy, especially at times like this, when his heart was racing and his mouth was dry with fear.

He made his way as quickly as he could down the steep little stair-case from his rooftop eyrie, very much afraid that his past was once more pursuing him.

It was on a December night a year and a half ago that Alexander had gone to a public house called the Swan in Vere Street, with a young man he had met in a nearby coffee house. The man was an Italian called Luca, olive-skinned and gently spoken, who told Alexander how much he loved music. Luca seemed to be known at the Swan, and a room upstairs was made immediately available for him. Alexander started to forget his own shyness after they had shared the first bottle of wine. There had still been moments of hesitation on his part; but Luca had extinguished the candles one by one in their chamber, and coaxed him smoothly into intimacy.

Alexander would never forget his shock, moments after it was all finished, when Luca asked him coldly for a large sum of money. Not in payment for the young Italian's practised services – Alexander would have expected that, he knew how these things were done – but as blackmail.

Alexander soon realised that he was not the only victim. Luca was one of a group of men who were systematically taking advantage of people such as Alexander at the Swan and other public houses in the vicinity of Vere Street. For a while sinister visitors called at Alexander's house by night to demand money, disturbing his neighbours and leaving Alexander himself shaking with fear. He sold precious belongings to pay them: his books, his gold watch, a much-loved telescope that had accompanied him on all his travels; but it was not enough, and his tormentors told him eventually that unless he could find more money, his name, along with those of several others caught in a similar trap, would be reported to the magistrates.

Alexander knew what kind of hostility such cases aroused. It was twenty years now since a man was last hanged in London for sodomy, but it was still a capital offence. Prosecutions were frequent, and they never failed to arouse an atmosphere of near-hysteria which left those accused, even if they were cleared, unable to resume their normal lives, while the news sheets whipped up fearful talk of foreign corruption, of the devil at work amongst honest Englishmen.

Alexander was forced to acknowledge, in the end, that he had no alternative but to go to his half-brother, Jonathan Absey, for help. It was Jonathan who rescued him, by using the powers of his office; Jonathan who saved Alexander from prison and put an end to the threats of the blackmailers; but Alexander found that the open scorn with which his half-brother dealt with the business was almost harder to endure than his fear of those night-time visitors. Jonathan had made it all too plain, when it was over, that he never wanted to see Alexander again.

So Alexander's emotions, as he entered his little first floor parlour, were in turmoil as he saw who was sitting there in the light of the two quavering candles. His heart seemed to shrivel within his breast, and what followed pushed the glory of the stars from his mind.

'Well, Alexander,' said Jonathan Absey. 'I've dragged you from your stargazing, have I? Come now. It's been a long time. You could make some effort to look pleased to see me. Even if it is only a pretence.'

He stood up slowly, and the acidity of his voice, which Alexander had not heard for a year and a half, seemed to etch the silence that followed. Alexander suddenly felt how shabby, how dreary this room was, with its empty grate and its dark oak panelling. The smell of the cheap tallow candles mingled unpleasantly with the faint but pungent odour of the malt distillery nearby, a smell that on certain nights always crept through his windows, no matter how close he fastened them. He said quickly, 'You. What do you want?' and his voice shook, because he was afraid that Jonathan had come to tell him that he was, after all, to face a belated prosecution over the Vere Street incident.

'You'll already have guessed,' Jonathan said, 'that this isn't a social visit, Alexander.'

'I never imagined it was,' said Alexander shakily. 'Please tell me quickly why you are here.'

Jonathan continued to regard him silently, and his blue eyes were cold, cold as Vega, it seemed. Alexander noticed that one side of his brother's face was badly, recently bruised, and he seemed to be holding himself awkwardly, as if suppressing some discomfort.

'Why does the sight of me make you so frightened, Alexander?' Jonathan was asking softly. 'You haven't been visiting that sordid little tavern in Vere Street again, have you? Or anywhere else of similar kind? Because if you have, I can't help you again. You know that, don't you? You understand that you must take all of the consequences upon yourself this time?'

Alexander was aware of a sharp sickness at the pit of his stomach and a breaking of sweat on the palms of his hands. 'I haven't been there. You must know that I haven't, that I would never go again . . .'

'Well, I hope to God that you mean what you say.' Turning his back abruptly on his brother, Jonathan began to prowl around the room, letting his fingers brush against Alexander's precious harpsichord, his music books, his Flamsteed's *Atlas Coelestis*, his delicate dividers. Alexander flinched at each touch until at last Jonathan stopped his prowling and faced him squarely.

'I've come for information, brother. And the sooner you answer me, the sooner I'll leave.' He thrust his hands into his coat pockets. 'Tell me. Do you know any French astronomers living here in London?'

Alexander was astonished. 'French astronomers?'

'You heard me.'

'I know of a few, yes.' His voice to his mind sounded babbling, stupid. 'I've heard of them occasionally because they have links with the Company of Titius, a self-named band of star-watchers . . . But you're surely not interested in these people?' He remembered all too clearly his half-brother's scorn for the subject of astronomy and all who dealt with it; and yet Jonathan, who was still studying him carefully, replied,

'I might be. Tell me what you know about them.'

'The Company of Titius,' began Alexander quickly in a low, toneless voice, 'is the name used by a group of astronomers from various countries in Europe, who have dedicated themselves to finding the whereabouts of an undiscovered planet, as predicted by a German professor called Titius, and others since him . . .'

He became distracted as he saw that Jonathan, hands still in his pockets, was leaning back against his harpsichord. 'Go on,' Jonathan snapped.

Alexander moistened his lips and struggled on.

'. . . as predicted by a German professor called Titius, and others since him. The lost planet is believed to lie between Mars and Jupiter . . .'

Only a little while ago, in the seclusion of his rooftop retreat, he had been contemplating the Titius theory with quiet rapture; but indeed he took no joy in recounting the German's theories now, to his half-brother. And Jonathan seemed to take no joy in hearing them, either; he listened, but the frown remained on his face as he heard out Alexander's halting account of the arithmetical pattern of the planets' distance from the sun.

'And so,' Alexander concluded, stumbling over almost every word, 'the members of the Company of Titius write to each other, to share their findings. There are members in Paris, and Rome, and Berlin . . . Please. My harpsichord. It is fragile, Jonathan, *take care* . . .'

Jonathan moved abruptly away from the instrument, setting every string vibrating. 'Enough of this talk of stars and planets,' he said. 'Just tell me one thing: do you know any of these people yourself?'

'Not personally, no . . .'

'Then how have you heard of them?'

Alexander stammered, 'My friend Perceval – Perceval Oates, the spectacle-maker – has corrected some instruments for them.'

'And did he give you the names of these people, these Frenchmen?'

'If he did,' replied Alexander desperately, 'I cannot remember any.'

Jonathan's mouth tightened. At last he walked stiffly over to the window, where the curtains had not yet been drawn, and for some moments he gazed out into the Clerkenwell night, while Alexander held himself still by a great effort of will, waiting. Then Jonathan turned away from the window, and in the flickering light of the candles Alexander saw that his brother's bruised face was more dissipated than the last time he'd seen him, and his blue eyes were weary, so weary that Alexander wondered if his daughter's death had taken from him something more vital than life itself.

'You know that you are in my debt,' said Jonathan, breaking the silence.

'Yes. Yes. I have always acknowledged it . . .'

'I don't think you realise quite how much you owe me, but let that pass. Listen, Alexander. I want you to do something for me. I want you to find out more about these French astronomers in London. I want you to join their company, their society, whatever they call themselves, and report back to me.'

Sheer disbelief dispelled Alexander's fear. 'But I don't know where they live. I don't even know who they are.'

'Then find out,' said Jonathan. His voice was still quiet, but the menace had returned. 'Visit them. Talk to them about the stars.'

'Why?'

'Because I'm interested in them, brother. Isn't that enough?'

'But what if I fail? What if they don't want me in their circle?'

'Alexander,' said Jonathan, 'Alexander, sometimes you exasperate me. You've had your moments of distinction, haven't you? Didn't you once help Herschel with some important work of his?'

'A few years ago I made some suggestions about the orbit of his new planet which he thanked me for . . .'

Jonathan shrugged. 'There you are then. What more do you need to impress them?' He took a step closer. 'I need to know about these Frenchmen. I want their names, their occupations. I want to know where they live.' He fixed his gaze relentlessly on his half-brother. 'I'll give you a week, no more. You know where I'm to be found, don't you?'

'Yes. But . . .'

'I don't expect you to fail me, Alexander.' Jonathan was already making his way to the door. 'And remember that the sooner you begin, the sooner this will be over, for both of us.'

With that, he left. Alexander stood at the top of the staircase, watching his brother disappear down into the dark hallway; he listened until he heard the slam of the big outer door; and he waited, wearily, for the inevitable.

He knew that the noise of Jonathan's going, at such a late hour, would disturb old Hannah, who lived in the rooms below. Whenever something agitated her, Hannah would recite feverishly from the Bible; and now Alexander, with a heavy heart, heard her voice rising in a demented, muttering litany:

'*The beauty of Israel is slain upon thy high places . . .*'

She lived with her spinster daughter. Alexander could hear the daughter's voice now as she tried to calm the old woman and persuade her back from the door she had opened into the unlit hallway. 'Hush, mother. Be still.'

Alexander went quickly down a few steps and peered into the gloom. Hannah stood in the hall in a faded cotton nightrobe, with her grey hair hanging loosely around her shoulders. Her daughter, who carried a candlestick, was tugging with her free hand at the old woman's arm. Alexander called down, 'My visitor has gone now, Hannah. There's no cause for alarm. I'm truly sorry you've been disturbed.'

Old Hannah looked up at him with beady, disbelieving eyes, but was silent. Her daughter finally managed to lead her back inside.

Alexander went up again on to the roof after that, but the night was no longer his. His hands shook on the telescope, his gaze was not steady; and after the glow of candlelight in the room below, he knew he would have to wait for his vision to adjust again to the darkness if he was to see anything other than the brightest stars. He realised also that in his agitation earlier he had not covered the speculum of his telescope properly, and it had become misted with the night dew.

He rubbed his right eye, which was misted likewise, but with blindness; and with his left eye he watched Vega, almost overhead, and unmistakable with its steely blue brilliance; but it reminded him of his brother's eyes, so he looked away quickly, and gazed at the Pole Star, lodged in the handle of Ursa Minor, age-old mark of constancy for men of the sea.

Constancy? Ah, no. The great scientist Laplace believed that the rules which governed the universe were immutable; but Alexander could not agree. How could anyone not realise that it was mere chance that ruled us all? How could anyone not see that the most dazzling calculations of which the human brain was capable could be overturned by the unexpected journey of a meteor, or by an exploding star, or by the gradual, relentless gravitational pull of the giants of the heavens?

Or by the arrival of one's blue-eyed half-brother, Jonathan, who had always despised his older sibling: Jonathan, the details of whose job were a closed book to Alexander apart from the fact that he worked on secret government business, in some nameless government office; Jonathan, with his badly bruised face, and eyes that were as steely as Vega when they were not mired by weariness, or bitterness, or both.

Alexander listened to the church bell of St John's striking midnight, and gazed one last time at the tantalising bounty of the night sky. Somewhere out there was celestial harmony, somewhere there was order and peace; and just for a moment his yearning heart soared high above the rooftops of lowly Clerkenwell, far from the sordid intrusion of Jonathan's untimely visit. He remembered Titius's pattern of figures, that he had tried so clumsily, so ineffectually to explain to his half-brother; and once more he wondered: Why did Jonathan want to know about these astronomers?

He shivered, and, since the night air was growing cold, started with a heavy heart to put everything away. He looked northwards, across the dark fields and heaths that stretched away beyond the lonely road to distant Hampstead. Far beyond the trees, he could see the smoking tile kilns at Bagnigge Wells, whose foul stench polluted the countryside even at this late hour. Turning, he went downstairs.

Daniel had sensed that his master's stargazing was over for the night and prepared a bath for him in his bedchamber. The boy had lit candles, and a fire too, to warm the chilly air; and now he waited to attend Alexander, but his eyes were still wide with fear of the late-night visitor.

'It's all right, my dear,' said Alexander tenderly. 'That man can do us no harm. But I'm sorry – so sorry – that he upset you. You must be tired; you should go to your bed.'

He divested himself of his garments and eased himself into the warm water, feeling distaste, as ever, for the flabby white folds of flesh at his stomach, for his spindly legs. He thought that Daniel had gone, but the boy returned, with a small earthenware phial in his hand. Silently, Daniel unstoppered the phial and began to rub the unguent it contained into his master's tense shoulders. Alexander felt the boy's fingers kneading away the aching knots of tiredness.

'I think you are weary,' Daniel said in his soft voice. 'Does this help?'

Alexander sighed in gratitude. 'Yes. Yes, it helps greatly. Thank you.'

He had bought Daniel when the merchant ship on which he served as navigator called in at Mauritius nine years ago, on a long voyage to the Indies. By then Alexander's career was already in decline, otherwise he would not have taken passage on board that more than disreputable ship.

They had spent some days in harbour at Port Louis, waiting for repairs. Most of the crew passed the time by drinking themselves into a stupor beneath the hot sun. Alexander, dazed by the tedium of it all, had wandered to the market place, and there he saw the boy, scarcely more than seven or eight and small for his age. He had been beaten, half starved, and abused in other ways. Alexander had felt the kind of anger that gave him courage. He bargained harshly with the boy's master, and bought him for a few coins.

It was not unusual for officers aboard ships such as his to retain a personal slave. Daniel became Alexander's, although he preferred to call him his servant. Slowly the young boy learnt to trust him, and his wounds healed.

The boy was beautiful, with his dusky skin and his dark, wide-set eyes that had not quite lost all their trust in humankind. How easy it would have been to betray that trust. Alexander could have made good money by selling him nightly on that long, becalmed voyage home, when the winds would not rise to help them on their way, and the Southern Cross, with its pointers Alpha and Beta Centauri, dazzled them overhead in the clear warm heavens, reminding them of their displacement, chiding their slowness. The sailors, bored and idle, indulged in many secret bestialities beneath the mocking stars; but Alexander kept Daniel away from them, feeding him and salving his sores, teaching him the rudiments of letters and mathematics, and pointing out the wonders of the heavens to him. He found to his pleasure that the boy was an apt and willing pupil, and when Alexander's sailing days were done, Daniel stayed with him.

Alexander's decision to leave the sea was forced on him, in the end, not only by the arthritis that was already starting to bite deep into his bones, but, more seriously, by the deterioration in his eyesight. On the lowly ships he sailed on, the position of the sun was still the mainstay of the navigator's art. Alexander had taken care of his sight as far as he was able, always using a backstaff to calculate the sun's zenith; but even so he started to become blind in his right eye. To use the left one would have inevitably led to that one, too, becoming as opaque, as milky white as its fellow; and so Alexander had to accept that his career at sea was over.

Once, before taking up navigation, he had been an apt scholar of music. On his retirement, he decided to set himself up as a music teacher and organist, and with the meagre pittance thus obtained was able to occupy one of the several little wood-and-plaster houses that lay close by the church where he played for services and tuned the bells. Daniel lived with him, his servant and his dear companion.

Daniel was reaching now for more of the unguent, but Alexander, seeing that the boy was slow with weariness, stopped him by saying gently,

'No, my dear. There's no need. You must be tired. Go to your bed; I will see to everything else.'

The youth bowed his head and silently put the ointment away. Alexander watched as Daniel prepared himself for sleep on the little truckle bed in the corner of the room, and realised that for a few precious moments he had forgotten all about his brother Jonathan.

My beloved is mine, and I am his; he feedeth among the lilies
Until the day break, and the shadows flee away.

VIII

*We can never hope that the circumstances as far as
they regard the state of France can be more favourable
than they now are. What must be obvious is the
infinite advantage of acting soon, and, at all
hazards, acting offensively.*

Foreign Office letter, Lord Grenville to Eden,
Summer 1795

Early the next morning, Jonathan Absey, bracing himself against
the bright sunlight, made his way on foot from Brewer Street,
down the Haymarket and past the King's Mews to Whitehall;
and as he traversed the familiar streets, it seemed to him that London
was more than ever in a state of armed readiness. Soldiers from the
Tower and from the barracks at St James's Palace were everywhere,
making the much-talked-of threat of invasion seem even more real;
and outside the Horse Guards, on the parade ground, was a battalion
of foot soldiers, whose scarlet and white uniforms blazed with colour
against the classic grey stone façade. Some officers rode slowly to the
front of the lines, mounted on fine horses; Jonathan stood and watched
them, until a sharp command rang out and the men marched off in
the bright sunlight towards Storey's Gate and Westminster.

These soldiers were the pick of the established regiments. Most of
the others to be seen in London were raw novices, callow youths invei-
gled into the army by sharp recruiting officers. Others were prison
scum, enticed by promises of pardons. Jonathan had heard that William
Pitt had announced in parliament only the other day that fifteen addi-
tional battalions of foot were to be raised urgently in order to cope
with the country's present danger; yet Jonathan wondered, as did many
others, where all those extra men would be found. He guessed that
even thirty battalions of foot would not be enough to make up for the
recent, catastrophic troop losses in the Flemish and West Indian
campaigns.

He walked on carefully. His body still ached from the beating he'd received outside the Angel two nights ago, and the skin round his eye was dark with bruises. Yesterday afternoon he'd paid a visit to a surgeon, to check if his ribs were broken. He was told they weren't; but whatever, they ached damnably.

Afterwards he'd visited the police office at Bow Street, where Bentham had suggested he might enquire about the death of the red-haired girl in the spring. They knew nothing there, but he'd visited other places, and he'd found out, by dint of stubborn, almost despairing questioning, that not one, but two red-haired girls were on record as having been killed since his daughter's death last June. The first of them, Jane Parsons, a young streetwalker, had been murdered last November. The second, Bessie Sharp, a seventeen-year-old who worked in a Whitechapel tavern and also earned money as a whore, had died in March. They were both strangled. Both had marks on their necks that corresponded to the use of something smoother than rope. And no progress whatsoever had been made in finding the killer of either.

Jonathan thought: I paid investigators to find out these things for me. I should have been told. I should have known of these deaths . . .

A surly constable answered his questions about Bessie Sharp almost monosyllabically at the Whitechapel police office; there was no one else there, at the time of his visit, with more authority; but at Hatton Garden, where Jane Parsons's death had been recorded, Jonathan found himself talking in a private room to the stipendiary magistrate, Aaron Graham, who listened to him with some sympathy.

'A young woman was killed two nights ago,' explained Jonathan earnestly as he leaned across the big table that separated him from Graham. 'She was strangled with a cord that left no abrasions. She, too – like these others – had red hair. Three deaths, and all so similar – Jane Parsons, Bessie Sharp, Priss at the Blue Bell; it seems to me that they could all have been killed by the same man . . .' He pushed forward the notes he had made on the deaths of Bessie and Priss.

'You haven't mentioned your daughter,' said Aaron Graham quietly. 'Are you thinking of her also?'

Jonathan was silent a moment. Then he said, 'I never stop thinking about her.'

'Yes,' said Graham. 'Yes, of course. I'm sorry.'

Aaron Graham was a direct appointee, here at Hatton Garden, of the Home Office; he was well respected, and his influence spread far beyond the official boundaries of his office. Jonathan leaned forward again. 'Would you do something for me, Mr Graham? Would you send a fresh report on the deaths of these girls to the Chief Magistrate? Surely, with the killing of the girl at the Blue Bell, some official action must be taken?'

Graham hesitated; Jonathan's heart sank. Graham said, 'I would like very much to help you. But—'

'But they were whores,' said Jonathan heavily.

Graham spread his hands. 'You know the system as well as I.'

'They were so young. They didn't deserve to die as they did.'

Graham stood up decisively and gathered the papers Jonathan had produced. 'I'll do what I can,' he said. 'Of course I will.'

Jonathan stood too, somewhat dizzily, because of his stiffening bruises and aching head. He shook Graham's hand. 'Thank you,' he said.

And so the next morning he came wearily to his place of work, climbing the stairs with care, because his injuries had stiffened overnight. His office was situated in the building known as Montague House, where the Board of Trade held residence on the ground floor, and the Home Office on the first. Here, as Collector and Transmitter of State Papers, he was the recipient of a seemingly never-ending stream of suspicious mail, forwarded to him with varying degrees of urgency by the port agents, by the clerks at the postal office, and by the county deputies, who seemed to write, in these times of trouble, of insurrection and treachery in all the shires of England. Gazettes, local news sheets, and even Corresponding Society journals were all grist to Jonathan's mill; but his chief responsibility was the examination of intercepted foreign mail, which had been temporarily withheld from its journey by packet ship to the Continent; much of it written by the countless French refugees who filled London, all of whom were suspected, by the watchful agents of the Home Office, of being spies. Sometimes those letters which were deemed important enough by Jonathan to be shown to his superior, Pollock, might be passed higher, sometimes very high indeed; for the Chief Clerk was responsible to the Under-Secretary, who in turn came under the direct command of the Secretary of State for the Home Office, the Duke of Portland himself.

As usual that morning there was work in plenty awaiting him; he was kept busy for two hours with the latest ship letters from the merchant captains of the southern ports, a whole batch of them, sent to him by the meticulous clerks of the postal office in Lombard Street. They thought that some, perhaps all of them might prove to be worthy of Master Absey's esteemed attention.

But Jonathan's attention, by eleven o'clock in the morning, was wandering; so much so that he got abruptly to his feet, scattering his papers.

They write to each other, he thought. Paris, Berlin, Rome – *they write to each other.*

This business on his desk could wait. That of the mysterious astronomer-doctor could not. He seized his hat and coat and marched out of the office. He knew, none better, where records of all foreign mail were kept.

The public mail office in Lombard Street, at the very heart of the city, was thronged with clerks scurrying to and fro, and the high ceilings and vaulted passageways echoed to the sound of their busy voices. Jonathan caught the eye of one of the clerks and said,

'A moment of your time. I want you to check your records for me, for some items of mail that are dispatched regularly from London to Paris.'

Jonathan was known there. 'Certainly, Mr Absey, sir. What name shall I look under?'

'The Company of Titius,' said Jonathan. He spelled the name out, and the clerk listened, frowning.

'Titius. Is that some mercantile concern, sir?'

'No, scientific,' said Jonathan, 'but they send letters regularly.'

'Very well. I'll look straight away, Mr Absey.'

Jonathan waited for him in the ante-room, where the clerks were busy with their official bags. The clerk had gone to check the registers of continental mails, of which there were plenty; Jonathan knew there were still four posts a week across the Channel, even in this time of war, depending, of course, especially in winter, on how the packet boats fared with the wind and the tide. With every dispatch and every arrival of overseas mail, these clerks sorted around a thousand letters, and in each consignment perhaps a hundred would be quietly intercepted – 'on suspicion' – and passed swiftly on to an adjacent office that nestled discreetly between Lombard Street and Sherborne Lane.

This was the crucial and secretive section of the Postal Secretary's department that the public never saw, but with which Jonathan was only too familiar. In the private Sherborne Lane office, the letters in question were pored over and copied until midnight if need be by senior clerks, so the originals could go on their way the next morning; and indeed, sometimes it would be two or three o'clock when the Decipherer himself was called out, yawning, to sharpen his quill pens and prepare to do his own kind of intricate work by the light of guttering candles. All through the rest of the night, young clerks would run through the dark streets of London, past St Paul's and Ludgate Hill, along the Strand to Whitehall and the offices of the great departments of state – War, Home and Foreign – where they handed over the packets they carried, marked PRIVATE AND MOST SECRET; and there more eyes would strain over crowded words, and more messengers would be sent to run up and down the quiet corridors of Whitehall. There was no evidence of such secrecy here in the main hall, as the clerks went about the business of sorting letters in the bright light of day, and the public came and went. But Jonathan knew that by day as well as by night all the business of a nation at war continued, behind closed doors.

More clerks hurried by, but there was still no sign of the one he'd spoken to. Restlessly Jonathan paced the corridor and looked again at his watch. Surely, surely he must have found something by now.

And then, the clerk came back. Again he looked puzzled.

'I'm very sorry, Mr Absey, sir. I've looked through the Paris files, and there's a brief record of several letters sent there from London in the name of the Company of Titius; but there are no copies.'

Jonathan was aware of a crushing sense of disappointment. 'But all mail to Paris should be copied and recorded – or at least its contents summarised. Don't you even have the name of the sender?'

The clerk looked crestfallen. 'Nothing, sir. Just some dates, and the name of the person to whom the letters were sent – someone called Master Titius, in Paris. That's all, I'm afraid.'

Jonathan rubbed his hand distractedly through his hair. Master Titius, in Paris. Hadn't his brother told him that Titius was a German professor? Confused and disappointed, he said at last, 'If anything should be sent under this name at a future date, will you let me know, straight away?'

'Of course, sir.'

'You'll remember the name? You'll put it on your list of interceptions?'

'Yes, I certainly will. The Company of Titius, sir.' He spelled it out. 'I'll file your instructions straight away.'

Jonathan, aware that he was becoming tedious in his disappointment, nodded curt thanks and walked slowly out into the courtyard. A hurrying messenger almost ran into him, and pulled up to apologise. Jonathan drew himself up sharply and felt the bruises on his ribs aching with renewed vigour.

He had hoped that the answer to his quest might be here, in the foreign mail office: he'd thought he might find the name of the French astronomer in the Angel; the name, he was almost sure, of the murderer who had haunted his thoughts for the long year since his daughter's death. He had hoped, for one brief moment, that the trail of her killer, which had seemed so cold, was opening up again, but it seemed he was wrong. Unless Alexander could help him.

The noisy squabbling of some sparrows in a corner of the courtyard roused him from his abstraction. He walked away at last from the Lombard Street office and turned along Poultry, intending to make his way back to Whitehall and his duties there; but then he thought of the paperwork awaiting him, and the noontide briefing, for which he would already be late. He turned aside into a nearby tavern and ordered wine, taking refuge in the dimly lit, anonymous surroundings of the tap room; and he found himself thinking again of his timorous half-brother, with whom he had shared a childhood nearly as tortured as the present.

Alexander, five years older than Jonathan, was the only son of Jonathan's mother's first husband, who had died of a lung fever one winter when Alexander was scarcely three years old. Jonathan knew that Alexander's father had been a schoolteacher and a musician, but he was rarely mentioned. Jonathan's father, Peter Absey, was, by way of contrast, a striving attorney, who tried to make up in bullying and ambition what he lacked in natural ability. He ruled his little family and his servants with a rod of iron in his big, echoing house in Soho Square; and he developed a total antipathy to his wife's first son, having no sympathy for Alexander's gentleness and musical tastes, which he saw as a sign of weakness.

Peter Absey beat Alexander regularly, and when Jonathan was very young he had believed that Alexander had brought his punishment on himself. Later Jonathan saw the way of it better, and he even came to secretly respect his older half-brother for the stoical courage with which he bore his situation; but by then the barrier was up between them, and it was too late to do or say anything to make amends.

The mother of the two boys, a reserved, devout woman who came from a genteel family and laid claim to distant links with some well-to-do cousins who were merchants in the City, had done nothing, as far as Jonathan could remember, to stop her husband's viciousness towards his stepson except, perhaps, to pray for them all.

Alexander, who grew into a plump and awkward youth whose clothes always seemed a size too small, found a refuge of sorts in his stars and his music. He was talented at figures, and was singled out for praise by the master of mathematics at the undistinguished private school in Great Marlborough Street which both boys attended. The masters wanted him to continue his studies. But this was declared impossible, by Alexander's stepfather and his subservient mother, and so Alexander was apprenticed to a watchmaker in Turnbull Street at fourteen.

Peter Absey, who was by now stout and prone to apoplexy, had given up the beatings. Correspondingly, as if his other energies were failing too, his business as an attorney began to decline. When Alexander was sixteen and Jonathan eleven, a new storm arose, because Mrs Absey discovered that her firstborn son was sharing the bed, and the embraces, of the unmarried, middle-aged watchmaker. Jonathan, who didn't quite understand such things at the time, asked a friend what this meant, and he was told succinctly, 'It means they're buggering each other.' Alexander left London silently, without a word to anyone; Jonathan discovered much later that he'd gone to sea, in the merchant service, where he put his mathematical and technical skills to some use by becoming a ship's navigator. Plenty of buggery too, Jonathan assumed.

The little family, with the father irate and mother distraught, sold up the big, cold house in Soho Square and moved to faraway Lambeth, to escape the punishing gossip.

Jonathan's father died. For a while their mother was incessantly at prayer, dressed always in black; and then she died too, in crucifying pain that Jonathan would never forget, of a malignant tumour at her breast, close to the very place where she always clasped her hands in prayer.

For Jonathan, meanwhile, unexpected good fortune had come. A distant relative, one of his mother's prosperous merchant cousins of whom they had heard much but seen little, recommended Jonathan as a trainee messenger in the lower echelons of Whitehall; and so his career had begun. He had worked hard, and soon proved his worth. On being promoted to clerk in the Home Office, he had married, and he and his wife Mary bought a cottage close to the river in Chelsea and had two children, a girl and a boy. But by the time their son was leaving infancy, it became apparent to his parents that the boy's mind was somehow damaged; and indeed, his mental age never advanced beyond that of a child. Mary, troubled by her son's affliction, was sometimes resentful; and as the intensity of Jonathan's work increased, his wife grew increasingly unhappy with his sometimes sour humours, and the fact that he was often called away for days at a time, leaving her to deal with the mysterious, occasionally aggressive visitors who called at their door looking for him. One evening, four years ago, he'd got back, tired, to their house in Chelsea village to find his things packed, and his wife standing in the doorway, insisting that he leave. His children, Thomas and Ellie, had watched silently as he turned to go.

He minded it all more than he could say. Mary and his son Thomas still lived in the cottage they had bought together, one of several pleasant dwellings that lay between the old timber sheds of the former porcelain factory and the open fields. He still visited them. But now his daughter was dead, and his son was a young giant of sixteen, with the mind of an infant.

Whenever he could, Jonathan would take Thomas for a walk along the river bank, where they would stand on the tide-scoured pebble shore and watch the boats passing by. Thomas, who towered over his father, would exclaim with delight at their coloured sails; he loved brightness and movement, just as he loved to have people around him. One of the things that distressed Jonathan most on his son's behalf was the way that strangers were frightened, even repelled, by Thomas's friendly eagerness to enjoy all the things around him. Afterwards they would walk slowly home with the treasures they had collected – coloured stones, leaves, flowers – and while Thomas played with them in a corner of the parlour, Jonathan's wife would tell him of the money she needed, to feed Thomas and keep him in clothes. She never spoke of Ellie. He guessed that she blamed him for the loss of their daughter.

Jonathan was brought abruptly back to the present as the door to the tap room was flung wide open, filling the room briefly with sunlight. A group of Cheapside carters made a noisy entrance. Realising that his wine was finished, Jonathan left, and wandered the taverns and coffee shops of Cheapside, enquiring about French *émigré* doctors and the Company of Titius; but the trail had gone cold. Many of those he asked looked at the livid bruise on his cheek, smelled the wine on his breath, and dismissed him, drawing their own conclusions.

By the time Jonathan got back to his office, it was past four o'clock. He had been absent much longer than he had intended. Sitting down at his desk, he began to sharpen his pens and gazed bleakly at the sea of documents that awaited him. Some of them had even strayed on to the faded little couch in the corner, one of the few concessions to comfort in the room; Jonathan had never used it, except as an extra surface for his many papers. Slowly he pulled the tray of new dispatches over in front of him.

The foreign mails always came in at three. There were none. The tray was filled with inland mail only. He frowned and looked again. Perhaps none had been intercepted in today's post, but that was rare indeed; in fact there had not been a single day for over a year now in which there were neither ship letters nor incoming mail from the packet boats that were considered worthy of his attention.

Just at that moment his door opened and John King, the Under-Secretary, second in administrative importance only to the Duke of Portland himself, came in. He was a little younger than Jonathan, tall and lean and sharp-nosed. A former Oxford and Lincoln's Inn man, he had been appointed to his current post last year, and he had lost no time in making his mark. He was known to have his favourites, and Jonathan wasn't one of them. Jonathan got to his feet quickly.

'Absey,' said King in his abrasive Lancashire voice. 'I see you're back.'

'Yes, sir. I was about to start on the foreign letters. But there don't seem to be any.'

King folded his arms and said tightly, 'There were, in fact, several. They arrived two hours ago. Some of them were marked as urgent. The Secretary of State expressed a wish to see them straight away, so they were passed to Connolly, who copied them and made notes on them for our files.'

Jonathan breathed in sharply. Connolly was a junior clerk, more than ten years younger than he was. Connolly was eager for promotion. Jonathan said, 'I'm sorry, sir. I had business elsewhere.'

'Not good enough, Absey. Your business is here. We have lowlier people, called messengers, to handle our lesser work.'

'I'm sorry,' Jonathan said again. 'This is the last time it will happen.'

'You're right,' said King. 'From now on, I've told Connolly to deal with the foreign mail.'

Jonathan was stunned. 'But I've been dealing with the foreign mail for ten years, sir. It's my chief work. I know so many people, so many names . . .'

King leaned intimidatingly across the desk, his hands resting on its edge. 'I've had my doubts about you, Absey, for some time. You need to show a little more caution in your private affairs. I know, naturally, about the unfortunate matter of your daughter. But to go round the watch houses, Absey, following up the murders of common street-walkers . . .' He shook his head in vivid disapproval. 'You're a Home Office agent, remember, not an officer from Bow Street.'

Drawing himself up to his full height again, he gave Jonathan a last, admonishing glance and left the room.

Jonathan waited till he heard his footsteps dying away into the distance. Then he closed the door and leaned back against it. How did King know about his fresh enquiries concerning the murdered girls? Was it Bentham who'd informed on him?

And then he thought of Graham. It could well have been Aaron Graham at the Hatton Garden office, who yesterday had promised Jonathan, with apparent sympathy, that he would send in a report on the deaths of the murdered girls to the Chief Magistrate.

Instead, he must have reported Jonathan's unorthodox activities to his Home Office superiors. Just for a moment, Jonathan had thought he had somebody on his side. The mistake would not be repeated.

Soon afterwards he had another visitor: William Pollock, the elderly Chief Clerk, who had set this whole chain of events in motion with his talk of the *émigrés* at the Angel. Pollock stood in the doorway, clearly ill at ease; he took a moment to meet Jonathan's eye.

'I gather you're out of favour with the Under-Secretary,' he said at last.

Jonathan replied, 'Yes. He's taken me off the foreign mails.'

Pollock cleared his throat and drew closer. 'I know you work as hard as anyone in Montague House, Jonathan. But it was most unfortunate that you were absent when today's mails came in. There were several urgent items, and the Under-Secretary was highly displeased that you weren't here to deal with them. Perhaps you have a little too much coming on to your desk at the moment.' He glanced ruefully at the heaps of paper strewn around the office. 'For the time being, let's leave Connolly to deal with the foreign interceptions, shall we? It means you'll be free to concentrate fully on the internal mail.' He patted the papers on Jonathan's desk. 'Still plenty for you to be getting on with there.'

Too embarrassed to say anything more, he quickly left the room.

Jonathan sat down at his desk. He lifted up the first of the letters that awaited his attention and started to glance through it. It was a report of rumours of insurgence amongst the militia in Norwich, from the county magistrates there; nothing new, then.

The Under-Secretary was right. Hunting for the murderer of street girls was not Jonathan's job. But one of the girls has been his daughter.

It was with a burdened heart that Jonathan worked his way through the rest of the account of the discontent at the Norwich barracks. He would be more careful, in future, of whom he asked questions. But he would not stop asking them.

Alexander, he intoned silently, *Alexander, you had better, just this once, be doing what I asked you* . . .

IX

*T*onight, *I saw a falling star, tumbling in glory from the heavens;
falling, as all men must fall, from grace.*

*Proud Hydra, the solitary one, shines as brightly as ever through
the vault of the sky, boasting his hundred heads in bold defiance; but soon
he will sink deep beneath the Lernaean marshes, not to be seen again until
the autumn equinox saddens the skies.*

*The Crab showed itself briefly at sunset. The pain was bad later, as
bad as I have known. Such corruption of the flesh, such failure. How cruel
is the creature we call God, to regiment so brightly the beauty of the
universe, and yet to allow such fetid decay here below.*

*It is impossible to gaze at the stars tonight, to seek the one which is lost.
The moon is too full, too bright.*

*The moon was full when Selene came, silent, to my door. On that night,
she shone so brightly that she drove the stars from the sky.*

Guy de Montpellier slammed down his pen, and splashes of ink flew
like tracings of black embroidery across the paper on which he had
been writing. He lifted his head, listening. There was no sound here
in his candlelit room. But in the nearby bedchamber of his sister, his
beautiful sister with her shorn, powdered hair; could he hear something there?

Guy rose from his desk and listened again. Still no sound, except
for a faint rustling that might have been the chafing of silken
garments as they slipped from soft skin, or might be nothing but
the movement of the heavy window drapes as they stirred in the
night breeze. No sound, except for a long, low sigh that could have
been the breeze once more, or perhaps an exhalation of scarcely to
be borne pleasure, or pain.

Guy reached out his hand and swept everything from his desk:
paper, pens, ink; everything crashed to the floor.

Silence, then. Silence throughout the house. No one stirred, except
Guy and one other; and he paced the hall below, with a crumpled
message clutched in his hand.

'*The Company of Titius is being watched. Be prepared, again.*'

At last Guy walked unsteadily to the open door and left his chamber. Moments later, in a far room of the house, the celestial sound of a harpsichord dazzled the air.

X

But first whom shall we send
In search of this new world; whom shall we find
Sufficient?

John Milton, *Paradise Lost* (1667), Book II

'Tell me, my friend,' said Alexander Wilmot diffidently, tugging at a frayed buttonhole on his fustian coat to conceal his underlying tension, 'have you heard anything lately of those French astronomers you once mentioned to me?'

He was asking the question of Perceval Oates the spectacle-maker, whose little shop nestled side by side with the workshops of the numerous watchmakers of Clerkenwell. Perceval had already lit candles, because outside the evening sun was starting to sink beneath the rooftops, casting the narrow street into shadow. The interior of the shop was crammed with all the articles of his trade, and it smelled, as always, of the snuff Perceval used, and of slightly stale linen.

Perceval was thin, spare, ascetic; a remnant of the old Huguenot intake into this northern parish of London; he was unmarried, and, as far as Alexander knew, he was subject to none of man's usual cravings for the pleasures of the flesh. Ensconced here in Townsend Lane, last bastion of suburban respectability before the prim little shops and cottages gave way to the roistering taverns and bearpits of Hockley in the Hole, Perceval was always dressed in plain brown suits of serge, dusty but serviceable, just like the furnishings of his shop; and he wore an old-fashioned peruke wig, thoroughly powdered, in defiance of the younger, freer fashions.

Alexander had brought the speculum mirror from his telescope for Perceval to polish. Normally he looked forward with eager anticipation to making the short journey here through Clerkenwell Green, past the open spaces where the children played. But tonight Alexander found difficulty in recapturing the simple enjoyment of his previous visits, because two days ago his brother Jonathan had made his intrusive demand for information; and so Alexander had come here, with the utmost reluctance, to extract what he could about the exiled star-watchers from his unsuspecting friend.

To make matters worse, Perceval, who was carefully examining the mirror to check that all the tarnish had been removed from its alloy coating, was slow enough in replying to his hesitant question. Alexander, wondering if he would have to repeat himself, brushed the perspiration from his forehead with his large, crumpled handkerchief and waited. Outside, a cart rumbled by, drawn by two weary horses. For a few moments the clangour of iron wheels and hooves on cobbles filled the little shop.

At last, Perceval, gazing at him from behind his wire-framed spectacles, said, 'French astronomers? You mean the Company of Titius?'

In the stuffy warmth of the shop, Alexander found himself almost shivering. 'Yes,' he said. 'That was the name. The Company of Titius.'

Perceval nodded. 'As it happens,' he said, 'I corrected some instruments for them only last month.' He paused, turning the speculum mirror carefully with his gloved hands. Once more Alexander was afraid that was all he was going to say, and he would have to press him again. But then the spectacle-maker glanced up.

'There's a small group of them in Kensington,' he went on, 'led by Guy and Auguste de Montpellier, who are brother and sister. They were prominent members of the Company in Paris, and were friends of several of the great astronomers: Bailly, Messier, de Saron . . . ah, such gifted men, dead now, all dead . . .' He shook his head sadly. 'Auguste and Guy de Montpellier escaped from the slaughter, but only just in time. They were forced to flee to England, as so many of their countrymen did. And here they continue their work, together with their astronomer friends, as best they can.' He was polishing the mirror again, rhythmically. 'You really should make their acquaintance.'

Alexander, as he listened, found that he was breathing almost painfully. 'Why should they wish to meet me?' he ventured at last. 'What do I possess, to recommend myself to such distinguished people?'

Perceval looked at him mildly. 'You are, as ever, too modest. You have considerable expertise in various fields of knowledge. Herschel himself acknowledged your work.'

Alexander blushed.

'And don't you correspond with Laplace, in spite of the blockades?' pressed on Perceval.

'Only by the good offices of the Royal Society, who send my letters,' demurred Alexander. 'The government would no doubt love to rescind its members' franking privileges, but for the present the Society's mail travels freely, in this country and abroad.'

'Well, well,' said Perceval. 'Long may the custom continue. If only such farsightedness prevailed in other spheres. What a foolish business war is.' He shook out his polishing cloth. 'Auguste de Montpellier and her friends would be delighted, I am sure, to hear both of your correspondence with Laplace and of your wide experience in the fields of navigation and astronomy.'

Someone else came in then, for a pair of spectacles that had been left for repair. Alexander moved back into the shadows and waited. The perspiration was trickling down his back beneath his ill-fitting shirt and too-warm coat. He drew out his kerchief to dab at his forehead again and waited, envying his friend his mild, precise certainty as he dealt with his customer.

As well as spectacles, and eyeglasses for optical instruments, Perceval made watch lenses too, for his neighbouring tradesmen. He managed to obtain the very best of materials, almost magically, it seemed, even in these difficult times. Alexander noted with silent wonder the stack of pristine telescope tubes of the finest quality, fresh from the workshops of Leiden and arranged neatly in the corner of the shop, waiting for Perceval's nimble fingers and exquisitely honed lenses to bring them to life.

Perceval also played the violin, with devout and precise rapture. Occasionally he accepted an invitation to Alexander's house for supper, and to Alexander the pleasure he gained from these evenings was something he could not express in words. The stars he could share, could talk about, at least to a degree. But music was a private joy; and to discuss the inspired precision of a Corelli sonata, to try to explain its mystical counterpoints and ravishing inner harmonies in terms of mathematics, as some did, seemed to Alexander to violate the music's wordless perfection.

The customer left at last with his spectacles clutched in his hand. The door closed behind him with a little tinkle of the bell, after briefly letting in the scents and noises of the darkening street. Some children were rolling a hoop down the cobbles, and the sound of their laughter faded as swiftly as a dream.

Perceval locked up in a small brass box the money his customer had handed over. Then he glanced across at Alexander, his thin, bewigged face with its pointed nose as bright as a little bird's and continued, as if nothing had interrupted them:

'Yes, you really should meet the Montpelliers. They brought their telescopes with them, from Paris.' He was carefully putting the brass box under the counter. 'Whenever they can, they are out watching the stars. And looking, of course, for the lost planet.'

Alexander's heart was beating hard. 'So they and their friends truly believe in it?' Perceval was one of the few people with whom he ever talked about his own search for the missing star; he knew that the spectacle-maker had a calm faith in its existence, and a certainty as to its eventual discovery.

'They are undoubtedly believers,' replied Perceval. 'In fact it is Guy de Montpellier's life work, his dream, to discover the lost star. Naturally he and his friends face some scepticism: hostility, even. But why should mankind, in its presumption, dare to conclude that everything has been discovered? Herschel assumed nothing; he studied the skies as if he was the first astronomer ever to observe its vastness, and so, without the preconceptions that have blinded so many scientists to what actually lies before them, he was able to discover a planet, the first person to do so since ancient times. Why should there not be another out there, waiting to be found?' He paused, and added in a quieter voice, 'And you, my friend. How close you have been.'

'It's almost two years since those sightings. I have seen nothing since.' Alexander's voice was wistful. 'My sight is a little worse, and my telescope is only modest.'

'But you still have the records of your observations?'

'Yes. I do.' Suddenly Alexander's face seemed alight with hope again. 'Perceval, if only I had proof of one more sighting, I truly believe that I might be able to plot its path.'

'The Montpelliers have a magnificent telescope,' said Perceval, 'and instruments for recording everything they've seen. They've built themselves an observatory on the roof of their house; and because they live well out in the country, far away from the lights and the smoke of the town, they have a spectacular view of the heavens. You must meet them.' He paused to lock the drawer into which he'd placed the box. 'Monsieur de Montpellier is, I believe, an excellent musician. They say he plays the harpsichord like an angel. His renderings of Rameau's sonatas are held to be particularly fine.'

Alexander felt his pulse stirring almost painfully, like numb fingers being chafed into life. 'So Monsieur de Montpellier is a musician as well as an astronomer?'

'Oh, yes. In fact he has an altogether brilliant mind, though I fear it is somewhat clouded from time to time.'

'You mean he's not well?'

'So they say. He's constantly attended by a physician, their friend Pierre Raultier, who came with brother and sister into exile here, from Paris. Doctor Raultier has lodgings in Holborn, but he spends a good deal of his time at Kensington, with the Montpelliers. He takes care of poor Guy when he is ill.' Perceval was polishing again, giving the speculum metal a final caress with a piece of soft leather soaked in some pure spirit, whose odour seared Alexander's nostrils.

You do not know, thought Alexander, *you do not know that I have been asked to betray these people to my half-brother Jonathan* . . . He found he was gripping the edge of the counter with tense fingers, his heart full of yearning at the thought of the lost star and the glittering company who pursued it.

'What would be the best way to offer my help?' he asked at last. 'What do I possess, to recommend myself to such illustrious people?'

'Write to Auguste de Montpellier. She is the one who issues invitations to their gatherings. Tell her of your various skills. Anyone with any interest at all in astronomy would be foolish not to be glad of your company,' replied Perceval serenely. He handed over the speculum, which was ready at last. 'I'm afraid,' he went on, 'that any more polishing will destroy the precision of the mirror. You'll perhaps have to consider getting a new one made.'

'Yes,' said Alexander, but he was cast down again, for he knew it would cost more than he could afford.

He paid Perceval for his work, and made his farewell, because he had no more excuses for lingering. He went slowly out into the street, where the lamplighter had started his work. Not yet ready to go home, Alexander walked for a while in the warm, close-gathering dusk in a dream of speculation, hardly noticing the smell of the tile kilns from across the fields as he wandered along Clerkenwell Green, past the churchyard and pillory to Milton Lane. Last summer, a violent crowd had attacked the recruiting officers when they set up their stand here in an attempt to enlist volunteers for the unpopular war with France. The officers had not been back.

Leaving the Green, he turned north along one of the paths that led up through the fields towards distant Islington village, past groups of shadowy cattle that grazed contentedly in the drowsy evening heat. As he walked, an owl swept past his face, beating the warm air with its wings. Alexander stood gazing at it until it was quite lost in the darkness. Then he turned, as the sound of voices reached him like ripples spreading out from a stone dropped in a pool.

From Clerkenwell a chain of marshy ponds ran all the way up to Islington, where in season the wildfowlers came. Tonight, there was a crowd gathered round the nearest one; a constable was amongst them, and there seemed to be some muted activity, some calling out. The constable was pulling something out of the water with evident distaste. It was a limp object, black with slime, which he dropped on to a piece of sacking lying in wait at the water's edge. Alexander saw the fragile limbs, the heavy head, and realised it was a newborn infant.

The ponds were a convenient place of disposal for such guilty secrets. Two years ago, at the time of the famine, many unwanted babies had been thus discarded. This doomed infant must scarcely have lived more than a few hours before the black waters engulfed it. The tiny body, enfolded in sacking, was picked up by the constable. The crowd began to disperse. Some of them caught sight of Alexander, standing there in the dusk. A man pointed in his direction, and he thought he heard laughter.

Alexander turned quickly round and headed back towards the Green, then hurried down Jerusalem Passage to his little house in the court behind the church. By the time he got to the shabby front door, it was dark, and Altair was a flickering point of light in the east. The wind from the south carried the faint, sweet stench of the tanneries to his nostrils. He went in and closed the front door quietly, hoping Hannah wouldn't hear him; but she opened her door and came hobbling out into the hallway, her eyes bright with curiosity, before her daughter could stop her. The daughter, tired and pale as ever, came quickly to fetch her in, with a low murmur of apology. Hannah resisted, toothless, moaning, and her daughter had to remonstrate with her. The stench of stale urine hung heavily in the stairwell, for Hannah was incontinent, and her daughter struggled to keep her clean. Alexander felt guilty for destroying once more the little peace they had.

He said to them, 'I have a singing pupil coming later this evening. I hope you won't be too much disturbed.'

He had found that if he warned them before he had visitors, the daughter was prepared, and kept her mother calm. Hannah was silent. The daughter nodded and said, 'We won't mind at all. We enjoy hearing your music. Don't we, mother?'

Still Hannah said nothing. Alexander hurried on upstairs as her daughter led her back into their ground-floor parlour.

Daniel was waiting for him. Alexander sent the boy for their usual supper from the Bull's Head, but the dish of mutton, when it came, was greasy and full of fat; they never sent him their best. He knew he should go himself, to complain, but he was afraid that people would stare at him and whisper, as they had by the pond earlier.

After supper, it was time for his singing pupil; it was his way of supplementing his meagre income. This one was a plump, eager girl who had been flattered into thinking she had talent. Her mother sat close by, dominating the little room in her huge feathered bonnet and fringed shawl, happily tapping out the time quite erroneously with her cane as Alexander struggled to keep the girl in tune with his harpsichord. His precious wax candles had burned down low by the time he got rid of them at last, with false reassurances as to the girl's progress that he despised himself for, and promises that she did indeed have a remarkable gift.

He went, then, up on to the roof. The breeze had turned from south to west, and the heavy clouds had driven in during the last hour. He gazed across the chimneys and spires of London to where the dome of St Paul's gleamed in the darkness. To the east he could see the sweep of the river and the masts of the great men-of-war, at ease in the deep water by Woolwich.

He thought of the places the ships sailed to, across the wide Atlantic to the southern seas, and found that his right eye was aching, as if the memory of those distant oceans had rekindled the glare of the noonday sun on the sea. Closing his eyes, he recalled with painful clarity everything his friend Perceval had told him about the Montpelliers in Kensington. He thought of Guy de Montpellier, who played the music of Rameau on his harpsichord, and searched for the lost star; and he found himself filled with yearning to see all this for himself. What could he do, to introduce himself to them? He realised that Perceval's gentle encouragement had raised his hopes almost too painfully.

Then he remembered Jonathan's visit, and the night breeze was suddenly cold against his skin.

XI

Curiosity is one of the permanent and certain
characteristics of a vigorous intellect.

Samuel Johnson, *The Rambler* (1751)

There was a building in Middle Scotland Yard which was officially part of the Secretary of State for the Treasury's domain; but because its cellars were regularly flooded by the Thames at high tide, and because its upper rooms were without fireplaces and therefore not favoured by the Whitehall clerks, who preferred their places of work to have at least a modicum of comfort, the building had fallen into a state of relative disuse, even though it was so central to the great offices of state.

But there was a particular chamber on the second floor, at the top of a winding staircase, that had become a general depository of paperwork for all the government departments that occupied the buildings nearby. It was a long, narrow room, almost a gallery, that stretched from one end of the edifice to the other; its walls were lined with presses and shelves, all of which were piled high with documents that had found their way here over the years, chiefly because they were considered of no great importance, and no one knew where else to put them.

So, once a day, or perhaps even less often, humble clerks from the Home and War Offices, from the Treasury and the Paymaster-General's department, scurried up the narrow staircase, bringing their obscure documents or copies of them up to this chamber. Some of the shelves were starting to spill their contents on to the floor, as if each sheet of paper was begging to be read, or docketed, or made useful in any way at all; generally in vain, because the room, which was cold even on a bright June morning such as this, only rarely attracted the attention of anyone other than the lowly depositing clerks. Certainly it did not often attract the attention of someone as busy as Jonathan Absey.

And yet here he was now, and he had, moreover, found something to engage his attention. Extracting a sheaf of papers from a cabinet marked FOREIGN MAILS, he carried them with the utmost care over to a narrow desk beneath the window, where the dust he had disturbed in this half-forgotten room danced in the shafts of the morning sun; and indeed, Jonathan's normally sombre face, which still bore the remnants of a four-day-old bruise, seemed to reflect that light, just a little, as he leafed through the papers and lifted one, at last, from amongst its fellows. 'The Company of Titius,' he read aloud, wonderingly. 'The Company of Titius . . .'

He stopped, because here was another surprise. It appeared that this humble room had attracted not one, but two visitors this morning. The sound of more footsteps could be heard at the far end of the gallery; the door opened; and in came Richard Crawford, carrying a bundle of documents under his arm. His look of astonishment at discovering another occupant quickly turned into a smile of greeting when he saw who it was.

'Jonathan,' he said, still a little breathless from his climb. 'Fancy finding you here.' He glanced curiously at the papers in front of Jonathan on the desk, and then at the open cabinet. 'I didn't realise there would be anything in this dreary place to engage your interest.'

Jonathan, registering with a certain resignation that his rebuff of Crawford the other day was apparently quite forgotten, said, 'It's a small matter only. Nothing at all of importance. Really.' The room already seemed tainted with the odour of Crawford's troublesome digestion, for which Jonathan knew that he took Dr James's patent powders as ardently as any communicant taking wine.

Crawford patted the documents that were tucked under his arm. 'Well, I have papers to file. Lists of supplies. Copies of the militia accounts which the Ordnance department has sent me.' He was craning his pallid face over Jonathan's shoulder to see what was in front of him. 'What are you reading?'

Jonathan hesitated, drawing the papers a fraction closer. Crawford was the only remaining colleague to consider himself Jonathan's friend; it probably made life easier, all in all, not to offend the over-sensitive little Scotsman. 'There's a group of French astronomers living in London,' he said at last, 'who write to others, in schools of astronomy across Europe.'

'Astronomers?' A frown had supplanted the smile on Crawford's face; and Jonathan, slightly unnerved by Crawford's change of mood, went on quickly: 'Yes. They call themselves the Company of Titius.'

For a few moments the silence in the room was broken only by the crooning of the pigeons on the ledge outside the window, until the Scotsman gathered his pallid features into an even deeper frown and said at last, 'Take my advice, Jonathan. Have nothing – nothing whatsoever – to do with these people.'

Jonathan's heart beat a little faster. 'What do you mean?'

Crawford leaned closer. 'I repeat. Don't get involved. I tell you this in confidence, as a friend.'

'But why?' Jonathan persisted.

Crawford looked behind him, almost as if he was frightened he might be overheard. 'I first heard of the Company of Titius when I worked for Huskisson and Nepean,' he confided in a low voice. 'One of our own men has been placed in this company.'

'An agent?' Jonathan asked in astonishment.

'Yes.' Crawford was nodding earnestly. 'One of the best.'

Jonathan leaned back in his chair and ran his hand through his hair. This wasn't what he'd been expecting.

Ever since the outbreak of the revolution in France, the Home Office had busied itself planting agents everywhere: in the London-based Jacobin clubs, in the Corresponding Societies, even in the county militias. Some were of use, others less so; but whichever category they fell into, their identities and their business were, of necessity, closely guarded.

No wonder, thought Jonathan, no wonder that he'd been unable to find anything out about the Company at Lombard Street, or in the office of the Chief Postal Secretary at St Mary Woolnoth, where he'd called yesterday. If there was an agent in place amongst the group of astronomers, the files would have been destroyed; it was always the way. And yet someone had slipped up, otherwise he wouldn't have found what he had found here.

'You had better tell me more,' he said.

Crawford pursed his lips. 'Oh, no. I've said enough. Quite enough.' He sniffed and moved away to file his papers. Jonathan walked to an adjacent cabinet and likewise replaced his own, bending over to ease them into the drawer. When he straightened up, he realised Crawford was watching him.

'Listen, my friend. It's not wise to meddle. Let the matter rest,' said the Scotsman, dusting his hands. 'You'll take my advice?'

'Yes,' Jonathan lied, closing the cabinet with a thud. 'It looks as if I've wasted my time.'

He left the gallery, and Crawford, smaller than he, had to hurry down the stairs to keep up with him. And so they walked back together, with Crawford chattering inconsequentially of minor Home Office business as they passed through Whitehall Yard to Montague House, where the Scotsman made his farewells at last and went bustling off to deal with his humdrum ordnance accounts and payrolls.

Jonathan, on reaching his own office, carefully closed the door and sat down at his desk. Then he drew out the folded sheet of paper he'd pushed deep into his pocket the instant he'd heard Crawford's footsteps coming along the corridor.

It was a list of dates. Both this list, and the one he'd had in his hands just before Crawford had entered, had been filed together under the name of the Company of Titius, in the bundle of papers he had pulled from the drawer marked FOREIGN MAILS. But this one had a name on it. On the back, someone – a clerk, perhaps one of those he'd seen two days ago at the mail office – had written: *Sender – Doctor Raultier of London. French citizen.* A French doctor who made a study of the stars, and corresponded with astronomers in Paris.

The evidence that should have been at Lombard Street had been destroyed. And now, thanks to Crawford's revelation, he knew why. But someone had forgotten to destroy this document which Jonathan had in his hand.

He was looking for a murderer; and now he had a name.

Part Two

12 June - 15 June 1795

XII

We quite often go wrong about the things that Nature
does impel us towards. For instance, sick men long
for drink or food that would soon be harmful to them.

René Descartes,
Meditations on First Philosophy (1641)

Guy de Montpellier let his fingers crash harshly down on the keys of the harpsichord, bringing to an end the exquisite cadences that had filled the room. He said in a low voice, 'I am well, Raultier. Look at me. See, I am well.'

He shifted restlessly as he spoke, scraping the legs of his chair against the parquet floor. His pale skin was sheened with perspiration.

Pierre Raultier hesitated in the doorway. Thinking Guy to be resting in his room, he had been writing in the study downstairs before the ride back to his lodgings in Holborn. But the sound of the harpsichord had drawn him to the music room, with the letter he had written scarcely dry in his hand. 'I'm glad,' he said. 'But it's late, Guy. You must rest.'

'Rest, rest. Soon there will be nothing but rest . . .' The younger man's voice was bitter, and Raultier saw, with a sinking of his heart, that the light of his terrible malady was in his eyes again.

Guy suddenly turned back to the harpsichord and played a dazzling arpeggio in contrary motion, his lace-ruffled wrists flying in miraculous counterpoint over the ivory keys. Then he stopped abruptly once more. 'You look anxious, Doctor Corvus, Doctor Crow. Poor crow, ugliest of birds, Jupiter's black spy . . . That's what my sister calls you; did you know? Auguste is cruel, isn't she, to those who love her?'

Raultier kept his heavy face expressionless; he said nothing, but his hand tightened round the letter he held.

'Perhaps we don't deserve such torment, Raultier, you and I,' Guy went on. He got up and moved towards the doctor, his over-bright eyes fastening on the paper Raultier held. 'But what have you been writing? A letter to my sister?'

'No. It's nothing . . .'

Guy smiled slowly. 'I think you're lying. I think it's a letter to her. Don't you know that she'll laugh at it, just as she laughs at you? She'll show it to Carline, when he comes to her in the night. Have you heard them together, doctor? Have you heard my sister when she calls out to him in her pain, her ecstasy?'

'I write of the stars,' Raultier interrupted him abruptly. 'Nothing more.'

'Then *show me*.' And Guy stepped forward to snatch the paper from the doctor's hands. He read the names of the stars aloud: Chara, Alkafazah, Alifa, Mirphak, and so many more, a familiar litany inscribed with such care in column after column all across the pale parchment; but as he read, a frown shadowed his intent face.

'Some of your figures are wrong. Look here, at Alifa; you've described it as a third magnitude star, when even at its brightest it's never higher than fourth.'

Raultier reached out for the paper quickly. 'You're right. An elementary mistake. I'll check it all in the morning.'

Just for a moment Guy clung to the sheet; but then his fingers relaxed, and he let Raultier take it back. Once more his tiredness seemed to overwhelm him. 'All the stars are there,' he said in a quiet voice, almost to himself. 'All except the missing one. I promised her I would find it, and I've failed. *Selene* . . .' He sank down again on the chair by the harpsichord, and Raultier moved closer to him.

'Guy. You must forget. You must put your memories of Paris behind you.'

Guy lifted his harrowed face. 'But I can't forget the prison,' he whispered. 'Sometimes I think I should have killed her that night when I visited her there. I should have put my hands round her slender neck and killed her, it would have been more merciful . . .'

'Hush. You are tormenting yourself. It's over.'

'*I cannot forget* . . .'

'Wait here.' Raultier hurried from the room, while Guy sat slumped in his chair, clenching and unclenching his hands. Raultier was back within moments, holding a small brown phial of medicine and a glass into which he poured a measure of the thick liquid. He watched as

Guy drank. 'You must remember,' he said, 'that Selene is now just the name of the lost star. The other never existed. Ever.'

Guy nodded. 'Only a star. And when I find her, then I may have peace . . .' He gazed at his tense hands, then looked up suddenly. 'Raultier —'

'Yes?'

Guy moistened his dry lips. 'Sometimes the pain is almost more than I can bear. I need to know: will it get much worse?'

Raultier's face was pale. 'I'll make sure it doesn't,' he said.

'You promise?'

'I promise.' Raultier put his hand gently on the younger man's shoulder. 'You'll rest now, Guy? You'll do as I say?'

'Yes.' Slowly Guy bowed his head.

Guy listened to the doctor's footsteps fading away down the passageway, then went to the window and leaned his forehead against the cold glass, preparing to surrender himself as the datura began its all too familiar work. It was as if cunning fingers were sending warmth stealing through his blood and surging through his veins to every nerve ending in his body; didn't the doctor realise that this medicine made him want to act, not dream? Didn't Raultier know that it made his mind run wild with fancies and cruel visions? How could a man rest, how could he sleep, when the blood pounded darkly in his loins, when sleep would only bring tormenting visions of a red-haired witch, a white-skinned succubus, offering herself to him, tormenting him with her beauty? *Selene . . .*

He opened his eyes and gazed out into the night and tried to remember the peace of the place where he was born; he tried to remember the names of the dazzling canopy of stars that arched over Clermont-l'Hérault, but he could not, it was no use, he could think only of how he had searched for her all that long night almost three years ago, and found her.

Death had been let loose in Paris that night, on the streets and in the prisons; death and worse. They told him she had been taken to one of the city's most desperate gaols, the Salpêtrière; and he hastened there with terrible fear in his heart, because he knew that many prisoners in the other gaols were already dead, dragged from their cells and butchered by the mobs who ruled the capital through those hideous September days and nights; while the guns of the Prussian army, less than an hour's march away, filled the air with a sound like muffled thunder.

But at the Salpêtrière, the warders had found a better sport for their female prisoners than handing them over to the mob.

They had taken Guy to her cell, in return for gold. Guy wanted to help her to escape, but her keepers thought he had come, like the others, to watch. At first he hadn't believed it could be her, because she looked up from the filthy straw of her cell and she laughed at him, with her red hair loose about her face, and her breasts bared to the light of the prison's dim lanterns, and her mouth swollen from her gaolers' kisses.

They clustered around her, those brutal men who guarded her so jealously from death, and waited to take their turn. At first Guy wanted to tear his way through the bars to them, and kill them for it; but then he realised. She knew what was happening. She wanted it. She teased them, she mocked them with her beauty, turning to show them her white breasts, her long red hair. And then she had beckoned one of them to her, with a smile; and Guy, who had come to take her, somehow, away from the horror of that place, by giving his own life if need be, had been almost sick at what he had seen.

Sometimes, he thought that was when his illness started, that strange, clawing agitation at the back of his skull that brought a darkness to his soul. Almost three years ago, and yet, dear God, he still heard her low cries of pleasure wherever he went.

He crossed the room to the bell pull by the door and jerked it furiously. A few minutes later there were heavy footsteps on the stairs, and Ralph the coachman was there at the door. Ralph was surly and strong, a fearsome sight indeed, with one side of his face split by a hideous knife scar. Guy beckoned him in and asked curtly,

'Has the doctor gone yet?'

'He has left, sir, yes.' Ralph was unhappy, uncertain.

'Then get the carriage ready for me.'

Now there was real fear in Ralph's eyes. 'Sir, I cannot. Last time they made me swear not to.'

Guy gazed at him steadily. 'Get the carriage ready. Otherwise I'll tell Auguste your little secret, and you'll be out on the street. Do you understand?'

'*Sir –*' Ralph held out his big, calloused hands in entreaty.

'No one else would employ you,' Guy continued emphatically, 'ever again, if they knew.' Ralph hung his head; his hands dropped to his sides, and Guy knew he had won. 'I'll be down shortly,' he concluded, crossing to the door and holding it open. 'Be ready for me.'

Ralph turned to go, his face unnaturally pale except for the livid scar on his cheek. Guy listened to him going downstairs again, then he went to his sister's room, to search for her gold. She had put it in a new hiding place, but he discovered it quickly enough, hidden beneath a skein of silks in a tapestry sewing box in her private parlour. Her bedroom was next door. She and Carline were in bed, but they did not sleep. He knew, because he could hear the sounds of his sister's pleasure.

He put the heavy coins carefully into his coat pocket. Then he went swiftly downstairs, and out to the front of the house.

Ralph was waiting for him with the cumbersome carriage. Guy climbed in and pulled the door shut. Then he looked back at the silent house.

As the carriage moved away, he thought, for a moment, that he saw a face at a second-floor window watching; but whose face was it? The servants would be in their quarters at the back of the house by now, their tasks finished for the night. His sister and Carline had eyes for no one but each other. Only Raultier would spy on him, and Raultier had gone now, back to his home in the city.

He must have imagined the face at the window. Such fancies came to him all too easily in these last days.

XIII

What female heart can gold despise?

Thomas Gray, 'Ode on the Death of
a Favourite Cat Drowned in a Tub of
Gold Fishes' (1747)

'Ah, yes,' said Georgiana Howes with a languishing sigh, whenever anyone asked her about her ambitions in life. 'I long, above all else, to be a famous opera singer.'

Famous and wealthy, like La Fanciola; that was her dream. The manager of the Drury Lane Theatre, Samuel Crisp, told her she had a voice like an angel, and looked like one too, with her sweet face and tumbling red hair. Tonight, because Madame Ottoline was ill, she'd been given the chance, young as she was, to sing Eurydice; and when the opera was over the audience had stood and cheered, throwing flowers on to the stage.

The man had been amongst them. He was a foreigner, a Frenchman; there were so many of them in London just now. When he came to her afterwards, and asked her so politely, almost shyly, in his charmingly accented voice for the pleasure of her company at a private supper, she'd acquiesced gladly, because he was young and well-favoured, this Frenchman. Even her friends, who were always telling her she should save herself for men who were old and rich and could advance her career, took one look at him and enthused over her good fortune. Almost enviously, giggling over the secrecy of it all, they helped her to scurry out the back way into the courtyard, before Samuel Crisp should see her. They were used to such adventures.

The Frenchman was waiting for her in Drury Lane. She was glad to see that he had a private carriage, even if it was heavy and old-fashioned. She climbed into it quickly, for it was raining and she didn't want her finery to be spoiled. She coloured a little with excitement as the man joined her and closed the door, but after that she kept her face prim, patting her unusual red curls into tidiness beneath her wide-brimmed bonnet and smoothing down her striped silk skirt as the carriage moved away.

The young Frenchman seemed restless, and anxious for them to make swifter progress, but the steady stream of people on foot and in carriages coming from the theatre kept their pace slow. He gazed out of the window, tapping his fingers impatiently on his thigh, and Georgiana watched him surreptitiously. Oh, he was a handsome one, and no mistake: slim and graceful, with a vivid, angular face and long dark hair and eyes that seemed almost to burn into you . . .

He turned to face her, and smiled slowly.

'You sang Eurydice wonderfully. I have not heard better in Paris,' he said.

She blushed again, and a pleasant glow of anticipation warmed her as they continued their journey.

He took her to a private dining parlour in the New Inn off Henrietta Street, where they sat before a roaring fire. He said little, but ordered dishes of hot buttered crab, and smoked turkey breasts with peas, followed by bowls of orange syllabub and cream. He ate some of it, but mostly he gazed at her face, her hair. He kept filling Georgiana's glass with sweet white wine, and she grew talkative and excited as he complimented her in his charming foreign voice on her sublime singing, and assured her that she had a bright future on the stage.

The wine was racing warmly in her veins by the time she greedily licked up the last of the syllabub from her spoon. She was stealing a look at his hands – long, fine, musician's hands, so unlike Sam Crisp's stubby fingers – when he suddenly leaned forward to grasp her chin, twisting her face towards his.

'Have you ever been to Paris?' he demanded.

'No,' she stammered out as his eyes burned into her; 'no, though I had a friend who was with the *Comédie* before the war . . .'

He let her go and sat back with a sigh. 'That was a long time ago,' he said. 'Everything is different now.' Then he smiled, and poured her the last of the wine, and she felt warm and a little breathless at the thought of what was to come. After they'd talked for a few minutes more, of music and the theatre, the man pushed away his own empty wine glass and started to rise from the table. He said, 'Earlier I heard you sing for them all. But now, my little songbird, I'm going to ask you to sing for me alone. Isn't that why you're here?'

'Yes,' she said. 'Oh, yes.'

He led her into another private room, just along the passageway. It was darker in here, and a little cold at first, but he poked at the slumbering fire in the grate until it roared up, and its flames sent shadows leaping all around the old oak panelling on the walls. In the corner was a heavily curtained bed. Georgiana felt another tremor of expectancy as she watched the Frenchman move gracefully about the room.

Sam Crisp, who assumed everything his girls did was his business, would tell her to ask for her money first. But she was sure that this man would pay her, which was more than Sam did, or his clumsy friends. When she'd first started at Drury Lane, she had been flattered at first by the theatre manager's attentions, by his promises to help her in her career; but now she was tired of him. He was coarse, clumsy, often drunk, and she had grown to secretly detest his heavy fumblings.

The man was taking his coat off slowly, and she expected him to come towards her, to make the first move, for that, surely, was the way of these things. But instead, he went across the room to the heavy damask drapes at the window and pulled them tightly shut.

As he turned to her, Georgiana Howes felt afraid, because that strange look had come into his eyes, and he said, 'There. We don't want the stars to see us, do we?'

Georgiana glanced quickly towards the door. But then he smiled, and started walking towards her, and Georgiana thought of the way he praised her singing, and the things he had promised her. 'Well, now,' she murmured, pleased enough with what she saw, 'well, now.'

Slowly she unlaced her bodice, so that the firelight gleamed on the smooth white skin of her breasts. He stood watching her; then he unpinned all her long hair, so that it fell in shining red swathes to her shoulders.

He caressed her intently with his hands, and kissed her mouth. Georgiana eased herself from his grasp and, taking his hand, drew him back with her to the big bed.

He dealt swiftly with all that was necessary of his own clothing and hers, thrusting back the layers of her petticoats so impatiently that he almost tore them. Urgently he kissed her face, her throat, her flushed breasts; Georgiana laughed at his ardour and pulled him close. Soon all the shadowy corners of the room were echoing to the soft sounds of her pleasure.

Then, without any sort of warning, he wrenched himself away. Georgiana opened her eyes and cried out in protest. He pulled himself to his feet, and stood with his back to her; he called out, as if he was speaking to someone else in the room, '*Selene, Selene, you are playing your old tricks*,' and she saw that he clenched his fists, as if embroiled in some secret agony.

Georgiana drew herself up swiftly on the bed, suddenly cold. 'Sir, are you all right? Is something the matter?'

He whipped round to confront her, and she cowered away, frightened by how strange his eyes seemed in the whiteness of his face. She wondered if he was ill, or on some kind of narcotic, an opium-eater; the pupils of his eyes were like pinpricks, and he was swallowing again and again as if something choked him, or as if a terrible torment possessed him. He looked at her as if she was a verminous creature that had crept from a dirty gutter into his bed; then he pulled on his coat and went unsteadily across the room to the door, where he called out to someone sharply.

Georgiana jumped from the bed and fastened up her gown with trembling fingers. She guessed what this was about. She'd heard stories of men who'd call in a companion to complete this kind of unfinished business, as if in revenge for their own failure. But before she'd even had time to assess her chances of escape, the Frenchman was coming back towards her, looking as if he didn't understand why he was here, in this room, with her; and while she watched him warily he drove his hand into a deep pocket and pulled out a handful of coins, gold coins, more gold than she had ever seen in her life. He counted out ten of them and pushed them at her. She saw that his hand was trembling.

'Here,' he said harshly. 'Take them.'

'No. There is some mistake,' she breathed. 'You cannot give me all this.'

He closed his hand over hers, almost hurting her as the coins bit into her palm. 'Indeed I can. That's all you want, isn't it, you and your kind? Money? Now go.'

'But—'

'My coachman will take you home.' He pushed her hand away and turned his back on her.

Georgiana moistened her dry throat. Oh, such a pity. Such a fine-looking gentleman, and all that money still in his pocket. But he wasn't in his right mind, to be ranting of stars and someone called Selene, and then giving her all this gold. The sooner she was out of here the better. He looked merely tired now, tired to death; not raving. But even so she quickly gathered up her shawl and bonnet and hurried from the room, tightly clutching the golden coins in case he changed his mind. Foreign gold, it was, with some foreign king's head on one side, and an angel on the other; she'd have to take it well away from Sam Crisp's prying eyes to change it, but she'd spend it then, and gladly.

The coach driver was standing at the end of the passageway in his shabby greatcoat, waiting for her. Seeing him close up like this made her afraid again, because he was so big, and he had an ugly scar down one cheek from a knife that must have almost taken his eye out. She was very careful to keep well away from him as he led the way out of the inn and into the courtyard where the carriage stood, with a boy holding the horses. The scarred coachman opened the door silently for her. She told him where she wanted to go and climbed hurriedly inside, anxious to get away from his disturbing gaze.

Once inside the carriage Georgiana leaned back, feeling a little easier. Well. A strange evening and no mistake. Soon she'd be home, back at the lodging house where she shared rooms with the other girls from the theatre. What a story she'd have to tell her friends, though she'd be careful to miss out things like the gold, and the foreign gentleman's disappointing failure to complete his vigorously begun task.

She pulled the coins out of her pocket, and gazed at them, and shook her head, still bewildered. Enough here, perhaps, to get her away from Samuel Crisp's greedy clutches. Enough for a new sort of life.

The carriage made slow progress; Tavistock Row was clogged with pleasure-seekers who'd spilled out from the theatres to dine and drink in the warren of low places that lay between here and the Strand. But Georgiana could see that they were getting near at last to Bridges Street, and Bear Alley, which was as close as any coach could get to the little court where she lived, and so she tapped on the roof and got ready to jump out and hurry off into the darkness.

She was quick, but the scarred coachman was quicker. Before she could make her escape, he'd leapt down and was standing in front of her, barring her way. She wished he'd stayed where he was, because his was the sort of face to give a girl dark dreams. She gave him a tight nod, and tried once more to move off; but he caught her by the arm with his brawny hand, swinging her round to face him, and said, hoarsely,

'I was watching. I know it was wrong, but I was watching, because the door to the chamber wasn't properly shut. You looked so beautiful. I couldn't help it. Please, I have not much money, but I have a little . . .'

The way he was looking at her, here in the pool of darkness by Bear Alley, with his eyes so anguished, so maddened for her in the midst of his scar-seamed face, made Georgiana shudder with repulsion.

'Take your hands off me,' she breathed. 'Let go of me, or I swear I'll scream so loud you'll have half the city at your heels.'

She pulled her arm away, but there was no need. Already he'd stepped back, ashen-faced, into the darkness. Georgiana gathered up her skirts and ran, her heart pounding. The brute, the brute; what did he take her for?

Not far to go now, and she would be safely home. She clutched the gold coins tightly in her hand. Nearly there. And then, as she passed the darkness of White Hart Yard, she heard footsteps coming swiftly up behind her.

Her heart pounding, she quickened her pace. She hoped, for a moment, that she had lost whoever was pursuing her. Almost sobbing in her fear, she turned round and saw no one, nothing in the near blackness. She drew a deep, steadying breath, and chided herself for her stupid fancies.

But there was nothing fanciful about the way the cord was suddenly flung round her neck from behind. Her head pounded; her eyes felt as if they would burst from her skull, and yet still she fought frantically, until she could no longer drag air into her lungs. Her arms flailed as the stars exploded in her head. The coins flew from her hand and rolled away into the gutter. Dimly she heard a voice, saying softly: '*A dead body revenges not injuries.*'

The rumbling wheels of a nearby carriage, gathering speed over the wet cobbles, stifled the sound of her last cries. A hand searched her body and the darkness around, gathering up the spilled gold.

XIV

*We are in a mixture of rage at the triumph of the
Jacobins, of mortification at our own disgraces, of
extreme indignation and horror at the turpitude of
some of the Allied Powers, and of grief and alarm
at the ruin which is coming upon Holland and upon
the whole European continent.*

Lord Auckland to Lord Henry Spencer,
November 1794

At the outbreak of the war with France a little over two years
ago, the English government had passed the Alien Act, which
required all foreigners resident in England to register their
names, addresses and business with the authorities. Initially, the effect
had been remarkable, in that many French exiles had instantly fled
the country, fuelling government suspicion that their status as refugees
was a falsehood, and that they were here either to spy for the
Republican French, or to stir up dangerous dissent amongst radical
Englishmen. And during the months immediately following the
passing of the Act, several *émigré* suspects were hauled in and charged,
including, most noticeably, those agents left secretly in place by the
last French ambassador. These were swiftly rounded up – betrayed, it
was said, by some obliging compatriot – and bundled home without
ceremony.

There had been no significant arrests of Republican spies recently,
but still the refugees from Jacobin France continued to cross the
Channel; and they registered with the authorities as requested,
generating such volumes of paperwork that a new department of
government known as the Alien Office had to be established to deal
with it all, in a rented building at number 20 Crown Street, conve-
niently adjacent to the Foreign and Home Offices.

It was here that Jonathan headed, on the morning after his visit to
Middle Scotland Yard.

Ostensibly, his purpose was to make official enquiries about a group of French *émigrés*, suspected Republicans, who were rumoured to be spying on the Royalist regiments that had been forced out of Holland and were lodged, temporarily, at the barracks of St James. He was left alone, and immediately began searching the files; but there was no file for a doctor-astronomer named Raultier.

Thomas Carter, the superintendent, returned just as he had finished. 'Was there anything else, Mr Absey?'

It was probably only his imagination, but Carter's sharp eyes seemed suspicious. Jonathan said quickly, 'No. There was nothing else.' He turned to go.

Nothing else; an apt summary indeed of his investigations, yesterday and today, into Raultier. Early yesterday evening Jonathan had gone to the College of Physicians in Charing Cross, to ask about any French doctors who might have registered there in order to practise their profession, but the clerk dismissed his query. 'The man you're looking for is probably some quack,' he'd shrugged. 'Some foreign mountebank, here today, gone tomorrow, before his customers realise he's swindled them out of good money for a jar of coloured water.'

Doctor Raultier covered his tracks well. Or someone did for him.

Jonathan went back to Montague House, where he reflected that if he'd thought his workload would be reduced by John King's removal of his foreign duties, then he was very much mistaken. He'd only been out a short while, but his desk was stacked with domestic documents awaiting his perusal: gazettes, and briefings from the county deputies, and intercepted letters from Lombard Street.

So he read them, and he recorded them, and compared them with his lists of suspicious persons and organisations. Some of the items he put to one side to investigate further; others he marked, to be passed on to other people who would do so, especially where such crucial places as the dockyards or the militia barracks were concerned. Later that afternoon he spoke with one of the officers who had recently returned from the Low Countries with the defeated English army; and what he heard displaced for a while even the matter of his daughter's death from his mind. The officer told him, bitterly, of the shambles of the badly led campaign, in which by December more than half of the twenty-one thousand infantry had been laid low by typhus, wounds and exposure. He told Jonathan of Dutch traitors and French secret agents; of the thieving English wagon corps known to the soldiers as the Newgate Blues because most of them were convicted criminals; he told him about the filthy military hospitals that were considered by those unfortunate enough to end up there to be mere short cuts to the next world.

And then had come the new year, and the most terrible frosts anyone could remember, which froze the rivers and canals of Holland so hard that the French cavalry were able to gallop freely across them in pursuit of the ragged English survivors. The remaining supplies were misdirected or stolen, so that basic rations and clothing were non-existent; there were pitched battles around some newly arrived food wagons between the Brigade of Guards and their traditional foes, the Hessians; while those too weak to fight for their share simply died of hunger in the icy wastes of Gelderland.

At night, the officer said, the men huddled together in what few tents they had, listening to the wolves howling in the woods nearby. It was so cold that your breath froze in your beard, and your piss turned to ice before it hit the ground. Men and horses died of exposure where they lay. Six thousand soldiers – nearly a third of the expeditionary force – had perished in four days. Jonathan listened to it all, horrified.

'Is it true, what people were saying, that we could have made a stand in Holland if the weather had been less harsh?' Jonathan asked. 'Could we have held on, and driven the French back?'

'Some blame the weather and some blame the supplies,' said the officer tiredly. 'But I'll tell you this. It was French intelligence that finished us off. The French knew everything. Week after week they were able to intercept our supply wagons and cut off our retreat. It was as if they knew our orders from London before our own commanders did. Their spies must be everywhere.'

He'd looked over his shoulder as he spoke, almost as if expecting someone to be listening, even though they were quite alone. When he'd gone, Jonathan returned to his desk with a heavy heart.

It was no wonder that the British government was setting agents to work in increasing numbers in London, in the provinces, and on the Continent itself, to find these enemy spies. But he asked himself the question: were agents like Raultier so valuable at this time of national crisis that they should be protected in everything they did, even if they committed murder?

That night Jonathan went to a crowded coffee house in the Strand to eat his solitary evening meal. But it was noticeable to any casual onlooker that he allowed his food to congeal on the plate; and though he drank his wine, he was hardly aware of tasting it. Everywhere he looked he was haunted by the face of the French doctor at the Angel.

He had heard nothing from Lombard Street about the Company of Titius; nor, after what Crawford had whispered to him, did he expect to. And there was still no news from Alexander. Four days had gone by since he visited his half-brother. Bitterly he regretted giving Alexander a whole week to find out more about the French astronomers; already, in his state of stomach-knotting tension, the wait was too long.

He became aware that someone was elbowing his way purposefully through the crowded coffee house towards him. It was Abraham Lucket, with a look of almost painful excitement written across his face. Jonathan shoved his untouched plate aside as Lucket eagerly tucked his long limbs into the vacant chair next to him and pushed back his pale, scrubbing-brush hair so that it stood even more upright. 'Sir,' he said excitedly, 'sir, have you heard the news?'

Something Jonathan saw in the boy's face filled him with dread. 'I've been hearing various items of news all day, none of them good. Are you going to surprise me with something I don't already know?'

Lucket positively shone with importance. 'I think I might be, sir. You see, there's been another murder!'

For a moment, Jonathan felt sick. He closed his eyes and opened them, but his empty stomach heaved at the renewed onslaught of the flickering candles, the stench of the dense tobacco smoke swirling around him, the noise of the people talking and laughing at neighbouring tables.

Pulling himself together, he said slowly, 'Another murder?'

'Yes! A girl was found dead this morning, sir, down by White Hart Yard! And I've come to tell you, because it was *like the other one.*'

'Explain.' Jonathan's voice was hoarse. 'Explain what you mean.'

Lucket obliged. 'She died like the other girl, sir. This one was a singer at the Drury Lane Theatre. Another redhead. She went off with a Frenchman straight after the performance, and she was killed in exactly the same way.' He leaned forward confidingly. 'Strangled, sir; same sort of cord; smooth, they say it was, didn't tear at the skin. They called Constable Bentham out to see her; and he said that everything about it seemed just the same as the murder of the girl from the Blue Bell, the one he told you about that night at the Watch House . . .'

He broke off expectantly, eyes bright. Clearly he was trying to temper his youthful relish at the story – but such news, such exciting news!

Jonathan said at last, in a voice that shook with anger and rising helplessness, 'How do they know it was a Frenchman?'

'The girl's friends saw him at the theatre. Heard him talking to her. These friends say they told her not to go, they said he looked dangerous, but she went, and *then* . . .' He pretended to pull a knot tight behind his own scrawny neck, sticking out his tongue in a mimicry of throttling; but his antics were cut short as Jonathan slammed his fists down on the wooden table and pushed himself to his feet; his wine glass toppled over with a crash, and the remnants of the claret spilled across the table. People turned to stare.

'Sorry, sir,' whispered Lucket. 'Sorry.' He was cowering away, his eyes wide.

Jonathan pulled himself together with a huge effort. He sat down again, but his fists were still clenched. He said, 'Did you learn anything else?'

'I think that's everything, sir,' Lucket stammered, shifting his chair so that the wine Jonathan had spilled wouldn't drip on his breeches. 'No. Wait. There was something else. The coins—'

'What coins?' Jonathan's voice was quieter now, but no less dangerous.

'They – they were found close to the opera girl. In the gutter. The two constables who found her arrived together, you see, and so neither of them was able to quietly pocket them. They were French coins, sir, four golden coins; they gave them some name. *Louis d'or*. That was it.'

'The Frenchman gave her *gold*?' asked Jonathan incredulously.

'Yes, sir, I swear that's what I heard,' said Lucket earnestly. 'It must have been payment. But why give her so much, and then kill her?'

'I don't know,' said Jonathan. 'I don't know.' He got up, leaving Lucket staring after him, pushed his way past the people who thronged the coffee house and went out through the door into the Strand. The night air was cool on his face. He breathed in deeply and gazed up into the black London sky.

Raultier. The killer must be Raultier. He needed evidence against this doctor; evidence of the kind that no one, no matter how powerful, could ignore. Turning up his coat collar against the rain that was starting to fall again, he set off along the busy thoroughfare towards the Piazza, and Drury Lane.

At the corner of Henrietta Street he stopped and looked back to check that the street was clear of carriages before crossing. Just at that moment, he thought he saw someone else, ten yards or so behind him, stopping too; but whoever it was stepped back into the shadows so quickly that he almost thought he'd imagined it. His spine tingling, he crossed and went on, more slowly this time, and turned to look again at the corner of Russell Street.

But this time he saw no one.

XV

*Reason, or the ratio of all we have already known,
is not the same that it shall be when we know more.*

William Blake, *There is no Natural Religion* (c.1788)

Samuel Crisp, manager of the Drury Lane Theatre, was well pleased with life. Tonight, Madame Ottoline, now quite recovered from the temporary indisposition that had put Georgiana on stage in her place, had sung to a packed house; and if some of the audience had come to marvel over the fact that Georgiana, last night's unfortunate Eurydice, had died miserably at the hands of a strangler within two hours of her last curtain call, well, that was up to them. Samuel Crisp found their money as good as anyone else's.

The theatre was empty now. The shabbily dressed musicians, grumbling about their pay as always, had packed up their instruments and gone home. The auditorium was silent, except for the sound of his own footsteps and the scurrying of mice. All the candles had been extinguished, except for the one he carried as he made his way to the dressing room where Madame Ottoline waited for him.

She was a sweet, pliable thing, even if she was almost thirty, which was just a little old for his tastes. At least she'd always been suitably grateful for the assistance he'd given her in her career. Now she allowed him to sit and watch her while she unlaced her gown and let it slide to the floor. Her breasts were still shapely, thanks to the boned corset she wore to uplift them. Glancing at him from time to time with a look that promised well for the night ahead, she stood before the mirror and began to brush her long hair. Her real name was Sarah Miggs. One of Samuel's first pieces of advice to her was that she should give herself a fancy foreign name, and she did. She always listened to him. Not like Georgiana.

He was just pouring himself a glass of brandy when the doorman came, with the news that there was someone at the entrance who wanted to ask him about the murder. Samuel Crisp frowned; he'd become heartily sick during the course of the day of being questioned by the Bow Street men about the violent death of Georgiana Howes.

'Tell whoever it is that I'm not here,' he snapped.

The doorman looked anxious. 'I think he's someone quite high up, sir. Not one of the Bow Street men.'

'Did he give you a name?'

'Absey, sir. Something to do with the Home Office.'

The Home Office? Then the doorman was right; unfortunately this intruder was rather more important than the loutish local constables. 'Very well. Show him in,' he said reluctantly.

He told Sarah to sit down in the chair in the corner. She offered to put on her gown again, but he said, no, she could stay in her corset and petticoat. He hoped her state of undress would unsettle this newcomer.

But when Jonathan Absey came in, he didn't even seem to notice her.

'I've said everything I've got to say about Georgiana,' Sam Crisp began importantly. 'Georgiana went off with a stranger, and that's all I know. I've always warned my girls about such things, always.'

Jonathan heard him out with barely restrained impatience. 'Is that so? And what about the strangers you sell them to for the night? Do you warn these girls about them?'

'I don't know what you're talking about. I look after my girls, they're like a family to me . . .'

He was floundering. Jonathan glanced at the half-naked woman in the corner. Then he said, 'Don't waste my time, Crisp. I've spoken to men who have paid for girls like Georgiana, from this very theatre. Did you take money for her the other night, from the Frenchman who killed her?'

'No!' Sam Crisp was beginning to sound alarmed now. Jonathan gazed at him, waiting. 'Very well,' the manager went on, still flustered, 'so some of my customers might have given me gifts of money. But that's because they are patrons, you see, of the theatre; the money all goes on my girls, to help their careers . . .'

Jonathan looked again at the woman, Crisp's companion. He saw that the natural colour had gone from her cheeks, and her pallor high-lighted the garish rouge she wore. Her skin was goose-pimpled with cold, and her nipples above her boned bodice were startlingly dark against her white flesh. She stared back at him, challenging him with her nakedness. Turning back to Samuel, Jonathan said, 'Who actually saw this Frenchman?'

'No one saw him! I've told the Bow Street men that already. Georgiana sneaked out round the back, soon after the performance was over . . .'

Jonathan gave a gesture of impatience and turned back to Sarah. 'Who saw him?' he repeated. She pressed her lips together and crossed her arms over her breasts. Jonathan said warningly, 'Soliciting for custom is a crime. I could close this theatre down. Then you and the other girls would be out on the streets.'

She tossed her head sullenly. 'I saw the man. Several of us did.'

'Tell me about him.'

Sam Crisp stared at Sarah angrily. 'No more, Sarah!'

Jonathan said to her in a hard voice, 'Perhaps you'd prefer to answer my questions at the Bow Street office tomorrow.'

She returned Jonathan's gaze thoughtfully and crossed her legs. 'No. I'll tell you now. Georgiana was a friend of mine. She was a lovely girl. She loved her singing, so much. I was with her when the foreigner came for her. I was too ill to sing last night, so she came to me after the performance with one of the bouquets she'd been given. She said it should really have been for me.'

Jonathan moved closer. 'You're sure he was French?'

'Yes, I'm sure. So many of them are French who come to the theatre, especially when it's *Orpheus*. Gluck wrote a version of it specially for the Paris Opera. I suppose it reminds them of home.'

'Did you hear what the Frenchman said to her?'

'He asked her if she'd come for supper with him. You'll know what they expect, of course, when they ask that.' She reached up to untangle an imaginary knot in her hair, taunting him with a glimpse of her naked breasts.

But Jonathan was not so easily distracted. 'Did this Frenchman expect the same?' he persisted.

'Well, yes.' She twisted a lock of hair thoughtfully round her finger.

'To be honest, having seen him, I'd have been disappointed if he *didn't* expect it.'

'Why?'

She smirked a little. 'Well, he was attractive. Dark hair, quite long, tied back with a black ribbon; a thin sort of face; dark eyes; striking enough. Above all, he was young.' She glanced meaningfully at the middle-aged Crisp.

Jonathan stepped forward. 'Young?' His voice was hoarse, strange to his ears; Sarah leaned back in her chair, watching him curiously, and said,

'Yes, young. Younger than me. About twenty-four, twenty-five.'

For a moment Jonathan was unable to move. He hadn't realised until that moment just how sure he'd been that the man who'd taken Georgiana away was Raultier. If it wasn't Raultier, then who was it? He rubbed his aching temples with his fingers. Everything was falling apart again.

Sarah Miggs was still appraising him, a small, sneering smile playing at the corner of her mouth. 'Was there anything else, sir?' she asked.

'No,' Jonathan managed at last. 'No more questions. I'll see myself out.' He backed towards the door, his mind in turmoil, and opened it swiftly before Crisp could do it for him. Outside, the corridor leading to the stage was dark, and as he felt his way blindly along it, he stumbled over some scenery that partially blocked his path. He halted and cursed, stooping to rub his bruised shin.

Behind him, faint candlelight spilled out through the open door to Sarah Miggs's dressing room. From behind that door came the golden tinkle of female laughter; a sound that was sexually alluring and at the same time utterly contemptuous.

On that same night, a packet of papers was delivered to a Dover fisherman, Stephen Hawkscliffe, by a man who'd ridden from London. The man asked Hawkscliffe to convey the papers as a matter of some urgency to a merchant in Boulogne.

Hawkscliffe, who owned a handy cutter, agreed, at a price, since the state of hostilities with France had by no means stopped his own trade with the Continent in brandy and fine wines, and he certainly wasn't averse to carrying other items as long as he was paid enough. He found it easy, as did many of his fishermen colleagues, to use quiet little landing places, and thus avoid the interference of officialdom on both sides of the Channel. If he sailed from Dover at the dead of night, he would reach the seaside hamlet of Wimereux, a mile or so north of Boulogne, just as dawn was breaking, and there would be no one at all to see him land except perhaps a few shrimpers on the deserted beach.

But before he could set sail on the midnight tide, his cutter was approached by a pair of stern-looking men sent by the port agent, who was the government's representative here in Dover harbour. They ordered him to hand the package over, and questioned him closely about it before proceeding to open it in front of him. It was found to contain a folded letter addressed this time not to the merchant in Boulogne, but to a Master Titius in Paris; and the letter itself proved to be a list of names, with numbers beside them: Chara, 3.9; Alkafazah, 2.1; Alifa, 3.6; and many, many more that covered the page.

They puzzled over them until Hawkscliffe himself, having some knowledge of celestial navigation, pointed out that they were the names of stars.

XVI

I know not who thou art, nor on what errand
Sent hither . . .

Thomas Gray, translation from Dante's
'Inferno' (1738), Canto XXXIII

It was the following day, early evening. Enveloped by the rays of the still-warm sun, Pierre Raultier was urging his horse towards Kensington, along the King's New Road. Already the lowly suburbs to the west of the city had given way to the deserted heathland of Hyde Park, where even nowadays footpads and bridle-culls were said to lurk; but his thoughts were not of highwaymen, nor even of the stars. Instead he was remembering Auguste's bright, fragile face as she roamed the big house and said to him distractedly,

'We need money, Pierre. More money . . .'

He was late; he should have been at the Montpelliers' house an hour ago. But shortly after leaving his home, he had passed the opening to Beadle Court, with its filthy tenements, and a man had come suddenly out of the darkness there. 'Doctor, doctor. You are needed.'

Raultier had stopped as the man, wretchedly dressed and stinking of tobacco, pleaded with him to save the life of his little daughter, whose throat, he said, was closing up with fever.

Diphtheria. Raultier had gone swiftly back to his lodgings for ipecacuanha and opium powder, the only medicines he had for this terrible scourge. And then he followed the man without question. Raultier had lived in this poverty-stricken district for almost two years now, and was known in these slums for his sober kindness; people turned to him in their distress, and he charged them little, often nothing, only wishing he could do more to prevent hunger, and wretchedness, and vice; he wished he could do more against the starvation that made children's limbs malformed, and more against the evil that transformed ten-year-old children into the bewildered, often gin-stupefied receptacles of old men's lusts.

In Paris, when his studies at the Hôtel Dieu were complete, he had worked as an *officier de santé* throughout the early years of the Revolution, doing what he could to alleviate the terrible poverty he saw there in the city's sunless, stinking streets. He almost understood what drove the men and women who had been deprived of nearly everything except the raw urges of survival to turn with such ferocious rage against those whose aristocratic heels had ground them again and again into the gutter.

Was it any better, now, in Paris? He had heard that the rich there had different faces, different names; but they still rode in their fine carriages, while the poor watched them silently, with hunger harrowing their faces. Raultier saw poverty as a disease, worse than leprosy; and he knew it was the children who suffered the most.

So he had let the man take his arm, had allowed himself to be led swiftly into the dark lanes behind Beadle Court, through a peeling, half-opened door, and up a crooked stairway into a low room where the walls ran with damp and a woman sat, with a child dead in her arms. The man began to sob, but the woman just stared at Raultier, quite silent, still holding her young child to her breast.

And so Raultier was late; and here was another delay, as he urged his mount on past the Knightsbridge turnpike. Now his thoughts did turn to highwaymen, because two men were riding out towards him from the shadows of the furzy thicket that clung to the edge of the road. They wore heavy coats, with hats pulled low over their brows, even though the evening was warm; and he thought he glimpsed the muzzles of sleek pistols peeping out from beneath their greatcoats. His heart was beating hard as he reined in his horse.

'Good doctor,' said one. 'Please come with us. Let us avoid trouble, shall we?'

'Who are you?' Raultier asked. 'What do you want?'

'You will know soon enough.'

One of the men took hold of his bridle and turned him back along the road he had just travelled. They rode so close that their big horses, one on either side of him, nudged the flanks of his own lean mount. Their faces were inscrutable, their pistols ever visible. Once past the turnpike, they turned north up Tyburn Lane and took him to a low tavern called the Blackamoor close by the burial ground of St George's church, where he was relieved of his horse. The tap room they led him into was crowded with ale-swilling market men and tannery workers, and after the silence outside the noise made his senses swim. His companions escorted him up a twisting staircase to another room; and here was silence anew, but of a different kind. Here was just one person, sitting at a table in the centre of the chamber: a middle-aged man attired in the sombre clothing of a clerk; bewigged, bespectacled, earnest.

Pierre Raultier felt the relief wash through him almost like wine, because he knew the man.

'You remember me?' asked Richard Crawford. As he spoke he gave a signal, and the two men who had escorted Raultier left and drew the door shut behind them.

'Yes,' said Raultier, swiftly suppressing the slight unsteadiness that had possessed him with the sudden release of tension. 'Yes, of course I do.'

'It's good to see you, Doctor Raultier. Please, make yourself comfortable.' The little Scotsman gestured to Raultier to take a chair, then got up himself, in order to light more candles. The flames flickered brightly, throwing the smoke-stained oak panelling of an earlier age into sharp relief. Raultier sat and waited, registering anew Crawford's familiar mannerisms as he tended the candles then sat down again; he seemed possessed, as ever, of some internal discomfort. Dyspepsia, thought Raultier.

There was a jug of water on the table, and a decanter of wine. Crawford poured wine for Raultier, and pushed it towards him. Raultier took it, quite calm now, aware that the close air of the room was heavy with the scent of hair powder, and of Crawford's handkerchief, which was laced with perfumed water to ward off the smells of stinking poverty that rose from below. Motes of dust danced solemnly in the shafts of candlelight.

Crawford clasped his hands before him on the table. 'Doctor Raultier,' he said at last. 'I must apologise for the manner in which you were brought here, but I could think of no other way in which our meeting would go unnoticed. And there is so little time.'

Raultier bowed his head briefly. 'I've told you that I'm always at your service.'

'Indeed. And I've remembered it. Just at present, I'm engaged on urgent government business,' went on Crawford, 'and you are one of the few men we can trust to help us with it. It's two years now, since the Chauvelin affair. Your assistance on that occasion was invaluable.'

Again, Raultier nodded in acknowledgement. Chauvelin was the French ambassador in London before the outbreak of war. When he left the country, he left behind a spy ring; but thanks to information given by Raultier, every single one of them had been captured.

'Now we need you again,' Crawford was saying in his soft Scottish lilt. He reached to pour himself some water, but instead of drinking it, he turned the glass round and round with his fingers. Then he looked up swiftly, and began to speak in a harder, surer voice. 'You'll have heard, doctor,' he said, 'that the Royalist regiments of d'Hervilly, and Hector, and Dresnay, are being equipped and armed here, in London. Soon they'll be sent down to Portsmouth, and from there to France.' Raultier listened intently. 'Embarkation is imminent,' Crawford continued; 'in fact final orders are even now being drawn up at the War Office and the Admiralty. Yes, even now . . .' He paused, looking down at his glass. Then he lifted his head. 'Unfortunately,' he went on in his clipped Scots voice, 'all those soldiers are going to their deaths.'

Raultier felt the physical shock of those words travel through him. He knew Crawford must have seen it too. 'I hope you are wrong,' he said, 'but I know you wouldn't say it unless your fears were real. How can such an outcome be possible?'

'Spies, doctor,' declared Crawford flatly, pushing at the glass with his finger. 'There are spies everywhere. We fear that nothing is secret – the army's departure date, its strength, the place of landing. Nothing.' He leaned back in his chair and studied Raultier for a moment. 'We need to know who the traitor is. And at the moment we suspect one man. He's here in London. He's a Breton – like yourself – and he holds the ears of those who are in favour of this crucial Royalist venture. Have you heard of Noel-François Prigent?'

'Of course,' responded Raultier earnestly. 'He's a Royalist agent who works from Jersey and helps refugees to escape from France.'

Crawford nodded. 'Indeed. This Prigent – also known as *Le Brigand*, I believe – has helped many *émigrés* across to England, using the Channel Islands as a stepping stone. But that's only the part of it. He has also worked for us. For English intelligence.' Crawford was fingering his water glass thoughtfully once more. 'The problem is that we no longer know if we can trust him.'

112

'Why have you started to doubt him?'

'Oh, he was never too trustworthy. A blabbermouth, as we would say. He was always taking risks – a vainglorious young fool – and in the end he took one too many chances and was captured by the Republicans last December during one of his secret trips to mainland France. He *says* he was treated badly, and was lucky to escape with his life. He *claims* that he managed to keep his identity as a English agent secret, and that some of his own men helped him to escape.'

'Don't you believe his story?'

Crawford leaned forward. 'Since Prigent was imprisoned by the Republicans, Raultier, some of our best agents on the French coast have been betrayed and captured. Prigent is back in London now, as full of himself as ever, boasting about his escape. He has the ear of the Comte de Puisaye, who is at the forefront of the Royalist cause; also that of Master Windham, Secretary-at-War. Consequently he knows everything about the landings. Everything.'

'What do you want me to do?' asked Raultier quietly.

'We need to act quickly. Prigent has taken lodgings near the old Artillery Ground at Moorfields. He's been sick with some kind of fever, which has left him with a weakness he can't shake off. He's tried several doctors, but has dismissed them all as quacks, which no doubt they are. What we would like, Raultier, if you are willing, is for you to attend Prigent yourself. Tomorrow, if possible.'

'So soon?'

'It's presumptuous of me, I know,' said Crawford quickly, 'but I've already made all the necessary arrangements, and I've ensured that you would come to him well recommended. We're not looking for specific information, Raultier; all we require is your opinion as to whether this man is to be trusted or not. I don't think you'll find it difficult to gain his confidence; he's known to have a fondness for physicians, and talking over his own health. And as I've said, we know him to be indiscreet on other matters. You are from Brittany, just as he is. You could talk about old times together, find out where his real loyalties lie.'

A sudden cacophony – the roar of voices in dispute, the shrill notes of a woman shouting – rose, muted, from beneath them to break the silence that had fallen as Crawford finished speaking. Raultier waited for the noise to die away then said, 'So you are asking me to form a judgement on the reliability of this man? In a matter of days?'

Crawford leaned forward again, his expression registering his recognition of the doubt he must have heard in Raultier's voice. 'Doctor Raultier. We know you have no love for the Republicans. You have already served us well by giving us the names of Chauvelin's men. But believe me, Prigent is a much greater threat than the ambassador's spies. Hundreds – no, thousands of lives may be lost if we cannot be certain of everyone involved in the invasion – and Prigent is at the moment the one we most suspect. Please. Help us.'

Raultier met his gaze steadily. 'Tell me what you want me to do,' he said.

For the first time Crawford let a slow smile lighten his pallid features. 'I'll confirm the arrangements for the meeting for tomorrow,' he breathed. 'I'll send a messenger to let you know where and when to contact Prigent. Thank you, doctor. Thank you. We'll reward you well, believe me.'

He got up then, to clasp Raultier's hand. He went to the door, to call for the men who had escorted Raultier, and told them to fetch Raultier's horse, then he came down into the courtyard with him, waiting at the doctor's side until he was safely mounted.

'I must beg your forgiveness again,' Crawford said, 'for the way in which you were brought here.'

Raultier gathered up his horse's reins. 'In these times,' he replied, 'one cannot be too careful.'

Then he used his spurs on his horse's flanks, and rode out of the courtyard; and as he urged his horse westwards, along the King's New Road, his sombre face seemed for a moment almost incandescent in the rays of the setting sun.

XVII

*All Celestial bodies whatsoever have an attraction
or gravitating Power towards their own Centres,
whereby they attract not only their own parts and
keep them from flying from them, as we may observe
the Earth to do, but that they do also attract all the
other Celestial Bodies that are within the Sphere of
their activity.*

Robert Hooke, *Attempt to Prove the Motion of
the Earth* (1674)

At about the same time that Raultier left the Blackamoor inn, a shabby hackney coach pulled up with a clatter of hooves and creaking of wheels outside the gates of a walled mansion in Kensington Gore; and Alexander Wilmot clambered down into the dusty road, a little dazed by his long journey, and breathing in the fresh air deeply to rid his nostrils of the smell of the old leather seats and of stale drink that permeated the interior of the carriage.

The Montpelliers' big house, set at the end of a broad drive that wound its way between thickets of overgrown laurel and stands of lime trees, looked forbidding to him in its isolation. The gabled wings, clad with ancient ivy, stood guard over the main body of the house; while a cluster of stable blocks and outbuildings spilled untidily out into the gathering darkness on either side. He felt that the house was watching him.

He looked up to where the steep roofs and high chimneys of the lonely mansion reached towards the first faint stars. Vega in Lyra burned through the encircling canopy of the twilight, while in the south-west Arcturus twinkled in the arms of the crescent moon. To the west, the familiar shape of the circumpolar Plough greeted him like a friend, as if to reassure him; but when he looked at the house again, he knew that he should turn his back on all of it, because he had come here as a spy.

The driver of the carriage was watching him from his high perch.

Alexander hesitated one last time, then paid him, thus making return an impossible option, and watched him go. He found that his palms were damp; he was about to wipe them on his brown serge coat, but remembered just in time how he and Daniel had spent the best part of an hour brushing and repairing it. He remembered too how Daniel had sewn a loose button on his breeches, and polished his sadly worn buckled shoes with patient care, while Alexander paced the room in a turmoil of conflicting emotions.

The invitation had arrived that morning. The handwritten card seemed at first a pure harbinger of joy; and almost with wonder, Alexander had pressed it deep in his coat pocket, where he kept touching it secretly during the funeral service for which he had played the organ that morning. He was conscious of it all through the warm heat of the afternoon, during which he had intended to transcribe a Missa Solemnis by Rameau for the church choir at the little desk in his first-floor parlour, but instead kept stopping to stare out, unseeing, over the roofs and fields beyond Clerkenwell.

And now he was here; the moment had come; but by the time he reached the wide stone steps that led up to the entrance, his chest felt tight with anxiety and his breathing was uneven. The flambeaux in their iron brackets suddenly seemed a seraphic warning of a place forbidden to him; he turned and looked instead, with longing, at the beauty of Antares in Scorpius, slowly rising above the southern horizon over the fields and leafy lanes that stretched towards Chelsea village.

In perhaps another hour, when true darkness began to hold its brief summer sway, it would be a wonderful night for the stars. Earlier rain had fallen briefly; and now the indigo sky, washed clean of dust, glittered with a tantalising brilliance. He absorbed its emerging treasures one last time, then he straightened his wig, pulled at the heavy doorbell and waited, clutching his invitation in his perspiring hand, mentally preparing the words with which to introduce himself.

The door opened abruptly and his thoughts were scattered. A man stood there; a big man in dark, loose-hanging clothes, whose face was made utterly forbidding by the terrible scar that split his cheek.

Alexander stammered as he announced himself, and dropped the invitation card on the floor. He bent to reach for it, but dropped it again, and by the time he had retrieved it at last, the scarred man's smile was almost a sneer as he beckoned him in.

The hall he entered was imposing and chilly, its black and white floor tiles interspersed with lofty marble pillars that supported a wide gallery running the whole length of the first floor. Empty of furniture, with vaulted ceilings that echoed at his every step, the big house seemed almost a carcass, a gaunt body deprived of life. And Alexander, as he followed the scarred man up the curving stairway, was assailed by a fresh onslaught of fear that his hosts and their guests would be speaking their own language. His command of the French tongue had once been competent, a necessity in his wide travels; but now? His presumption in seeking this invitation all but overwhelmed him. Shaking with apprehension, he followed his stern guide into the big drawing room, where he was dazzled in equal measure by the blaze of candlelight and the throng of curious faces all turned towards him.

Almost immediately a woman detached herself from the group she was with, and came swiftly towards him. She paused to speak briefly, almost sharply, to the scarred man, then she was standing close to Alexander, laying her slender white fingers on his arm, and saying in a musical, vibrant voice, 'My dear Monsieur Wilmot. So it was you who sent me the pretty, the enchanting little toy! I am Madame de Montpellier, you see.'

Alexander, who was normally shy of beautiful women, was captivated. She was young, graceful in every movement, every gesture; her pale powdered hair was cropped fashionably short, and crowned with some delicate head-dress of feathers that nodded as she moved. Her gown was a gossamer sheath of pale green silk, and she wore long cream gloves that just reached above her elbows. A single strand of pearls adorned her slender neck.

Alexander tore his eyes away from her face to the place where she was pointing, and he saw that she had placed his little model of Jupiter and its four moons on a satinwood table close by. Since his visit to Perceval's shop three days ago, Alexander had stayed up late each night to complete this miniature orrery. Daniel had anxiously brought him cup after cup of fragrant coffee to keep him awake as he worked, while his fingers grew raw with sanding, and his eyes ached with the straining after perfection; but perfect it seemed now, even to his own critical eyes, as he gazed at it.

He said at last, in her own language, 'It was no less than you deserve, madame. I had heard of you and your companions' reputation as watchers of the skies, and wished to pay homage. Since my tongue is poor, and my pen even poorer, I thought to send you this little toy, in hopes that it might amuse you.'

'So humble,' she said, her hazel eyes dancing beneath arched, expressive eyebrows. 'So humble, yet so fluent, so clever!' She bent over the model and turned the little key that Alexander had asked Perceval to make; and the four moons, Io, Europa, Ganymede and Callisto, moved around their parent planet in a slow, elliptical dance. 'Indeed, this toy, as you call it, has delighted me for hours, and my brother Guy as well; sometimes we call my brother Ganymede, you see, after the brightest of Jupiter's moons, and he calls me Io, beloved of Zeus – but did you know this already, I wonder, that you made the model? – and so we have had much amusement together, plotting the errant courses of our little moons, so near to one another, yet destined never to meet . . .' She broke off, her eyes suddenly over-bright, it seemed to Alexander, and went on, 'You are too modest, I think, about your own talents, Monsieur Wilmot. You told me in your letter that you, too, seek Titius's missing planet. Tell me, I implore you, what progress you have made.'

Other people surrounded them, but to Alexander at that moment they seemed insubstantial, ephemeral. 'Madame,' he said, 'like many others, I have spent some time studying Titius's calculations. I was far away from England when Herschel made his great discovery. But I shall never forget how I felt, on my return, when I learnt that his new planet lay exactly where Titius had predicted that it should be.'

'And how did you feel, Monsieur Wilmot?' she asked quietly.

'I could not sleep,' he said simply. 'I could not think of anything else. I pored over my papers by day, and gazed at the sky night after night, seeking the lost planet.'

'Ah, yes,' murmured Madame de Montpellier. 'Selene.'

'Selene?' He was startled, wondering if she was talking of the moon; but she looked at him, smiling, and explained,

'Selene is the name we give to our missing star, after the goddess of the moon and sister of the dawn. You must know the story of how she laid flowers on her lover Endymion's sleeping body, and enchanted him with the music of her voice . . .' She closed her eyes and began to hum to herself softly, only to break off her low song and put her hand on his arm. 'Have you ever seen her, Monsieur Wilmot? Have you seen Selene?'

He hesitated, confused by her nearness, by the warmth of her slender fingers on his sleeve, by her strange humming. He said at last, 'Yes. Yes, I think that I have . . .'

'Please. Tell me.'

Alexander cleared his throat self-consciously. 'It was in the autumn, almost two years ago, in the constellation of Pisces.' He hesitated, aware that his hostess was gazing at him with almost painful eagerness. 'I saw her for two nights in a row,' he went on. 'But then the clouds came, and I was unable to find her again.'

'*Ah.*' She hung her head. 'But it *was* her? You're sure?'

'I believe it was the object you call Selene,' he replied quietly. 'But since then my sight has grown worse, madame; and in those days I had the use of a better telescope. I've not seen the lost star again.' He remembered with renewed regret how he had been forced to sell off his old refractor to pay off his debts to his blackmailers.

'But if you had the use of a better telescope,' demanded Auguste, clutching his arm more tightly, 'if you had one completely at your disposal, would it help you in your search?'

'Undoubtedly,' he replied. 'But even without a telescope, madame, there are other ways to plot her course.'

Her eyes never left his face. 'How?'

'Through the science of mathematics,' he said.

'Of course,' she breathed. 'Of course. And you are a mathematician . . .'

All his nights, and days, of work; all his hours poring over the Titius figures; it seemed to Alexander now as if here at last was the culmination of all his research, here in the belief that shone from Auguste's face. He nodded. 'All I need,' he said, 'to complete my work, is one more sighting.'

Her grip on his arm was by now almost painful. 'My brother Guy has seen it,' she whispered.

Alexander's heart leapt. 'He has figures?'

'Yes. Oh, yes.' She looked around the crowded room, searching, and Alexander eagerly followed her gaze, but it was clear from her frown that Guy had not appeared. She turned back to Alexander. 'He isn't here yet,' she said, 'but I will get you his figures.'

'Madame,' he replied fervently, 'I would be most honoured.'

'My dear Monsieur Wilmot.' She gave him her bewitching smile again. 'Any man who can create a thing of beauty such as *this* —' she pointed again at the orrery — 'bestows a privilege on others with his presence, not the reverse.' Warmly she pressed his hand, and turned, almost with reluctance, it seemed, towards her other guests. 'We'll talk again later. I'll ask Guy to give you his calculations as well, but for now I mustn't monopolise you. Come, my little English friend. I think that you are a discovery in yourself. I shall call you — "mouse". And now I'll introduce you to my other friends.'

She had a glass of wine brought for him, which in his elation he drank too quickly. His mind was still racing with the discovery that Guy de Montpellier had sighted the star, and actually had figures that, together with his own, could lead to an all-important confirmation of its path. But gradually, as he was introduced to one group after another, he had to concentrate on lowlier, if still gratifying matters, as he realised that the people Auguste led him amongst already knew of him as the creator of the Jupiter model, and wished him to describe, in detail, the making of his miniature orrery. He did so with shy pride, and they watched raptly as he turned Perceval's little key and Io, Ganymede, Callisto and Europa began their slow dance around stately Jupiter. After a while he had another, less welcome observer when Madame de Montpellier, who had briefly moved away, came towards him again; this time, to Alexander's surprise, she had at her side the scarred doorkeeper, who looked no less forbidding to Alexander than he had earlier.

Was this man a friend, or a servant? His attitude towards Madame de Montpellier was protective, almost ardent. Towering over her slight figure, the doorkeeper watched her silently all the time; yet he seemed the only one who, like Alexander, did not really belong to this glittering company.

Though how could he, Alexander, feel that he was not one of them when Madame de Montpellier herself rested her hand so intimately on his sleeve, and lifted her face so brightly to his, in defiance, it seemed, of the man's scarred scowl? Alexander's heart beat more rapidly, his blood moved more warmly in his veins when she took him by the arm and led him gently away from the model and its admirers to meet yet more of her companions. As she guided him round the room, her beautiful voice teased and cajoled her guests, gently mocking, yet at the same time caressing, like some rare music.

'Ah, there is my Doctor Corvus,' she exclaimed, guiding Alexander swiftly towards another group. 'Good Doctor Corvus, come and meet my Mouse, who made the exquisite Jupiter toy for me.'

'Doctor Corvus. I am pleased to meet you,' said Alexander, holding out his hand as a tall, dark-haired man in clothes that hung loosely on his big frame stepped forward towards them. At the same time he heard Madame de Montpellier's soft laughter and he hesitated, confused. The doctor, who had a heavy-featured face with sad eyes, reached to shake his hand and explained quickly, 'Corvus is Auguste's familiar name for me. I am Raultier, Pierre Raultier.'

Alexander gave a start of glad recognition, for this was another name his friend Perceval had mentioned. He would have liked to talk to the doctor, but Madame de Montpellier was eager to move on, pausing only to explain to Alexander, in Raultier's full hearing, 'I call Pierre by the name of Corvus because he watches over us, just as the great black crow watched Juno. He rescued us from the Revolutionaries, Mouse; he is an unlikely-looking saviour, is he not?'

She looked challengingly at Raultier, then once more gave her low laugh and moved on. But Alexander looked back over his shoulder, and saw Pierre Raultier staring after their hostess as if he could not take his eyes from her.

There were many others, both French and English, whose names he could not remember at the time. They seemed, to the marvelling Alexander, to gather around their beautiful hostess as she circled the long room like the moons of Jupiter orbiting in due homage. He stood and watched, wondering at it all; and suddenly he heard the sound of a harpsichord being played, in some distant room. He thought he recognised the closing bars of a sonata by Rameau. Then someone slammed a door, and he could hear it no longer.

The elusive music was still haunting him when Madame de Montpellier came to him once more with a tall newcomer at her side: a fair-haired, impossibly beautiful young man who made his heart miss a beat. Could this be the brother whom she had called Ganymede, the beloved of the gods? The brother who had seen Selene?

'I am delighted to meet you, monsieur,' said Alexander shyly in the man's own language, bowing a little.

'There is no need for your French, Monsieur Wilmot.' Madame de Montpellier lifted her hand in admonition. 'My dear friend William

Carline is as English as you are. But you must not expect him to reply. He is mute.'

'I'm sorry,' said Alexander, blushing.

'Then do not be,' said his hostess quietly. 'He needs no one's pity. William Carline is one of the most skilled star-watchers I have ever encountered; his knowledge of the necessary instrumentation is formidable. You will, I think, enjoy working with him.'

So he was to work with them? *Phaethon. Ah, Phaethon, beware,* his mind warned him, but quickly he dismissed the inner voice. 'Indeed,' he said earnestly, 'I should be most glad to.'

Madame de Montpellier bowed her pale, shorn head in brief acknowledgement. 'We will speak of this later.' She smiled radiantly at him. 'But now it's time for all my guests to eat. I am sure you must be hungry after your long journey.'

Alexander could already smell the food that was being brought in; the delectable aromas of roasted meats and dainty savouries filled his nostrils. As Madame de Montpellier moved amongst her other guests, with Carline silent at her side, Alexander joined the people grouped around the damask-covered table that ran the width of the room, and a servant proceeded to heap slices of roast venison and helpings of buttered peas and asparagus on to a plate for him.

Alexander, nodding his thanks and responding to the friendly comments of the nearby guests who recognised him as the distinguished maker of the Jupiter model, picked up his plate and started to move away from the table. But some unseen person behind him knocked his elbow, his plate jumped in his hands, and the rich madeira sauce that adorned the venison splattered the front of his coat.

Colour rushed to his perspiring face. He swung round, an exclamation still on his lips, and saw the scarred doorkeeper moving quickly away. Was it he who had caused the accident? Why? People were staring at him; he felt hot and confused. Turning round to put his dripping plate back on the table, his hand shaking with mortification as the meat juices ran down his coat, he saw Madame de Montpellier standing nearby, watching him, with William Carline at her side, his beautiful blue eyes wide and mocking.

Suddenly the doctor, Pierre Raultier, appeared in front of him with a large, clean napkin. 'Here, my friend,' he said. 'This should remove the worst of the damage.' Alexander began to stammer out his thanks, but Raultier cut him short, kindly, with an upraised hand, and helped him to tidy himself. Then he produced two clean plates, handing one to Alexander.

'Time to start afresh, I think,' he said. 'I am ready for food myself, and madame's chef is excellent: yet another exile from France, as are so many of us. Would you join me?' The doctor's English, though lightly accented, was exquisite, precise.

Alexander replied, 'You're very kind. But to be honest, I'm not sure that I feel hungry any more.' The memory of Madame de Montpellier's pitying hazel eyes still mortified him.

'Nonsense,' said Raultier, heartily biting into a fragrant venison pasty. 'Eat, monsieur, and confound the boorish Ralph. He is endeavouring, I think, to demonstrate the revered Herschel's theory that a tiny random action – that is, the deliberate jolting of your elbow a few moments ago – can have massive and multiplying reactions: notably, not only the ruin of your suit, and your minor humiliation; but possibly, even, your premature departure from our little company.'

So Raultier too had noticed the doorkeeper's malice. 'Why would he bear me such ill will?' Alexander exclaimed.

Raultier shrugged. 'Ralph is jealous of any newcomer,' he replied. 'We are all, I suppose, anxious not to lose our place in Auguste de Montpellier's charmed circle. Take no notice of him.'

Much heartened, Alexander began, like Raultier, to help himself to the savoury food. 'You mentioned Herschel's theory earlier, sir,' he reminded the doctor earnestly after a few moments, 'about a small action having incalculable results. Are you a follower, then, of Herschel's propositions?'

'I have great admiration for the man, yes,' said Raultier, 'as have all of us in this company.' He paused to pour Alexander some wine. 'He combines observational brilliance with a capacity for great humility. In spite of his wonderful discoveries, he still believes that in reality we understand very little.'

'Yes,' agreed Alexander, 'yes, true modesty is a quality, surely, of some of the greatest minds.'

Raultier continued to look steadily at Alexander. 'Talking of modesty, I hear from Auguste that you yourself are a mathematician of considerable skill. We are all hoping very much that you will join us.'

'I could wish for nothing better,' responded Alexander fervently. 'Are you also an astronomer, Doctor Raultier?'

Raultier waved his hand in self-deprecation. 'I can hardly lay claim to any kind of distinction. When time allows, I work on my own modest project, which is to compare the magnitudes of the brightest stars; but my knowledge must be insignificant compared to yours. Tell me, though: how did you hear about our little circle?'

'We have, I think, an acquaintance in common,' replied Alexander eagerly. 'Perceval Oates the spectacle-maker, of Clerkenwell.' Just for a moment he was afraid that he had made a mistake again, because Raultier seemed to go very still; but then the doctor was nodding heartily, and saying with approval, 'Perceval. Of course. He's an excellent craftsman.'

'He helped me with the mechanics of the Jupiter model. He made the key for me.'

The doctor turned to look appreciatively on the nearby orrery, which still had its circle of admirers. 'I take it that the moons of Jupiter are of particular interest to you. Do you work on the intricacies of this subject entirely by yourself?'

'Not entirely, no. I have the honour, you see, to correspond with Pierre Laplace on the matter of planetary orbits and Jupiter's moons.'

'You correspond with Laplace himself? In Paris?' Raultier's astonishment, and admiration, were evident.

'Yes,' said Alexander. 'Of course Laplace writes to many others on the subject, and encourages their opinions. You'll know that he and his colleagues are hoping that their work on the movements of Jupiter's moons might help in the matter of longitude . . .' His face suddenly fell. 'But perhaps I ought not to mention Monsieur Laplace here. You are all exiles from your homeland; I doubt if any of you feel anything but hostility to a man employed by its government. Forgive me for my tactlessness.'

Raultier refilled both their glasses and shook his head. 'Not at all. Don't apologise. Laplace's life has been in danger too, you know. He had to make a hasty escape from Paris last summer, towards the end of Robespierre's reign of terror. But things have changed. Laplace was recalled to Paris in December, along with other men of science. To win a war, Monsieur Wilmot, to sail great ships across the seas and to build bigger and better guns, a government – even a Jacobin government – needs scientists.'

'But you yourself would not go back to your homeland, doctor?'

Raultier hesitated briefly. 'No,' he said. 'I would not go back to Paris.' He reached for his own wine. 'But, you know, I have often thought, lately, that it would be good to get in touch with an old colleague like Laplace again, especially now that his exile is over. And yet it can be difficult to send letters to Paris, especially now that so many of my old friends in the Académie are dead, or exiled . . .' He regarded Alexander thoughtfully. 'Tell me. If I were to give you a letter for Laplace, would it be a great inconvenience for you to enclose it with your own packet for the Bureau?'

Alexander felt his heart expand. 'It would be no trouble at all, doctor. But I had no idea that you and Laplace were old friends.'

'Colleagues, rather,' explained Raultier hastily. 'I worked with him once, when I was a doctor at the Hôtel Dieu. Laplace was writing his treatise on probability. As part of his work, he spent some weeks in the hospital, making a study of the likelihood of death amongst the patients.' He paused, and went on, a little grimly, 'He discovered that if you were poor, and ill-nourished, you were only half as likely to survive as someone who came from a more prosperous background. We doctors, of course, could have told him that at the outset, but Laplace, though he is an excellent soul, is one of those who enjoys reducing everything to statistics.'

Alexander nodded. 'Yes. Laplace's certainties can at times seem presumptuous. Yet in our correspondence I find him to be effortlessly brilliant.'

'Indeed,' agreed Raultier. 'But isn't your mail intercepted? Don't you face problems in sending and receiving these letters?'

'I write to him through the Royal Society,' said Alexander with some pride. 'The Society has special franking privileges. Its members' letters go directly to their various destinations, whether at home or in Europe.' He inclined his head in a gesture of self-deprecation. 'Of course my work is of minor importance . . .'

'You are over-modest, my friend. I think your achievements must be considerable. And how reassuring to know that the pursuits of astronomy and science are deemed important enough to be allowed to continue even during these difficult times.' Raultier lifted his glass in a toast. 'To the men of science.'

'To the men of science,' echoed Alexander. They drained their glasses.

'I'm afraid I've monopolised you for too long,' said Raultier, glancing at his watch. 'But there's one more matter, before I let you move on. Auguste tells me that you've done some work on Titius's theory of planetary orbits. Tell me, in confidence: do you believe that this lost star really exists?'

'Don't you, doctor?'

Raultier hesitated. 'I would dearly like to believe. And yet so many others have tried to prove its existence, and failed.'

'But Guy has seen it. He has recorded it,' exclaimed Alexander, astonished.

'Yes, perhaps,' said Raultier, frowning. 'Although I cannot help but see the physical and mental effects of such a difficult endeavour . . .' Again he hesitated. 'I'm afraid it does Guy no good to have his hopes raised so painfully, only to be cast down again.'

He broke off abruptly. He was gazing over Alexander's shoulder to a far doorway; Alexander turned and saw Auguste de Montpellier standing there alone, her face pale and anxious as she searched the busy room.

'Alas,' said Raultier quietly. 'This could be an example of what I was just talking about. Will you excuse me?'

He hurried over to Auguste. She spoke a few words of what looked like quiet but desperate entreaty to him, then left the room again. Raultier came quickly back to Alexander, and his face too was shadowed with anxiety.

'It's as I feared. Madame de Montpellier's brother is taken ill. I am sorry, I shall have to leave you.'

'Of course. I didn't realise he was in the house . . .'

'You heard him earlier. He was playing the harpsichord.'

The celestial music. Guy. Ganymede. 'I'm so sorry he's unwell.'

Raultier nodded curtly. 'I must go to him immediately. But if I may, I'll call on you soon, with a letter for my old colleague Laplace.'

'Of course,' said Alexander fervently.

Raultier pressed Alexander's hand briefly and hurried towards the door through which Auguste had left the room.

XVIII

That Comets are capable of destroying such Worlds
as may chance to fall in their way, is, from their vast
magnitude, velocity and fiery substance, not at all
to be doubted; and it is more than probable, from
the great and unoccupied distance betwixt ye planets
Mars and Jupiter, that some World may have met
with such a final Dissolution.

Thomas Wright of Durham (1711–1786)
Letter I: Second Thoughts

A ll the Montpelliers' guests were preparing to depart, their spirits subdued as the news swiftly spread that Auguste's brother had been taken ill. Alexander was following them slowly along the wide first-floor gallery to the head of the staircase, when his attention was caught by the sight of a harpsichord that was half hidden behind the open door of a smaller chamber. He moved towards the door as if drawn by some unseen presence. The instrument was silent now, and yet the candles that illuminated it were still burning brightly, as if in expectation of the return of someone recently departed.

Alexander gazed into the room with yearning in his heart. The walls were hung with straw-coloured silk that glittered in the light of the candles in their sconces. Three empty telescope tubes, similar to the ones from Leiden in Perceval's shop, lay on a small table, their burnished mahogany gleaming darkly.

He found himself walking past them towards the harpsichord; and he felt in his solitude as if he were the only person in the house. Gazing at the ivory keys that were worn with use, he let his finger-tips brush them tenderly, hearing once more in his mind the music that the sick man had coaxed from them.

Sheets of manuscript paper lay on top of the harpsichord. Alexander saw that they were covered with spidery, delicate musical notes; and some writing.

Il est impossible de contempler les étoiles cette nuit pour chercher celle qui est perdue . . .

It is impossible to gaze at the stars tonight, to seek the one which is lost.

He pulled himself away jerkily. He was spying. How pleased his brother would be with him.

Filled with a sudden self-loathing, he left the room and made his way down the broad staircase to the entrance hall. Most of the other guests had already departed. A footman held the door open for him, and he hurried through it, feeling like an intruder in the now-quiet house. Outside, he stood uncertainly on the steps in the flickering light of the flambeaux, together with the few remaining guests who were waiting for the last of the private carriages to be brought round to the front of the house. Alexander watched them depart one by one down the drive that led to the Kensington Road; and standing there alone in the shadows, he thought, How am I going to get home to Clerkenwell?

There were no hackneys here, no link-boys to summon him a chair. How foolish he was, not to have anticipated this dilemma. He would have to walk, at least as far as the Knightsbridge turnpike, and hope to hire some conveyance from there. The distance was no more than a matter of a mile or so, but the road was lonely where it passed through the exposed heathland of the park, and he was afraid of foot-pads. He looked up at the sky for inspiration, but none came, for the clouds had gathered and only the moon rode high above them, casting her faint silver light over the dark woods that surrounded the house as the last of the carriages disappeared into the distance.

And then, a deep voice at his shoulder said sonorously,

'I see you view the outer darkness, good sir, where the damned are forever condemned to dwell, their best hope a distant glimpse of the stars that cluster round the Abode of God.'

Alexander had jumped at the sound of the voice. Turning, he now saw a middle-aged man, tall and sturdily built, with a loose black coat and a wide-brimmed hat pulled over his long iron-grey hair. He had noticed the same man earlier, deep in conversation with Madame de Montpellier, and he remembered thinking fleetingly that he looked like a priest. Certainly his strange words just now confirmed that supposition. Alexander felt the automatic, shrinking fear that he felt in the presence of any man of the cloth, for they brought back memories of his pious, devout and deeply unhappy mother. But then he noticed the deep lines of dissipation carved down the man's lean cheeks, and saw the twinkle in his eyes, and smelled the brandy on his breath.

'I am indeed a man who makes a study of the stars, sir,' Alexander replied. 'But at this moment I feel I am lost eternally in the outer reaches of rural darkness, unless I can find some miraculous way of conveying my tired and unfit body back to Clerkenwell Green.'

The man laughed delightedly. 'You see Clerkenwell Green as the Abode of God?'

'No,' said Alexander, 'but it is, for better or worse, where I live.'

The big man pondered this with some appreciation. 'So Clerkenwell is your home. Is it possible to view the heavens from Clerkenwell?'

'I have a small rooftop observatory. My instruments are simple. But on a clear night I can watch the stars with as much joy as the Astronomer Royal himself.'

'Excellent, excellent! So your home is therefore a celestial palace, a heavenly dwelling, of sorts.' The man held out his hand in a dramatic gesture and began to declaim,

'Before the starry threshold of Jove's court
My mansion is, where those immortal shapes
Of bright aerial Spirits live insphered . . .' He paused expectantly, staring at Alexander, who smiled and continued the verse quietly.

'*. . . In regions mild of calm and serene air*
Above the smoke and stir of this dim spot
Which men call earth.'

The man, grinning anew, clapped him on the back. 'Well said, friend, well said! But I haven't yet introduced myself. My name is Matthew Norland.'

'Alexander Wilmot, at your service.' They shook hands.

'Alexander Wilmot,' said Norland, 'you are clearly a man of character, and, what is more, a lover of England's greatest poet; so let me make a proposition to you. My servant had instructions to be here with the coach at midnight, but he is always late. He blames the horses; he says they are fit for nothing, but I assure you that if he can still coax some action from them he will be arriving here at any moment, to take me back to the metropolis: Hockley in the Hole, to be precise; and you, good sir, shall accompany me.'

Silently thanking heaven, and his knowledge of Milton, for his good fortune, Alexander quickly agreed to share Norland's carriage, which they could already hear coming up the drive. Once inside, he was also given the chance to share the man's leather flask of rough brandy; and as the heavy vehicle moved slowly eastwards along the darkness of the King's New Road, with the wastes of Hyde Park enclosing them as the sea embraces mariners on some well-charted but still hazardous voyage, they talked of poetry, and the stars; until Alexander, mellowed by the strong spirits, ventured to say at last, his words a little slurred,

'Do you know, good sir, when I first saw you, I thought – for a moment only – that you must be a priest.'

Norland leaned forward to touch Alexander's knee, and said with an air of collaboration, 'Do you know, for a while I thought I was one as well. For several years, to be precise. But the delusion lasted no longer than that.'

So he had, indeed, been a man of the cloth. After that disclosure Norland rambled on about himself with some fluency, telling Alexander that when he was a priest he had lived for some years in Paris, attached to the Jesuit seminary of St Firmin in the rue Saint-Victor. He had been introduced to the Montpelliers, he said, in the year before the Revolution, because of their shared interest in the study of the stars.

Alexander wondered when and why Norland had ceased to be a priest; but it was not, of course, a question he could ask. A pleasant alcoholic haze enfolded him more and more securely as the carriage made its rolling way along the rough paving stones of High Holborn. He listened eagerly to Norland's talk of the mysteries of the heavens, and broke in at last,

'What about Selene?'

And Norland looked suddenly, shockingly sober. He said, agitated, 'Selene? What do you know of her?' He must have seen the puzzlement on Alexander's face, because he broke off, took a deep breath, and smiled, but with an effort, it seemed, and said,

'Ah, yes – you are speaking of their lost star.'

'Could the name mean anything else to them?' asked Alexander anxiously.

'Yes,' said Norland in a serious voice, 'yes indeed. They call the star Selene because it was the name of the woman Guy loved, in Paris.'

Alexander strained to hear his words as the carriage clattered over rough cobbles. 'I did not know. What became of her?'

Norland frowned and hesitated. 'A bad end, I'm afraid. Those were dangerous times for lovers. Though Selene was of noble birth, she dedicated herself to the ideals of the Revolution, and was a friend to many of its leaders. But then she made the mistake of supporting Lafayette, who tried to save the king and his family and then defected to the Austrians. Dangerous times indeed; the fortress of Longwy had fallen, Verdun was threatened, and the Prussians were pouring deep into French territory. The road to Paris lay open to the enemy. Tales of treachery from within swept the city. Selene, who had dared to defend the traitor Lafayette, was branded a traitor herself and thrown into prison.'

He was silent for a moment, and Alexander waited with painful intensity. 'It was the autumn of the massacres,' Norland went on at last. 'You will have heard. The prisoners in the gaols were dragged out and killed by the mob on the Paris streets.'

Alexander breathed, 'Did Guy's Selene die too?'

'They were all killed,' repeated Norland solemnly. 'Priests, nobles, women and children . . . Many of them were tortured first then torn to pieces by the blood-crazed rabble.' His hands clenched round his bottle. 'Guy was bereft. The Montpelliers fled Paris, as did so many during those terrible weeks. Guy vowed, then, that he would find the missing star for his lost Selene, and name it after her. It has become, I think, a kind of quest. His own search after redemption.'

The big carriage jolted onwards. It was Alexander who broke the silence that had fallen between the two men. 'Do you believe that Guy will find his star?'

'I do not.' Then seeing the look on Alexander's face, Norland went on quickly, 'Oh, perhaps this lost star, this lost planet that they believe in, did exist once. Perhaps it was destroyed in some primeval collision with another celestial body. That would, at least, explain the great and unoccupied distance between Mars and Jupiter. But to assume so ardently that it still exists, to search for it as if it were his soul's salvation; ah, how Guy deceives himself, and his sister cruelly supports his hope . . .' He leaned forward and gazed at Alexander with drink-hazed eyes. 'Others, the greatest astronomers in the world, have tried to prove its existence and failed. Surely, with all the fine instruments we now have available, it would have been discovered by now, were it an object of any significance. Raultier has his doubts too. But the Montpelliers believe in it, oh, how they believe. Nothing I say, nothing anyone else says, deters them. And who am I, to refuse my help?' He raised his brandy bottle and drank deeply.

I believe in it, thought Alexander fervently. *I have seen it. I will help them.* He found he was swaying rhythmically with the carriage, the brandy fumes making his head heavy. Aloud he said, 'She is a beautiful and fascinating woman, Auguste.'

Norland laughed, and again Alexander detected a note of bitterness in his sonorous voice. 'She is indeed. But beware, my friend. She is a fallen angel, and would take us all with her, down, down . . .' He gazed out of the window into the black night. 'Like Satan. Beautiful, lost Satan.

> *From morn*
> *To noon he fell, from noon to dewy eve,*
> *A summer's day; and with the setting sun*
> *Dropt from the zenith like a falling star . . .'*

He turned back suddenly to Alexander. 'What did Auguste tell you about Carline?'

His voice was harsh; Alexander felt uneasy as he remembered the mute Englishman's cold blue gaze. 'I met him only briefly,' he replied. 'I learnt that he cannot speak. And that he helps with the telescopes—'

Norland let out a coarse laugh. 'Ah,' he said. 'If only that were all. He has an interesting if enigmatic history, our Carline. Raultier found him one night last summer, in July, lying on the turnpike. He had somehow travelled up from Portsmouth, perhaps in a drover's cart bound for London; we never learnt it all. He was near death; his back had been laid open by the cat o'nine tails. He was a Navy man, a purser, who had been caught stealing, and this was his punishment, though I have never heard it given to an officer before, and he has never spoken of it, for the trauma of his injuries has rendered him mute. I have heard of such things after a battle, in men who have been wounded or been close to men who've died. Something goes in their mind and they lose the faculty of speech.'

'Then how do you know all this about him?'

'The good doctor found his warrant card on him, stamped "dishonourably discharged". And we all know of the harshness of the punishments that the Royal Navy metes out to its delinquents.' Norland took another draught from the brandy flask and failed to cover up a hearty belch. 'Still, Carline fell into good hands. Raultier had studied similar cases in Paris – felons who had been whipped to within an inch of their lives, whom he'd brought back to life, no doubt only to face Madame Guillotine. But here was a man who would live; and so the good doctor tended him as assiduously as any mother her firstborn till after a month or so he could get back on his feet. And yet Carline's speech never returned. He communicates only in writing, or sign language. But his arrival proved a boon of sorts, for some time during his naval career he had picked up knowledge of telescopes and celestial navigation, so now he helps with the star instruments and makes himself useful to the Montpelliers.' He gave a slow grin. 'More useful, in fact, than Raultier ever imagined.'

Again Alexander felt uneasy. 'What do you mean?'

Norland leaned forward confidingly. 'Perhaps you hadn't noticed, but poor Raultier is infatuated with Auguste. It was his devotion alone that enabled her to escape the Commune. For this, I know for certain, he enjoyed but one night of her favours, and afterwards she treated him like a dog; while he, his carnal appetites only temporarily satiated, behaved like one, following her with pitiful despair wherever she went, still hoping for another scrap from his mistress's table. But Auguste is one who scorns weakness, and soon she grew tired of him. Her eyes wandered and settled on the very cuckoo that Raultier had brought into her nest. Soon she was spending every night in Carline's arms; perhaps she knew that, unlike the besotted doctor, she would never have to hear from his mouth words of endearment and affection, for they are the things she despises above all else in a man.'

For a moment the vision of heaven Alexander had glimpsed at the glittering mansion seemed to have vanished like a dream. Could all this be true? Could the beautiful Auguste really have taken to her bed a flogged criminal who had lost the power of speech? He felt cold, and quite sober again; then he realised that Norland was gazing out of the window once more, and beckoning curtly to Alexander to do the same. The carriage was making its way tortuously up Greville Street, where one of the low-class taverns was spilling its noisy customers out into the street. The faces of the men who had gathered there were surly and aggressive as they milled around, while a group of prostitutes stood by, passively watching and waiting for trade.

'Look at them,' said Norland. He spat through the open window in the direction of the women. 'Damned whores. Look at their faces. Surely they were made for the darkness, every one of them.'

Norland's big fingers clenched and unclenched in his lap. Alexander was alarmed by the welter of emotions at war in the ex-priest; jovial good humour one moment, then bitter anger the next. His long, sagging face that must once have been handsome was twisted with rage. Here, thought Alexander, was a man who hated all women, Auguste included. What he had said about her and Carline had been said in spite, surely?

He found himself relieved that their journey was almost done; indeed, it was only a few moments later that Norland was rapping on the roof of the carriage to instruct the driver to stop. 'Well, my friend,' he declared, turning back to Alexander. 'Here is Clerkenwell Green. I trust I'll see you again soon, in the place of outer darkness which is a lodestar for all we souls who are damned.'

Norland's dark mood had still not evaporated. Alexander looked at him, freshly disturbed. Was he talking of the Montpelliers' house? It sounded as if the ex-priest was talking of hell itself. Alexander began to clamber out with difficulty, and his confusion must have shown on his face, because as he shut the door, Norland, wiping a smear of liquor from the corner of his mouth, suddenly grinned out of the open window at him and said, 'I refer, of course, to Madame de Montpellier's celestial mansion. I speak of it in that manner because it's so far from town. From the way they were talking so admiringly of your skills, I'll see you there again before too long. Farewell until then. Time for me to *drive far off the barb'rous dissonance, of Bacchus and his revellers.*' Once more Norland was himself again, smiling broadly as he lifted his hand in a parting salute.

Alexander stood by the side of the road and raised his hand likewise, watching as the carriage moved slowly off. The mud thrown from its big wheels spattered his coat, but he hardly noticed it. 'The Company of Titius', he murmured under his breath, 'the Company of Titius . . .'

It was late indeed. The Green was deserted, the Watch House silent, the pillory empty. The smell of the malt distillery, pungent and sickly, hung in the air. All the windows of the little houses were dark, their lamps extinguished, as were the stars.

Alexander, standing there, could hear the far-off rumble of the night-soil men, bringing their malodorous cart up from Turnmill Street to gather their nightly cargo of excrement. Who would want the daylight to shine on such a task? And, he thought, there were many people in this teeming city who likewise sought the darkness. He recalled the sparsely lit upstairs rooms of the public house called the Swan in Vere Street, where men met furtively behind locked doors. He remembered how several men were stoned in the Cheapside pillory for their part in the Vere Street scandal, because the London mob got to them before the constables could protect them; indeed, perhaps the constables didn't try too hard to keep the pilloried men safe.

If it hadn't been for Jonathan, Alexander would have been there with them. Jonathan told him those men were lucky not to have been hanged.

It was the brutal lack of privacy involved in such a death that horrified Alexander the most. He had once seen a hanging; and he would never forget how the victim had kicked out at the empty air. The crowd had bayed with laughter at the dying man's antics, and roared encouragement as he danced his way to death. Alexander had hurried away before it was over.

Now, his spirits perturbed, he made his way quickly along Jerusalem Passage, past the silent Bull's Head into the little court behind St John's church. There, he fumbled with the key to his home, his fingers clumsy with Norland's brandy, and got the door open at last. He climbed the stairs quickly and quietly, anxious not to wake Hannah from her God-fearing slumbers.

Daniel was asleep, of course. He had clambered into Alexander's bed for warmth, and he sprawled beneath the threadbare counterpane with one hand curled by his cheek like a child's. His lips were parted; his breathing was quiet and untroubled.

Alexander undressed as quietly as he could, and pulled his cold linen nightshirt over his soft white flesh; then he eased himself into the bed and took the boy tenderly into his arms, telling himself that he had no intention of waking him. But when Daniel opened his eyes sleepily, and smiled at him through his dreams, Alexander was more glad than he could say.

For Daniel's beauty, at times like this, caused Alexander's heart to stop; it was a gift, a bounty almost too great to bear. Still, Alexander could not help but think about the ex-priest Matthew Norland, whose face told of a lifetime of intemperance in one form or other. Was this Norland's sin? Was this why he looked at Alexander so knowingly, as if recognising his forbidden love?

The thought shadowed Alexander's desire, his sharp easement. And his peace, for the time being, had gone, because as he lay there in the darkness with his love asleep in his arms, and the church clock striking two outside his window, he remembered his brother Jonathan. A cold chill seeped through his body.

Daniel, lost in dreams once more, cried out in a language Alexander did not understand.

At around the same time, Jonathan Absey was disturbed by a persistent knocking at the door of the house in Brewer Street. Unable to sleep, he'd been sitting by his dying fire, his head bowed in intractable thought. Somewhere in the Company of Titius was the killer of the red-haired girls, the killer of his daughter; perhaps not Raultier, but the younger Frenchman who'd been seen taking the singer from the theatre. And yet just as Jonathan was sure of the guilt of one of this company of French astronomers, so he was also sure that Raultier and his circle were being protected. Where could he go from here?

The sound of the caller below took some time to penetrate his absorption. When he finally heard it, he pulled himself up quickly and made his way downstairs, straightening his rumpled coat as he went, his mind running feverishly through the various possibilities. Lucket? A messenger from Lombard Street? Alexander, even?

He opened the door and saw an exhausted-looking stranger, clad in a dusty coat and riding boots, standing there in the darkness. With one hand he was holding the reins of his horse, which was lathered with exertion. With the other he was holding a letter.

'Master Absey? Master Jonathan Absey?' the stranger asked.

Jonathan nodded curtly. 'Yes?'

The man let out a sigh of relief. 'Then I've got something for you here.' He held out the letter.

Jonathan took it and turned the waxed package slowly in his hands. 'Who sent you?'

'The port agent in Dover, sir. He thought the letter might be important.'

Jonathan was instantly alert. The Dover agent had often sent Jonathan information in the past. But this package must be of exceptional urgency if the messenger had gone to the trouble of rousing him at home.

'What's in here?' he asked sharply.

'A letter, sir. It was delivered late last night to a fisherman called Hawkscliffe, who's a scoundrel, a known smuggler. A stranger paid him to carry this letter to an address in Boulogne. Hawkscliffe was due to sail on the morning tide.'

So this letter was foreign mail; and thus not Jonathan's business, but Connolly's. He was about to say as much, when the man scratched his head and went on,

'It's a funny sort of letter, mind. I was there when they opened it. It's addressed to someone called "Master Titius", and full of outlandish names . . .'

Jonathan broke open the port agent's seal and pulled out the intercepted letter. In the dim light of the street lamp, the first words danced before his eyes. '*A Monsieur Titius . . .*'

The messenger stepped forward. 'Is something wrong, sir?'

'No,' breathed Jonathan at last. 'No. You've done well.'

The man seemed pleased. He expected money, naturally; Jonathan dug into his pocket and pulled out some coins for him, which the messenger took eagerly. Then, knuckling his forehead, he departed.

Jonathan closed the door and climbed the steps to his room, his eyes never leaving the letter. '*A Monsieur Titius . . .*'

Under the greeting was a list of stars and numbers. That was all.

Chara	*3.9*	*Alkafazah*	*2.1*	*Alifa*	*3.6*	*Mirphak*	*2.7*
Capella	*0.1*	*Chaph*	*2.27*	*Giansar*	*3.9*	*Alioth*	*1.8*
Mizar	*2.1*	*Ati*	*4.03*	*Kocab*	*3.6*	*Alkaid*	*1.9 . . .*

And so it went on; line after line of careful writing, covering the entire page; the names of dozens of stars, names familiar from his childhood, thanks to Alexander. Jonathan sat at his desk, and pulled the candles closer.

Letters had been removed from the archives; legal records had been erased. But now, thanks to the port agent's blunder in failing to replace his name with Connolly's, this letter had come to him.

The letter should still go to Connolly, but it wasn't going to.

He sat there with his candles burning low, and the London night enfolding him; he asked himself again and again the very question the port agent must have asked: why send a list of stars in such a secretive way, unless it wasn't what it appeared to be?

Of one thing only was he sure. No one in government must know that Jonathan had the letter in his possession, and so all his usual channels of investigation were barred to him. But there was one other person who ought to be able to help him in this matter of the stars: Alexander, from whom he'd still heard nothing.

It was late: he felt exhausted, emotional, even. He found himself suddenly remembering what he'd so often tried to forget: how when they'd taken him, last June, to see Ellie's body, she had looked to him like a child as she lay on the mortuary slab. A sleeping child. He'd stood helplessly staring down at her, impotent tears in his eyes, his gaze fixed on her small hands. The nails were badly broken. She must have struggled with her unseen attacker, clawing at his hands and arms uselessly, and crying out for help. Perhaps, in those long, agonising minutes before she died, she had called out to her father, as she had as a small girl when she'd hurt herself.

Gripping the letter with both hands as if to wrestle its secrets from it, Jonathan felt a surge of anger, almost of rage, engulf him. Everywhere he turned in his search for his daughter's killer he met with conspiracy, incompetence, indifference. But somehow, some-where, he would discover the truth about her death.

XIX

In strange way
To stand inquiring right is not to stray;
To sleepe, or runne wrong, is.

John Donne, 'Satyre III' (*c.* 1593-7)

The next morning Jonathan made his way to Montague House and climbed the stairs to his office, where more letters awaited him, more reports from watchers around the city and the country; letters concerning Frenchmen, and rumours of sedition, and hints of unrest that were something or nothing; yet in these times of peril, none could be ignored. It was noon before he was able to get away and make his way through the bustle of Whitehall to Charing Cross, where he hired a sedan to take him to Clerkenwell; but on reaching his brother's house at last, Jonathan was discomposed when Alexander's soft-skinned little black catamite opened the door to him, trembling and barely able to stammer out that his master was playing the organ at a service.

Jonathan, made uncomfortable by the boy's evident fear of him, turned away swiftly and made his way to the church. Even before he got there he heard the faint resonance of solemn music, and saw the hired carriages in the street outside. There was a shabby hearse waiting, with half-starved black horses that shuffled their sackcloth-covered hooves mournfully on the cobbles. A funeral, then, and his brother played the music.

He opened the heavy door, which creaked slightly, and slipped into the cool gloom of the church. The music had just ended, and the pipes wheezed out ghostly echoes as of lungs expiring. Time for the prayers now; though too late, thought Jonathan, for the corpse in the coffin, which was no doubt starting to stink already in the early summer heat. The organ was set back behind the choir stalls in some privacy, and there Jonathan saw his fat half-brother sitting, with his perspiring face bowed in prayer like the rest. Jonathan walked quickly up the shadowy aisle towards him and touched his shoulder.

Alexander nearly jumped from his seat at the touch. His face became drained of colour and his hands shook like leaves; he had to clench them in his lap. From the chilly nave, the responses rose in mournful dirge.

'*The days of man are but as grass; for he flourisheth as a flower of the field; for as soon as the wind goeth over it, it is gone.*'

'What are you doing here?' whispered Alexander.

'I've been waiting to hear from you, brother,' said Jonathan tersely. 'Have you made any attempt to do as I asked you?'

Alexander flinched visibly. 'You should not have come here. I must play again very soon—'

'Just answer me, will you? It's six days since I called on you. Have you found out anything yet about the Company of Titius?'

'Please. Not so loud . . .' Alexander's voice shook too, as well as his hands. 'I've been there once, to the house where they meet; but it was so brief that I learnt nothing . . .'

Jonathan was incredulous. 'You've actually been there? And you haven't let me know?'

'It was only last night . . . I was going to get in touch with you, Jonathan, I promise I was!'

'It seems I've saved you the trouble,' responded his half-brother grimly. 'Where do they live? Whom did you meet?'

Alexander spoke so quickly that his tongue tripped over his words. 'They live in Kensington Gore, and there were so many people that I can't recollect all their names. I met Madame de Montpellier, she lives there with her brother Guy; and they both study the stars—'

Jonathan found that he was clenching his hands. 'Did you meet this brother?'

Alexander looked fearfully around the church, clearly afraid of the attention Jonathan's urgency might draw to him. 'No, because Guy de Montpellier was sick – he kept to his room.'

'How sick is he? Is he able to leave the house?'

'I tell you, I don't know. I don't even know what's wrong with him—'

'How old is he?'

'Younger than Madame de Montpellier.'

'And she is?'

'I cannot tell these things – still young, not yet thirty, I would guess . . .'

Jonathan bowed his head, his mind racing furiously. So Guy de Montpellier might indeed be the man who had taken Georgiana from the theatre. 'Who else was there?' he rapped out. 'Did you meet a doctor?'

Alexander looked surprised, and freshly afraid that Jonathan knew so much already. 'Doctor Raultier, yes, I met him. We talked, he was kind—'

'Describe him to me.'

'He was dark-haired, with heavy features. He was dressed in sombre clothes; a tall, gaunt-looking man . . .'

Surely this was the doctor Jonathan had watched in that low Piccadilly tavern seven nights ago. He forced himself into a semblance of calm. 'Does this doctor tend Guy de Montpellier?'

'Yes. In fact he was called to attend him while I was there. He is most concerned for the young man's welfare . . .'

'Is Raultier an astronomer too?'

'Yes – he makes a study of the magnitude of the brightest stars . . .'

Jonathan was silent a moment. Then he pressed on with renewed intensity, 'Who else was there?'

Alexander was shaking his head in distress. 'I can't remember them all. There was a priest, an English priest, who was in Paris with them, who drinks too much brandy . . . And there was a man who is the doorkeeper, and seems to watch over them all . . . dear God, what more can I tell you?'

'Their business.' Jonathan's voice was rough.

'Their business . . . They belong to the Company of Titius. They search for a missing star, as I told you before. They call it Selene. I can think of nothing else, Jonathan, nothing . . .' Alexander's lips were dry, spittle-flecked with anxiety.

Jonathan's gaze was relentless. 'Then you'll have to go to them again. And soon,' he declared. 'Or I will take to visiting you here more often, as you play with your precious bells and tend your pretty choirboys.'

From further down the nave, the voice of the priest continued mournfully. *For when thou art angry, all our days are gone; we bring our years to an end, as it were a tale that is told . . .*

Alexander swallowed nervously.

'Do as I say,' repeated Jonathan. 'Visit these people again, and learn more, and report, in detail if you please, back to me as soon as you are able. Do you understand me?'

'Yes,' whispered Alexander.

The choirboys were shuffling their feet and clearing their throats, preparing for their next anthem. Alexander raised his hands and flexed his fingers over the keys, looking rather wildly at the music resting on its stand.

'Oh, no. I've not finished with you yet.' Jonathan swiftly put another sheet of paper that was covered with names and numbers across the music. 'Look at this, brother mine. Look at it, and tell me, when your playing is over, what it means.'

Silence had fallen throughout the nave of the church. The choir was waiting; the congregation looked curiously towards the recess where the organist sat; and Alexander, his face sheened with sweat, struggled through the Gloria with considerably less than his usual competence, for his gaze kept being dragged unhappily towards the piece of paper that Jonathan had thrust in front of him. It was the Dover letter. As soon as the music was finished and the solemn prayers had begun again, Alexander pulled the paper on to his knees, ever conscious of his brother's eyes boring into him, and gazed at it anxiously.

He looked up at Jonathan at last. 'I don't understand. Where did you get this from?'

'That's hardly your business.'

'I know. It's just that I wouldn't have thought it would interest you . . .' Alexander looked again at the letter, his face still riven with anxiety. 'It's a list, you see, of the brightest stars.'

Jonathan was listening intently. 'I had guessed as much. I've heard of some of them. But what do the numbers mean, Alexander?'

Alexander continued to scan it, his brow furrowed in perplexity. 'They must be the magnitudes of the stars. Someone has been studying them in extraordinary detail, to get such exact figures. But I can't understand why some of them are wrong.'

'Wrong?'

'Yes, I'm sure of it—'

Jonathan seemed to have gone very still. 'Tell me more.'

Alexander stared up at him, his blind eye opalescent in the gloomy light of the church. 'Some of them, though not all, are incorrect. The visible stars, you see, are generally grouped by astronomers in magnitudes of first brightness down to sixth. But look here at the number given for the star Adhil.' He indicated a name on the closely written list. 'It's a star of the fifth magnitude, but the number given for it in this list is 2.11. And Edasich is listed here as 1.8, but that's incorrect too, it's only a third magnitude star. Yet many of these figures are correct, the one for Capella for instance; and the whole list has been prepared with some care. Why have these errors been made?'

Jonathan's heart was beating faster: he had learnt to listen, and wait, for moments like this. 'I've heard that some of the stars vary considerably in brightness,' he said. 'Couldn't that explain it?'

Alexander blinked up at him. 'Oh, no. None of these are variables. Every star can vary a little, of course, from night to night, depending on atmospheric conditions, and the telescope being used. But not to this extent. Not to the extent of several magnitudes, as some of these do.'

'There must be a logical reason for it.'

'If so, I do not know it.'

Jonathan took the letter back slowly and folded it up. The mournful congregation had risen from prayer once more, and its members were looking to the organist, expecting music again. Alexander jumped to attention, and reached to straighten his music while his short legs stretched for the pedals. His fingers knocked the spidery sheets to the floor, all in a heap. Some of the choristers chuckled openly with mirth as Alexander stooped and struggled to collect the scattered sheets. Jonathan turned and made his way swiftly towards the door, leaving the coolness of the church behind him to face the noonday glare of the sun.

In the far corner of the churchyard, the two gravediggers leaned on their shovels and waited for the coffin, their work almost done; otherwise there was no one in sight. Jonathan walked slowly round to the shade at the side of the overhanging porch, and settled himself on a lichen-covered memorial stone. Then he gazed at the letter again, feeling more and more sure that it had to be in code, just as the port agent must have suspected.

As a junior clerk, many years ago, it had been one of Jonathan's regular tasks to carry suspect documents such as this to a man called John Morrow, who had no official title, but was known simply and almost reverently as the Decipherer. The elaborate encryption methods used by foreign embassies and envoys and other, more subtle enemies of the state were child's play to Morrow, who had been trained in Hanover, centre of the cipherer's subtle art.

Once the Decipherer had shown Jonathan a code which, he said, had as nearly beaten him as anything he'd dealt with. It was devised by an Englishman, Jenkinson, who was a cartographer and an enemy spy during the American wars fifteen years ago.

Outwardly it was a list of places and their latitudes, sent to a fellow cartographer in Paris, supposedly for some new atlas he was compiling. Jenkinson was already under suspicion in London, and so Morrow was given a copy of the intercepted list to study. But the Decipherer was baffled, and it was only when a friend, a geographer, pointed out to him that some of the latitudes were wrong – by barely a degree – that Morrow at last began to unlock the cipher. For only the incorrect numbers made up the message . . .

The heavy doors of the church creaked open. The service had ended at last. The coffin, borne by six black-coated mourners, was emerging from the gloom of the porch into the bright sunlight.

Jonathan stood up. Folding the letter with the utmost care, he slid it deep in his pocket and made his way swiftly out through a side gate.

XX

*It must not be wholly overlooked that M. de Puisaye
is interested to counsel this expedition at all hazards.
Without it his situation is desperate. If it succeeds it
is to give him an opening to great distinction and
probably splendid fortune.*

Letter from General Moira to William Pitt,
summer 1795

A ll the church spires of London glittered in the afternoon sun
as Pierre Raultier, carrying his doctor's bag, made his way on
foot to the old Artillery Ground, just to the north of
Moorfields and a little over half a mile to the east of Clerkenwell
church. By the grey stone walls of the burial yard, Raultier stopped
and watched as ranks of weary Frenchmen clad in various semblances
of the scarlet Royalist uniform marched to and fro to the barked
accompaniment of their officers' orders. Groups of ragged children
watched too, and jeered from a distance.

Raultier saw one section of the marchers fall into disarray. Angrily
the soldiers pushed at one another and argued with raised fists. Another
section joined in the altercation. Their officers bawled for order, but
to no avail.

Before his exile, Raultier had seen regiments of blue-coated
Republican soldiers marching in their hundreds through the streets of
Paris to fight the Prussians at Valmy. They had been ragged and half
starved, many of them shod in nothing better than wooden sabots.
But oh, the look in their eyes, the fervour in their step, as they sang
the Marseillaise and marched off proudly to die for their homeland.
Those who had stayed behind had also played their part; he remembered the old men making tents for the soldiers, the women sewing
up their uniforms, and even the children tearing up scraps of linen to
make bandages for the wounded. The Luxembourg gardens, ruined
pleasure-ground of royalty, had been taken over for the forging of

cannon, and the Tuileries itself was transformed into a vast smithy. All day and all through the night Paris had glowed like an inferno with the light of the blacksmiths' furnaces; and the city's streets echoed to the clanging of anvils as gun after gun was forged.

With the same terrible fervour, the common people had sought the extermination of their enemies within the city's walls as well as without; and thus had begun the infamous slaughter of the prisons, from which the Montpelliers had only just escaped. No wonder the Republican army had gone on to defeat half of Europe, and had cowed what enemies remained. This army in Moorfields had nothing of that chilling ferocity.

To Raultier's right, the marching men, sweating in the heat, wheeled and halted and started off again uncertainly to the sound of a barrage of commands. A boy with a little drum walked in front, rapping out the time; somewhere a fife whistled shrilly. A dog ran up and down, yapping. Two lines of men collided, and someone cursed them loudly. What chance, wondered Raultier, had these dishevelled exiles of reconquering their native France?

Rousing himself with an effort from his troubled thoughts, Raultier approached one of the officers and enquired after Noel-François Prigent.

'Prigent? He's over there. See the young man arguing with the lieutenant whose arm is in a sling? That's him.'

'My thanks.' Raultier turned and walked towards the two figures the officer had indicated. Birds twittered in the yew trees that edged the burial ground, and the June sun beat down from a cloudless sky. In the shade of the trees two men stood gesticulating at each other, their voices raised in argument. Raultier approached them and said, 'Monsieur Prigent?'

The younger man, the one not in uniform, broke off what he was saying to reply, 'I'm Prigent. What the devil do you want?'

He had long brown hair framing a narrow face that was lit up with passionate fervour, and with anger too, Raultier noted, at being thus interrupted. He was wearing a loose riding coat and buckskin breeches, and his white shirt was unbuttoned at his throat. *Le Brigand*, they called him. He was perhaps only a little older than Guy de Montpellier.

Raultier gave his name. Prigent looked momentarily puzzled, and then realisation dawned and a smile swiftly dispelled his irritation. 'Of course. The doctor.' He looked Raultier approvingly up and down. 'They told me you would come. You were certainly given good references. I'm glad to make your acquaintance.'

'And I yours,' said Raultier.

Prigent said something in an undertone to the lieutenant he'd been talking to, who quickly left them to rejoin the ranks. Then Prigent turned back to Raultier and encompassed the activity on the Artillery Ground with an expressive sweep of his arm. 'Look at them, will you? These officers have no more idea of fighting a war than they have of running a baker's shop. They argue amongst themselves about rank and precedence, and these poor soldiers, kicked out of Flanders and Spain and Toulon and just about everywhere else in Europe, are shortly going to be landed on the shores of France, God help us all.' He broke off and drew a bottle from his pocket, which he unstoppered with relish and drank from deeply. Then he handed it to Raultier, and wiped his mouth with the back of his other hand. 'Try some of this, doctor – it's straight from the vineyards of France. The wine you buy in English taverns is piss. The food is hardly any better, but one has to eat. I was half starved for three months as a prisoner of those damned Republicans, and I'm only just starting to get some flesh back on my bones.'

Raultier swallowed just a little of the wine and handed the bottle back. 'I hear you've been suffering from bouts of fever, Monsieur Prigent. Did the symptoms start during your captivity?'

'Yes. The gaolers treated me abominably. And just when I think I've shaken the illness off, why, there it is again; the unsteady pulse, the fever, the sweating. I perspire in my bed like a pig, and afterwards I'm so weak I couldn't lift a sword if General Hoche himself was charging at me, and all his Republicans roaring up with bayonets behind him. I've tried all sorts of powders and potions, and some of them tasted like poison.' He lifted his bottle and drank again. 'Look, doctor. My lodgings are close by. Why don't I send for food, and more wine, and then you can examine me there?' He clapped Raultier on the shoulder and grinned. 'Let's leave this devil of a mess for the time being, shall we?'

Two hours later, Raultier was concluding his examination of Prigent, who was lying submissively on the bed in his breeches and shirt.

'Well? What do you think?' asked Prigent anxiously. 'What's your opinion?'

'I think,' said Pierre Raultier, putting the plessor, the little rubber-tipped hammer that he used to sound out the lung cavities, back into its case, 'that you'll live, Monsieur Prigent.' He replaced the plessor in his medical bag, which lay open on a table beneath the window; beside it were three empty wine bottles, and plates that now held only pastry crumbs. For the duration of his stay in London, Noel-François Prigent had taken two rooms at the corner of Black Raven Court and Chiswell Street, above a baker's shop. He and Raultier had consumed two of the baker's good pies, along with the wine, during a friendly discourse prior to Raultier's examination of the young man, when their shared Breton background had been discussed exhaustively, along with a long list of mutual acquaintances. Prigent had more than once expressed his amazement that they had not met before, because, he insisted, if they had, they would surely have been firm friends by now. Raultier, who had taken less of the wine, had smiled encouragingly.

Now Prigent pulled himself up from the bed and started to pull on his boots. Then he hesitated. 'You don't think,' he said, 'that I could have caught a consumptive fever, do you? When I was in that damned Republican prison in Lorient, there were sick men coughing all around me, and the air was vile.'

'No, I don't,' said Raultier soothingly. 'But I'll prepare a restorative medicine for you, with iron and sulphur to build up your strength. And a little extract of wild chervil would be beneficial. It helps to purify the blood, in cases such as this.'

Prigent pulled his coat sleeve back down over his wrist. His face was slightly flushed. 'Chervil; that's an old Breton folk remedy, isn't it? I've enjoyed our talk, Raultier. It's been good remembering the old times, when Brittany was free of those Republican devils. I suppose you've heard that Puisaye needs sound medical men to attend to his troops when this expedition sets sail. Would you consider going with him?'

Raultier was carefully placing his equipment in his bag. 'Regretfully I'm needed here.'

'Of course.' Prigent nodded and picked up his glass to drain the last of his wine. 'But let me know if you change your mind, will you? Puisaye's down at Portsmouth now, preparing the first body of troops for embarkation.'

'Already?' Raultier said with surprise.

'Believe me, my friend, it's not before time. We've suffered the most damnable delays.' Prigent had begun to pace to and fro, with his hands behind his back. 'Even the decision over the landing place has taken months. It's to be Carnac, of course; you and I, Raultier, could have told them from the very beginning that it was the only possible place.'

Raultier closed his bag. 'Indeed, it's the best site. Well, let us wish them every success.' He indicated the bottle of medicine he'd left on the table. 'There's enough there for one week, Monsieur Prigent: two spoonfuls per day. I'll write you a note for more, and you can collect it from any apothecary.'

Prigent, who had picked up the bottle and was examining it, frowned suddenly. 'That's no good. I'm leaving for Portsmouth myself tomorrow. The expedition sails in two days' time, on the 17th.'

'Then I'll call at the apothecary's shop in Bunhill Row on my way home,' said Raultier, 'and ask him to send you a good supply of the mixture immediately. How much will you need?'

'Let me see. It will take the convoy a good seven days to reach Quiberon Bay. And then a day or so more to sail on to the Vilaine estuary . . .'

'The Vilaine? I thought you said Carnac was the landing site.'

'The *main* landing site,' said Prigent with a smile. 'But Tinténiac and I are going to lead an outflanking column westwards from the Vilaine, back towards the peninsula, so we can surprise the Republicans from the rear. It's a master stroke.'

Raultier nodded. 'An excellent plan,' he agreed. 'And we must ensure that you're able to play your part fully. I'll write you a prescription for a month's supply, and I'll see that you get your medicine later today.' He picked up his bag. 'I wish you the best of luck, Monsieur Prigent. France and Brittany need more men like you.'

The two men shook hands, and Raultier went down the stairs and emerged into the daylight, next to the bow-fronted baker's shop. The thoroughfare was busy, because it was market day in nearby White Cross Street. He was jostled as he accidentally stepped in someone's path, and it took him a moment to adjust his senses to the shouts of the vendors and hucksters. Holding his doctor's bag close, he set off along Chiswell Street in a westerly direction, but it wasn't long before he became aware of someone following him. He stopped in the entrance to an alleyway and turned slowly, to see Richard Crawford hurrying towards him.

Crawford looked hot and sticky and out of place in this mean street. 'Raultier,' he said breathlessly. 'I know you'd promised to contact me this evening, but time is so short . . . How was your meeting?'

Raultier drew back a little into the alleyway, and Crawford followed him, clearly grateful to be a little apart from the crowds. 'It went well, I think,' said Raultier in reply. 'Exactly as planned, in fact. He accepted me immediately.'

Crawford looked anxiously back over his shoulder to the street, as if still afraid someone would overhear him. 'And? We have to know now, Raultier, if Prigent is to be trusted. Tell me, what did you think of him?'

'The meeting only lasted a couple of hours. But the relationship between doctor and patient always inspires a certain intimacy . . .'

'Yes? Yes?'

'From what I've seen, Prigent is entirely trustworthy. He appears to be as committed to the Royalist cause, and to Puisaye himself, as anyone I've ever met. I see no reason at all to doubt his loyalty.'

Crawford seemed visibly to relax. 'Thank God. It's been a worry, Raultier. I can't begin to tell you.'

'He seemed to me to be the soul of discretion,' Raultier continued. 'We talked, of course, on general matters – old times in Brittany, the course of the war, and so on – but nothing more.'

Crawford, clearly much relieved, wiped the sweat from his brow. 'That's good. Thank you once more, Doctor Raultier. I hope we can call on you again for your help. There will also be the matter of payment for all this.'

Raultier said, 'I am glad to be of assistance.'

Crawford nodded. 'Of course. You certainly have our heartfelt gratitude. I'll be getting along, then. This infernal heat . . .'

He shook hands earnestly and hurried off towards White Cross Street, looking for a sedan to hail. Raultier stayed where he was for a moment and watched the little Scotsman disappear from sight. Then he set off along Chiswell Street once more, and turned up Bunhill

Row to the busy apothecary's shop. When it was his turn, he asked the man to send two bottles of iron and sulphur mixture to Monsieur Prigent's lodgings directly.

'I'll do it as soon as I can,' said the apothecary, 'but you must realise, sir, that I am pressed for time.'

Raultier reached into his pocket for money. 'I understand,' he said. 'But so, I think, are we all.'

XXI

The misfortune of our situation is that we have too
many objects to attend to, and our force consequently
must be too weak at each place.

King George III,
'On the War with France' (1794)

'The Montpelliers?' the clerk was saying. 'How very strange, Mr Absey. Someone else was asking about them only the other day.'

It was later that same afternoon, and Jonathan was at the Alien Office again, asking questions. He had headed there shortly after his visit to his brother at the church in Clerkenwell; and he was faring rather better than on his last peremptory visit two days ago, because this time the eagle-eyed superintendent, Thomas Carter, was absent; and his clerk, who knew Jonathan by sight, was helpful and unsuspicious. Besides, Jonathan knew better now than to ask directly after Pierre Raultier.

So someone else had been enquiring about the Montpelliers. He managed to respond, casually enough, 'Oh? Who was it?'

The clerk was looking through his record book of daily business to find out. 'It should be here,' he was frowning. 'Every enquiry should be noted, however brief. But I can't find it.'

'It doesn't matter,' Jonathan said; though he thought, very much, that it did. 'Could I perhaps see their files for a few moments?'

'Of course.' The clerk was searching through the *émigré* records, which were arranged by order of date of registration. 'The Montpelliers. Tell me again, Mr Absey, when they arrived in England, will you?'

'It was in the autumn of 1792, I believe,' said Jonathan. 'September, October, maybe.'

'Ah, yes. Soon after the prison massacres. So many of them fled Paris then. A dreadful time.' He shook his head. 'In that case, they would actually have been living here for some months before the Alien

Act was passed . . .' As he spoke he was turning over page after page with purposeful competence. The staff at the Alien Office were known for being meticulous in their work.

'Here you are, Mr Absey,' the clerk announced at last, with satisfaction, 'you can look through the Montpellier notes yourself if you like. They came here in the autumn of '92, as you said – late October, four months before war was declared. They're well born, the brother and sister, connected by birth and marriage with some of the noblest families in France. It's all in there. And it looks as if Madame de Montpellier is still on the list of proscribed *émigrés*. That means she and her brother would face trial for treason if they returned to France.'

Jonathan noted silently where the Montpelliers were living. Kensington Gore, as Alexander had said. A comfortable exile for them, then, and a lifestyle that would be expensive to maintain.

He read the notes on Auguste and found out that she and her brother had spent their childhood on a wealthy estate in the south-west corner of France. At the age of twenty Auguste had married the Comte de Féraud, and gone with him to Paris; but at the outbreak of the Revolution her husband fled. Auguste renounced him, and embraced the new regime. But it seemed that its wheel had turned against her.

Why? wondered Jonathan. Perhaps her husband had joined the exiled *émigré* army at Koblenz, and raised arms against the Republic. Yet for three years Auguste had lived on safely in Paris. He noted the fact silently, and moved on. There was less about her brother, Guy. He was younger than she was, and would be twenty-five now. Guy had gone with his sister to Paris at the time of her marriage. Like her, he was proscribed some time in the summer or early autumn of 1792 – which, it wasn't quite clear – and forced to flee.

Aware of the clerk's interested gaze, Jonathan quickly scanned the rest of the file. Included in the records were, as required by the Act, details of the people associated with their household: the servants they had brought with them from France; an English manservant, Ralph Wallace, who had served the previous occupants of the house; a list of friends and acquaintances, including a former priest whose name was Norland, who was presumably the man Alexander had met. Jonathan ran his finger down the list of visitors and known contacts, looking, with aching eyes, for just one name.

And just as he was about to give up, he found it. The name of Pierre Raultier, whose own file had been carefully obliterated from the Alien Office records; but once more, someone had been careless, just as they had been careless at Middle Scotland Yard. Someone had forgotten that the French doctor's name would still be listed here, for he was a close friend of the Montpelliers.

Raultier's address was given as number 28, Eagle Street, Holborn. There were a few more lines, giving his date of birth, at Auray, in Brittany; an account of his training in medicine at the military college in Beaumont; a brief summary of how he went next to Paris, to work first as a surgeon at the Hôtel Dieu and then as an *officier de santé*, tending the poorest people in the city.

Jonathan was able to read that Raultier was proscribed also, just as the Montpelliers were, according to the information acquired through some intricate route by the secretive but efficient Alien Office. Jonathan knew that since the fall of Robespierre last summer, many *émigrés* had returned to their homes, to live safely if cautiously under the somewhat more moderate régime of the National Convention. But return was, it seemed, not an option at present for the exiled Montpelliers and their friend Doctor Raultier.

He handed the files back to the clerk, and thanked him. 'As a point of interest,' he said, 'most of the refugees arrived here without any money, didn't they?'

'Oh, yes, sir. Most of them left everything behind. They considered themselves lucky, at the time, to escape with their lives. Any money or jewellery they managed to carry out would have been spent on bribing their way over here. That's why so many of them live in penury, or have to find work of some kind or another.'

Jonathan was thinking of the gold given to Georgiana. 'Presumably some of them still get some sort of income sent over, though, from France?'

'How could they, Mr Absey? All *émigrés* automatically had their estates and possessions confiscated by the Revolutionary Committee. You don't get an income from nothing.'

'Perhaps friends would send them money?'

The clerk sniffed. 'You've heard of the worthless paper money that they issue over there? *Assignats?* What use would they be to them? They hardly buy anything in Paris, let alone here.'

Jonathan said, 'I was thinking of French gold. *Louis d'or*.'

The clerk smiled wistfully. 'Now you're talking, Mr Absey. Gold is different. Of course, as I said, some of the *émigrés* might have managed to bring small quantities of gold with them; but the last time we came across a significant number of *louis d'or* was when those spies were arrested a couple of years ago, the ones left in London by Ambassador Chauvelin. Dozens of the coins were found hidden in their lodgings. They were being paid regularly, by the government in Paris. Spies need to pay informants, so they have to be given the very best currency.'

Jonathan nodded thoughtfully. 'I've heard that our agents in France are paid in French gold as well, by the English government.'

'That's true, sir. As much as twenty-five *louis* per month.'

'So couldn't *louis d'or* just as easily be an indication of agents on our side?'

'An interesting point, Mr Absey. But agents working for the English are paid in old gold.'

'Old gold?'

'Minted prior to 1793,' the clerk was happy to explain. 'Before the king was executed. The English Treasury hasn't been replenished with French gold since the war began. The old coins are still valid currency in France, of course. But the spies who are set in place by the Revolutionary Committee are paid in the *louis d'or* of the constitutional kingdom of 1793. They've got the king's head on one side, and a winged angel on the other. In large, fresh-minted quantities, they're a giveaway in this country. We've caught two or three Frenchmen with them recently, before they had a chance to sell them on or get them melted down by the Jews in Clare Market. And each of them was a spy.'

'What was on the old *louis d'or*, then?'

'The king's head, of course. And, on the reverse, the royal coat of arms.'

Jonathan thanked him and went slowly back to his office, thinking again about the Titius letter.

Why had it been sent so secretly, when correspondence – especially of a scientific nature – was still permitted with the Continent? Was it because Jonathan had placed the interception order, and the sender, Raultier, had been warned of it?

Who was the letter intended for? Some Parisian astronomer? Yet it was addressed to Titius, who Alexander had told him was a professor at the German university of Wittenberg. Was the name 'Titius' used as a greeting by members of the Company of Titius to one another? Yet it couldn't be a genuine exchange of information, surely, not with its burden of false magnitudes. Jonathan fretted on, trying to make sense of the little he knew. Raultier, sender of the letter, must be the agent employed by the English; he was proscribed by the Republicans, and faced automatic trial for treason if he returned to his homeland. To whom, then, in Paris, could he be directing a letter that made no apparent scientific sense; a letter, moreover, that he didn't want the English authorities to see?

Jonathan was aware that there were many different factions among the *émigré* Royalists. They were united, naturally, in their aim to destroy the Republic; but after that, all was division. Some held that only a radically revised form of constitutional monarchy, with royal authority curtailed by democracy, could hold the tumultuous country together now; while others, Royalists to the core, were adamant that nothing short of a full return to the *ancien régime* of the days before the Revolution, with a king restored to the almost despotic power of the Bourbons, would serve.

In Paris, Jonathan knew that the secret Royalist Agency, headed by the Comte d'Artois, uncle of the imprisoned boy king, was working by means of intelligence and persuasion towards the restoration of an absolute monarchy, distributing to that end the last of the Bourbon fortunes by a secret network to armies and informers. The English government's involvement in French affairs was tolerated, just, by the Royalist Agency because England was the only country now that seemed fully committed to pursuing the war against the Republic; but Pitt and his ministers were lukewarm about the restoration of the *ancien régime*, whose excesses had, in the eyes of many English moderates, driven the desperate populace to revolution.

Another faction was led by the Comte de Puisaye, who was to lead the proposed invasion of France. Puisaye was a constitutional monarchist, and in favour of the restoration of the king to the throne, but only if royal power was curtailed by certain democratic safeguards. For these beliefs, Puisaye, though a valiant soldier who had roused and led large peasant uprisings in the western regions of France, was despised and resented by the haughty d'Artois and the Royalist Agency. They gave him a certain amount of reluctant acknowledgement as the leader of the planned expeditionary force; but only because it was Puisaye who had boldly come to London and persuaded first Windham and then Pitt and the rest of the Cabinet to give full backing to this expedition; the details of which were still classified as 'Most Secret', even though it was public knowledge that troops and ships were already being prepared on the south coast.

And now Jonathan wondered: Is Raultier keeping the Royalist Agency informed of the latest developments in Puisaye's enterprise? Is the French doctor perhaps in the pay of d'Artois, as well as the pay of the British? Is that his game?

If so, then little harm could come of Raultier's activities, in that both sets of masters were on the same side, at least for the present. Though there was the risk, if he was sending information to the Royalists in Paris, that his letters might be intercepted by the enemy . . .

Jonathan stood at the entrance to Montague House and kneaded his aching forehead. Stop, he told himself, stop; the Dover letter could still be just a list of stars, perhaps being sent to some scientist colleague who lived under threat from the authorities in the continuing turmoil of Paris; someone who perhaps didn't want it known that he was corresponding with an exiled enemy of the Republic, Pierre Raultier.

But why were some of the numbers wrong?

Jonathan had reached the lobby. He looked up to see the Chief Clerk coming towards him, frowning.

'You've been out a long time, Absey.'

'Yes, sir.' Jonathan bowed his head in acknowledgement of the rebuke. But Pollock had been in a meeting all morning at the Treasury. So someone must have reported him.

He turned, his mind still in turmoil, to go to his office, but Pollock hadn't finished.

'Jonathan.'

'Sir?'

Pollock beckoned him closer. 'I think you should know that the landing on the west coast of France is to go ahead. The Royalist troops will be departing in a matter of days. The details are still classified as top secret, but no doubt you'll have heard rumours.'

'Yes, sir.'

'Now is the time for great diligence,' Pollock exhorted him. 'We need you at your desk.'

Nodding, Pollock moved on; and Jonathan went on his way also, to his office. Once seated at his desk, he pulled out the Dover letter and looked at it again.

When he was newly married, his wife had hung a beaten brass plate in their little parlour, by way of ornament. Jonathan used to tease her about it, because she loved to polish it herself, and make it shine like gold. Ellie loved the plate too. When her brother Thomas was still a baby, she liked to show it to him. She used to hold a candle very carefully up to the plate on the wall, and tell him to watch its bright, dancing reflection.

One day Jonathan, watching over his beautiful little daughter and her candle with all the love in the world in his heart, suddenly noticed how the scratches and ancient polishing marks on the brass dish always, without fail, made a series of perfect circles that centred on the point of the glowing flame's reflection, no matter where the candle was held.

And so it seemed to him now: wherever he went he was ringed by his sense of foreboding about French star-watchers, and letters to Paris, and red-haired girls who had died on London's dark streets. The murder of his daughter seemed suddenly to be no longer simply a private agony, his to bear as best as he could alone, but part of something larger, more ominously far-reaching.

One thing was for sure. It was more than Jonathan's job was worth to be seen asking more questions about the killer of his daughter. If he had been treading on dangerous ground before, knowing there was a English agent in the Company of Titius, then how much more was he risking his position now, by keeping, in secret, a letter that was no business of his.

Jonathan forced himself to work till six to clear the backlog on his desk. Then he walked to Charing Cross to find a hackney, and told the driver to take him to the Bow Street police office, where the high-ceilinged hall echoed to the clamour of people queuing to report petty crimes or disputes. Jonathan looked round swiftly to check that there were no officers there who knew him, and then he homed in on a young, fresh-faced constable, to ask if he had the records of the death of Georgiana Howe.

It had been a dreadful affair, that, observed the constable; such a young girl, and so pretty. He pulled out the file for Jonathan, who let him believe that he was an attorney here on behalf of the dead girl's relatives. 'A pity there were no witnesses,' the constable continued. 'And precious little evidence. Not much to go on, now, sir, is there?'

Jonathan said casually, 'I heard there was the gold found close by her body. Do you know what happened to it?'

'Ah, yes. French gold, wasn't it? I remember. That's Home Office business, that, sir. They'll have it locked away somewhere and signed for. You'd need a warrant from the Under-Secretary to get your hands on that.'

Jonathan tried again. 'Were you on duty on the night she died? Did you see these coins yourself?'

'No, no. You'll have to try the Home Office, as I said.'

Jonathan, with that now familiar sense of powerlessness, said, 'Yes. Thank you.'

After that Jonathan ordered the coachman to take him to a dingy bookseller's shop that he remembered in Piccadilly, purporting to sell, according to its sign, books of a scientific nature. Telling the driver to wait, he went inside to ask the shop's owner if he had any books about the stars.

The man was stooped and elderly; his little shop was ill-lit, and cobwebs festooned the higher reaches of the shelves. He looked as if he could scarcely make a livelihood from his profession. Jonathan was the only customer present. Yet his face lit up at Jonathan's question.

'Stars,' he echoed rapturously. 'The study of the stars; a noble pursuit indeed. But what kind of book did you require? Did you want charts? Tables? Almanacs? Are you perhaps looking for Flamsteed's atlas, or de Lacaille's? Or maybe you require a copy of the Messier list?'

Jonathan said, rather helplessly, 'I just want something that gives the brightness of the stars. Is there such a work?'

'Is there?' Again, the old bookseller seemed delighted with his request. 'Well, now. There's James Gregory's book, of course. He compiled his list, you know, by comparing all the stars to the sun; a laborious task, and not entirely accurate, but still most useful. I have a copy here somewhere. But then –' and he turned to Jonathan enquiringly – 'you might just want the most basic of catalogues, might you, sir? Giving the stars of the first to the sixth magnitude, as originally compiled by Hipparchus the Greek?'

Jonathan shook his head. 'I really don't know. I have very little knowledge of the subject, as you can tell. But I think that I want a list with some degree of accuracy. Whole figures are not enough; I need a little more precision.'

'Gregory's, then,' said the bookseller decisively. He pulled a book down with his gnarled fingers and caressed it lovingly. 'This is the best I have. Of course, what we're all waiting for is the catalogue Herschel has in preparation. He's making a study of the comparative brightness of the stars, with his sister's help. It should be worth waiting for.'

Jonathan leafed through the book the man handed to him, drawn to it in spite of himself. 'How do they do it?' he said. 'How can they actually compare the brightness of the stars? Of course, I can see that even with the naked eye one might appear very much brighter than another. But how can these astronomers reach such a degree of accuracy?'

The bookseller was more than happy to display his own knowledge. 'The technical capabilities of their telescopes are the key,' he explained. 'As I said, Gregory used the sun as his reference guide – a somewhat crude method; but nowadays the accuracy they can achieve is amazing. Shall I tell you how William Herschel does it? He takes one star, of undisputed brightness – let us say Mirach, in Andromeda, of the second magnitude. He trains his telescope on it. Then he sets up another telescope, identical in every feature, and turns it on another, lesser star – Alita, perhaps, in Ursa Minor. Next he adjusts the apertures of both telescopes until each star appears to be of exactly the same brightness; and then, by checking, with his usual mathematical precision, by how much he has closed the aperture on each telescope, he can calculate the relative magnitude of the lesser star.'

'So the use of telescopes, as you describe, enables an astronomer to judge the relative brightness of a star to a precise degree?'

'Oh, yes. The magnitude can be expressed using a logarithmic scale of brightness, with amazing accuracy.' Carefully the old man began to wrap the book, and Jonathan reached into his pocket for money to pay him.

'Clearly the stars are a passion of yours,' Jonathan said.

'Ah, yes. And surely, sir, surely it has to be good to turn our eyes from the hateful turmoil of war and lift them to the skies!'

Jonathan agreed, and thanked him, and went out into the street again to rejoin his waiting hackney.

His mind was still absorbing what the bookseller had told him so it took him a second to notice that his coachman had dismounted and was standing by his horse with his back to the approaching Jonathan. Another man, whom Jonathan couldn't see clearly, was engaged in conversation with him; but as Jonathan drew nearer, this stranger seemed to notice his approach, and broke off abruptly. The driver turned round, and also saw Jonathan, and straightened up. The other man, meanwhile, turned and hurried off, away from Jonathan, down Piccadilly.

Jonathan experienced another of those moments of unease that seemed nowadays to assail him all too frequently. There was nothing wrong at all in his coachman chatting to someone as he waited for his passenger to return – an acquaintance, perhaps, or merely someone passing the time of day. Why, then, had the man hurried off so swiftly when he saw Jonathan coming?

'Who was that?' Jonathan asked the coachman, who was climbing back up to the carriage seat.

'No idea, sir. He asked me who you were and where you'd gone. But before I could reply, you showed and he ran off.'

Jonathan looked along the road in the direction of the questioner. So he was being followed, as he'd thought. But for the moment there was little he could do about it.

'Where next, sir?' the coachman called down as he gathered the reins.

'Brewer Street,' Jonathan replied curtly, and climbed inside.

Once home, he sat at his desk, and laid the letter to Titius alongside his star book. He pored over them both with increasing frustration, and all he could see was what Alexander told him: that some of the numbers were wrong.

XXII

Now Ev'ning fades! Her pensive step retires,
And night leads on the dews, and shadowy hours;
Her awful pomp of planetary fires,
And all her train of visionary powers.

Ann Radcliffe, 'Night' (1791)

To the north of the city, in the parish of Clerkenwell, where St Sepulchre's bell could be heard tolling the hours of approaching death for Newgate's chosen, Alexander heard someone knocking at the door below. The caller knocked again and again in the darkness, disturbing old Hannah, who awoke from her urine-soaked mattress and lamented the passing of peace for ever, it seemed, for her weary daughter had much to do to soothe her.

Alexander hurried down the steep little staircase in the dark with a fast-beating heart, because he was afraid that the midnight caller might be his brother Jonathan. But his fear was replaced by something almost approaching joy when he opened the door to find Pierre Raultier there.

Raultier was holding out a package. He said in a low voice, 'I am sorry to disturb you. But will you send this to the Bureau for me, as you said you would last night?'

The doctor seemed agitated; Doctor Crow indeed, with his long dark coat hanging loosely from his shoulders, and his tall black hat, and his harrowed face. Alexander took the package quickly. 'Of course I'll send it.'

'Tomorrow?'

'Yes, I'll go to the Society's office straight away in the morning. As soon as it opens.'

'I'm sorry for the inconvenience of my call.'

'Not at all. I'm glad to be of help.'

Raultier nodded. 'Perhaps I'll see you soon at the Montpelliers' house.'

'Yes,' said Alexander eagerly. 'Yes, I do hope so.'

He stood there on the doorstep with the packet clutched in his hands, his face shining with fervour as he watched Raultier walk quickly back to the carriage that was waiting for him further along the street. Alexander waited till the doctor's coach had disappeared into the darkness beyond Clerkenwell Green; then he locked up again, and hurried up the staircase, guiltily closing his door on Hannah's moans.

So quickly, then, this privilege had come. So swiftly was he to prove useful to his new friends. Holding the packet close to a candle, he read the address: *A monsieur Laplace, aux bons soins du Bureau des Longitudes à Paris.*

It so happened that Alexander himself had a document that was ready to be sent to Laplace. He had been working once more, when his time permitted, on the motion of Jupiter's satellites, finding himself inspired to fresh mathematical labours by the work he had done on the miniature orrery. Now that he had summarised his findings, Laplace would surely welcome them as a useful addition to his own work on planetary orbits.

Late though it was, he went straight to his desk to get out his pen and his ink, and prepared to enclose Doctor Raultier's little packet within his own.

'To Pierre Laplace.' He addressed it with some pride. 'At the Bureau des Longitudes, Paris; through the courtesy of the Royal Society, London.'

Letters. At Lombard Street, the busy mail rooms were at peace for just a few short hours before the dawn brought more urgent work for their busy clerks. But a letter of a more singular kind had been dispatched that night by private courier from Lord Grenville to the Earl of Bute, Britain's ambassador in Madrid, begging him to keep the vacillating Spanish government in the war on the side of the English; *'for,'* wrote Grenville, *'great things are afoot on the coast of France'.*

The Royal Catholic French army of his most Christian Majesty Louis XVII was to sail from Portsmouth at last: d'Hervilly's twelve hundred, Hector's regiment of naval officers and seamen, Dresnay's seven hundred, and Rohan's light infantry – all of them veterans of Flanders, and Germany, and Toulon; a total of four thousand men. The troops at Moorfields were to be sent to reinforce the veterans. After weeks of vacillating and dissent in high places, the sealed orders had been delivered, both to the English admirals who were to have responsibility for the safe passage of the French troops, and to those who would command them: the generals Puisaye and d'Hervilly.

The ships that would carry them, under the command of Admiral Sir John Borlase Warren, were to weigh anchor in the Solent on 17 June. Admiral Bridport was detailed to attack the enemy fleet in the Channel, and to blockade it at Lorient. Sir Sidney Smith, commodore of the small but swift-moving naval flotilla which guarded the Channel Isles, received orders to use his ships as decoys to confuse the Republicans as to the expedition's landing place. And the convoy itself, bearing the Royalist army clad in British-made uniforms and bearing British arms, was preparing to make sail in hazy weather for Quiberon, and its point of landing, Carnac.

In Paris, the news that the boy king, Louis Capet, had died alone in the great tower of the Temple was suppressed, for fear of repercussions in the turbulent Royalist regions of the country. The Committee of Public Safety, having shied away from executing him, as they had killed his father and mother, had chosen instead to poison his young life with noxious air; and in his wretched cell, where he was tended roughly by Simon the Cobbler, he had contracted a disease of the bones and nerves which his doctors despaired of curing. All his wasted finger joints were covered with nodules; his lungs were irreversibly damaged, his stomach shrunk. His last days were spent lying silently on his cot, scarcely able to breathe, unable to eat or drink.

On shores near and far, armies waited for orders and soldiers primed their arms, while proud generals stirred in their sleep and dreamed of fierce and bloody wars beneath the cold light of indifferent stars.

Part Three

20 June – 7 July 1795

XXIII

Saturn was high in Pisces last night. I found him in the darkest hour of all, the hour before dawn, floating serenely within those pale rings. The summer nights are not long enough, I think, for such beauty.

We must find the lost star, before Praesepe returns, before the crab bites again.

It is too early for sleep. The midsummer nights are so short, so light. There is scarcely time for the moon and stars to rise, for Venus, more brilliant than any, to voyage in the east and look on our secrets, before the gaudy, prying, violent sun marches forth to obliterate the majesty of the heavens. They say that to the north, in the frozen wastes of Russia, there are days on end when the sun never sinks. The people of that land feast and carouse, giddy with the constant light. But winter comes, and, as if in atonement, there are days, weeks of constant darkness when the Aurora Borealis flickers, ghostly, on the Arctic horizon.

These nights are not made for sleeping.

Guy de Montpellier put down his pen and went to the window of his room. It was ten in the evening. The sun was sinking below the horizon, but its dying rays still glittered beguilingly on the far-off spires of the city.

Raultier had called at the house earlier. He had examined Guy at length, and told him he must rest; but to Guy it was Raultier who looked as if he had been spending sleepless nights.

Afterwards they had talked about the stars, and then Raultier had spoken in private with Auguste. Raultier had refused to give Guy more of the medicine that eased him so, but Auguste had brought it for him, as soon as the doctor had gone.

When night came, and Auguste disappeared to her bedroom with Carline, Guy went to the chamber where the harpsichord was, to envelop his senses in music. But the music was not enough, and his sister was lying oblivious in Carline's arms; so he went to take more of the medicine, the datura, until its warmth surged familiarly through his veins and he felt his pulse throbbing, heavy and uncomfortable. Outside, darkness was falling. It was time. He collected his remaining gold and went carefully downstairs, pausing to listen when he reached the hallway; but he could hear no one stirring on the floors above. Quietly he let himself out of the front door.

He found Ralph brushing down one of the horses in the stable. The coachman recoiled on seeing Guy's figure emerge from the gloom; he dropped the brush, which clattered on the cobbles. The big horse in its stall whickered and stamped with fright.

'Get the carriage ready,' said Guy. 'You and I are taking a journey.'

Ralph shook his head in agitation. 'Sir, you know I mustn't; your sister has forbidden it—'

Guy stepped closer. 'Who is master here, Ralph? You, or me?'

'You are, sir.'

'Then,' said Guy with quiet menace, 'you must do as I say. Mustn't you?'

Behind Ralph, the horse was tossing its head, trying to pull free of its halter. The coachman clung to the lead rope with one hand and said, desperately, 'Sir, sir, I must answer to your sister as well—'

'*Answer* to her?' Guy brought down his clenched fist on the rim of the stable door; his voice was harsh with agitation. 'You would do more than answer to her. I know your secret, Ralph, and if you dare to cross me, Auguste will know it too. Then you'll be out on the streets begging, as you should have been three years ago.'

The big horse had gone still, and Ralph seemed to shrink back into its shadow. 'I shall be out on the streets anyway,' he whispered, 'if I take you to the city.'

Guy folded his arms across his chest and put his head on one side, considering the trembling coachman. 'Come, Ralph,' he said, in a voice that was suddenly conciliatory. 'My sister loves me. She will forgive you if I ask her to, just as she has in the past.'

Ralph muttered, 'I barely escaped a beating when I took you before.'

'Ah, Ralph, Ralph, there will be no beating, I promise you! Do this for me, one last time.'

The scarred coachman was still unhappy, uncertain. 'As long as this *is* the last time.'

'Don't worry,' Guy reassured him, patting his arm, 'don't worry, it will be.' He smiled, but his eyes glittered as if with a fever.

In another part of the house, William Carline kissed Auguste's warm flesh and exhausted her with pleasure, while the velvet stillness of the summer evening gathered all sounds into silence.

Afterwards she ran her fingers slowly up and down the silken muscles of his back. She cried out softly, as she so often did, at the cruel ridgings of scar tissue that wealed his skin.

Raultier had tried to cure Carline of his muteness. He had explained that all illnesses, whether physical or mental, had their origins in the nervous system; and thus could be treated through manipulation of the spinal cord. But Auguste found her own way of making Carline resigned to his affliction, for he seemed content enough to be silent, in her bed. Now she stroked the scars on his back as he lay naked in her arms. 'How could they have done this to you?' she whispered. 'How could they?'

Carline reached to take her hand and to make love to her again.

Afterwards she covered herself with a loose silk robe and lay on her bed, half lost in dreams. Carline dressed and went up on the roof with his telescope and his sheaves of paper, to work in concentrated silence on the variable brightness of Beta Lyrae, high in the east.

An hour later, Auguste came to him. She was fully dressed, and her face was deathly pale in the darkness. 'Guy has gone,' she whispered.

Carline looked away from the stars, and down to the empty road that wound its way towards the city. So Guy was awake and bound again on some nocturnal voyage of his own.

Carline gathered his writings together, and put the telescope away, and prepared for another kind of search.

XXIV

Why should the weeping Muse pursue her steps
Through the dull round of Infamy, through haunts
Of public lust, and every painful stage
Of ill-feigned transport, and uneasy Joy?

William Whitehead, 'The Sweepers' (1754)

Rose Brennan clutched her flowers to the tattered lace at her bosom. There were so many of them, they seemed almost to cover her thin frame, the stocks and gillyflowers and daisies; but all her blooms were wilting badly now. Too hot, too airless, especially with the coming of darkness; sweet Christ, she found it difficult to breathe on summer nights like this. The smell of food from the crowded alehouses – chops, pastry-pies, rich gravy – was sickly on the warm evening air.

Rose Brennan sold her flowers in Covent Garden. Unlike the other market vendors, her trade was mostly at night; for the darkness gave men the chance to come up to her and bargain not for her flowers, but for her favours.

She tramped slowly past the tumbledown shacks that lined the northern edge of the Piazza, her thin-soled shoes slipping in the discarded waste of the market. 'Buy my flowers, sir? Sweet flowers for your lady?' Worried that she might look as faded as her blooms beneath the dim street lamps, she patted at her tousled auburn hair beneath her little straw bonnet.

The sudden raucous cackle of the Punch and Judy show up by the arcade made her jump. She hated Punch and Judy, especially the big, gaudy male puppet, with his vicious tricks that always made the customers laugh. There was a good crowd there now, pressed against the railings of the church, laughing at the lantern-lit show. She wandered past them slowly. 'Buy my flowers?'

There were too many other girls out tonight, pale, wan-faced like her, raking the taverns and coffee houses of the Piazza for custom. Business had been harder to get these last few months – worthwhile business, at any rate. The gents with money were turning lately towards the nunneries of King's Place and St James for their pleasure – more private, more discreet, Rose had heard tell, at least for those who could afford them. Still, there should be plenty of customers pouring out of the theatres soon and coming down here for a taste of the low life. Quick trade, that was what Rose Brennan liked. She liked a man merry, and generous with his purse, but not so drunk as he couldn't finish what he'd begun.

A gang of ale-sodden sailors swaggered past, on their way to the Nag's Head in James Street, their faces all bloated with ale and cockiness. Rose dipped quickly into the shadows beside the church. Oh, no, not them. They'd grab hold of her in a dark alley and take her one by one, and afterwards they'd give her nothing.

She could hear noise and music coming from a seedy brothel that was crammed into one of the shacks that lined the Piazza. A door slammed; there was the sound of shouting, and swearing, and heavy, stumbling feet as someone started to run. It sounded as if a fight was breaking out. Damn them, thought Rose. They'd have the officers out soon enough, from nearby Bow Street, and peaceful traders like herself would have to move on, quickly. She hurried on into the shadows and relative quiet of King Street, just beyond the church. The cackle of Mr Punch followed her. She wondered whether to be done with it all for the night and head back to her dingy room amidst the rookeries of St Giles with just the few coins she'd collected so far.

Rose was an orphan, and had been brought up in an asylum for foundlings in Lambeth. She was considered fortunate to have been taken in there. She was a small and skinny child, and no one really noticed her, until, when she was twelve, one of the doctors who attended the orphans when they were sick, a swarthy, pockmarked man who smelled of gin, had told her that he needed to inspect her, privately, and that she must tell no one of it, or she'd get into trouble and be thrown out.

She'd done everything he'd said, let him touch her, let him do other things too, and he'd offered her a little money, which surprised her. Sometimes he hurt her. He always looked frightened when it was all over, and furtive, but the other, older girls laughed when she timidly asked them about it, and told her that all men were like that, and was the old bastard paying her well?

So she said nothing else to anyone, even though she didn't like the doctor's pockmarked skin, or his gin-soaked breath, or the things he asked her to do. But then, one spring, her monthly course didn't begin, and when she told the doctor he was angry, and had her thrown out of the home anyway.

She'd been taken in by some older girls, who were looked after by Mother Gardiner in a house in Grape Street. They'd given her something to get rid of the baby, and for some weeks she'd been very ill. Then she was told she could stay with the girls in Grape Street, as long as she earned her keep and kept well away from the constables. For a while Rose did well. Her thin, childlike frame, her huge blue eyes and long auburn hair appealed to some of the customers; she was kept busy, and secretly she dreamed of meeting someone who would take care of her, someone kind.

But then Covent Garden began to decline in fashion with the moneyed set, and the more vicious elements began to take over. Tonight, considering it was midsummer, was as bad a night as any Rose could remember. She gazed up into the darkening sky, looking for the moon – a full moon brought luck, the other girls said, for it made men lustier – but she couldn't see any moon, full or otherwise. She looked away in disappointment. The smell of hot pies from a stall drifted, warm and sickly, along the rubbish-strewn street.

Then she went very still. Here was a likely-looking prospect, coming slowly but surely towards her from the Piazza. The lamplight was behind him, so at first she couldn't see his face, but, judging by the cut of his coat and the set of his shoulders he was a gentleman, even if his clothing was a little shabby. He came up to her cautiously, looking around him as he went; and Rose, seeing his young, vivid face, felt her hopes rise.

She thought suddenly, when he was almost up to her, He's not used to this game. He's afraid of someone seeing him. If I'm not quick, I'll lose him.

Swiftly, she moved up to him swaying her thin hips in emulation of the older prostitutes. She offered him a coy, dimpled smile from beneath her lowered lashes. 'Buy my flowers, sir?'

She had a shock when he came right up to her, because his eyes looked strange, as if he'd come from strong light into blackness. He was looking at her face, her hair, her flowers, as if she somehow puzzled him; he hardly seemed to have heard what she said. She wondered if he was ill.

'Is there somewhere we can go?' he said at last in accented English that showed he was a foreigner. 'A place where it's dark?'

She understood. 'Away from the crowds, you mean, sir?'

'Away from the stars,' he said.

The stars? thought Rose, astonished. Was he raving? Perhaps it was a turn of phrase they used in his country. Well, she didn't mind what language he spoke; he could be a Hottentot or a Hindu, as long as his money was English.

'We'll go somewhere nice and private,' she said, pressing his hand. 'Trust me, sir.'

Quickly she led him down the little twisting alley that lay in the shadow of the churchyard to a walled-in courtyard where scarcely any lights shone. A couple of dogs were growling over a bone, and she shooed them away. Then she put down her flowers by the wall. It was dark here, and smelled strongly of piss, but at least the Watch wouldn't catch them.

The man still seemed anxious, preoccupied. She tried to study his face again, but it was too dark to see much. Surely it couldn't be his first time with a girl like her. Perhaps he was just nervous, in which case she would have to help him along a little.

She reached up, to start unbuttoning his coat, but he caught her hands and held them tightly. 'She would do it with anyone,' he said abruptly, 'for flowers, for money, for pretty things. Would you? Tell me, would you?'

He was still gripping her hands, and his eyes seemed wild again, with pupils like pinpricks. This time Rose was frightened by his ramblings. He must have taken something that had unsettled his brain; either that or he was mad. She pulled herself away from his grasp and backed up against the wall, watching him warily. But then he seemed to grow calmer. He drew in a deep, steadying breath, and held out his hands. 'I'm sorry. Please don't go. There's something I want you to do. I will give you money.'

And that was hard enough to come by, on bad nights like this. Rose nodded. She thought she knew what it was he wanted; she was good at guessing the customers' tastes. 'Two shillings?' she said sharply.

'Yes,' he said. 'Yes.'

She squatted down quickly, her skirts spreading out on the grimy cobbles, and began to unfasten the man's breeches. She was surprised at how unready he was. Well, she thought, he's nervous. He'll take some working on. She glanced up at his face doubtfully, trying to read his expression in the darkness. 'Mister? Perhaps this might help?'

She was unbuttoning her patched bodice while she spoke, to free her small breasts. Carefully she guided his hands towards them, and heard him gasp as his fingers discovered the smoothness of her flesh there, and the prominence of her nipples. Soon enough he was ready. She crouched down again before him, and his hands moved this time to her thin shoulders, gripping her so hard that he almost hurt her. She felt him tremble as he submitted to the heat of her mouth; his body began to move, and soon she heard his sharply indrawn breath. 'Selene,' he cried out. 'Selene!'

A strange name, thought Rose. Well, it wouldn't be the first time that a customer, hers or anyone else's, pretended that he was with someone else while he was at it; she just wished he wouldn't make so much noise, because it was enough to bring the Watch on them. She was relieved when he was finished at last, and she wasted no time in moving away and fastening her bodice again. Even in the darkness here by the churchyard wall she could see that he looked as pale as one of the mortally sick patients she'd seen taking the air over at St Bartholomew's hospital. She gathered her flowers together, watching him warily as he fumbled in his pockets.

He held out some coins at last. Clutching her flowers to her chest with one hand, she reached out with the other for his money; but her flowers tumbled to the ground again when she realised what he was giving her, and she breathed, 'No. Jesus, no. There must be some mistake . . .'

But he was already hurrying off, while Rose stood there gasping, her hands weighed down with golden coins.

Dizzy with disbelief, she watched him head towards Henrietta Street, where a heavy carriage stood, its horses straining restlessly against their harness. The driver, perched high on his seat with reins and whip in hand, turned slowly to look at Rose; and as the light of the street lamp caught his face she felt a cry of horror rise in her throat, because the terrible scar that split his cheek made him look like the devil himself.

The foreigner climbed into the carriage. The door closed. The driver gathered up the reins and urged the horses on, towards Bedford Street.

She drew a deep breath, and closed her hands tightly round the coins. Well. With this gold, she could certainly stop work for tonight. For good, perhaps, at least at this kind of business. Shaking her head, she slipped the coins into her pocket and bent to pick up her scattered flowers, scarcely yet able to believe that she might not need to ply her trade ever again.

It was then that she heard the footsteps coming swiftly up behind her. They seemed ominous; quickly Rose looked for somewhere to run, but by then it was too late – the cord had been flung round her neck, and she was being choked to death. She kicked out, her thin arms lashing at her attacker, but the ligature tightened relentlessly. She was fighting for breath. Her pulse was throbbing, her head exploding, and she heard a man's voice say quietly: *A dead body revenges not injuries . . .*'

A hand reached into her pocket for the gold. Even in her extremity she was aware of acute grief at its loss.

But then distant shouts broke through the haze of her impending unconsciousness. More heavy footsteps intruded on the darkness, breaking into the sound of her own gasps as her agonised lungs struggled for air. 'The Watch!' a voice called out in the darkness that enveloped her. 'The Watch!'

Rose was only dimly aware of the blazing light of lanterns swinging before her eyes, the pounding of nearby feet. As pale faces loomed over her, she sank back into a mist of pain.

XXV

For evil news rides post.

John Milton, *Samson Agonistes* (1671)

Abraham Lucket was watching a cockfight in the pit beneath the Red Rose tavern off Drury Lane. In fact, he'd practically made himself hoarse cheering on the black-feathered newcomer, who clawed, strong-legged and bloody-backed, at the much-fancied champion. The battle was almost over, and Lucket was looking forward to winning a good purseful of shillings from the black cockerel's victory, when the warning cry suddenly erupted from the tap room above. 'The crimping men! 'Ware crimping men!'

It was the signal for chaos. Stalwart fellows who moments ago had been yelling for the cockerels now bellowed in a different fashion as they fought their way to the stairs to escape, but it was too late; they were being felled as they emerged into the tap room, by villains with stout cudgels. Lucket stayed put and watched from the bottom of the stairs in disgust. He knew, as did any male of fighting age who walked the streets of London, that this was the end result of the government's new recruitment measures. Talk of voluntary enlistment was a joke; no one with any sense wanted to go off to war, and so, to any rogue capable of raising recruits for the new battalions, ample reward in the form of cash was offered, and no questions asked.

Lucket had heard that these self-styled crimping captains were contracted by the War Office to supply raw men at twenty guineas a head. For the 'captains' to raid a cockpit was new to Lucket, though the lower class of brothels were used commonly enough to lure young men to their fate, and a few weeks ago Lucket had heard that the two famous pugilists, Mendoza and Ward, had been bribed by a crafty trio of crimping captains to draw a crowd to St George's Fields by advertising a fight. The fight began, sure enough; but soon many of the watchers found themselves felled in turn and dragged off senseless to join a different kind of battle. They woke up far from home, and dressed in the uniform of His Majesty's army.

The crowd down here milled and bayed for the blood of their would-be captors, but the narrow staircase made effective action impossible. Fighting started at the foot of the steps, and soon it was the blood of men's noses, not the blood of cockerels, that spilled on the sawdust. Abraham Lucket looked around and saw his chance of escape.

A narrow window, set high up into the wall, let air in at the level of the street outside. Lucket was thin and agile. Swiftly he piled up ramshackle chairs to scramble on, and then proceeded to wriggle his way out through the opening, twisting and swearing as he did so.

He rolled out on to the pavement, blinking in the darkness, and dusted himself down. He had avoided the fight, but he'd lost his prize money. Feeling thoroughly disgruntled, he set off to another tavern and ordered a pint of ale to soothe his throat, which was still raw from cheering on the black cockerel. It was then that he heard the talk of how a redheaded flower girl had been almost throttled to death by a Frenchman in an alley off King Street.

Interested, he listened with some care. Then he loped off to track down Jonathan Absey in his lodgings. Absey was in his shirt-sleeves, his grey hair rumpled by his own fretting hand; and Lucket saw, in some puzzlement, that he had a book of stars open wide on his desk, with sheets of paper, scrawled with his own writing, spread out all around him.

He looked tired, and not over-pleased to see his messenger. A nearly empty bottle of brandy and a drained glass stood on the table nearby. So Lucket proceeded warily; and as he began to tell his employer, with untypical reticence, about the girl and the Frenchman, he half expected to be clouted for his pains.

But he wasn't. Jonathan sat up and listened with the utmost attention. Then he stood and reached for his coat and, with the great effort of one who is trying rapidly to clear his fatigued brain, he said, 'Where is this girl now?'

'At the Bow Street Watch House, sir. With the parish constables.'

Jonathan was already searching for money in his pocket. 'Do you remember the doctor I asked you to follow? The doctor who was treating his patients in the Angel tavern?'

'Of course.'

'Would you recognise him again?'

'Easily, sir.'

Jonathan gripped his shoulders. 'Then listen. His name is Raultier. He has lodgings at number 28, Eagle Street, Holborn. I want you to see if you can find out exactly where he was at the time the girl was attacked.'

Lucket's eyes widened in conjecture. Jonathan said swiftly, 'No questions. Just do it.' He handed him the coins.

'Yes, sir. Holborn, sir.'

Jonathan held the door open and quickly followed Lucket down the stairs and out into the street. The sour smell of smoke hung in the air, and there was a faint glow over the rooftops to the south; for Lucket's former companions, the mob from the Red Rose, had overcome the press gang and gathered fresh allies. Marching over Westminster Bridge to St George's Fields in full force, they attacked the Royal George public house, which was suspected of harbouring crimping men; then they threw all its furniture out into the road and set fire to it. Afterwards they gutted another suspected recruiting house in Lambeth Road, calling out against vile crimps and kidnappers, and the perfidious French war encouraged by their own King George, who everyone knew was really a German; then they proceeded cheerfully back across the river to Mr Pitt's house at Downing Street, where they broke several windows before they were finally dispersed by the militia.

XXVI

Return we to the Dangers of the Night . . .

John Dryden, *Third Satyr of Juvenal* (1693)

Rose Brennan cowered in the chair as if she was waiting for someone else to hurt her. There was a line of livid bruising round her neck, like a collar.

'This Frenchman who paid for your services,' the man was saying to her tiredly. 'We wish to know more about him. That's why you were brought here. We mean you no harm. You'll be taken back home shortly.'

Rose, hardly hearing him, looked round her with wide, fearful eyes. She'd never been anywhere like this before. When they'd brought her inside the building, she'd followed them up dusty staircases and past lots of dark rooms, empty rooms, until at last they came to this one, which wasn't empty, but felt as if it was, because the ceiling was so high, the panelling so dark. As well as the man who asked the questions, there was an elderly clerk sitting at a small writing table over by the far wall, scribbling away with his quill pen, not lifting his head, not even when there was a long silence, like there was now.

The big desk in the middle of the room had piles of books and papers on it, as did the little couch beneath the window. Behind the desk sat the weary-looking man with iron-grey hair and pale blue eyes, who spoke to her in a soft yet steely voice. She thought she could see the faint remnants of a bruise along one side of his face; and his eyes were slightly bloodshot, with tiredness, or drink, or both.

'I ain't a bad girl,' she whispered. 'I ain't . . .'

The two constables from Bow Street had brought her here, one sitting on either side of her in their dark, shuttered carriage with mouldering straw on the floor. She was afraid at first that they were going to keep her at the Watch House, to lock her up for being out on the streets; but no. In fact once they'd got her here, to this strange, dead building that no one seemed to live in, they'd asked her if she was warm enough, and comfortable as could be expected, which was a rare kind of civility, she supposed, for people like them to show to someone like her; and then they took her up the narrow, echoing flight of steps to the room where she was sitting now.

She was tired and frightened. Surely it must be almost one in the morning. But the man with the blue eyes wasn't ready to sleep, though he'd had a long night of it already; couldn't she smell the stale liquor on him? She watched him warily as he pressed on with his questions.

'This gentleman, your client,' he was asking now. 'What did he look like?'

Should she tell him he had a madman's eyes? Rose shuddered a little, and her hand flickered nervously at her throat. 'He was a gentleman, sir, like you. Well dressed. Dark, plain clothes, expensive-looking, if a bit the worse for wear.'

The man was tapping impatiently with his fingers on the desk, making Rose nervous again. 'His face? Colouring?'

'He had – he had a thin sort of face, sir. Long nose, dark eyes – strange eyes. His hair was dark too, long, and tied back from his face.'

'Was he young?'

'Yes. Yes, he was.'

'Twenty-five, perhaps?'

She was surprised. 'Why, yes. He might have been . . .'

The man suddenly slammed his palm down on his desk, and let out a low exclamation that could have been an oath. The clerk eyed him cautiously, coughed, and said, 'Mr Absey, sir. Should I be writing all this down?'

'Of course. Why else are you here?' The man called Absey turned impatiently back to Rose. 'And he was French, you say?'

'He was certainly a foreigner, sir, from the way he spoke; most likely French, though I can't be completely sure . . .'

'So what did he say to you, this foreigner?'

What did customers usually say when they picked up a girl? Rose struggled to remember. 'He asked if – if there was somewhere we could go, somewhere away from the crowds. No, not away from the crowds. Away from the stars. Yes, that was it. Away from the stars.'

She was aware of a sudden deep silence in the room. The clerk's quill had stopped, once more poised over the white paper. The man with iron-grey hair leaned slowly forward, and his voice, when it came, frightened her again.

'You're quite sure that's what he said? That he wanted to go somewhere away from the stars?'

'Quite sure, sir.'

'What do you think he meant?'

She hesitated, shrugging, more than a little frightened by the look that had appeared in this man's eyes. 'Don't know, sir. He was probably a little drunk, or something.'

'What do you mean, *or something*?'

'I've seen it before, sir. Like being drunk, only different.'

'He had taken opiates, you mean? Laudanum, perhaps?'

Rose had friends enough who numbed their senses with the poppy drug. Opium and liquorice cordial, that was a favourite. Who could blame them? 'Could have been,' she said warily.

'He paid you?'

She tensed. 'Only a shilling. The usual.' Her hand clenched round the solitary gold coin deep in her pocket, the only one not to be taken by whoever it was who'd tried to kill her. She tried to remember the way she'd felt, the happiness inside, when she realised how much gold the man had given her, but she couldn't.

The man who was asking the questions said suddenly, 'So he didn't give you any gold?'

She fought to hide her astonishment. Did he know? Was this a trap? 'Jesu, no,' she said rather shakily. 'Gold? You must be jesting.'

The man's face hardened. 'This is no jest, Rose. Because, just as you were turning to go, this same man came up behind you, and tried to strangle you. Didn't he?'

Rose lifted her head suddenly. 'No! I told the other men. I can't be sure!'

The man leaned forward with his elbows on the desk, his fingers steepled, his pale blue eyes almost scornful. 'Are you telling me now that it *wasn't* the man who'd just paid you a shilling for your services who tried to murder you?'

She trembled a little, because his voice was so hard. '*Someone* came up behind me all right, just after the customer had gone. But it can't have been him; I was watching him, see, I saw him go—'

'On foot?'

'No! There was a carriage waiting for him. I remember because it was driven by an ugly, scarred brute of a coachman . . .'

'A hired carriage?'

'I don't know. I don't know!'

'The Frenchman could have come back to attack you. After you thought he'd gone.'

'No. He didn't. Because I heard the man who tried to kill me *talking*. And he wasn't French, like the other one. He was English. He had an English voice—'

'*English?*' The man behind the desk sounded stunned.

'Yes! He was counting, as he pulled the cord around my neck. And he said – he said . . .'

'Yes?'

'He said something strange. Something that I thought was most likely the last thing I'd ever hear.' She bowed her head and whispered, '*A dead body revenges not injuries.* English. Like the Bible. I thought I was done for. And I've had enough of your questions, enough . . .' Her voice trailed away and she covered her face with her hands.

The man took a deep breath. He settled back again in his seat and pushed his papers to one side. 'Very well,' he said. 'Thank you, Rose. You've been most helpful. I will have you taken home now. You're quite sure you don't want a physician to examine your injuries?'

'No! Lord help me, no!' She got to her feet too quickly, and her legs trembled with tiredness and shock. 'It's just a little bruising,' she added in a quieter voice. 'I'll be all right again by morning, sir.'

And pounding the streets again in search of custom by nightfall, thought Jonathan wearily as he closed the heavy door after the girl. He'd sent the duty clerk to escort her down the stairs, and to procure a carriage for her. Now he poured himself a glass of brandy, letting himself acknowledge, for the very first time, just how badly her bruised, fragile body in her threadbare dress had disturbed him.

Another one who looked like his daughter. She had the same red hair, the same translucent skin; and an air of natural grace, of beauty, even, that couldn't be extinguished even by the tawdriness of her clothes and the squalor of the life she led.

The attempted throttling had been done with a smooth cord, about half an inch wide; the constable who attended her had commented on the uniformity of the markings round her neck, as if he'd almost admired the attacker's handiwork. No abrasions, he said, such as a rope would leave; no fibres. Some fabric like silk, soft but strong; and lethal enough when pulled tight. Another few moments, and she would have been dead. Killed by some madman; an Englishman, Rose had insisted, or perhaps a Frenchman who spoke English fluently. Surely, this was the same man who had murdered his daughter.

Jonathan sat at his desk and covered his face briefly with his hands.

He had to accept that the Frenchman who talked to Rose of the stars before he paid for his pleasure was not Raultier, and, moreover, that Raultier was nowhere near; Lucket had done his work well, and had reported to Jonathan, just before Rose arrived here, that he had tracked down Doctor Raultier of Holborn, and the physician had in fact been dining alone at an inn in Compton Street at around the time Rose was attacked. Could Jonathan even be certain that the Frenchman Rose described was Guy de Montpellier, deluded with opium, muttering about the stars? And if it was Guy, how could he be the killer, when Rose Brennan claimed that she saw the young Frenchman getting into the carriage? *A dead body revenges not injuries* . . . Chilling words to hear indeed at the moment the breath was being choked from your body; almost biblical in their finality. Some madman: not Raultier, not Guy, but a man who spoke English. Was there perhaps another accomplice?

Jonathan rubbed his eyes wearily. If Rose had been given the gold too, then it was just possible that it would have helped him to unravel the mystery; but no. A shilling, she said. And of course, that was all a poor street-girl like her could have expected. She had looked at him as if he was mad when he asked her about gold, and no wonder. Perhaps his bitter, obsessive mind was pulling all this into a pattern that was a dangerous mirage, just as the candle flame held by his little daughter had drawn all the glittering imperfections of the brass dish into an illusion of perfect, concentric circles.

When Lucket had visited him tonight, with his news of the girl, Jonathan had sent to the Watch House for her quickly, and hurried back to his office in the darkness, to the surprise of the night clerk and the porters. He felt almost sure that this victim, the only one to survive these attacks, would somehow help him to track down his daughter's murderer. But disappointment was all he was left with, again.

He poured himself more brandy. It was past one o'clock, and he knew that he should go home, but his mind was too full for sleep.

The liquor was just starting to warm his stomach when he heard footsteps in the passageway outside, followed by a knock at his door. Jonathan opened it and saw the clerk standing there.

'Yes?' Jonathan spoke tersely.

'The girl wants to see you again, sir. Seems there's some problem about her going home. She says it's too far to walk.' The clerk made no attempt to hide the contempt in his voice as he spoke of Rose. Jonathan, remembering her exhaustion and the bruises on her neck, said,

'I told you to get her a carriage. You were to summon a carriage . . .'

He stepped forward angrily. 'I'll come down to her. You may go.'

'Very well. Goodnight, sir.' The clerk went downstairs again. Jonathan followed him swiftly, just in time to see the clerk's scarcely hidden expression of lechery as he took a last, surreptitious look at the girl.

Rose had seated herself on the only chair in the hallway. Her hands were clasped tightly around her knees, and she was shivering. Her blue eyes seemed huge in the pallor of her fragile face; her auburn hair was hanging in a tangle of matted curls around her drooping shoulders.

'I'm sorry, sir,' Rose whispered as she gazed up at him. 'I'll be all right to go soon, honest I will. It's just that it's so late, and there's all kinds out there at this time of night.'

She was pitifully thin beneath her tawdry gown, except where the tattered lace of her bodice clung to the rounded swelling of her bosom. Her dress was too short for her, probably passed on; he could see the little laced-up half-boots she wore, fastened tightly over the grubby cotton stockings that covered her thin calves. Jonathan was shocked by the sudden, unprepared-for lust that surged in his blood, shocked and ashamed when he saw how the candlelight gleamed on the translucent skin of her throat, highlighting the livid marks of the cord. Against the dark panelling of the hallway she looked like a bruised angel.

'You should have been provided with a carriage,' he said. He could hear that his voice was thick with tension. 'Come upstairs, and I'll find you money for one.' He thought he saw her smile, secretly, though when he looked again her face was expressionless as she followed him obediently back up the stairs to his room.

Jonathan started looking for money in his drawer. While his back was turned, he heard her crossing the room to the couch beneath his window. He heard her brushing the papers strewn upon it to the floor, and he turned abruptly to see her sitting down on it, and carefully lifting her feet in their little laced boots until they were just resting on the edge. Slowly, she began to ease up her skirt and petticoats, leaning her body back against the wall; and this time she watched him unblinkingly with her wide blue eyes.

'I saw the way you was looking at me earlier,' she said, as if by way of explanation. 'I saw. I knew. Come, then.'

Jonathan was breathing heavily. He stood, unable to move, his hands clenched at his sides.

'What's the matter, mister?' she taunted him softly. 'Your wife don't like you going with girls like us? Is that it?'

He lurched towards her unsteadily, and she whispered rude, triumphant endearments in his ear as she took him in her arms. She had pulled her gown up around her waist, and he saw that above her threadbare cotton stockings, which were tied with faded red ribbons at the knee, her flesh was quite naked. Her thighs were already opening for him. He felt her small, childlike hands fumbling with his clothes; her fingers were cool and knowing against his hardness. He pressed himself against her with a groan, and soon the feral heat of her thin body engulfed him completely, as did the degradation of what he found himself doing. After it all, he could hardly bear to look at her quietly exultant face. Dazed, he pulled himself away and turned his back on her as he covered himself.

'I will pay you well,' he said hoarsely, forcing himself to face her. 'But you must go now. You must go home. Here, here is money, for a carriage . . .' He fumbled stupidly on his desk for the coins, pushing them towards her, not wanting to touch her again. 'You will say nothing of this to anyone, nothing. You understand me?'

'Oh, yes,' said Rose Brennan. Her big, childlike eyes were certainly mocking him now. 'I understand. You'll find me at the Piazza when you want me again. And I'll know where to find *you*. Won't I, sir? My name is Rose.'

'I know,' said Jonathan dazedly.

She regarded him coolly. 'Do you? You called me another name just then.' She nodded towards the couch.

Jonathan froze. A name? He could remember nothing, nothing . . .

'Doesn't matter, though,' she went on. 'I get called all sorts. Some men babble of their wives while they're at it, some of their sisters, some of their little girls . . .'

'Please. Go.' Jonathan, perspiring freely, was moving towards the door. He put more money in her hand and held the door wide open.

'And the Frenchman,' Rose went on pensively, 'now, he called me something strange. Some foreign name.'

Jonathan released the door handle slowly. 'What did he call you?'

'Selene,' she pronounced, almost with relish. 'Funny name, ain't it? But as I said, I've been called stranger.' She smiled at him and walked past him to the door, swaying her hips in her own kind of mockery.

Jonathan could hardly breathe. He caught her roughly by the arm. 'He called you Selene? You're quite sure?'

She shrugged. 'Why, yes. I'm sure.' She pulled her arm free. 'Goodnight, Mister Absey.'

Jonathan let her go. He was hardly even aware of her footsteps fading away down the stairs.

Selene: the name the Montpelliers gave to their lost star; yet more confirmation that he was drawing close, so close to his daughter's killer. But who would listen to his accusations, when the Company of Titius was so powerfully protected?

A feeling of despair assailed him, until he remembered that he might, perhaps, have a crucial weapon already in his possession: the list of stars. If he could only prove that it contained a ciphered message, the document might give him the authority he needed to demand that the killer be exposed. But he could do nothing unless he unlocked its secrets. He needed help. And after tonight he could wait no longer.

He sat at his desk again, pulled pen and paper close, and began to write a message to the retired Decipherer, John Morrow.

XXVII

From harmony, from heavenly harmony
This universal frame began;
From harmony to harmony
Through all the compass of the notes it ran
The diapason closing full in Man.

John Dryden, *A Song For St Cecilia's Day* (1687)

Here, four nights later, was Alexander Wilmot in a mood of happiness; a sensation so transient, and for him so rare, that he felt as if such occasions should be used to mark the passage of time, like the transits of Venus. He knew that the moment would pass all too soon, and yet he was indisputably content, sitting on this warm summer evening in his little first-floor parlour over-looking the churchyard of Clerkenwell parish. Sunlit fields stretched away northwards beyond the rooftops up to distant Islington village, in a landscape that was dappled with trees and cows grazing in their shade; while for once the smoke from the reeking tile kilns was no more than a wisp of mist on the horizon.

He was host to his friend Perceval Oates the spectacle-maker. They had eaten supper together: a steak and oyster pie, and a bottle of claret, brought by an eager Daniel from the Bull's Head. For once, the fare had been good, the meat succulent, the gravy rich with juices, and now, in warm contemplation, the two men were about to play; Alexander on the harpsichord, Perceval on his violin.

It was three nights after the summer solstice and the pale, dusty sky still shimmered with the heat of the day that was ending. Alexander had left a small-paned window open for air, and the smells of the malt distillery by the Green drifted faintly into the room. A fly buzzed angrily against the window, not realising it could escape, determined to beat out its life against the illusion of its imprisonment; while from below came the drone of old Hannah's voice reading tonelessly from her worn bible, for her window too was open. A brewery dray rumbled slowly by, followed by a farmer on foot, driving some recently purchased young heifers in a slow, late journey from Smithfield up to the open fields that lay alongside the New Road.

Alexander let his fingers release Corelli's notes in steady joy as the pure sostenuto of his friend's violin soared in counterpoint. Later, when the desire for music was temporarily sated, he hoped they might go out on to the roof together, to observe the white star Denebola, the lion's tail; then perhaps Perceval would linger to see Saturn rise in the east, and the chance might even occur to talk with his friend of the Montpelliers, and the lost planet that they too searched for: riches in store indeed. Daniel sat on a little stool before the window, watching his master, his hands clasped round his knees as he listened to the incandescent music falling away to a perfect resolution and silence.

A sharp knocking at the door below broke rudely into the still air. Daniel jumped up and ran downstairs to answer it, while Alexander rose from the harpsichord and began, with apparent calmness, to pour more coffee for Perceval. But his fingers were shaking as he awaited the intruder.

'Mother, be still.'

Alexander could hear the sad spinster daughter below, trying to calm old Hannah, whose voice had risen in a crescendo of agitation as the knocking became louder, more urgent. The knocking stopped abruptly, only to be replaced by footsteps, Daniel's and someone else's, coming swiftly up the stairs; and it was only when Daniel came back in, followed by Pierre Raultier, that Alexander realised just how afraid he had been that the visitor might have been his brother Jonathan.

Instead, the arrival of Raultier caused Alexander's spirit to leap with secret joy, along with a surge of pride that the French doctor-astronomer should see him here with his friend Perceval, and not alone, as he more usually was.

Raultier took off his hat and looked quickly round the candlelit parlour, taking in the sheets of music on their stands, the silver pot of coffee, the empty dinner plates on the side table that Daniel hadn't yet removed.

And then the doctor saw Perceval there, placing his violin in its open case, meticulously polishing rosin from fingerboard and strings; and it seemed to Alexander that Raultier hesitated, just for an infinitesimal moment of time. But then he stepped forward to greet him, and Alexander thought, of course, they had already met; hadn't Perceval told him that he'd done some work for Raultier? In fact Perceval was already shaking the newcomer by the hand, his bright, birdlike face peering up at the taller man. 'Doctor Raultier,' he said. 'What a pleasant surprise.'

Raultier returned the greeting, then turned to Alexander and said, 'I interrupt. I apologise.'

Alexander said quickly, as though it was every hour he was so busy with such distinguished company, 'Ah no. Think nothing of it. My friend Perceval and I often meet to play music together. It's one of our favourite activities, second only to looking at the stars. Of course, you already know each other.'

'We do,' acknowledged Raultier. 'I've had cause in the past to use Perceval's skills. In the spring he repolished a damaged speculum for my telescope.'

'Has the mirror served you well, doctor?' Perceval asked earnestly.

'Indeed,' replied Raultier. 'Earlier this month I was able to view the moons of Jupiter with perfect clarity.' He turned back to Alexander. 'Mr Wilmot, I come to you with a heartfelt request, but I fear it comes at an inconvenient time for you. My friends and I – that is, Madame de Montpellier and our little company of star-watchers – were most earnestly hoping that you might be able to join us, tonight. But I see that you are already engaged in other activities.'

Alexander, as he listened to Raultier's request, felt the joy sear through his uneventful life like a meteor speeding through a forgotten part of the heavens. It was over a week now since his visit to the far-away mansion in rural Kensington Gore. His memory of it was somehow illusory, as if an unknown, glittering landscape had been illuminated for him, only for the vision to be obliterated without warning. Sometimes, it seemed his recollections of that evening were more real than the event itself; as if the world of the Montpelliers was on a different plane, in a parallel orbit to his own mundane existence. Surely, if he and they were fated to meet again, it would be climactic, all-changing. During these hot airless nights of late June, when he was unable to sleep but was anxious not to disturb Daniel slumbering beside him, he would try to hear again Auguste's voice and Guy's exquisite playing, Guy whom he had not yet seen.

And now Perceval, kindly, thoughtful friend that he was, had stepped forward and was saying, 'You interrupt nothing, Doctor Raultier. As you see from my violin, secured and fastened in its case, we had in fact finished our music-making for the night.'

Alexander looked at him in speechless gratitude. 'Will you come another night, soon, Perceval?' he said humbly.

'Indeed, I will, my friend.' Perceval picked up his violin case. 'But now I must leave you. I told my housekeeper, you see, that I wouldn't be out late. She worries,' he went on, explaining to Pierre Raultier, 'lest I catch a chill, even on a warm, clear evening such as this. She fears that stargazing is an unnatural obsession, believing like the ancients that the comets in particular are bringers of death and sickness, and that only madmen would dare to study them.'

'Perhaps she is right,' said Raultier, so quietly that Alexander was not sure that he heard him correctly.

Perceval was fastening up his coat, ready to go. Amidst mutual addresses of appreciation, Alexander escorted him downstairs. Then he climbed hastily back up to his parlour.

Raultier was standing at the open window, gazing out as the evening sun lingered over the little village of Clerkenwell. He turned as Alexander came into the room. 'I shouldn't have troubled you without warning,' he said abruptly. 'But Guy particularly asked me to come to you. His sister has told him of your interest in the lost star. Guy feels that, with your help, he might be able to predict its path with more certainty, and perhaps even see it again.'

Alexander's heart was beating fast. 'Has the young man recovered, then, from his sickness?'

Again Raultier hesitated. 'He is well, for the moment at least. Will you come? I have a carriage waiting outside.'

'Of course I will come,' said Alexander quickly. 'But you are an astronomer yourself, Doctor Raultier.' He gestured towards the shimmering evening sky. 'This is midsummer, and the hours of darkness are brief. You will know that this is the most difficult time of the year for such work.'

'I know.' Raultier seemed agitated. 'But we cannot afford to wait. We have no time to wait. If Guy's estimates of the object's path are correct, then within a month it could well have moved too close to the sun to be seen . . .' His voice increased in intensity as he spoke.

'I have no exceptional skill as an observer,' said Alexander, still anxious. 'I fear that your faith in me might be misplaced. That you might be disappointed in me.'

Raultier said quickly, and more warmly, 'My dear sir. Isn't our preoccupation with stargazing a lifetime's story of strong endeavour and constant disappointment, the latter always outweighing the former? Look at Galileo, look at Kepler – they broke their hearts in constantly searching after the unattainable, did they not? And yet – and yet, all astronomers live in hope, longing to be blessed like Herschel: to discover some new wanderer in the skies, to open up fresh mysteries for mankind. And Guy so needs to have something to believe in . . .' He paused and added more quietly, 'Perhaps we all do. We need your help.'

Alexander said, 'I will do whatever I can.'

'Thank you.' Raultier pressed Alexander's hand. 'Thank you . . .' He started towards the door, then turned suddenly. 'Before we go, there's just one other small matter. Did you manage to send that message for me?'

Alexander nodded earnestly. 'I took it the very morning after you brought it, to the Royal Society for dispatch, sealed inside a packet of my own.'

Raultier took a deep, steadying breath. 'I am grateful to you,' he said.

Alexander told Daniel where he was going, and the two men went downstairs together. Hannah was disturbed by their departure; they heard her voice rise with urgency as she intoned her well-worn words. Then they heard her daughter admonishing her tiredly, and Hannah's voice became harsh in protest, almost shrill, as she lamented with Isaiah that there was no peace to be found; *'There is no peace, saith the Lord, unto the wicked . . .'* Alexander's steps faltered as they went by her room, past the stench of urine and soiled clothing, and he saw Raultier too pause at the noise. Alexander said quickly, 'She is a good woman at heart.'

'Perhaps,' said Raultier, 'we were all good at heart once. Perhaps the woman is fortunate in that, through her madness, she has stayed so.'

The sun was sinking low. Scarred Ralph drove the carriage, but Alexander felt secure in Raultier's company as they proceeded along the airless, dusty London streets to the turnpike road to Kensington, and then through the deserted park, where the great trees broke up the milky twilight with their overarching branches, hiding the emerging stars. As they travelled westwards they spoke of the present glories of Vega in Lyra, of Cygnus the swan with its brilliant star Deneb; and of the eagle, Altair, shining in the south-east. Alexander had already resolved that he would tell Jonathan nothing of this visit. The Montpelliers deserved his loyalty, not betrayal.

All his life, Alexander had felt excluded from normal companion-ship. All his life, there had been a barrier between himself and other people, that could only be broken through by means of an excess of wine, or music; and afterwards, his solitude returned. So he had given up envying others their easy talent for comradeship, their conversa-tions that drew people around them, instead taking consolation in his work, in his studies, and in Daniel's heartwarming need for him.

But now, he felt that the barrier had been broken. He was to be a friend to these people; he was to be part of their company. *'We need you . . .'*

Only one thing troubled him, and that was his knowledge that Raultier's letter had not gone on its way as swiftly as he would have wished. Alexander, on delivering his package to the Society's head-quarters in Somerset House the morning after Raultier's night-time visit, had been informed that the next foreign mailing, which should have departed the following day, would be delayed owing to some obscure technicality concerning the renewal of the Society's franking privilege. And so, Alexander was told, his packet of papers would of necessity be held for perhaps a week or so before its dispatch.

Alexander had been disappointed, but he felt there was no need to trouble the doctor with news of this minor inconvenience. After all, the letter would be safely delivered, sooner or later, and that, surely, was all that mattered.

Raultier needed him. They all needed him, and he was going to help Guy to search for Selene. Alexander's joy shone as transparently as the evening stars.

Alexander's departure was noted by Abraham Lucket, who had been kicking his heels in the Bull's Head in Clerkenwell. In fact, Lucket had spent the evening checking up on Jonathan Absey's half-brother, the brother he suspected Absey would sooner be without; and one of the most interesting things Lucket had learnt was that he wasn't the only person lately to have been asking questions about Alexander Wilmot. He had tucked the intelligence away at the back of his mind, and was just leaving the Bull's Head at close on sunset when he saw a carriage draw up close by the pillory on the Green. A man had got out of it, and hurried purposefully down the alley that led to Alexander's house. Lucket, standing back in the shadows, recognised him instantly. It was the French doctor from the Angel, with lodgings in Eagle Street: the doctor Jonathan had asked Lucket to check up on, on the night of the attack on the flower girl.

Lucket watched the Frenchman knock at the door until the black boy let him in. Once he was safely inside, Lucket went to chat to the driver of the carriage, a big, surly man with a scarred face.

He smiled with satisfaction at the replies he eventually received to his questions, and also at the things he had seen. He watched the carriage set off westwards, then set off himself, on foot, south towards the city as darkness fell, with his hands in his pockets, his stiff hair jaunty, and his lean belly well warmed by a pint of the Bull's best ale. He was confident that Jonathan Absey would be suitably grateful for the information Lucket was about to bring him.

XXVIII

*For, methinks, the understanding is not much unlike
a closet wholly shut from light, with only some little
openings left, to let in external visible resemblances,
or Ideas of things without.*

John Locke, *An Essay Concerning Human
Understanding* (1690)

Joshua Whitcomb, garrulous landlord of the Blue Bell tavern where Priss had worked, was relieving himself copiously against the wall of one of the dark wynds that adjoined his hostelry when the two men came up to him. They walked slowly, but with purpose. They didn't look as if they were after light-hearted entertainment. They watched and waited as Joshua let the stream of amber liquid die away against the cobbles.

Joshua, who'd left his tavern in the capable hands of his wife for an hour or two while he went to sup several good pints at Mistress Lambert's alehouse in the Strand, and give her a good pleasuring into the bargain, suddenly felt all the mellowness leave him. Struggling to fasten up the placket of his breeches, remembering with fleeting wistfulness how what was concealed therein had earlier elicited satisfying exclamations of delight from the lips of the buxom Mistress Lambert, he turned briskly towards the exit from the alley, and the welcoming lanthorn that hung over the battered sign for the Blue Bell.

But they were on him long before he got to it, the two watchers, grasping him and swinging him round as if he were a stripling, not a sturdy ox of a man, as Mistress Lambert had so rapturously called him in the throes of her pleasure. Josh swung a punch at one of his assailants, and the answering fist in his guts, hard as steel, set all the ale in his belly a-reeling, and drove his sweet thoughts of Mistress Lambert heavenwards.

Jesu. He fought for breath. 'I've no money,' he gasped out, 'if that's what you're after. Leave me be, or I'll cry for the Watch.'

How they laughed at that. It suddenly struck him, looking at their thin, mean faces and their sober dark coats, that perhaps they themselves were Bow Street officers. He wondered even more when he saw the third man, who lingered in the shadows, waiting and watching with tired blue eyes.

The man who'd hit him said, 'Listen to me. We're here to ask you some questions, and we expect honest answers. You understand?'

Joshua was afraid that they'd found out about the stolen goods he'd handled for Tobias Greenway of the Seven Dials; or about that batch of counterfeit coinage he'd helped on its way last spring. He pulled himself together, tugging at his rumpled coat, and muttered, 'I've got nothing to hide.'

It was then that the third man stepped out from the shadows. 'You had a girl,' he said, 'working for you. Her name was Priscilla, and she was murdered two weeks ago, only yards from here.'

Joshua shrugged, almost relieved that it was just another question about Priss. 'Aye, she was a pretty wench. Perhaps a little too easy with her favours.'

The man stepped forward suddenly, and his grip on Joshua's chin made him flinch. 'You enjoyed her favours, landlord Joshua? Is that right? There are some who whisper that it was you who sneaked out and throttled her with those big hands of yours.'

Joshua paled. 'No. There's no truth in that. How can you think it?'

'But you took your turn with her often enough?' The man's voice grew harder. 'Took your pleasure of her, between drawing pints? We've heard the wench was getting ambitious, was suggesting you send your wife packing and make her mistress of the Blue Bell instead; was that a lie too?'

'Yes,' said Joshua hoarsely. He was struggling now. 'All lies –' He tried to break away again, but one of the man's assistants caught his arm behind his back and wrenched it up with such force, he thought the bone broken. The agony screamed through his nerves. The stench of the puddle of urine close to his feet rose insistently to his nostrils, warm and sickly. He felt his testicles shrinking into his abdomen, and he clenched his teeth together. It struck Joshua Whitcomb that they might be going to kill him here in the darkness of this alley. So close to safety, just as Priss had been . . .

'Tell us,' said the man with the pale blue eyes softly. 'Tell us what you remember of that night. The girl, Priss: she'd gone out walking with a Frenchman, hadn't she? She told you so; what else did she say about him?'

Joshua struggled against the fierce pain as his arm was slowly pushed up his back. 'I told them,' he whispered. 'The constables – I told them every damned thing I could remember.'

'Then tell us again, Master Whitcomb.'

'He was a Frenchman,' Joshua gasped. 'I don't know any more—'

'Did she mention his age?'

'No. She didn't. But she thought – she thought he was ill, or rambling on something stronger than beer –'

'And what did he ramble of?'

'The stars. She said he talked of the stars.'

'Well. So you said before, to Master Bentham of the Hanover Street Watch House, on the night of her death. But I think we want a bit more. Try a little harder, Master Whitcomb. Or your fine tavern might receive some interesting visitors soon, who have a suspicion that your cosy tap room is housing a nest of thieves.'

'No – *shite* –' Joshua Whitcomb tried to break away again, but his captive arm was twisted tighter, and the agony almost made him faint. He swallowed, and said, white-faced, 'What more can there be, damn you? She said he talked of stars, and seemed to think she was someone else—'

'*Who?*'

'I can't remember. Some strange, god-damned foreign name . . . *Jesus Christ* . . .' The sweat was standing out in beads from his forehead. 'Selene. It was Selene . . .'

The man who questioned him seemed to go very still. Then he took a step forward. 'What else?'

'He – he gave her a coin, a gold one, a French one; she showed it to me, and laughed about it, and said, what would I say if she told me he'd given her a whole purseful of the stuff?'

The man said slowly, 'A purseful? Do you think she meant it?'

'No, of course not. She was teasing me, she liked teasing me; she waved this gold coin in my face—'

'Did you look closely at it? Did you see what was on it?'

'No. She took it back quickly enough, and kissed it, and went off to serve some other customers, and within an hour, she was dead . . .'

A sob broke in his throat. The blue-eyed man jerked his head impatiently towards his henchmen, and they let Joshua Whitcomb go. He fell back against the damp-stained wall, weak with pain and fear, his arm hurting as if the bastards had broken it; while the three men disappeared into the darkness at the back of Maiden Lane just as quickly as they'd come.

A cat wailed from the high wall, mocking him. He felt quite sober now, and rather sick.

Jonathan dismissed his men and set off home, on foot, dizzy with tiredness and speculation. Selene. The talk of stars. The red hair. And the coins, the gold coins given to both Priss and Georgiana; had Rose received them too? Rose, with her bruised child's body and her knowing woman's smile; how carefully she'd avoided his eyes, when she told him of her shilling. Had she lied to him?

He tramped slowly past the gaming dens of Leicester Fields, thinking of the Frenchman searching London for red-haired prostitutes who were alone and vulnerable on London's dark streets. Paid with gold. Killed by a man with an English voice, after the sick young Frenchman who called them Selene had finished with them.

A crowd had gathered at the corner of Princes Street, watching a group of Italian jugglers with swarthy skins and sequinned clothes that glittered brightly in the light of the torches they carried; his way was blocked, so Jonathan ground his hands into his coat pockets and thought: They are being silenced, these girls, but why? Because Guy de Montpellier wasn't supposed to leave the house? Because someone didn't want him giving away the Montpelliers' secrets?

What secrets? Could it be, as Jonathan had suspected before, that Raultier was working clandestinely for the Royalist Agency, and sending the plans of his English masters to d'Artois in Paris? Or could it be that Jonathan was wrong altogether in his suspicion that the letter was in code?

The Italian jugglers were moving on, their torches leaving a trail of sparks against the dark night sky. The crowd began to melt away. Jonathan continued homewards with his head down, and on reaching Brewer Street he climbed to his rooms, took off his coat, and looked for the star letter, then realised he'd left it at his office, locked in a drawer. He'd sent his message to the old, retired decipherer, John Morrow, whose protégé he'd once been; but he'd received a curt missive in reply saying that Morrow was in a critical state of health and couldn't see him. Another failure, amongst many, in his struggle to track down the killer of his daughter. And yet he must be getting closer, day by day, hour by hour, in his search for revenge.

He was just lighting more candles when Lucket called, with his news of Alexander's journey.

'How long ago?' Jonathan rapped out.

'It's two hours since your brother set off, sir. I've been waiting for you.'

Jonathan, dashing the weariness from his brain, hurried down the stairs, pulling on his coat again as he went. He would go to Clerkenwell and await Alexander's return, all night if necessary.

XXIX

I saw Eternity the other night
Like a great ring of pure and endless light,
All calm as it was bright;
And round beneath it, Time, in hours, days, years,
Driv'n by the spheres,
Like a vast shadow mov'd; in which the world
And all her train were hurled.

Henry Vaughan, 'The World' (1650)

'Our little mathematician,' said Auguste de Montpellier affectionately as she came forward to offer him her hand, and Alexander, bowing low as she welcomed him to their rooftop observatory, felt dizzy with happiness. Her fingers in his were gently confiding, and he was aware of some delicate fragrance lingering in the air as she moved.

It was still warm up here, even though it was past ten at night. The newly darkened sky was a backdrop of velvet against which the stars blazed with midsummer brilliance, dominated by the clear beacon of Jupiter in the south-east, brighter than any star.

All around them, the woods and fields of rural Kensington melted into nothingness, indistinguishable from the horizon; there were no night factories here, no street lamps, nothing to distract from the majesty of the heavens except the clear trilling of the nightingale, and the owl's lonely call. The splendour of the Milky Way, stretching overhead from pole to pole, seemed their only confinement.

Alexander had hoped, of course, that Guy would be there, but he did his best to conceal his disappointment at Auguste's brother's absence as Raultier took him to meet the other dozen or so people gathered up here; and as if to console him, there were some that he recognised: Matthew Norland, the former priest who loved Milton, who greeted him warmly; the silent William Carline, with his almost perfect blond beauty, who nodded to him from where he stood; and in their midst Madame de Montpellier herself, just as entrancing as he remembered. A full cap of lace-trimmed white lawn all but covered her hair, and she wore a fringed silk shawl draped carelessly across the bodice of her muslin dress.

She looked different, in some subtle way that Alexander couldn't at first define; but then he realised that she had not powdered her hair. Delicate tendrils of it gleamed like burnished copper around the edges of her white cap, and as Alexander lifted his head after touching his lips to her hand in homage, he noticed also that round her neck she was wearing a bright scarlet ribbon.

She saw his eyes on the ribbon, and laughed aloud. Her hazel eyes were so bright as to be almost feverish.

'Do you like my ornament, monsieur mouse?' She was clearly amused by his confusion as he dragged his eyes away from her throat. 'It's all the fashion in Paris to wear a red ribbon around one's neck – *à la guillotine*, they call it. Does that shock you? Tell me, please tell me, my English friend, that you don't disapprove of me too dreadfully . . .'

Her face, to Alexander, was dazzling, almost hallucinatory. He struggled to find a reply but before he could think of one she moved laughing away, with Carline following her like a shadow. Alexander saw that they were going to a little table set up in the shelter of the wall, with raised sides to protect papers and quill pen from sudden draughts; Carline began to write something, and Auguste, bending over intently to read his words, whispered a reply.

Alexander started as a hand was laid on his arm.

'You stare at them as if you find them more wondrous than the stars,' said Matthew Norland drily in his ear. 'She's beautiful, isn't she? No wonder she torments men so. But come, my little astronomer. Let me show you some of our inanimate rooftop treasures.'

Relieved at the distraction, Alexander followed him, and was soon enraptured, because the chief treasure was the wonderful telescope, which Norland proceeded, with some knowledge, to demonstrate to him. It was a Dollond achromatic, with a tripod base and lengthy tube cunningly crafted from polished mahogany, and a finder made of brass mounted alongside. The ex-priest, as he showed it to him, seemed quite sober, and genuinely appreciative of Alexander's company. Afterwards Norland asked with some astuteness about the calculations Alexander had completed for Herschel; then they talked of the respective merits of refractors and reflectors, and recollected how the intrepid Herschel, finding no instrument suitable for his work, had decided to make his own by casting huge metal mirrors of five feet in diameter in the cellar of his Bath home. They paused briefly in their conversation when wine and dishes of cold food – pickled salmon, tiny quails' eggs, and venison pasties – were brought out by servants and placed on trestle tables around the observatory, which was faintly lit by lamps whose flames danced in the warm still air. Afterwards, to Alexander's joy, he was offered a turn at the telescope. He used the brass finder tentatively at first, for this was far superior to any other instrument he had used, but soon Auguste de Montpellier came to his side to encourage him.

'Here, *monsieur* mouse,' she breathed, 'you must handle it confidently. We are relying on you, all of us, to find the missing star, and to bring us fame and fortune.'

Alexander feared at first that she was mocking him again. But then he realised that all of them, including Auguste, were watching him with almost reverent attention as he adjusted the telescope fractionally and gazed through the eyepiece at the red alpha star of Hercules, with its fifth magnitude blue-green companion. Everything was very still, very clear in those brief midsummer hours of darkness; and behind him no one moved.

And then he heard footsteps on the stairs, and low voices, and Guy de Montpellier arrived, followed by Ralph.

He knew without being told that it was Guy, for he possessed the same kind of beauty as his sister. Gazing in silence at the young Frenchman, who was flamboyant in black velvet, with a tumbling white cravat at his throat, knotted with careless perfection, Alexander felt painfully conscious of his own rotund figure and shabby clothing. A mouse indeed. He hung back in the darkness, and for a while the stars and telescope were forgotten as the others hovered in this creature's bright orbit. The scarred guardian of the house, Ralph, who had humiliated Alexander so on his first visit here, placed cushions on the couch in the corner, which Guy impatiently disdained. Then Auguste, who of course had her own minor satellite, Carline, constantly at her side, teased her brother with gentle adoration; while Raultier looked on, silent, with a physician's watchful eye.

Only Norland, the big priest, seemed unaffected by Guy's arrival.

He made his way to where Alexander sat in the darkness, close to the low wall that bordered the balcony, and his deep-lined face was haggard as he arranged his long limbs in the chair he had pulled up.

'Quite a couple, aren't they?' he said, gesticulating at Auguste and Guy. His breath, as he leaned close, now reeked of brandy; and Alexander realised that Norland was, after all, deeply drunk. 'Ralph spoils the perfection of the scene, of course,' Norland went on. 'Poor Ralph, like myself, is but a foil to their beauty. Sometimes Auguste calls him her Cerberus, her keeper of the gates of hell.' He laughed a bitter laugh, and poured himself some wine from a nearby bottle. His hands, Alexander saw, shook a little; they were large and strong, their backs almost covered with wiry dark hairs.

Alexander too turned his gaze on Ralph. 'Why do they have him with them all the time? Ralph is a mere servant, not an astronomer, surely?'

'Ralph is their minion, another of their acolytes. He's lived in this place for many years; he was coachman to the former owners, and Raultier, when he took over the lease of this place for the Montpelliers, persuaded him to stay. He's here because he's useful. You can see for yourself that the man is as big and strong as an ox. He tends the heavy telescopes, when Carline gives him permission, and carries Guy when he is ill. He drives the carriage for them, and acts as madame's body-guard. And he works for very little, for a pittance merely, which is important, as the Montpelliers lost their wealth in fleeing from Paris. Their estates were appropriated, like the property of all exiled *émigrés*, in the name of the glorious Revolution.' He sipped his wine thought-fully. 'Ralph is besotted with Auguste, of course.'

Alexander looked again at Ralph, who was carefully moving the big telescope at some whim of Auguste's. He had a thickset body, formi-dable in its impression of brute strength; Auguste scarcely came up to his shoulder. Auguste, beautiful, graceful, untouchable, was on tiptoe, whispering something in his ear, teasing him. Ralph bent his head to listen, and his badly scarred face flushed with delight. Clearly, he worshipped her.

Norland, at Alexander's side, chuckled contemplatively. 'Poor Ralph. He was almost as devastated, I think, as Raultier, when Carline became Madame's lover. In fact, if I'd been Carline, I would have been wary of Master Ralph. His passions run deep beneath that brutal exterior. Many years ago, he tried to strangle his wife.'

Alexander's skin crawled. A mocking bitterness tainted Norland's veneer of expansive good humour, yet would Norland dare to say such a thing if it were not true? He turned slowly to Norland. 'Was there a reason for it?'

'Oh, the usual kind of thing. Ralph married one of the serving girls at the house, but she was a lustful wench by all accounts, and was unfaithful to him many times. She taunted him with her lovers, in fact. A bitch, a heated bitch. They still talk of all this in Kensington village; the story is well known.

'It was his wife who scarred poor Ralph with a knife during an argument, and then told him she found him too repulsive to merit her attentions.' He reached for his wine and drank deeply. 'Some months later Ralph found her with another man, a servant from the house, in his bed. He tried to strangle her with his bare hands. The manservant managed to stop him, before she was really harmed; otherwise Ralph would surely have killed her.'

Alexander felt tense with shock. 'What happened after that?'

'The wife ran off with her lover. Ralph took to wandering the lanes and fields around Kensington, looking for her; some said he was losing his mind. But the family who lived here were good to him, and saw to it that no charges were pressed. They realised that his wife had driven him to his violence. Besides, he was good at his work, and devoted to them.

'And then the Montpelliers moved into this house, two and a half years ago; and the rest, I think you know. Madame de Montpellier took a fancy to Ralph, in spite of his grim past. She has a passion for devotion, you see, even if it leads to a man killing the thing he loves. Indeed, I think that Ralph would kill, to protect her.' He stretched out idly for a cold venison pasty and bit into it with relish, suggesting to Alexander that he should eat some more of the delicacies on offer; but Alexander was no longer hungry. Such devotion was surely dangerous, thought Alexander, seeing how Ralph's despairing eyes followed Auguste as if he were under some malign enchantment. He watched Ralph's hands too as they adjusted the heavy telescope to her fancy; they were huge yet dextrous as he moved the mountings to their new position; and all the time the blond Carline was at Auguste's shoulder like some mute archangel, his cold, blue eyes on Alexander.

Alexander shivered. Norland's tales had fuelled his imagination unhealthily. He rebuked himself, and tried to push his dark thoughts from his mind. Norland, meanwhile, who'd beckoned to a servant for more wine, was sliding into complete inebriation. He began to question Alexander hazily about his travels; and Alexander, as much to hide his embarrassment at the ex-priest's drunken condition as in a true sense of conviviality, found himself telling him of his long voyages as a navigator through the southern oceans; of the glory of the Magellanic clouds, with their giant stars wheeling overhead like a newly discovered universe to him, while the flying fish leapt in the midnight phosphorescence that trailed the ship. And then a shadow fell across the table where he sat, and a younger man's voice broke in,

'Matthew, you are disgustingly drunk, even more so than usual. Leave us, will you? Master Wilmot and I have things to discuss.'

Alexander swung round, and saw that Guy de Montpellier was standing behind him.

Norland got up quickly, colour suffusing his face. He picked up his glass and his plate of food and moved away. Guy settled himself in his place and turned to Alexander.

'I'm sorry Norland has been bothering you,' he said. 'He's a drunken bore. And he can sometimes be indiscreet. I wonder what secrets he's been telling you about us all?'

Alexander had longed for this meeting ever since Perceval had described Guy to him, with his love of stars and music; and now that the moment had come, he wished that he had not been caught listening to Norland's sordid tales. 'We were talking about the southern oceans,' he said quickly, 'and the stars to be seen there.'

The young Frenchman looked amused. 'Is that all? Didn't he tell you any secrets? He will.' He rested his hands on the arms of his chair. 'Norland has secrets of his own. He was a priest once – did he tell you? But even his drab priestly garments quite failed to conceal the lusts of his body . . .' He broke off and his expression darkened. 'Sometimes I grow weary of the fools with whom my sister surrounds herself. They all watch me, and each of them thinks that my salvation rests in their hands alone. Norland is an ageing, lecherous hanger-on who rambles of darkness and the devils that are within himself. Ralph is scarcely human, though devoted enough. As for Carline . . .'

He paused, and Alexander saw how tightly the young Frenchman's hands were gripping the arms of his chair. 'As for Carline,' Guy went on at last, 'he keeps my sister happy, and there is no more to say. Although I could add that she is entranced, I think, almost as much by his ruined back as his beautiful face. She attracts such people like moths to a lamp; and, just as easily, she destroys them with the brightness of her flame.' He smiled as he gazed across at his sister, but beneath his words and his smile there seemed to lie a bitter tension. He turned quickly back to Alexander. 'But you didn't come here to learn such things. Your mind, I know, is on weightier matters altogether. They've told me that you too believe in our star. They say, even, that you've seen it. Now I want to hear about it for myself.'

Alexander was astonished by the way in which Guy, a complete stranger, had taken him into his confidence so quickly. Wishing fervently that he had not drunk so much wine with Norland, he gathered his rambling thoughts.

'Two years ago,' he began, 'I saw an object that could well have been this lost planet, on two consecutive nights.' Guy was nodding eagerly. 'But then,' Alexander went on, 'the moon grew too bright, and by the time I was able to search for it again, the object had moved too close to the sun to be seen. I never found it again.'

Guy listened raptly, his face etched with shadows. 'But surely you haven't given up hope?'

Alexander lifted his eyes, briefly, to the star-scattered sky overhead. 'No,' he said, shaking his head. 'Oh, no.'

'I have seen it too,' breathed Guy, reaching out to touch Alexander's arm. 'I will show you my figures. I saw it two months ago, when I charted its movements throughout the night. I have studied these figures, but I cannot make sense of them alone; I need the help of someone with mathematical expertise, of the kind you possess . . .' His hand tightened on Alexander's coat sleeve, and his eyes were dark with the strength of his passion.

'In Paris,' he went on, 'I talked often with de Saron. He believed he had seen it too. But he was betrayed by those who were jealous of him; and his enemies sent him to the guillotine.'

Letting go of Alexander, he reached for his wine and drank. Alexander said, 'I'm sorry.'

Guy was frowning, and looking down at his hand which tensely gripped the wine glass. He pushed the glass aside. 'De Saron was a friend of mine. He must have been afraid. Do you know, I've often wondered what it must be like, to die like that. You would think it would be quick – wouldn't you? – but those who have seen such things say that the pain, at the moment of execution, is so intense that the trunkless face goes into distortions of agony, as every nerve end from the parted body screams out its own little death . . .' He clenched his hands on the table till the knuckles shone white. 'The guillotine was invented as a humane means of killing criminals. But is there such a thing as a humane death, a peaceful end to the pain of living? I've thought about it, so often . . .'

He gripped Alexander's arm again unsteadily. 'There isn't much time. Will you look at what I've written, and see if you can chart her voyage through the sky? This time she must, she must be within my grasp: *I must find her.*' His voice had risen in pitch, become almost frenzied. Suddenly he got up and paced agitatedly to and fro, then he turned to Alexander and once more tried to smile, but his face was so pale that it seemed bleached by starlight.

'I talk of Selene, of course,' he said. 'The planet that eludes us all. But sometimes I think of her as a woman, with her tricks, her cunning.'

Alexander felt his blood run cold at Guy's strange words and his expression of harrowed intensity. 'I'll begin the work straight away,' he said quickly. 'But it could take time.'

'We have no time.' Guy was becoming agitated again, staring wildly at the heavens. 'The stars are gathering, crowding in; don't you see?'

Alexander was frightened again as he saw how the young Frenchman seemed to look without seeing, stabbing with his finger at the vastness of the night sky. 'Guy,' he begged, struggling to his feet himself, 'I think you are becoming tired; please, calm yourself—'

Guy whirled back to face him, and Alexander saw with horror that spittle was running from one corner of his mouth down his chin. 'They are watching me. All of them. The sea-crab, Praesepe – you know her? You know of her poison? She hides from me on summer nights, but I know she is there, just below the horizon, waiting to grip me with her claws as soon as autumn comes . . . Ah, yes, Praesepe watches me, but I will vanquish her, tread her beneath my heel, as Hercules did—'

To Alexander, Guy seemed to be hallucinating. Desperately Alexander looked round for help, and saw to his utmost relief that Raultier was coming swiftly towards them.

'Now, Guy,' the doctor said calmly. 'You will take a chill out here, without warmer clothes on. Come inside with me for a little. Come.' He took the younger man by the shoulder.

'No!' Guy knocked Raultier's hand violently aside. 'Don't touch me—' He continued to back away until he was only inches away from the low wall. Behind him a dizzying blackness beckoned.

Suddenly Auguste was at her brother's side. 'The doctor is right, Guy. Go inside, just for a while. I'll come and join you if you wish. You are tired.'

Guy stared at her as though she were a stranger. She had removed her lace cap, and her cropped, unpowdered hair gleamed redly in the light of the dim lamps that flickered around the balcony's low walls. Guy reached out his hand to her. 'Your hair,' he whispered. 'Oh, your beautiful hair.'

'Guy. Come with me,' Raultier said sharply, throwing a warning look at Auguste. Guy stared at the doctor almost with hatred; then he turned and started to go slowly down the staircase, with the doctor following behind.

Auguste came to stand beside Alexander then, bareheaded, with her fringed shawl pulled tightly round her shoulders against the rising breeze that made the lantern flames shiver and dance. 'Poor Monsieur Wilmot,' she said lightly, but her usual teasing smile flickered as uncertainly as the rooftop lanterns, and her face, too, was very pale. 'You look bemused by my brother's mercurial conversation. For weeks he is calm, he is lucid. Then this illness strikes him, and you see what happens. Pierre has to give him medicine, to soothe him, but then my brother's mind is clouded in a different way.'

'Will he recover?' asked Alexander, still shaken by what he had seen.

'Yes, oh, yes. His illness will pass. All things pass . . .' Her voice faded away; her forlorn gaze seemed drawn far away, by the constellation of Coma Berenices in the west, whose vast cluster of faint stars was dimmed by the brightness of Arcturus close by. Suddenly the legend of Berenice came to Alexander's mind: he remembered how the Egyptian queen cut off her beautiful hair as an offering to Jupiter, to save the life of the man she loved. And here was Auguste, shorn, desolate; was she trying to tell him something?

She shivered, then seemed to recover her composure. Turning back to Alexander, she said quietly, 'We need your help. Will you look at Guy's figures?'

Alexander realised that Carline was at his shoulder watching him, and once more the intensity of the Englishman's blue gaze made Alexander uneasy. 'Of course,' he said. 'I'm at your service. I've already told Guy that I will do so.'

All of a sudden, he heard the faint music of a harpsichord. The notes trickled like liquid into the clear night air. The sound ravished him; it was so ethereal that he almost wondered if he could be imagining it, but then he saw that Auguste was listening too.

'That is Guy,' she said. 'He is better, you see? Sometimes the sickness passes swiftly. Music is a great healer, better by far than opiates. There are times when my brother remembers too much.' She hesitated. 'Once there was a woman whom he loved greatly. She wasn't free to be his, but my brother was ardent in his pursuit, and who could resist him? Their time together was brief. Sometimes, when he is ill, he talks of her.'

'I know,' said Alexander quietly. 'Her name was Selene.'

She bowed her head in acknowledgement. When she lifted it again, her eyes were unnaturally bright. Alexander thought that he saw tears in them.

'Indeed. Sometimes he finds it hard to accept that he's lost her. Sometimes I think that is why he's ill.' She made an effort at a smile. 'But he will recover completely, I know he will, when he finds his lost star. Hear him play . . . Oh Monsieur Wilmot, little mouse. We are so glad to have you here with us.'

Alexander breathed, 'I will help him to find his star.'

'Yes,' she said. 'Yes.'

XXX

With trembling Heart
Gazing he stood, nor would, nor could depart;
Fix'd as a Pilgrim wilder'd in his way,
Who dares not stir by Night for fear to stray.

John Dryden, 'Cymon and Iphigenia'
(*Fables Ancient and Modern*, 1700)

Alexander had thought that Guy's departure would break up the gathering, but instead the watchers on the roof continued their work quietly and took turns at the telescope to gaze at Cassiopeia riding high between Perseus and Cygnus in the midnight sky. After a while Raultier returned and they gathered round to hear the news that Guy was now resting calmly in his room. Carline, meanwhile, silent master of the instruments, tended the Dollond telescope, almost lovingly checking its every feature, and finally rubbing the object glass with a soft piece of leather moistened with spirit.

Alexander thought of the whip marks on Carline's back. Then he looked at Ralph's scarred cheek, and wondered at Auguste de Montpellier's secret nature, that she had men who were so damaged, in mind or body, all around her.

They watched the stars for a little longer. Then Auguste disappeared, and a faint breeze stirred again around the observatory; they could hear it rustling the full summer foliage of the big lime trees in the garden below. Ralph started to uncouple the mountings of the telescope, and Alexander realised that Carline had gone too.

Alexander drew Raultier to one side and said, 'I feel I should be leaving. I do not wish to impose.'

'Of course,' said Raultier quickly. 'You don't impose in the slightest, but it's growing late, and you have a long way to go. I'll summon the carriage; Ralph will drive you home. But first, I'll fetch you some copies of Guy's observations, so you can study them.'

'I only hope,' said Alexander rather desperately, 'that I won't fail him.'

'You cannot fail,' Raultier assured him, 'because you've given him hope. Perhaps nothing is more precious.'

They went below, and Raultier left Alexander waiting at the head of the wide staircase that led down to the pillared entrance hall. From this vantage point Alexander felt more than ever aware of the lonely emptiness of the big house, which seemed only half furnished; yet there was money enough here for food and wine, and for the plethora of costly wax candles that burned with almost profligate expense in the gilt sconces that adorned every wall. On his way through the house he'd glimpsed rooms that were empty, and others where dust-sheets covered the furniture; he wondered now if the Montpelliers intended to stay here much longer, or if, in fact, they had even intended to stay as long as they had.

Alexander hadn't thought that Raultier would take so long. His bladder was starting to cause him discomfort, and he wished that he hadn't drunk so much wine. As the minutes went by he grew increasingly agitated, wondering if perhaps he'd misunderstood the doctor, if perhaps he was supposed to have gone straight outside to wait for the carriage in the courtyard. Remembering that Raultier had gone along one of the corridors that led from this spacious landing, Alexander decided to follow, to see if he could find him anywhere, and also to look surreptitiously for some private room in which to relieve himself. In an imposing dwelling such as this, built for frequent entertaining, there were usually discreet ante-rooms equipped for such a purpose.

All the doors were closed. As he walked further and further along the passageway it seemed to him as if this part of the house was deserted and in darkness. There was no sign of Raultier. But just as Alexander was about to give up, he saw one room where the door was ajar; and the betraying gleam of candlelight revealed that it might well be occupied. Alexander, moving nearer, heard a slight sound. Wondering if it might be the doctor, searching for the papers he'd promised him, he progressed tentatively towards the room and pushed open the door a little.

And now, for Alexander, time stood still. *What is this?* he wondered dazedly, *what is this?* As the scene unfolded before his eyes it took no more than moments for him to absorb what was happening; and yet it took for ever.

The room was relieved from darkness only by the faint light from a candelabra. There were two people in the room, Guy and Auguste de Montpellier. Auguste was seated, and Guy knelt at her feet with his head cradled in her lap.

'Ah, Guy,' Auguste was whispering as she stroked his long hair. 'You must not stray again. You must not.'

She was wearing only a loose silk robe, that was slipping from her shoulders to reveal her nakedness. Guy was gazing up at her, and as Auguste drew him into her arms, Guy kissed her throat, her shoulders, her breasts. She murmured to him as he caressed her, and she pulled him closer.

Alexander stood in the doorway, unable to move. He knew this picture would be forever etched on his mind, in the gold and umber chiaroscuro of the candlelit room.

Suddenly Auguste cried out her brother's name and pressed his dark head fiercely against her breasts. Alexander, dazed and disorientated, backed clumsily away from the open door and turned to stumble back along the passageway that led to the stairs. And then it was his turn to cry out in shock, because Matthew Norland was standing at the end of the corridor, watching him.

Alexander froze. He had to force himself to confront Norland's watchful face; he thought he could see the mocking laughter in the man's eyes.

'Well, well,' said the former priest softly. 'I thought you'd left us long ago, little mathematician.'

Alexander rubbed his damp palms agitatedly against his coat. He said, in a voice that was hoarse with tension, 'I'm waiting for Doctor Raultier. He promised to bring me some of Guy's writings.'

'And in the meantime you've been making more discoveries, I would guess, about this strange, God-forsaken household?' Norland's grin revealed his big, horse-like teeth; his sagging face was blurred now with drink. Did he know? Did he guess what Alexander had just seen? 'Don't be frightened, monsieur mouse,' Norland went on, in his slurred voice. 'We're not the kind of people you're used to, are we? Didn't I warn you about this place? We are all obsessed by Auguste; she is the candle to which each of us is drawn. I have seen how she fascinates even you; though somehow, I think your tastes lie in different directions . . .' He looked at Alexander consideringly, and the hot, suffusing flush of guilt spread through Alexander's body anew. His palms were still sweating, and his heart was racing with embarrassment. He muttered,

'I must go downstairs. Perhaps Doctor Raultier is waiting for me outside, with the papers – perhaps I misunderstood him –'

He was terrified that at any moment Auguste and Guy would emerge from the chamber, and that Norland would tell them he had been spying. He tried to move on, but Norland barred his way. 'No. You didn't misunderstand the good doctor,' said the ex-priest, folding his arms across his chest. 'He's gone to his room all right, but for something else, something he wouldn't tell you about. For laudanum.'

'For Guy?'

'No, my dear. For himself. Our Doctor Raultier is an opium user, as are many of his calling. He enjoys the substance in a tincture of alcohol, in regular, precise doses. Unless, of course, something upsets him, in which case he is prone to take a little too much . . . He hides his weakness well, doesn't he? He gives some to Guy, to alleviate his pain, and then he takes more of it himself. It makes up, I think, for not having Auguste.' He shook his head thoughtfully. 'Now, if only Guy could ease his frenzy over his own lost love in the same way, how much better it would be. But his memories are too vivid, and that is his torment.'

Did Norland know what was happening at this very moment a few yards down the corridor? Alexander tried desperately to press onwards, and suddenly the ex-priest seemed to relent, moving aside to let Alexander go past. But Norland followed him out on to the landing, where Alexander hesitated at the head of the staircase, not knowing what to do, where to go.

And Norland was close behind him once more, his breath sour with wine, his voice sly and insinuating. 'Yes, it's the memory of Selene that drives Guy mad,' he continued in Alexander's ear, even though Alexander shut his eyes and motioned with raised hand for him to stop. 'He saw her in prison. He was forced to watch her at play with the brutes who were her gaolers.'

Alexander went cold. Slowly he turned to face his tormentor. 'Are you saying that he saw her raped by her guards?'

'Raped?' Matthew Norland laughed brutally. 'Ah, no. Guy and Raultier like to pretend that it was rape. But from what I heard, from what I knew of her, she offered herself willingly to her gaolers, in as many ways as could be devised; for there were murderers out on the streets of Paris that night, dragging all the prisoners from their cells; and she knew they would reach the Salpêtrière very soon, so why not saturate her body with pleasure for those last few hours before the darkness closed in? The human spirit is weak in the face of death. Guy saw it all too clearly there in the Salpêtrière; and it drove him mad. Now poor Guy seeks consolation of a loftier kind in his search for the lost star.'

And in his sister's arms, thought Alexander agitatedly.

'But there is fresh agony for Guy even in his star-watching,' went on Norland, jabbing at Alexander's chest with his finger, 'because the quest for the lost planet drives him to madness. He should have learned to live with human weakness, like the rest of us. Raultier eases his own pain with laudanum, while I, I relieve mine with drink, and the bitter truth of poetry: *ah, demoniac frenzy, moping melancholy, and moon-struck madness*, as the stern Milton would say . . . We all have besetting sins, don't we, friend Wilmot?'

His grey eyes pierced Alexander knowingly. Alexander turned away abruptly, his heart hammering, and thought of Daniel, waiting for him in the darkened bedchamber of his home in Clerkenwell; only in his imagination Daniel's face suddenly became Guy's. Ah, God. This place was bewitching him. He put his shaking hand on the balustrade and stammered out despairingly, 'I must go. The doctor can perhaps send me the papers by messenger in a day or two. I will find my own way home—'

But before he could make his escape there were footsteps, and Raultier was coming along the corridor towards them with a sheaf of papers in his hand. He looked at Alexander, then sharply at Norland; but Norland just grinned and said, 'Monsieur mouse is waiting for you, Raultier.'

Raultier said tersely, 'Leave us, will you? Our business is private.'

The ex-priest seemed unaffected by Raultier's curt dismissal. 'As you wish,' he shrugged, and sauntered off.

Raultier watched him go, then turned back to Alexander. 'I'm sorry to have kept you. Here are Guy's papers. How long will it take you, do you think, to make something of them?'

Alexander, still shaken, ruffled through sheet after sheet of close-written figures. 'There is a good deal to be done. A month, maybe longer . . .'

Raultier's austere face fell. 'As long as that?'

'I will see.' Alexander lifted his head from the papers. 'I have several other commitments – I have my living to earn –'

'Forgive me for my obtuseness,' exclaimed Raultier. 'Of course, I should have explained earlier. We are hiring you for the task, and we will pay you in a manner commensurate with your skills.'

Alexander was freshly distressed. 'I didn't mean to ask for money.'

'Please don't argue. It will be seen to. Have you got everything? Ralph waits, with the carriage, outside.'

His eyes, Alexander was thinking, Raultier's eyes were different somehow; darker, more opaque. *'Our Doctor Raultier is an opium user, as are many of his calling . . .'* Was it opium, or was it something else? Had Norland been lying? Had the drunken ex-priest been lying about everything, filling Alexander's overwrought mind with gross falsehoods that were seething now like Bedlam fancies in his spinning brain?

Alexander turned unsteadily to go; but Raultier touched his arm and said, 'One more thing. Norland does not always tell the truth. Will you remember that?'

'He told me he was once a priest. Can that be true?'

'Yes.' Raultier hesitated, as if deciding just how much to say. 'There was a time when they killed priests in Paris, just as they killed the scientists. Norland was imprisoned. He renounced his religion, in order to save his life.'

Alexander said quietly, 'I am not sure that I would be any more brave.'

'Nor I,' said Raultier.

They shook hands gravely, and Alexander turned to go, with the papers clutched under his arm.

Outside the house, he drew in deep breaths of the clear night air to steady himself; then he got into the carriage driven by Ralph, who quickly whipped on the horses. Alexander was hotly embarrassed at having to call out to Ralph to stop when they had gone a little distance, so that he could relieve his long-suffering bladder behind the trees that lined the desolate road. He was sure that he saw a look of scorn in the scarred coachman's eye as he climbed back in.

He was calmer now, but he felt that he had violated both brother and sister by observing that moment of intimacy to which no one should have been a witness.

His hands tightened around the papers Raultier had given him. At least he had his chance, now, to absolve himself for his unwitting intrusion, by doing this work for Guy. Alexander's exhausted mind moved on in endless speculation, and his tired body was shaken to and fro by the movement of the carriage's iron-rimmed wheels over the uneven cobbles of High Holborn. As he thought about Guy he remembered his strange preoccupation with Praesepe, the misty cluster of faint stars that lay in the constellation of the sea-crab, Cancer.

Auguste had told him that her brother would recover. But Alexander knew, now, that Guy was dying.

XXXI

*Now sunk the Sun, now twilight sunk, and Night
Rode in her Zenith; nor a passing breeze
Sighed to the groves, which in the midnight air
Stood motionless.*

John Brown, 'Rhapsody' (1776)

The big carriage took Alexander at snail's pace all the way to Clerkenwell Green, past the pillory and the Watch House, then stopped at the entrance to the darkened alley beyond the church where his home lay. Alexander was ashamed, as he had not been before, of the narrow, dark-windowed little court, with its heaps of ancient detritus accumulated in damp corners, and the faint, pervading smell of the distillery; he imagined he felt Ralph's disapproving look on his back as he hurried along the lane and fumbled with the key to the peeling front door. Having made his way up the staircase as silently as he could, so as not to wake Hannah and her daughter, he carefully pushed open the door to the parlour and was surprised to see that the candles were still burning. 'Daniel?' he called out gently. 'Daniel?'

And then he realised, with a feeling of cold shock, that someone was sitting in the armchair over in the shadows by the window; someone who was watching him silently, expectantly. His half-brother Jonathan.

'What are you doing here?' Alexander whispered. 'What do you want?'

Jonathan got up slowly. His face had always been harsh and uncompromising; but Alexander saw a fresh kind of weariness now in the furrowed channels that ran from nose to jaw.

Jonathan said, 'You know as well as I why I am here. Now tell me what you've found out about the Montpelliers this evening.'

Alexander's first reaction was to wonder how he knew about his visit; but of course, Jonathan knew everything. Jonathan had watchers.

Alexander looked round the shadowy room in the grip of renewed fear. 'Where is Daniel?'

Jonathan walked swiftly over to the door and closed it. 'I sent the boy to bed. He's safe; which is more than I can say of you.' He placed himself in front of the door as if to prevent any escape. 'Are you playing games with me, Alexander? Why didn't you tell me you were going there again?'

'Because I didn't *know* I was going!'

Jonathan watched him narrowly. Disbelievingly.

'The doctor – Doctor Raultier – came to fetch me,' faltered Alexander, 'in a carriage. He arrived quite unexpectedly—' Breaking off, he drew out his crumpled handkerchief and mopped his brow. 'This is pointless, quite pointless, Jonathan. I've found out nothing, I tell you. We talked only of astronomy, and how can that possibly be of any importance to you?'

'You've met them,' said Jonathan. 'You've talked to them. I've told you before – I want to know everything about them, no matter how trivial the details might appear to you.'

'But this is a gross betrayal of trust . . .' Alexander's voice was shaking.

'*Trust?*' echoed Jonathan. 'What have any of them done to earn your trust, Alexander? I tell you, no one in that group of people is above suspicion – no one.'

'What do you mean?' Alexander's voice was still fearful. 'What are you accusing them of?'

'First answer my questions. Then I'll tell you.'

Alexander sat down slowly, suspiciously, on the edge of a seat. Jonathan remained standing. 'Did you meet Guy de Montpellier?'

'I met him briefly tonight, yes.'

'You said last time that he's sometimes ill. What's wrong with him?'

Alexander flinched and said in a low voice, 'I believe he has some disease of the brain. The symptoms of his illness can strike him suddenly, but can just as soon be gone.'

'So he's not house-bound? Not a cripple?'

'No. Sometimes you wouldn't even realise he was ill.'

'Does he take medicine for this malady?'

'Yes. The doctor prescribes it.'

'What is it? Some narcotic?'

'Laudanum, I think – but I can't be sure . . .'

'Does Guy de Montpellier sometimes take too much of this medicine? Does it affect his mind?'

'Sometimes,' replied Alexander hesitantly, 'he's confused by his illness.'

Jonathan's eyes burned into him. 'Does he ever speak of the star he's looking for as a woman?'

Alexander was stunned. Selene. It seemed as ominous as anything his brother had yet said that Jonathan knew this. *Sometimes I think of her as a woman with her tricks, her cunning . . .*

'Occasionally, yes,' he said. His voice was shaking again.

Jonathan began to pace the little room with his hands behind his back. He turned suddenly. 'Who else did you meet there?'

Alexander wondered when this ordeal was going to end. 'They have a friend who was once a priest . . .'

'The priest. Norland. You told me. Who else?'

'There's a man called Carline, William Carline.'

'He is English too? How long has he been with them?' He was still prowling the room as he asked his questions.

'I think, almost a year . . .'

Jonathan stopped. 'A year? Tell me about him.'

Alexander rubbed his furrowed forehead. 'He tends their telescopes, especially the lenses. They have to be protected, you see, and put away with the utmost care after each use; he has considerable knowledge of such things—'

'So he's a servant?'

'In a sense,' said Alexander tiredly. 'He's also Madame de Montpellier's lover.'

'And he's English? You've heard him speak?'

'No one has heard him speak.'

'No one?'

'He's mute, Jonathan. He was whipped out of the Navy for theft a year ago. The severity of his injuries caused his affliction. He came to the Montpelliers last July—'

'You're quite sure it was July?'

'Yes. They told me so. Raultier tried to treat him, but to no avail.'

In the silence that followed, the stench of the distillery seeped with fresh malice into the darkly panelled room. Jonathan closed his eyes, looking wretchedly tired again. 'What about the servants?' he asked at last.

Alexander spread his hands despairingly. 'There are some, of course. But I don't know anything about them. How could I?'

'Think, Alexander! If Guy de Montpellier wished to leave the house, if he wanted to go to the city, would he go alone, or would someone accompany him?'

Alexander felt a presentiment of alarm. 'There's Ralph,' he said. 'I almost forgot. Ralph is their coachman.'

Jonathan took a step forward, then stopped. 'Ralph. Ralph Wallace . . . *What does he look like?*'

'He is big, and quiet. He has a terrible scar down one cheek . . .'

And Jonathan was grinding one fist into the other, saying to himself, 'Not a hired coachman, then, but the Montpelliers' servant. Ah, how stupid I have been . . .' He turned abruptly back to Alexander. 'Tell me. What else do you know about this Ralph?'

Alexander hesitated; a mistake, because Jonathan moved quickly forward, like a hunter closing in on his quarry.

'Tell me,' he repeated, and Alexander, seeing the cold determination in his eyes, flinched and drew back.

'They told me,' he stammered, 'that once, many years ago, Ralph tried to murder his wife. He was sick in his mind, they said, and his wife had tormented him unbearably, and in fact, she did not die . . .'

Jonathan said quietly, intently, 'How did he try to kill her?'

'He attempted to strangle her.'

Jonathan bowed his head, as if in silent acknowledgement. Alexander waited, this time really afraid; and he said, when he could bear the silence no longer, 'You made a promise, Jonathan. You said that if I answered your questions, you would tell me what all this is about.'

Just for a moment Alexander thought Jonathan hadn't heard him, wasn't listening even; and then he looked up at last, and the expression in his tired blue eyes was one of almost inexpressible bleakness. 'I'm looking for a murderer,' he said.

Alexander let out a low cry of disbelief.

'Ellie's murderer,' went on Jonathan, his voice growing in intensity, 'and the killer of more girls, here, in London.'

'But what has this to do with the Montpelliers?'

'The last victim survived, Alexander. She told me that the man who lured her into the attack talked of the stars, and someone called Selene.'

Alexander shook his head. 'No . . .'

'Perhaps it was Guy – or someone working for him,' Jonathan continued, seeming to become conscious at last of his brother's distress. 'Whoever it was, this killer must be found, Alexander. He's being protected, but he must be stopped before he strikes again—'

He broke off as the door opened and Daniel came in, shivering. The boy looked first at Jonathan, then at Alexander, and whispered, 'I heard people shouting.'

Jonathan stepped back. Alexander went over to the boy quickly and drew him into the room. 'It's all right, Daniel. There's no need to be afraid.'

Jonathan had gone across to the open doorway. 'Alexander,' he said, 'you must promise me that you will find out more about these people. You must go again, tomorrow night.'

'*Tomorrow?* I cannot go again, so soon—'

'You must!' Jonathan took a step into the room, towards him; his voice was harsh, and Daniel started to whimper with fear. 'You must ask about Ralph, Alexander, and whether he always goes with Guy into London. Remember the girls.'

'All right,' said Alexander distractedly, putting his arm around the shivering Daniel. 'All right. Now please go . . .'

'Tomorrow,' repeated Jonathan. 'I'll be waiting to hear from you.' He turned at last and left the room.

Outside, the church bell tolled the hour. It was two in the morning. The flickering street lamps had been extinguished at midnight, and it was starting to rain, so the stars were extinguished too. Alexander gently told Daniel to go back to his bed; then he followed his brother down the stairs, so he could lock the door behind him. He heard the distant clatter of the night-soil men with their heavy cart, busy about the filthy but necessary task that ostracised them from the daylight, from the living world.

Alexander was still trembling. He would have given anything, at that moment, to have taken back what he had told Jonathan about Ralph. Ralph, a cold-blooded murderer? No, it couldn't be true.

Alexander owed Ralph no kindness, but he still felt pity for the man. His original crime was surely one born of private torment, not cold-blooded evil. He hoped that Jonathan's suspicions would founder, as they surely must, in the cold light of dawn. His brother was still distracted by grief over his lost daughter. He'd demanded that Alexander return to the Montpelliers tomorrow – but how could he intrude on them again, so soon?

He returned to his apartment and drew out the packet of papers that Raultier had given him earlier. He opened it and gazed at Guy's carefully inscribed recording of his sighting of Selene, in an effort to force the memory of Jonathan's intrusion from his mind. Here lay calm and beauty; here lay purpose. Folding the papers away reluctantly after a few precious moments of absorption, he resolved to start work on them tomorrow.

He began to move around the parlour, closing the curtains, straightening the chairs, extinguishing the few candles. But all the time, despite his efforts at calmness, his hands were shaking, because the man Jonathan suspected of murder had talked to his victims of the stars and Selene.

Alexander went to bed at last, trying to be quiet. Daniel was asleep again; but he awoke from a dream, and his eyes were wide with fright. 'It's all right, my dear. It's all right,' said Alexander, holding him in his arms. Daniel slept again. Alexander slept too, heavily and badly. He dreamed of Guy and Auguste; Auguste wore the red ribbon round her neck, and Guy's fingers lingered on the ornament with tenderness. Then Guy somehow became Ralph. His scarred face was twisted with some terrible emotion as his big hands tightened round the red ribbon and he began slowly, lovingly, to choke Auguste de Montpellier to death.

Alexander struggled up from the dream, his heavy body damp with sweat. He lay there for a long time as the rain beat against the window panes and fell on the cobbled street outside.

XXXII

No light, but rather darkness visible
Served only to discover sights of woe.

John Milton, *Paradise Lost* (1667), Book 1

It was raining still, at almost three in the morning, as Jonathan made his way on foot through Holborn, past Lincoln's Inn Fields and down Drury Lane to Covent Garden, where the night and the rain had brought no peace. The noise of music and gaming spilled even more loudly from the shacks and taverns of the Piazza, and drunken revellers, as if in defiance of the inclement weather, staggered from the portals of the Swan tavern at the corner of St Paul's church-yard to take advantage of the all-night hospitality of Tom King's coffee house, some falling on the way, or turning aside into the gutter to spew. There were prostitutes too, wet and bedraggled, still plying their trade.

Jonathan roamed the Piazza from Russell Street to King Street. He was looking for Rose. In the shadow of the church, a cluster of street-walkers had congregated, sheltering from the rain, laughing with one another, yet still ever-watchful for passing customers. He thought he saw someone in their midst, someone young with red hair, but when he drew near she had vanished.

And he was being watched. From amongst the crowd of whores a woman with a garishly painted face gave him a sidelong, assessing glance. 'Looking for something, mister?'

'Yes,' he said, agitated. 'Someone.'

'Don't be shy, now.' They all laughed.

He wiped the rain from his face with the back of his hand. 'You don't understand. I'm looking for a girl with red hair; I saw her here, just a moment ago—'

'Red hair? No redheads here, mister. But Moll will put on a wig if you like, or one of the girls will take you round by the churchyard where it's dark enough to pretend her hair's red, black, or whatever colour you fancy; would that do you, now?' They laughed, how they laughed.

'No,' Jonathan said, 'I'm looking for one girl in particular, her name is—' He broke off, and the sweat broke out on the palms of his hands, because he realised he'd nearly said his daughter's name. 'She is called Rose,' he managed at last.

An older woman dressed in ragged silk, who had bad teeth and sour breath, leaned close and said, 'Shove off, mister. If you're not here for business, then make way for those who are.'

Jonathan drew back, dazed, into the darkness. A crowd of drunken apprentices swaggered by, almost knocking him over. He backed up against the church wall to steady himself.

Though it would soon be dawn, there was no night-time peace for the people who made their living here: the all-night tavern keepers, the food sellers, the man over by the hummums who peddled his obscene prints to the leering drunkards who loitered at his stall; no respite for the pale-faced bawds who paced past the shacks of the Piazza with increasing desperation, their thin clothes soaked, their hair like rats' tails, looking for a shilling for the next day's food; no sleep, till the market men arrived with the coming of dawn to set up their stalls. Only then would Covent Garden's night-time inhabitants vanish like wraiths in the wan light, to snatch what sleep they could before preparing to offer the next night's requisite pleasure, or oblivion.

Jonathan went into Tom King's for coffee, and some of yesterday's bread. The people in here were subdued, lost between night and day. The coffee tasted vile to him, but it was strong, and he felt his weary senses reviving.

He paid his bill, and left Covent Garden to turn down Henrietta Street towards the Strand. Peace had enveloped the city as dawn broke. A cold mist was curling up from the river, and the earliest of risers were already about their business: the water carriers, the coalmen, the market-men bringing in their produce. And there were people like himself, ill-shaven, in crumpled clothes, who had not yet been to bed, but were now furtively hurrying along the streets with collars turned up, as if ashamed to be caught by the daylight.

Whitehall was deserted, except for the sparrows in the yard, and the porter on duty, who bade Jonathan a curious good morning as he paused in his sweeping of the steps before Montague House to hold the door open for him. 'You're first in this morning, Mr Absey, sir,' he commented cheerfully. 'Even Mr King isn't here yet, and he's an early bird, if ever there was one.'

'Yes,' Jonathan said. He hurried up the stairs to his office, pulling his keys from his pocket as he went along the corridor. Clumsy with tiredness, he unlocked his door and went in, then hunted for the key to the drawer where he'd locked the letter to Titius before leaving work yesterday.

It took him some time to register that the drawer he had locked it in was, after all, not locked; and even longer to accept that the letter had gone.

Jonathan searched every corner of the room for his letter, and found nothing. Nothing else was missing. He went downstairs again to find the porter, to ask him who else had keys to his room, and who might have the keys to his desk. The porter had been joined by the day man, who would shortly relieve him of his duties; and together they came up to Jonathan's room and listened to him almost pityingly as he explained how he had found his drawer unlocked. To him their eyes seemed to linger on the couch by the wall, where Rose had swept his papers to the floor and reached out for him.

He wondered if perhaps the sharp odour of his lust still lingered in here, even after four days. He thought he saw the porters glancing at each other slyly as Jonathan, his clothes and hair still damp from the rain, asked his questions. They told him that although they had access to all the rooms in Montague House except those of the Chief Clerk and the Under-Secretary – he could see the keys for himself, behind the porter's desk in the lobby – no one else should hold the keys to a private desk. Oh, no, Mr Absey, sir. Never that.

'So something's missing, sir?' asked the day porter.

Jonathan hesitated. 'I'm not sure.'

'You should report it, sir.'

They made various other suggestions which they thought helpful, until Jonathan thanked them for their assistance and told them they could go. They nodded sympathetically and left him alone in his room.

Jonathan took off his wet coat and hung it on the back of the door.

The grey morning light seeped into his room. He sat down at his desk and rested his head in his hands. Someone must have stolen the letter. But who? Who even knew that he had it in his possession?

The port agent at Dover knew that he had it. The agent had sent it to him mistakenly, thinking that Jonathan still dealt with intercepted foreign mail. The messenger who brought it to Jonathan knew. Apart from that, he had shown it only to his brother, who would have no idea of its significance. But significant it must be; at least he could be sure of that now, because someone had gone to the trouble of stealing it.

Who? Raultier's masters?

Whoever it was would know, at the very least, that Jonathan had it, and should not have had it. He tried to imagine the expression on John King's face if he should try to report its loss to the Under-Secretary, as the day porter had so cheerfully suggested.

'It was a list of stars, bright stars, sir. But I think it was in some sort of code.'

'How did you come to be in possession of this letter, Absey?'

'It was delivered to a smuggler in Dover, for dispatch to Paris, sir. It was intercepted by the port agent.'

'Foreign mail, then. It should have gone to Connolly, surely?'

Silence.

'You entered it, of course, Absey, in the book of intercepted mails, and copied it, and sent it for examination?'

'No, I didn't, sir.'

'Why not, Absey?'

Silence again.

'I think you had better explain yourself, Absey. Explain yourself . . .'

And Jonathan, exhausted, rested his head heavily on his arms, with King's imaginary and unanswerable questions ringing in his ears.

He'd fallen asleep. When he awoke, his limbs were stiff and cramped. Daylight was pouring into his room, and through the window he could see the sun shining between broken clouds. He glanced in agitation at his watch: it was past ten o'clock. A true sign of his new insignificance here, he thought bleakly, that he could sleep at his desk for so long, and not be missed. But someone was thumping with some vigour at his door now. He struggled to his feet and tried to straighten his crumpled coat, just as the door opened and one of the clerks came in carrying letters. The clerk, who was called Ellis, pulled up abruptly when he saw him.

'Dear God, Absey. You look as though you've spent the night at your desk.'

Jonathan made an attempt at a smile. 'I was in rather early. Perhaps I'd better go home and change my clothes.'

Ellis nodded, still watching him curiously. Then he started to leaf through the letters he carried, singling out those for Jonathan. 'Here you are,' he said. 'Quite a few for you this morning.'

But Jonathan ignored him. There was something other than letters, or a change of clothes, on his mind; something that had only just occurred to him.

He'd realised some time ago that he was being followed. And now someone had broken into his office to steal the letter. Perhaps the theft was intended to let him know he was still under surveillance; a warning to him to leave the Montpelliers and their circle alone.

The warnings to others were not so subtle. Prostitutes were dying when they got too near to the truth. Should he be prepared for more direct intimidation? Even physical assault? His mind raced on: perhaps such action would not be aimed at him, because of his position, but there were others who were close to him, and more vulnerable than he. Mary. *Thomas* . . .

Without a word he pushed past the startled clerk, ran down the stairs and out into the now-crowded courtyard. He hesitated a moment, looking up to the end of Whitehall where the hackneys waited for trade, but then turned and walked at a swift pace down to Whitehall Stairs and the river, where he hailed a boat to Chelsea. The Thames was crowded with ferries and barges, but he offered the waterman good money, and they made swift progress upstream. Jonathan jumped out of the boat at the ramshackle jetty near the old porcelain factory almost before the vessel had a chance to draw alongside, then made his way quickly along Cheyne Walk in the shade of the old elms. As he drew nearer to the place where Mary and Thomas lived he saw that the door of the cottage was closed and the shutters were drawn against the sun.

He stopped by the front gate, and found that his stomach was knotted with tension. He rebuked himself for being foolish. Perhaps they were out, and he'd wasted his time over some stupid, nameless fear bred of a sleepless night. He remembered that it was the servant's day off; Mary had probably taken their son to the market, or perhaps they'd gone along the river bank to watch the boats.

He walked more slowly up the path, and found the silence overwhelming. Once more he felt the chill touch of fear. Trying the door and finding it unlocked, he went in, calling out his arrival, and discovered his wife and son in the parlour at the back of the house, in the near darkness; the window was small and the sun hardly shone in here. At first he felt relief that they were here, together. But he saw straight away that Mary had been crying. Thomas, his childlike, giant son, was curled up in a chair beside her, long limbs askew, with tears in his eyes too, and his thumb in his mouth, and fresh bandaging adorning both his wrists and his hands.

Jonathan began, 'For God's sake—' but Mary was getting up from her chair, hurrying him tensely into the tiny front room, where she shut the door and said, in a low voice that pierced him raw,

'Enough. Enough of all this. Does the boy have to suffer too? Doesn't he already have enough to bear by being so alone, an object of scorn, of fear, of contempt?'

Jonathan shook his head. 'I don't understand. Tell me what's happened.'

'Very well. Your son, Jonathan, your sixteen-year-old son, who would not hurt even a flea, and who only wants people to love him, was outside in the sun, playing, looking for flowers, as he does, when some men came by and offered to take him to the fair—'

'You were with him? You saw them?'

She looked wearier than he had ever seen her. 'How can I be with him, every single moment of the day? He is sixteen. I cannot hold his hand any more, and put him in his cradle, and sing him to sleep. I was fetching eggs, for our meal. I was as quick as I could be, but when I got back, he was gone. I searched everywhere. He came stumbling down the road, a little over an hour ago, and – and . . .'

'What had they done to him?' He gripped her arms, almost hurting her; but she didn't even seem to notice.

'They burnt him, Jonathan. His arms, his hands. He says they held his arms over a brazier, until he screamed. He thought they were taking him to the fair, and they did that to him . . .'

'Dear God.' His throat was almost closed with shock.

'Oh, it will heal. The skin is blistered only; I have soothed the worst with ointments, and bandaged him.'

He breathed, 'Why? Why did they do this?'

She gazed up at him. 'At first, I thought it was mere cruelty. As boys will stone a stricken animal. But they gave him a message, Jonathan. They made him recite it as they held him over the fire. They told him to tell his father to stop asking so many questions. You understand? To stop asking so many questions . . .'

He let her go then, and went blindly into the back room where his son, taller than he was, knuckled tears from his eyes and whimpered with pain and unhappiness that such things could happen.

Jonathan went towards him, to touch his hair, his cheek, to comfort him in whatever way he could; but the boy flinched from him. His eyes were wide with accusation, with the disbelief that his father had not been there to stop all this.

Just as Jonathan had not been there to help Ellie.

'Stop – asking questions,' Thomas whispered. 'Stop asking questions.'

Jonathan left them, his mind numb with horror, now that all his worst fears had been realised. He took a boat back to Whitehall, and made arrangements privately, and paid heavily, for men that he trusted to keep a secret watch on Mary and Thomas and their house. After that he went back to Brewer Street.

In the desk at his lodgings were the pieces of paper on which he had attempted to make some sense of the missive from Dover. He drew them all together and began to attempt to recreate the lost letter to Titius, because he knew now that it must be important, even if he didn't understand why. Yet even as he laboriously tried to reconstruct the list of star names and numbers from his jotted notes, he realised the futility of his actions; no one would believe him without the original.

No letter, no proof. Now he had nothing with which to point an accusing finger at the Montpelliers. Someone in the government,

perhaps in Montague House itself, knew it too. They had delivered
their warning. They had told him that the Montpelliers, though they
harboured a murderer in their midst, were above the law, above
vengeance; and any further interference on his part would destroy him
and what remained of his family.

XXXIII

To Mr Alexander Wilmot.
 I beg to inform you that I am terminating our arrangement viz. my daughter's singing lessons. Of late she has not made the progress I would have expected of someone of her undoubted talent and capabilities.
 Consequently I have engaged another teacher for her.

The letter was signed with a flourish by the domineering mother of Charlotte, the pupil who was memorable only for her utter inability to recognise whether or not the notes she sang were in tune. Alexander read it, then crumpled the letter up and threw it away. He had received other dismissals like this recently.

Alexander knew that all this was his own fault. He had allowed other matters to distract him; he had neglected his musical duties. Soon his only source of income would be the meagre stipend from the church.

Three days had passed since his journey to the Montpelliers' house and his meeting with Guy. Three days since Jonathan's visit, and Jonathan's ultimatum that he must go back there and find out more, about Ralph; but how could he, when he had yet to finish his work on Guy's calculations, and had no excuse to contact the French astronomers until he had done so?

It had rained hard all yesterday and today, and was unseasonably cold for the end of June. After dealing with the letter from Charlotte's mother, Alexander donned his well-worn coat, thinking to himself that if Kepler's theory regarding the planets and their influence on the weather had any roots in reality, then this inclement day could most surely be blamed on the ominous conjunction of the sun and Saturn. He made his way doggedly through the rain to the church, to prac-tise the organ for evensong. Afterwards, deciding against a cab because of the expense, he braved the elements once more, and walked just over a mile to the river: the rain was sweeping across the grey expanse of the Thames and lashing it into spume so that the boundary between air and water was indistinguishable.

With rain dripping from his coat and hat, Alexander entered the reception hall of the Royal Society's rooms in Somerset House, and asked if there was any acknowledgement yet of the package he had sent to Pierre Laplace. The clerk examined a pigeonhole full of mail and replied, 'There's nothing for you here, Mr Wilmot.'

'Could you perhaps confirm for me that the package has at least been dispatched?' Alexander asked anxiously. 'I was warned, you see, that there might be some delay.'

The clerk checked his record book. 'It's gone all right, sir. It should be well on its way by now.'

Alexander thanked him and left.

He went home again and shut himself in his study, and began to read once more the notes that Guy had made about his sighting of the lost planet. But his good eye ached in the flickering light of the candle, and try as he would to concentrate, he seemed able to think of nothing but Jonathan and his questions, which had brought the night of his visit to the Montpelliers to such a jarring close. Every time he heard footsteps in the lane outside he was afraid it was his brother, come to remind him of his promise to go back there – a promise he had failed to keep.

He turned back to Guy's papers, and read a little more. He found himself, in fierce self-doubt, regretting that he too was playing a part in raising the sick young man's hopes to an almost painful degree of expectancy.

The rain continued, all that day and during the night also, so that he was unable to go up on to the roof and watch the stars. He continued to work almost despairingly through Guy's figures, but his spirits were low.

The following day, he returned from his duties at the church to learn from Daniel that someone had called – not Jonathan, but a messenger with a package for him. He opened it, and found that it contained a letter from Auguste de Montpellier and a purse full of coins.

He held the letter up to the light. *'My dear Monsieur Wilmot,'* he read. *'We trust that you are making good progress with Guy's figures. I hope this money will help a little with your expenses. If you need more, please contact Doctor Raultier at his lodgings in Eagle Street. Guy believes that his lost star is due to appear again, very soon.'*

Alexander opened the purse. It contained ten guineas. A little shaken by the generosity of the amount, he read the letter again. 'They still want my help,' he said to himself. 'They still trust me. They are my friends.'

Once more he shut himself in his study and continued his work on the notes that Guy had made. Guy's writing was swift, careless, brilliant, like his mind; he had jotted down sightings, positions, and the relative brightnesses of the nearby stars with the ardour of someone possessed.

Alexander found himself, this time, catching Guy's fervour as if it were infectious. His lingering doubts and worries about his brother were all for the moment dispelled. He went to fetch his own figures, of the sightings he himself had made. Two observations alone had not been enough to allow him to plan even a conjectural orbit. But with Guy's figures as well, he had something of substance to work on.

His mild face radiant with hope, he began the final search for Selene.

XXXIV

*Astronomers are as able as other men to discern that
gold can glitter as well as stars.*

Fanny Burney, Letter, 1788

It was the last day of June, and bright sunshine had driven away
the lingering rain. Jonathan was not at his desk as he ought to
have been, sifting through sheaves of paper for plots and rumours
of insurrection. Instead he was out on the streets again, looking for
Rose. He was afraid that someone would try to kill her, and that this
time they would not fail.

Since his visit six days ago to his brother in Clerkenwell – from
whom he'd heard nothing whatsoever since his ultimatum, another
failure to which he must shortly turn his attention – he'd spent the
nights struggling by candlelight to reconstruct the Dover letter from
his scraps of notes; and the days – whenever he could get away from
his desk – searching for Rose, just as obsessively as he'd once looked
for his lost daughter. And just before noon that morning he saw her
at last on the corner of King Street, hovering in the scant noontide
shadows of an abandoned hovel with her flowers clutched tightly in
her hands. Something about her pale, waif-like face, her bruised-
looking blue eyes, made him think of Ellie. For a moment he was not
able to speak, to move.

When she saw him, her demeanour altered instantly. She put one
hand on her hip and gazed up at him, her eyes slanting in speculative challenge. 'Well,' she said. 'Mister Absey. Come looking for me,
have you?'

'Yes,' he said a little hoarsely, because his throat was parched from
the heat. 'I've been looking for you. Where have you been?'

She laughed. 'My, my. You must have fond memories. Wouldn't
another girl have done for you?'

'No,' he said quickly, 'you don't understand. I was worried about
you, when I couldn't find you—'

'You needn't worry about me, mister.' She was watching him curiously. 'I've been busy these last few days, that's all. There's been lots of timber boats coming in down at the wharves. Plenty of sailors, plenty of easy trade.'

Her gown was slipping from her thin shoulders. Jonathan could see the curve of her small breasts, and he remembered how warm her flesh had been against his hands.

He said, 'I need to talk to you again, Rose.'

'Jesus.' She looked disappointed. 'Talk? What about?'

Jonathan tried desperately to find the words. He had planned what he was to say, but now all he could think of was the mockery in her young eyes. And her loose gown had fallen further from her shoulders, surely, for now he could glimpse the tip of one tender nipple. He struggled blindly for control. 'There are some questions I must ask you. Is there somewhere private we can go?'

'Oh, yes. Plenty of private places, Mister Absey.' She laughed at him openly then, as if she already knew of the tumult in his breeches. She took him down one of the dark little alleys behind the church, where the beggars had made their lean-to night shelters. It was filthy round here; the noonday heat nourished the ripe stench of dung from the draymen's horses and the rotting, discarded fruits. But as she moistened her lips with her darting pink tongue, and glanced up at him speculatively, in truth he forgot to notice such things.

She seemed agitated, almost feverish for the business to be under way; and so their coupling was correspondingly swift, there in the stinking shadows where no one could see them. She steadied herself against the wall and wrapped her arms around his neck as he fumbled with her skirts; she uttered soft little cries as he took her, whether in a feigned or real transport of pleasure Jonathan couldn't tell. Afterwards he moved back from her, avoiding her eyes. His limbs and his body were for the moment almost overwhelmed with heaviness.

She let her skirts fall back around her legs and watched him as he adjusted his clothes. 'Like an eager lad, Mister Absey,' she grinned. 'A green, hungry lad.'

He wondered whether she would expect him to pay her. *Of course she will*, he chided himself, *she's a whore, money is what she is here for.* Nevertheless he was bitterly ashamed of his own eagerness, and all he could think of, for a moment, was the almost childlike fragrance of her skin.

He said hoarsely, 'I am sorry. I did not come here for that.'

'Jesus, mister. Don't apologise. It's when you fail that you apologise. Don't you know that?'

He drew a deep breath. What was happening to him? He had allowed himself to be carried away by lust, when this girl was in danger of her life, and murderers roamed free. He dragged his eyes away from the pale gleam of her breasts, which she still had not covered, and said with an effort,

'I came to ask you some questions, Rose, about the night you were attacked. Do you think you would recognise the Frenchman who paid for your company?'

She buttoned up her bodice at last and watched him quizzically. 'My, but you have a quaint way with words, Mister Absey. Yes, I would. He was younger than you, for a start; much younger, in fact. Dark-haired, dark-eyed; maybe a little on the thin side, but handsome enough, and vigorous too, with all a girl could wish for nestling between his thighs—'

Jonathan said tightly, 'For God's sake. How can you joke about it? You were nearly killed!'

She shrugged her shoulders, and he thought again how young, how young she was, to have forgotten so soon.

'I've told you,' she said. 'It wasn't him who tried to kill me.'

Jonathan said, in a low voice, 'That's exactly why I wanted to speak to you. Tell me again. I want to be sure. Why couldn't it have been him?'

'Because the man who attacked me spoke,' said Rose, 'and his voice wasn't the same as the Frenchman's. Besides – and I told you this as well – the Frenchman walked on down the street after he'd finished with me, and got into a carriage. The driver was perched up on his seat, waiting for him. He was so big. He had a scowling face. And he was scarred, all down one cheek. I shan't ever forget how he was watching me . . .' She shivered.

Jonathan said carefully, 'Did you actually see this carriage leave?'

'Yes. I saw it go, with the Frenchman inside. It had stopped close by the Unicorn tavern, for the young man to get in. Then it had to move off slowly down Henrietta Street because of all the people there watching the Punch and Judy show.' She shivered again. 'I was watching that brute of a driver whip up his horses when I felt the cord go round my neck.'

Jonathan felt her words hit him one by one. 'You're quite sure?'

She shrugged. 'Of course.'

So the scarred coachman Ralph couldn't be the murderer. It couldn't be as he'd conjectured: that Guy and Ralph were working together, with Guy luring the prostitutes into the darkness, and his coachman killing them in some strange, sick ritual. But if he was honest with himself, he'd never held out much hope for this solution anyway; because hadn't Rose told him, at his first meeting with her, that she'd watched both men leaving, in the coach?

Rose was biting her lower lip and frowning at her memories; her bravado and apparent unconcern had only been a front. Jonathan reached out to touch her arm.

'You risked much for that paltry shilling you were given.'

She gazed up at him in defiance now, pushing a stray red-gold curl back from her cheek.

'Not a shillin', mister,' she said almost with pride. 'Oh, no. It was a fistful of gold, French gold. But it was thieved from me, see, by the man who tried to kill me; I just had one coin left, deep in my pocket, and I wasn't going to tell anyone about that.'

He stepped back, stunned again. 'But you said he gave you a shilling . . . Where's this gold now? Do you still have it?'

She looked up at him with scorn. 'Jesus Christ, can I live off a piece of gold? Can I eat it, can I sleep on it? No. I changed it, didn't I, down at Clare Market, for silver.'

French gold. *Louis d'or*, the currency of spymasters. Someone had followed Guy, to kill the girls and snatch it back . . .

'This gold,' he said tensely, 'can you remember anything about it? Can you remember what was engraved on it?'

Rose was gathering up her flowers now, smoothing down her skirt. 'You ask me some strange questions,' she said. 'Talking about money, are you going to pay me, mister, or what?'

He fumbled in his pockets and handed her all the coins he had. 'The gold,' he repeated urgently.

She was looking around restlessly, anxious to be on her way. 'Well, now,' she said. 'I remember a man's head. And on the other side . . .' She paused.

'Yes?'

'There was an angel,' she said slowly. 'An angel, writing.'

The world stood still for Jonathan. *Republican gold* . . .

Rose was watching him curiously, waiting. He asked her at last, 'So you had this coin on the first night I spoke to you?'

Again she looked defiant. 'Oh, yes. It was in my pocket. But I wasn't going to show it to you, was I?'

She was already turning to go; he caught her arm, but she shrugged him off. 'Enough,' she said. 'Leave me alone. I have money to earn.'

Jonathan walked back to his room in Montague House, and looked immediately through his incoming mail to see if there was anything yet from the decipherer Morrow, to whom he'd written yet again in desperation because there was no one else he could think of turning to for help in the matter of the Titius letter; but there was nothing, and nothing either from Alexander. He swept the letters aside. As he stood there the walls of his small room seemed to be closing in on him, stifling him. All he could think of now was what Rose had told him about the gold coin with the angel on it.

If Raultier was sending coded letters not to the Royalist Agency, not to fellow scientists, but to the Republican government in Paris, then, indeed, the killing of the girls – Jonathan's daughter amongst them – would be a necessity. They would have to be silenced, because the gold Guy de Montpellier bestowed on them so indiscreetly in his drug-induced confusion could be vital evidence that the Montpellier circle concealed an enemy spy.

And yet Raultier was proscribed by the Republicans, and under sentence of death if he ever returned to Paris . . .

Jonathan's mind was in turmoil. He had no proof of anything; the letter had gone, Rose's gold had gone.

But he had to act.

He went downstairs, and headed along the main corridor to the Chief Clerk's room. He knocked on the imposing door, but there was no reply. Jonathan stood in the ante-room, looking out of the window at the government clerks and porters bustling to and fro in the court-yard outside.

The Most Secret files, for the attention of the Under-Secretary, were kept in this room, locked in a cabinet. The records relating to the Brittany expedition would be in there. Jonathan wondered what was happening to the French Royalist troops, who had sailed in such high hopes for the coast of France. They should have landed by now; messages bearing news of victory or disaster might already be on their way to London.

The Chief Clerk, Pollock, came in briskly. He saw Jonathan and halted.

'Absey. You've not been spending much time here lately. I thought you were ill.'

'There were some private matters I was forced to attend to, sir. I'll make up for my absences, of course.'

Pollock nodded. 'Good. I was looking for you this morning. I wanted some of your files, on those troublemakers in Chiswick; they've been printing seditious leaflets full of all the usual sorts of nonsense, which are turning up at the dockyards. Do you know the people I mean?'

'Yes, sir. I'll look the files out for you straight away.'

'Do that.' He made to go into his room, then realised Jonathan was still waiting. 'Was there something you wanted, Absey?'

'I need to speak to you in private, sir.'

Pollock ushered Jonathan inside and closed the door. 'Well?' He looked harassed, and not pleased at this demand on his time.

Jonathan took a deep breath, aware that he'd almost exhausted his old mentor's patience. He knew that he was staking his career on what he was about to say; he knew, too, that he had no choice. He said, 'I came into possession of a confidential paper a while ago, sir, addressed to someone in Paris. I have reason to believe it contains a message to the Republicans, sent by a French agent in London.'

Pollock's expression changed from harassment to horror. 'Where is it now?'

Jonathan swallowed hard. 'I haven't got it any longer, sir. It's been stolen.'

Pollock's face tightened. 'Stolen? Who by?'

'I don't know. But I think it was probably someone who was trying to protect the spy—'

'So you've no longer got this letter. But surely you registered it? Surely you made a copy in the record books?'

'No, sir. I didn't get the chance.'

'What was in the letter?'

'It looked like a list of stars. But I think it was in some sort of code.'

'Stars,' said Pollock. 'Stars. How did this letter come into your possession?'

'It was intercepted by the port agent at Dover. It was being sent privately, in a suspicious manner . . .'

'When was this?'

'A couple of weeks ago, sir.'

'So it was addressed to Paris, and it was intercepted by the port agent. Why didn't it go to Connolly? Connolly was handling foreign mail by then, surely?'

'I know, sir, but there were other suspicious circumstances connected with the letter, and I thought it best if I handled it . . .' Jonathan was struggling now.

'Handled it? You mean *lost* it?'

'It was stolen, from my desk.' Jonathan pressed on, but already he could see the trust in which this man used to hold him dissolving into blank anger. 'There's something going on, sir,' he continued. 'I think I'm on the trail of something important, something sinister. I've not spoken to anyone else about it. There's a French spy involved, I'm sure, who's paid with Republican gold, and girls are being killed, to cover his trail . . .'

His voice faded away as he registered Pollock's incredulous expression.

'Have you any evidence? Can you show me this gold?'

Jonathan hesitated. 'No. But—'

'Enough,' Pollock interrupted him, waving his hand in dismissal. 'You've no gold, and you've no letter. I've heard enough. I used to think I could rely on you, Absey. I've always defended you, as one of my strongest men. But here we all are, with riots breaking out in the heart of London in support of these damned revolutionaries; here we are, waiting for news of the vital expedition to Brittany, and I find you, who surely must have enough work waiting on your desk after your frequent absences, telling me about mythical gold, and some letter, some list of stars; you don't know what it says, and you can't even produce it!'

'Sir—'

'Enough, I said. These absences of yours, these stories I keep hearing about you interviewing tavern landlords and prostitutes, are making me wonder.'

Jonathan thought, *How does he know?*

'And as for your drinking, Absey! Is that why you fall asleep at your desk? You interview street-girls in your room; you dig out files in Middle Scotland Yard that are none of your business; you lurk around the Alien Office asking obscure questions; and meanwhile your real work lies unattended on your desk. I suggest that you go and deal with it! And before you do anything else, bring me your file about those damned Chiswick radicals who'd have our naval yards in a state of mutiny, will you? That is, if you haven't lost it.'

Jonathan said desperately, 'Sir. I know where some of the gold is. There was a girl killed, just over two weeks ago, called Georgiana Howes. She'd been given some of this gold, by one of the spying group, and four coins were found by her body. I asked about it at the Bow Street office, where the murder was reported, and the constable there told me the gold had been locked away, in the care of the Home Office. It's Republican gold, sir, I'm sure of it, being used to pay the spy who sent the Dover letter —'

Pollock listened to his story with weary resignation. 'Very well,' he said after a pause, 'very well, I'll make some enquiries and I'll get back to you.'

Jonathan went slowly back to his office. He called up a messenger to deliver to Pollock the file he'd asked for; and then he waited.

He didn't have to wait long. Less than an hour later he was summoned to Pollock's room, and Jonathan could tell instantly from his expression what had happened.

'There was no gold,' said the Chief Clerk heavily, 'French or otherwise. There was nothing at all in the records of this girl's death that hinted at any kind of coins at all being found on her body.'

Jonathan knew, then, that it was useless to go on. He listened, dazed, as Pollock muttered something about how sorry they'd all been about his daughter, and how her death must have affected him worse than they'd thought; and that perhaps some consideration should be given to a further lightening of his duties.

'No!' said Jonathan. 'I'm all right. I can still do everything that's asked of me.'

Pollock ran his hand through his hair in a gesture of exasperation. 'Then do something useful instead of roaming the streets, will you? Check on this dockyard business for me; visit the places yourself; see just how far these seditious leaflets have spread.'

'Yes. Yes, I will, sir.'

Pollock turned on his heel and left. Jonathan returned to his office, knowing that now his career must be in jeopardy; for once a clerk lost the trust of his superiors, his usefulness was virtually at an end.

He began to deal with his backlog of paperwork by delegating most of it to a junior clerk who was eager for promotion. At five he left his office, walked down to the riverside, and went by boat to Chelsea. He took Thomas for a long walk along the sand and shingle of the river's edge; then he made his son a windmill out of twigs and feathers, and they sat on a half-ruined jetty watching the boats together till twilight fell.

XXXV

Thoughts speculative, their unsure hopes relate;
But certain issue, strokes must arbitrate.

William Shakespeare, *Macbeth*, V. iv

'**A**chernar,' said Jonathan slowly, writing as he spoke. 'Acrux. Adhara. Agena, Aldebaran, Altair – what next? What comes next? Antares. Yes, Antares . . .'

It was five days since his interview with Pollock. He'd been away from London, briefly, because he'd done as the Chief Clerk ordered and gone himself, first to the Woolwich arsenal, and then to the naval dockyard at Chatham, to make enquiries about the circulation of the seditionary leaflets. The business at Woolwich was dealt with swiftly enough, but his errand to Chatham had necessitated an uncomfortable journey by coach, followed by an even more uncomfortable stay in an inn close to the dockyard that Jonathan suspected of harbouring fleas; and it was with little hope of achieving anything that Jonathan spoke the next day to the commissioner and senior officers at the yard, who promised to be vigilant but knew as well as he that these places, with their low-paid, often transitory staff, were hotbeds of simmering discontent whose inhabitants could easily be stirred into more active kinds of troublemaking.

He showed the officers the leaflet, which began, '*Men of England! Why labour to fulfil the ambitions of tyrants? Why build and arm the ships that only serve to increase the power of the German king George who sits on our English throne?*' And he told them to be on their guard against traitors.

He travelled back to London overnight, and discovered he had developed a feverish cold that did little to improve his spirits. Deciding without much difficulty against making the long journey in person to the other naval dockyards, he struggled into work next morning to the accompaniment of a streaming nose and hacking cough. There he wrote to the port commissioners at the Plymouth and Portsmouth dockyards, enclosing copies of the broadsheet and urging them to be watchful; and by the evening he was once more sitting at his desk at his lodgings in Brewer Street with the detritus of careless living scattered around him – dirty plates, dirty linen, half-finished glasses of wine. He was making patterns of the stars.

He had succeeded at last in recreating the Titius letter from his copied notes. He was putting the names of the stars into alphabetical order, and slowly, unsurprisingly, facing the conclusion that the process left him no wiser than before. Earlier he had tried listing the constellations in which each star lay, picking out for special attention those stars for which the magnitudes given were wrong; but still he was aware of no revelation, no startling moment of comprehension.

He had made no plans for the remainder of the evening. His landlady, who lived in rooms below his, had knocked at his door earlier to see if he required supper. She seemed anxious about him; she glanced swiftly round his room and told him he looked ill, but Jonathan waved her away. He found he had no appetite for food; just the hunger to be done with this star letter once and for all.

He wanted to confront his daughter's killer. But how could he get any closer to him when the circle in which he moved was so powerfully protected – even though Jonathan suspected this very same circle might be harbouring a spy who was deceiving his British masters?

All official sources of help – Home Office files, police records – were closed to him. All he had was the letter – and even that was only a copy. In an effort to uncover its meaning he had played with all the patterns he could think of, both letters and numbers; he had composed squares, and shifted columns, just as he had seen the Decipherer doing in his methodical, painstaking way; but he could not discover the method of encryption. There must be a key, and without it the letter was indecipherable.

Lucket came to his door just after eight, wearing a newly acquired, no doubt second-hand tan coat with pewter buttons that was a little too big for him. He looked excited, and full of self-importance. Jonathan waited.

'I've come about the French doctor, sir,' Lucket said. 'Doctor Raultier. The one who lives in Eagle Street.'

Jonathan blew his nose and sat up.

'You asked me to listen out for any further news of him, sir. Well,

I've just found out that he's acquainted with Monsieur Prigent, the Jersey man!'

This time Jonathan got up quickly from his desk. Some of his papers fluttered, unheeded, to the floor. Prigent. The Channel Islands agent, the Comte de Puisaye's assistant, who had spent some time recently here in London, was now on his way to France.

Jonathan was learning, if nothing else, to be wary of reaching for conclusions too quickly. He said to Lucket, 'Both the men you speak of are Frenchmen, both Bretons too. That they should know one another isn't remarkable.' Lucket looked crestfallen. Jonathan said more gently, 'Tell me more. Tell me how you know this.'

Lucket shrugged. 'Oh, I've been asking around, sir, about the French doctor. On the streets.'

Jonathan nodded. He knew that Lucket, and others like him, had their own private networks – some honest, some not so – for sharing and imparting information, at a price. 'Go on.'

'Someone,' went on Lucket, his pride bubbling up again in pleasure at his own performance, whatever his master thought of it; 'someone I know, who works – in a manner of speaking – at the market in White Cross Street, told me the French doctor from Eagle Street was seen around two weeks ago, calling in at the apothecary's in Bunhill Row, well away from his usual patch in Holborn. So I called in there myself with my friend, and managed to look at the apothecary's list of prescriptions. He has to write everything up carefully, you see, the amounts, the medicines, like all apothecaries are supposed to do—'

Jonathan nodded. 'I know. What I don't understand is why any apothecary would let you see such a list.'

At least Lucket had the grace to blush. He scratched his head and said, shrugging, 'My pal distracted him. He grabbed some bottles from the counter – nothing of great value, sir – and ran off down Chiswell Street. The apothecary ran after him, howling with rage, and so I helped myself to his book of prescriptions. I didn't steal it. I just borrowed it for an hour or two, and then I popped it back, when he wasn't looking.'

Jonathan wished he had never asked. He should have known by now that many of his lanky assistant's tactics were better left uninvestigated. 'And?' he prompted.

'There was a note of a prescription, sir, ordered by the French doctor,

Raultier, for Monsieur Noel-François Prigent –' he pronounced the name with considerable care – 'who had lodgings in Black Raven Court, off Chiswell Street. He's not there now, though. I checked.'

'He's set sail for France, with the rest of them,' said Jonathan. 'But Raultier made out a prescription for him? You're quite sure?'

'Quite sure, sir!' Lucket was becoming happier with the response he was eliciting. 'I had plenty of time to read it.'

'Was there a date on this prescription?'

'Yes, sir. The 15th of June.'

So Raultier met up with Prigent just two days before the expedition set sail.

Jonathan knew that Prigent had been a minor intelligence agent for some time. Lately he'd heard other things about Prigent. He had been captured by the Republicans on one of his missions last December, and held near Lorient for almost three months. But he had been released, and there had been rumours ever since that Prigent might be a double agent. The rumours were only whispered, because Prigent still retained the confidence of Puisaye, and Windham in the Cabinet, and other important supporters of the Royalist cause. But even so, the doubts lingered.

And now Lucket was telling him that Raultier had visited Prigent, and prescribed medicine to him. What else had occurred during that meeting?

He swung round to face the expectant Lucket. 'I think we'd better pay a visit to Eagle Street, you and I.'

Lucket grinned. 'I thought you might say that, sir. In fact I came past Monsieur Raultier's lodgings on my way here. And I saw the doctor go out. He took his horse – he keeps it stabled close by, at the White Boar Inn – and he had his doctor's bag with him. But he might be back by now—'

Jonathan was already pulling on his coat. 'Oh, I hope not,' he said softly.

Evidence. He needed evidence.

They walked swiftly from Brewer Street to Holborn, and in less than fifteen minutes they were turning the corner of Eagle Street. It didn't take long for the useful Lucket, having ascertained that Raultier's horse was still absent from the stables round the back of the inn, to pick the lock of the door to the doctor's rooms.

The parlour smelt faintly of camphor. Bookshelves lined the walls, and there were glass-fronted cupboards filled with carefully labelled bottles. Jonathan looked round quickly, in the light of the evening sun that filtered through the window, and walked over to the desk in the corner. He found that his heart was racing.

A quill pen, recently used, still sat beside an unsealed pot of ink. Raultier must have gone out in a hurry; called to some patient, perhaps. Sheets of paper inscribed with writing lay carelessly across the desk's surface, confirming that the writer had been interrupted.

Jonathan leaned both his hands on the desk and gazed down at one of the letters. Even before his eyes had properly focused, he knew what he was going to see.

Star names. Star numbers. Dear God, he recognised them well enough by now.

He was breathing hard, and his hands had gripped the edge of the desk. So similar, so very similar, to the Dover letter, the one that had been stolen from his locked desk. Was this a copy of it? And were these other lists lying here, these other pieces of paper that were full of star names; were they duplicates of more letters that had been sent to Paris?

There were some sheets of blank paper on the desk, in a neat pile. Jonathan reached for pen and ink and said curtly to Lucket, 'Watch the street. Tell me if you see Raultier coming back.'

'Sir.' Lucket posted himself importantly by the window, where the dying rays of the setting sun glinted on his pewter buttons.

Jonathan wrote furiously, glad for once that he was now familiar with these obscure names. First he copied the one that looked like the letter he no longer had; then he started on the next. Stars, numbers, magnitudes again, ranging between one and six: were some of these figures wrong too? *Capella, 0.1*; *Chaph, 2.27*; *Alifa, 3.6*; *Giansar, 3.9*. He dipped the pen in the black ink again and again, covering one sheet and starting another. This second letter was longer than the first. He noted the date at the top of the list: 15 June. If this was a copy, and the letter was already sent, what information did it carry? Was it information that Raultier had obtained from Prigent?

Almost feverish with conjecture, Jonathan sanded the pieces of paper on which he'd written, and then he restored everything on the desk to its original state. It was growing darker, and he didn't want to light candles. Time to leave, before Raultier returned. His head ached, his throat was sore; and the smell of camphor assailed his senses, reminding him of his mother's darkened bedchamber, and her slow dying.

He put the folded papers in his pocket. Then, just as he was turning to go, he saw a small book lying on the corner of the desk. It looked well worn, and the gilt lettering on its spine was faded. He picked it up, and read the title: Lefèvre's *Mythologie*.

It was a French reference book, with alphabetically ordered headings and line drawings; the kind of volume carried by schoolboys to their lessons. As he'd lifted it, it had fallen open at a place that was marked by a lock of red hair, tied up in a dark blue ribbon. The shock of seeing the red hair had an almost physical impact on him. He realised that his hands were shaking. He forced himself to calmness and saw, at the top of the page, the name *Séléné*, followed by a line drawing of a woman with flowing robes and a coronet of flowers. Once more his heart seemed to stop. The name the Montpelliers gave their lost star. The name by which Guy de Montpellier, in the throes of his opiate-induced confusion, called the red-haired girls, while the scarred coachman Ralph waited nearby . . .

Lucket was calling him anxiously. 'There's a horseman coming down from the far end of Eagle Street, sir. Could be the doctor, I think. He's stopping now, sir, by the lane that leads to the stables at the back of the White Boar . . .'

Jonathan was scouring the marked page with hungry eyes.

'Séléné. Dans la mythologie grecque, déesse de la lune et soeur du soleil. Pendant qu'Endymion, son amant, dormoit d'un sommeil éternel dans une grotte du Mont Latmos, Séléné s'y rendoit chaque nuit, lui chantoit et parsemoit de fleurs son corps étendu . . .'

'Selene. In Greek mythology, goddess of the moon and sister of the sun. When Endymion, her lover, lay sunk in eternal sleep in a cave on Mount Latmos, he was visited nightly by Selene, who sang to him and strewed his body with flowers . . .'

Lucket was tugging at his shoulder. 'He's dismounted, sir! It is the doctor! He's leading his horse up the lane . . .'

Jonathan slammed the book down, with the lock of red hair still in

XXXVI

The human mind delights in extending and expanding its knowledge.

Bishop Berkeley, *De Motu* (1721)

John Morrow, seventy-seven years of age and one of the most formidable decipherers to have worked for His Majesty's Secret Office, lived now at St James's Place, about half a mile from Whitehall, but only a few steps away from the old Southern Department on Cleveland Row, where he had once been such a familiar figure.

His sitting room was on the first floor. It was a big room, and chilly even in summer. Now the fire was dying in the grate, and no one had been to attend to it. Pulling himself up from his chair with the aid of his stick, he limped crossly over to the doorway and pulled the bell to summon his housekeeper.

She should have known, he muttered to himself; the woman should have known that the fire needed more coals, that the room was growing cold as the sun sank behind the rooftops. Now that he was old, he needed the warmth. It was his lifeblood now, he couldn't be cold, and neither could his precious companions, his cats, who lay supine on the rug before the hearth, but watched him as he moved with green and amber eyes. Cats kept their secrets; they yielded to no one. For many years secrets had been the vital essence of his life: the secrets of governments, and spies, and soldiers. No one had been able to read secrets as well as he.

The housekeeper came, nervous, defensive. He told her, angrily, to build up the fire and bring him tea to warm himself; then he hobbled back to sit on the sofa that faced the hearth, and stroked the silky grey cat that nestled there. Its tail moved to and fro in irritation: at what? At the dying fire? At him, for intruding on its peace? He respected his cats more than people: they didn't respond to love, or to efforts at care; they simply demanded their due.

A knock came at the door. His housekeeper with coal, no doubt. 'Come in!' he called impatiently.

Then he stared with rheumy eyes, and the cat next to him arched its back and rose, because it wasn't his housekeeper, but a man with iron-grey hair and pale blue eyes, who stood there in the doorway with books and papers clutched in his hands and said,

'Mr Morrow. Sir. Didn't you get my letters?'

Morrow reached for his stick and pulled himself angrily up. 'Who are you? They had no business letting you up here, no business! Don't you know that I've been ill?' He hobbled across the room to confront this intruder, who took a step forward to meet him and said quickly,

'I'm truly sorry to disturb you, Mr Morrow. My name is Jonathan Absey. Do you remember me? I work in the Home Office. I used to bring letters to you, when you worked as a decipherer for the Secret Office—' He broke off, coughing. He looked ill himself. Morrow said surlily,

'So?'

'I – I need your help, sir.'

Morrow leaned on his stick. 'Why should I give you help? I don't work for the government any more. Too many new men, young men, who think they know everything. Go to one of them.' He shook his grey head in disgust. 'Clever young people. They pay them more than they ever paid me, and I was the best of all of them.'

'I know you were, sir,' said Jonathan quietly. 'That's why I've come here.'

Morrow threw him a sharp look. 'That fellow King didn't send you, did he? The new Under-Secretary? Can't bear the man. Bumptious upstart . . . I resigned completely, you know, when he took over. Before then I'd helped whenever they asked me; but not once he was in charge. Pollock, now, he was a better man, but they reckoned he wasn't clever enough for promotion.'

'John King didn't send me, Mr Morrow. I decided to come myself, because I truly think you're the only person who can help me.'

One of the cats had got up from the hearth and stalked over to its master, rubbing itself against his legs and staring up at the intruder with amber eyes. Morrow did remember Absey, yes, though he hadn't intended to say so at first, because they all thought you'd forgotten everything, these younger fellows. Absey had been a clerk he had admired, one of the brightest of them all; loyal, discreet, with a good nose for trouble. And he had shown a suitable respect for his elders too.

'So you're not Chief Clerk yet, Absey? They used to say you'd go far.'

He saw Absey breaking into a rueful smile. 'So you do remember me after all . . . No. Not Chief Clerk, I'm afraid. Nor ever likely to be. Not now.' He paused, then met Morrow's eyes directly. 'Do you remember, sir, how once I brought you a letter that seemed to be about navigation? It had been sent by someone who was under suspicion, but no one else in the Secret Office could make anything at all of it. You spotted the secret, though. You found out that some of the latitudes were wrong, and that was the key to it all. You deciphered the message within the hour, and it turned out to be vital.'

Morrow grunted and nodded. Flattery came sweetly to the ears, the older one got. 'I remember. I could still show those youngsters at the Secret Office a thing or two. Well? What have you come for? I assume you've got something you want me to look at?'

Jonathan, holding his books and his papers tightly to his chest, said earnestly, 'Yes. Oh, yes.'

An hour later, John Morrow leaned back in his chair, took off his spectacles, and rubbed his eyes. Jonathan, who was sitting opposite him at the lamplit table in the corner of the room next to the bookshelves that were crammed with a lifetime's scholarly reading, waited in silence. The copies he'd made, of the Dover letter and of the star lists he had found on Raultier's desk, lay spread out in front of the elderly Decipherer. The star books and catalogues Jonathan had brought with him lay open too. The fire had been stoked up by the housekeeper, and the cats – there were five of them – purred contentedly on the hearth. Jonathan, still a little feverish from his cold, found the room almost unbearably hot. He had taken off his coat, and was in his shirt-sleeves. He was aware of his pulse beating rapidly in anticipation.

Morrow said at last, 'You say there are some errors in the list. But are these star names all accurately written? All spelt as they should be?'

'Yes. I've checked them all, sir. It's just that some of the numbers are wrong.'

Morrow nodded. 'But most of them are correct . . .' He pored over the list again. 'I don't think there can be a substitution cipher involved here, because there's no repetition of names. I feel you must search deeper, Jonathan, for some other, more subtle explanation. Have you had any thoughts?'

Jonathan said quickly, 'I've made a note of the constellations, sir, in which each star lies, and written the names down here, on this piece of paper. Might that be of any use?' He handed Morrow another sheet; Morrow repositioned his spectacles and scrutinised it.

'Interesting, yes. Are there by any chance any numbers associated with these constellations?'

Jonathan's heart was beating fast again. 'I'm not sure. I hadn't properly thought of it before now. There's something in one of my books.' He pulled a volume towards him and opened it carefully. 'Here's a list of them, in alphabetical order. There are eighty-eight of them, from Andromeda to Vulpecula.'

'Eighty-eight. And that number is generally accepted?'

'It seems to be, yes.' Jonathan was looking further down the page. 'The last constellations were added by –' he ran his finger down the column – 'by de Lacaille in 1752.'

Morrow nodded. 'So. We have the numbers one to eighty-eight. A useful range, that. Let us look, then, at our first wrongly numbered star. It's – let me see – Alifa, in Ursa Minor, which is the eighty-fourth constellation.' He wrote carefully next to Jonathan's notes. 'Next: Mirphak in Perseus, which is the sixty-third . . . You see? More numbers. Always grist to the code-breaker's mill . . . What else? What else is there, Absey, that might enrich our list of stars?'

Jonathan cleared his throat. 'It might be nothing, sir. But I do know that each of these stars, as well as having a name, is identified by a letter of the Greek alphabet.' He rummaged, and found another piece of paper on which he had written out more letters and numbers; almost despairingly, it had seemed at the time, but his hopes were suddenly brighter. 'You see, here? Alifa is known also as Zeta Ursae Minoris; Mirphak as Alpha Persei, and so on.'

'You are knowledgeable about the stars.'

'No. No, I'd never studied them at all, until this business began.'

Morrow said quietly, 'There are other people to whom you could have taken this matter.'

Jonathan met and held the old man's gaze. 'There's no one else.'

'Didn't you think of the Secret Office?'

'I couldn't have taken it there.'

'In Vienna,' said Morrow, 'they call the deciphering room the Black Chamber, because of its dark secrets. Long ago the breakers of ciphers were taken away and killed once they had done their work, because their knowledge was considered so dangerous; far more dangerous to those in power than the possession of arms or wealth.'

'Have things changed, sir?'

Morrow continued to watch him. His eyes, though rheumy and almost buried in folded skin, were still sharp, still brimming with fierce intelligence. 'No,' he said, 'I think not. Well, young man. We have numbers in plenty here. Let us look, this time, at Tania Borealis. A beautiful name. According to what you've told me, it could also be called Lambda Ursae Majoris. Lambda is the eleventh letter of the Greek alphabet, and Ursa Major is the eighty-third constellation. And the magnitude given here, which you tell me is wrong, is 4.3. Eleven, eighty-three, four and three . . .' He leaned back and nodded. 'I think the answer, my friend, is staring you in the face. What you need is a book.'

'A book?'

Morrow pointed to the star list. 'It must be a book cipher. At least, that's how it seems to me. Look at these numbers. All the ranges are feasible, for pages, lines, letters, words. Of course there's some work to be done; and with a book code you always have the problem that the encipherer might have encoded the letter "e", for example, in a different way, using a different page of the book each time. Nevertheless, these problems are not insurmountable. Find your book, find yourself those crucial first few words, and the rest will be easy.'

Jonathan's spirits had soared, but now they sank again. 'How do I even begin to look for this book?'

Morrow looked at him, bright-eyed. 'You got these letters from somewhere. How did they reach you, I wonder? Were they intercepted? There are no names on them, apart from the name of Master Titius in Paris. Have you any idea at all of the sender? If not, then your task is difficult indeed. Identity is the key to this particular puzzle.'

'What do you mean, sir?'

Morrow waved his hands expressively. 'If you don't know the sender,' he said, 'you're working in isolation. It means you've no idea of how the encipherer worked, or where; no knowledge of the person, his home, his habits; the books he might have around him, the type of person he was. The recipient, of course, would have to possess the same book; but presumably he too is a mystery figure. Have you any idea who sent these letters?'

'Yes. I do know.' Jonathan looked directly at Morrow. 'I think you already suspect something of the sort. I broke into his house. I saw the letters, of which these are copies, on his desk.'

'Ah. Good man.' Morrow's eyes twinkled. 'You're enterprising.'

'My superiors would use another word.'

'Ignore them. So: you know the writer; you know his home. Is he a learned man, this encipherer? Presumably he's an astronomer? Otherwise the writing of a list such as this would immediately arouse suspicion.'

'He's an amateur astronomer, yes, but a doctor by profession.'

Morrow nodded and frowned. 'So he would have medical books. But they might be too esoteric, for a code book . . . Remember, the recipient would have to have a copy also. He might even have to carry it around with him without it looking suspicious. Could he be a doctor too?'

'I don't know. It would be a coincidence.'

'Yes. I can see that.' Morrow drummed his fingers on the table and then indicated his own crammed bookshelves. 'It would have to be a book that could be in everyday use,' he went on. 'Dictionaries are always popular for the science of encryption, as are common reference books. They're readily available, and wouldn't be regarded as suspicious if left lying about, or if found in more than one house—'

He broke off, because Jonathan had risen abruptly to his feet. 'Selene,' he was saying dazedly. 'Selene, goddess of the moon, sister of the sun . . .'

Morrow said quietly, 'You've thought of something.'

'Yes.' Jonathan gazed at him, his eyes suddenly full of hope. 'There was a book lying on the man's desk A reference book; a classical dictionary of mythology . . .'

'Good. Can you get a copy?'

'I will, somehow . . .'

Morrow smiled. 'If not, you can always break in again.'

'But I'd need the book for some time, wouldn't I? Its loss would be noticed. And I don't want him to suspect. Not yet. If there's another copy in London, I'll find it, believe me.' Jonathan was already starting to gather his things together. 'Sir, I don't know how to thank you.'

'You've enlivened a tedious evening for me. You've almost made me miss the business. Come back if you need more help.'

'I will. I'm truly grateful.'

Morrow had also got to his feet, and was making his way towards the door to open it for him, when Jonathan's eyes suddenly fell on the crowded bookshelves that lined the walls. 'Mr Morrow,' he said suddenly. 'I've just thought of something else you might know about.'

Morrow turned expectantly. 'Another code?'

'No. Not in that sense, though it could be just as important . . . It's something somebody said. I need to know where it's from. It could be from some obscure part of the Bible, but I haven't been able to find it anywhere.'

Morrow waited. 'Well?'

Jonathan said, slowly, carefully, '*A dead body revenges not injuries.*'

Morrow was nodding. 'I know it,' he said. 'The author is a strange man, a visionary; some believe him seditious. His name is William Blake. I've read his works. The line you mention is one of the Proverbs of Hell, from a recent work of his, *The Marriage of Heaven and Hell.* Blake is much influenced by the Bible, especially the Book of Revelation. Is this connected to your stars?'

'I don't know. I don't know . . .' Jonathan was shaking his head. 'It's something that an unknown person was heard to say, and I thought that knowing its origin might help me to discover the identity of the speaker; but now I'm not sure where it leads.'

'The stars are Blake's symbol for power and military might,' said Morrow. 'And he believes they can also control human destiny. Have

255

you heard of his work, *The French Revolution?*' He closed his eyes, and in a clear voice began to declaim from memory:

'When the heavens were sealed with a stone, and the terrible sun clos'd
  in an orb,
and the moon
Rent from the nations, and each star appointed for watchers of night,
The millions of spirits immortal were bound in the ruins of sulphur
  heaven
To wander inslav'd.

'I have no copies of Blake's works,' he went on. 'They're hand-printed and illustrated by the poet himself, so there are few in existence. Have you set yourself another challenge?'

'If so, it's one that will perhaps have to wait,' replied Jonathan. 'I'm hoping that the deciphering of these star letters will answer all my questions. I'm truly grateful to you, sir.' He hesitated. 'Before I go, there's a final favour I would ask of you . . .'

'You've already made yourself clear,' said Morrow gently. 'You want me to say nothing of all this to anyone. Otherwise you'd have used the more usual channels.'

Jonathan nodded. 'Yes. Some day I may be able to explain.'

'I understand. I wish you luck.'

'Thank you.' Jonathan shook his hand and made his way towards the door, which Morrow was holding open.

'One more thing, Absey!' It was Jonathan's turn to stop. 'Remember that you'll have to investigate for both words and letters. The message could be encrypted in either or both.'

'How will I know?'

'Trial and error. Think of common words again; they're most likely to be encoded by word, whereas the names of people and places are most unlikely to occur in the book, and so would be enciphered by letter. Unless some sort of system of codewords has been agreed in advance, in which case you'll face difficulties.'

'I'll remember,' Jonathan said. He started down the stairs. Morrow, standing in the doorway behind him, called out after him,

'And don't forget about nulls!'

'Nulls?'

'Symbols or letters that mean nothing. They're put in to deceive the code-breaker, and to defeat his attempts at rational analysis. The

Hanover men are the ones to watch for tricks like that.'

He beamed and raised his hand in a gesture of goodwill. Jonathan's last memory of Morrow was of the old man standing there at the top of the stairs, with two cats purring in the doorway behind him.

XXXVII

Now would I have a book where I might see all
characters and planets of the heavens, that I might
know their motions and dispositions.

Christopher Marlowe, *Dr Faustus* (1604)

I t was much later that night when Jonathan finally got home to
his lodgings. He made his way to his desk, past the piles of clothes,
and news sheets, and half-opened books about the stars that lay
on various surfaces, vaguely registering that his room was becoming
as unkempt as he was. Lighting candles at his desk, he threw his coat
across the back of the chair, and closed the curtains against the
encroaching darkness. He spread out the copies of the lists of stars
he'd found in Raultier's study, and carefully laid down his star books
beside them.

Then he drew another book from his pocket, and held it almost
reverently in his hands. It was smaller than the others, this book; well
worn, and bound in faded black leather. A copy of Lefèvre's *Mythologie.*
Turning the pages till he came to Selene, he gazed intently at the
familiar little picture: the flowing robes, the long hair, the coronet of
flowers. '*Séléné. Dans la mythologie grecque, déesse de la lune et soeur du*
soleil . . .'

After leaving Morrow's house in a state of mingled hope and despair,
Jonathan had taken a hackney through the dark streets of the metropolis to Field Lane. This was a neighbourhood full of once fine houses
that had been divided into crumbling tenements as the richer inhabitants moved westwards; and he knew that these lowly dwellings had
attracted many of the exiled French refugees. One end of Fuller Street
was even known to locals as 'Little Paris', because it harboured a wine
seller's shop where the Frenchmen congregated, and a butcher's shop
run by a Parisian where the womenfolk of the *émigrés* gathered to
lament old times. There were also second-hand shops and pawnbrokers,

and these were what attracted Jonathan's attention; for these lowly establishments, open till late every night, were filled with the evidence of recent impoverishment. Forlorn remnants of finery lurked in shadowy corners: shawls and ribbons, faded silk waistcoats, pieces of lace bearing some hint of lingering perfume; a broken silver watch or two.

And of course there were books.

Some seemed untouched, unread, while others had that faint patina that showed they were much-loved volumes, relics of childhood, perhaps, that had been brought into exile and now, in their owners' extremity, had to be sold for a few pence, to pay for fuel, or clothes, or food for hungry children. Other books had been brought to these shops because their owners had died; they lay unsorted, piled almost to the ceiling sometimes, in musty recesses, and Jonathan almost despaired as he asked, again and again, only to be told,

'Lefèvre's *Mythologie*? I have heard of it, monsieur, of course I have. It might be here. But then again, it might not. Take a look, if you wish.'

Jonathan looked, by the light of sparse candles, and soon the names of the popular French authors were rattling around uselessly in his brain: Crébillon, Marmontel, Saint-Pierre. He was on the verge of giving up, of rebuking himself for even thinking he could succeed at such a hopeless task, when he was directed to a tiny shop set back in an alleyway off Holborn Court, that sold books, and only books, English as well as French. The English bookseller listened to him, and said, 'Lefèvre? Yes, I know his *Mythologie*. It's popular with the *émigrés* who set themselves up as French teachers over here, because of course the stories are familiar to their English pupils . . . Wait a moment, would you?'

He picked up a candlestick and went into a store-room that adjoined the shop, and a few moments later came out smiling. 'Here you are.' He held out a book. 'It's rather a battered copy, I'm afraid, but still readable. Lefèvre's *Mythologie*, sir.'

Jonathan took the little book and turned to Selene. He gazed at the familiar picture and said quickly, as if the precious volume might at any moment vanish from his hands, 'Thank you. Thank you . . .'

Now, back in his rooms, he opened it again, and prepared to start work. But he found that he was almost afraid of beginning, in case he faced failure. What if his intuition was awry, and this wasn't the key after all? It had seemed so obvious, so simple, when Morrow had explained the type of volume he must look for; but what if he was wrong? And even if it was the right book, what if it was a different edition to the one Raultier had? It was a popular work, the bookseller had told him so, and must have been reprinted several times; just the slightest alteration of text or page numbers could be enough to destroy his chances of discovering the code . . .

It was in mingled hope and despair that he sat down at his desk and prepared to start work. He'd decided to begin with the letter intercepted at Dover, the stolen letter, which he had carefully recreated from his own scraps and jottings as he tried to make sense of it. *Chara, 3.9. Alkafazah, 2.1* . . . He thought of the Decipherer, and remembered all the possibilities the old man had suggested to him. His head ached, his throat seemed on fire again as he drew his pen, and ink, and paper towards him, and doggedly began work. Using his astronomy books, he compiled a fresh list of all the star names for which the magnitude was wrong; and then, beside each star, he wrote first the number of the constellation in which it lay and then the number in the alphabet of the Greek letter which represented it, and finally, the false magnitude.

Chara	*13*	*2*	*3.9*
Alkafazah	*83*	*22*	*2.1*
Alifa	*84*	*6*	*3.6*

'Think of your range,' Morrow had urged. 'Look at your sequences of numbers. What are they most likely to represent? Pages? Lines? Letters? Words?'

The constellations were numbered up to eighty-eight – too high a number for words, or even letters, within each line. He scanned the pages. Too high a number as well for the lines on each page of this small volume. The numbers to eighty-eight could be counted, in letters or words, from the beginning of each page, but that was laborious, surely. No, he decided: there were one hundred and fifty pages in the book; he would assume, at least for the time being, that the constellations must stand for the numbers of the pages.

He began with Chara, in Canes Venatici, which was the thirteenth constellation. He turned to the thirteenth page of the book. *'Atalante; chasseuse célèbre d'Arcadie, qui participoit à la chasse au sanglier de Calydon . . .'*

What other numbers could he explore? The Greek letter for Chara was beta, the second in the Greek alphabet: could this indicate the second line? The second letter? The second word on the page was *chasseuse*, huntress; an unlikely word, surely, as part of a message. Unless it was an agreed codeword, as Morrow had suggested, in which case his task was truly impossible.

He paused, fighting against a sudden wave of despair. What about counting letters? That gave him 'T'; surely a feasible opening letter. But what if beta represented the second line of the page, with a further variable to define the word or letter in it?

He still had the brightness figures to deal with: 3.9. But should he treat three and nine as separate numbers, or as one? He drew his candles closer and gazed at the star list, endeavouring to suppress the rising fear that he could not deal with all these possibilities. 'Try them all,' Morrow had urged. 'At first the task might seem overwhelming. But you only need one word to emerge, and you will have broken the cipher, you will have found your key.'

He tried using the third letter of the ninth word of the second line, and then the ninth letter of the third word. He tried ignoring the decimal point, and counting the thirty-ninth letter of the second line. He tried adding the numbers, to make twelve, and did the same again; until finally, using these variations on his basic system, he had six possible letters for Chara: the letter D, another D, P, M, S and O.

He moved on to the next star: Alkafazah, in Ursa Major, the eighty-third constellation; its Greek letter was the twenty-second of the alphabet, chi; its magnitude had been given falsely as 2.1. Turning to the eighty-third page, he started again.

He carried on tortuously, trying to think how John Morrow would have approached it; feeling a clumsy novice at all this. He worked through the first four stars for which the magnitude given was wrong; and, by assuming the constellations were pages and the Greek letters lines – if they weren't, he acknowledged, in a renewed moment of despair, he would have to start all over again – he eventually created six rows of possible letters, with a column for each star.

Chara	Alkafazah	Alifa	Mirphak
D	A	E	S
D	U	D	F
P	U	I	S
M	C	I	N
S	E	N	S
O	V	E	A

He looked along each line. He stopped, his heart beating fast, at the third line, which he'd achieved by ignoring the decimal point of the magnitude figure and using the whole number to count the letters along the line. *PUIS* . . .

Puis. The French for 'then'. An unlikely opening word for a coded letter. Unless it was only the first part of a word . . .

He found that he was breathing heavily. The light of his candles seemed for a moment to recede and then almost dazzle him; his head was swimming with conjecture. He put his hands over his eyes and tried to calm himself. Using the same method, of ignoring the decimal point in the false magnitude figure, he worked on, more speedily now, with Ati, and Kocab, and Adhil.

PUISAYE . . .

Surely, surely, this was the moment that confirmed everything he had most feared to find. He pressed on.

'Puisaye demande des . . .'

His heart was beating fast with mingled excitement and anger as the message began to reveal itself more fully. But then, just as he was writing with growing confidence, it all went wrong. He was working on the star Menkib; fourteenth letter, sixty-third constellation; its false magnitude was given as 2.15. He stopped abruptly. This was the first figure he had come across with two numbers after the decimal point. If he ignored the point, he was left with 215, and to count to the 215th letter on the fourteenth line was clearly impossible because there wasn't one. For a moment Jonathan despaired.

He sat back in his chair and tried to think of everything Morrow had said to him. Range, frequency, words, letters . . .

'*Don't forget about nulls,*' the old man had called out as he departed. '*Symbols or letters that mean nothing.*'

He looked at the fourteenth line, on the sixty-third page of his book, and on his sheet of paper he played with the numbers of Menkib's false magnitude. 2.15. Add the single numbers together? Ignore one number? Use 2 and 1, 1 and 5, 2 and 5?

He tried all these methods, and obtained the letters T, X, O and U. He worked on.

The next four stars were just two-figure numbers and gave him no trouble; they produced the words *et* and *de*. The problem was that none of the letters he'd deduced from Menkib would fit in front of *et*. What was he to do, then?

He thought, only for a moment, of going back to St James's Place. The old Decipherer would solve it all within minutes. But Jonathan would then have to burden him with his own knowledge. He remembered what had happened to Thomas, and the times he was sure he was being followed, and he knew that he could not share this with anyone else, until he was ready to resolve it.

Puisaye demande des . . . et de . . .

He rubbed his hands against his tired eyes. What letter could possibly go before *et* in this context?

'*Remember that you'll have to investigate for both words and letters. The message could be encrypted in either or both.*'

'*How will I know?*'

'*Trial and error . . .*'

Jonathan looked again at Menkib. The fourteenth line. The number 2.15. This time he looked for words. He tried the numbers separately and together; he added them to make eight; and he ended up with the words, *Hermes, mauvais, etait,* and *armes.*

Puisaye demande des armes et de . . .

Armes was the fifteenth word on the line. He had obtained it by ignoring the whole number of the magnitude, and using only the two numbers after the decimal point. It seemed to be the solution. There were some more stars with magnitudes containing three numbers; they would confirm or negate his discovery. He bent to his task again almost fiercely. He came to another star whose magnitude contained two numbers after the decimal point. He ignored the whole number and used the numbers after the point to count along the line. '*Puisaye demande des armes et de l'argent anglais . . .*'

'Puisaye asks for English arms and money . . .'

He was almost there now. He worked swiftly, and with growing confidence, until at last he was finished. He held what he had written up to the candlelight and translated aloud,

'Puisaye asks for English arms and money for a Royalist invasion of western France.'

To Jonathan everything in the room seemed clearer, sharper than usual; he felt he could almost see through the candlelit brightness of his room into the darkness outside.

The original of this document, Raultier's letter, had been stopped by the port agent at Dover, whose suspicions had now been fully justified. Surely it was the message of a spy to his masters in Paris, who paid him in Republican gold; but it was no longer of any use, because now everyone knew that Puisaye had got everything he asked for.

But what about the later letter, the one he had found a draft of on Raultier's desk? Jonathan drew out the copy he had made. It was in scraps, because he hadn't been able to fit it on to one piece of paper. He began on the first section, and this took him longer to decipher because of the haste with which he had copied it. Almost feverishly, he began by inscribing the number of the constellation and of the Greek letter next to each star whose magnitude was false. He realised that midnight had come and gone; his head ached ferociously, and his candles were burning low. Soon enough, though, he stopped noticing such things. '*L'expédition à destination de la Bretagne quittera Portsmouth le 17 juin. Quatre mille soldats royalistes, payés et armés par les Anglais, débarqueront aux environs de Carnac. Date prévue le 24 juin . . .*'

Soon he was aware of nothing but a feeling of growing despair, and anger, and helplessness, as he wrote and translated,

'The Brittany expedition sets off from Portsmouth June 17th. Four thousand Royalist troops, paid and armed by the English, are to be landed near Carnac. Estimated arrival 24th June.'

There was more yet.

'*Des bruits non-confirmés courent: une armée sous Tinténiac sera transportée par mer jusqu'à l'estuaire de la Vilaine en vue d'attaquer Hoche du côté est.*'

'There are unverified reports that an army under the Chevalier de

Tinténiac is to be taken by sea to the Vilaine estuary, to attack Hoche from the east . . .'

He thought, There could still be a reason for all this. It could be a false dispatch, sent by Raultier on the orders of his English masters to mislead the government in Paris.

But Jonathan could see little reason to doubt the veracity of the message. He knew that the expedition had indeed embarked on the 17th, with four thousand *émigré* troops; the landing place, kept so secret at first, was now widely known to be Carnac, again as the message said.

A message to the Royalist Agency? He clung to this, almost as if clinging to his sanity; but he knew he no longer believed it, because if it was so, then why had everything else happened? The killing of the girls. The stealing of his letter. The torturing of his son . . .

A letter to the Comte d'Artois and his outdated Royalists, who dreamed in exile of an impossible return to past glories? Oh, no. This was intended for a far, far more ruthless enemy.

When did Raultier send this message? Did he send it in time for the Republican army to take action against the unsuspecting Royalist troops? If so, what Jonathan had here on his desk was surely enough to justify action at the very highest level.

The next morning Jonathan entered the Home Office building almost before the porters had unlocked the main doors. He was holding the *Mythologie* book in one hand, and his copies of Raultier's letters, together with his deciphered translation, tightly in the other. He saw the porters looking at him oddly. He'd hardly slept, he hadn't shaved, and he knew how dishevelled he must look; he had been wearing the same clothes for days. But such things hardly mattered now.

Early though he was, he knew that the man he wanted to see might be here even earlier. He went straight up to the lobby on the first floor, where the main offices were.

'Is the Under-Secretary in yet?'

'Yes, but he's busy, Mr Absey. He—'

Jonathan went quickly across to the Under-Secretary's room, and knocked. A clerk opened it, and looked surprised to see him. The

Under-Secretary, John King, was standing by his desk, examining some papers intently; he glanced up in some irritation and said, 'Absey. What is it? You're lucky to catch me in. I have a meeting with the Secretary of State very shortly.'

King's mind was clearly on other business, but at least he wasn't outrightly hostile, as Jonathan had feared. Jonathan stepped forward and said,

'Sir. I must speak to you. It's most urgent.'

King frowned. 'Make it brief, will you?'

'It's the Brittany landing, sir. I'm very much afraid that it's been betrayed.'

King's mouth opened and closed. He seemed at first to go pale, but then the colour suffused his face. His Lancashire accent was harsher than ever as he growled out, 'What the devil do you mean, the Brittany landing has been betrayed?'

'I've been watching the movements of a suspected spying ring for some time now, sir. There's a group of French *émigrés* in London who are astronomers, and one of them is sending messages to Paris in the guise of lists of stars. One of these letters was intercepted.'

'Do you have any of these letters?'

'I have copies, sir. The only original I had was stolen.'

King slammed down the papers he'd been reading on his desk. 'Who by?'

'I don't know, sir.' Jonathan broke off, to cough. 'But whoever stole it from my desk knew that I had it, and knew of its importance. I'd always suspected that it was in code, but I've only just managed to decipher it. The French astronomer who sends the letters is supposed to be working for our own intelligence service, but he's betraying them. He has a book of Greek myths, called Lefèvre's *Mythologie*, that he uses to change his messages into lists of stars. And one of his letters gives the exact date, the destination, and the strength of the Brittany landing. I have a copy of it here . . .'

He proffered his papers, but the Under-Secretary made no move to take them; he was simply staring at Jonathan. Some moments ago he had gestured to his clerk to leave the room.

Jonathan took King's stunned silence as encouragement to continue. Emboldened, he went on, 'And there are girls being killed, sir. One of this group of Frenchmen, who is sometimes ill, goes out to find prostitutes and gives them gold, some of the Republican French gold that's sent from Paris in payment for the messages. But because his colleagues realise that this sick man is in danger of giving them away as spies, the girls are followed, and killed, and the gold is taken back . . .'

He broke off, because King was still staring at him. Jonathan's heart sank. He was beginning to know that kind of look. He had seen it before.

'Are you quite mad, Absey?'

Jonathan ran his hand through his dishevelled hair. 'It sounds far-fetched, sir, I know. But the chief thing is this: the Republican govern-ment in Paris has been informed of the arrival date of the Royalist expedition, and the exact place of landing – look.' He held out his papers. 'Puisaye has been betrayed, sir, and it might already be too late to warn him!'

The Under-Secretary's face was dark with displeasure. He didn't even glance at the papers in Jonathan's hand. He said, sonorously,

'The Comte de Puisaye and his troops have not been betrayed, Absey. On the contrary. The Brittany landing has been a complete success.'

Now it was Jonathan's turn to be silenced. At last he repeated shakily, 'A complete success? You are sure?'

'Of course I'm sure.' King gestured angrily towards his desk, where he'd put the papers he'd been studying when Jonathan came in. 'News was brought in at dawn, by an officer carrying dispatches directly from the fleet in Quiberon Bay. This officer landed at Dover late last night. The Comte de Puisaye and his troops disembarked safely a week ago near Carnac; they were delayed in their voyage a few days by bad weather, but otherwise everything has gone according to plan, and there was no resistance whatsoever. General Hoche and his Republicans were miles away in the hinterland and could do nothing.'

'But these letters,' said Jonathan desperately. 'These letters are still being sent, I am sure; I'm certain there is more. This spy is still at large, and he's pretending to work for the English . . .'

'For God's sake, Absey. What proof have you?' King snatched Jonathan's documents and the book, and scanned them angrily. 'Letters that are in your handwriting? Letters about stars? A children's book?'

'There was gold—'

'Where?'

Jonathan was silent.

The Under-Secretary eyed Jonathan narrowly. 'Perhaps you'd better keep these wild ideas to yourself from now on, Absey. Fortunately the Brittany expedition is in more secure hands than yours. Don't interfere with what you don't understand. I think I'd better have a word with Pollock about your future role in this department. I've been patient with you, and those who've tried to defend you, for a little too long. Now, if you'll excuse me, I've rather more important things to get on with.' He started towards the door, then stopped. 'And do something about your appearance, man. You look more like a tinker than a Home Office official. You look as if you've not slept, or washed, for days.'

He marched briskly from the room. Jonathan stood there, stunned, until the clerk came in again and curtly ushered him towards the door. He was still clutching the book and his papers as he went out.

So the Royalists had landed safely. The news was of victory. And yet Jonathan had been utterly convinced that Raultier must be an enemy spy. Perhaps the second letter had been intercepted, just like the first . . .

He stood there outside King's office as other clerks hurried by and pressed his clenched fist to his forehead. Stop, he chided himself, stop tormenting yourself; accept that you are wrong. Be glad that you are wrong.

He started to walk unsteadily back to his office, a headache like a hammer pounding inside his skull. One thing was certain. No one else would ever listen to Jonathan's stories about French spies and murderers now.

Feeling drained of energy and hope, he returned to his desk, only to be visited shortly afterwards by Pollock, who avoided Jonathan's eyes as he told him that his responsibility for domestic letters was to be taken from him immediately, and that his duties would now include only the routine scanning of Home Office circulars, gazettes, and general reports from the colonies. He would have to move from this office; he would have no more access to the confidential material that was sent to Montague House.

Slowly Jonathan gathered his things together. He had gambled and lost. But within him the anger continued to burn. Somewhere within that circle of French astronomers there was a murderer; the killer of his daughter. And in spite of King, in spite of Pollock, in spite of all the might of the British government, Jonathan was going to find him.

XXXVIII

*Depart Sir, and announce to your Princes the first
successes of our expedition. Tell them that they will
soon have an army of 80,000 men ready to die for
them. I can enter into no details, not having a
moment to spare. But I will limit myself henceforth
for some days to writing with the sword.*

Letter from Puisaye to Calonne, former French
Minister of Finance, living in exile in Wimble-
don. Received in London 6 July 1795.

It was late afternoon the same day, and Pierre Raultier was in the
shop of Perceval Oates the spectacle-maker in Townsend Lane.
Perceval was serving a customer, so Raultier waited his turn silently
and looked out through the small panes of the bow-fronted window
to the street, where a horse-drawn cart had come to a halt in the
bright sunshine.

The cart was face to face with a coal dray. Because there was not
enough room for them to pass in the narrow lane, the drivers
were standing their ground, cursing each other; and Raultier watched
them without really seeing them. The man in front of him was
buying a new eyeglass, and Perceval was attending to him with his
usual benign thoroughness. At last the purchase was completed, to
both buyer's and seller's satisfaction; the customer paid and left the
shop. The bell on the door tinkled loudly, then faded away into
silence.

Perceval looked up at Raultier, and his eyes were bright behind the
lenses of his wire-framed spectacles. 'Monsieur Raultier. This is a
surprise. So you have come for the telescope lens you left to be
checked?'

Raultier moved jerkily towards him. 'I had to see you—'

Perceval gripped the edge of the counter. 'You fool. I told you never
to come here. Never. Don't you realise I'm being watched?'

Raultier backed away. 'I must speak to you. I've just heard that my letter did not get through—'

'So I have gathered.' Perceval went to lock the door, then looked quickly through his window, scanning the street outside. 'The expedition was a success. What went wrong, Raultier?'

'*I don't know . . .*' Raultier seemed to be endeavouring to pull himself together with a huge effort of will. 'I don't understand. I did what I was supposed to do. I discovered vital information; I sent it, in time, through a new, and I thought trustworthy messenger . . . It was you who put Alexander Wilmot in my path. Wasn't it?'

'I made sure he came to you,' answered Perceval curtly. 'But after that it was up to you to make use of him as you saw fit. So. I ask again: what happened? Did you tell Wilmot of your letter's importance? Of the need for speed, and discretion?'

'Yes! He promised to send it immediately, and he has assured me that he did so!'

'Where is this letter now? Has it been intercepted? Has anyone else got the means to decipher it?'

'I don't know, God help me, I don't know . . .'

Perceval stared at him. He said at last, 'You are failing badly, Raultier. You know that, don't you?' He went slowly back to stand behind his counter.

Raultier whispered, 'I just need more time. Perhaps a little more help.'

'And how much more help can you expect?' Perceval's voice was rising again. 'What more can we do? You were given the names of those French spies, Chauvelin's agents, to betray when you first arrived in England; it was a sacrifice of good citizens of the Republic, Raultier, made to earn you the trust of the government here; but what have you done since?'

'I've sent letters regularly through the normal routes.' Raultier's voice was still hoarse with tension. 'But someone started to ask questions, at the mail office. So then I tried a different route, but my letter was intercepted—'

'What did the letter say?'

Raultier rubbed his hand against his furrowed brow. 'It was encoded, of course. It was about Puisaye's request for British arms and money to support the Royalist landing in western France.'

Perceval gestured scornfully. 'That's no loss, then, even if it was deciphered. The southern ports have been rife with such rumours since May, thanks to the movement of the troops down there. But you've sent another message, you say, a more important one, through Wilmot, that clearly did not get through; what was in that message?'

'It forewarned Paris of Puisaye's landing. It gave the place of arrival, and the expected date; numbers, arms, ships . . . I gave it to Wilmot on the 15th of June. Dear God, it should have reached Paris in time . . .'

'If it had,' said Perceval curtly, 'we would not be hearing these boasts of Royalist success today. How did you get this information?'

'Indirectly, through Prigent—'

'One of Puisaye's henchmen?'

'Yes. Yes . . . I was put in touch with him by someone at the Home Office, a Scottish clerk who has remained a reliable contact ever since the business of Chauvelin's spies. He thinks I am to be trusted. He asked me to visit Prigent, to check that he was still loyal to the Royalist cause, and so Prigent was encouraged to confide in me fully; he told me everything I wanted to know.'

'But your message failed to get through.'

'Yes,' whispered Raultier again.

'I can't help you any more,' said Perceval shortly. 'I told you two months ago never to return here; you endanger both of us. What about the gold I sent you? Did you receive it?'

'Yes. But I must have more . . .'

'There is no more. Fréron let me know, shortly before all contact ceased, that you were to get no further payments until he had results. And now my lines of communication with Paris are quite broken. No more letters. No more gold.'

Raultier clenched his fists on the counter. 'Perceval,' he said, 'please, there must be some way you can communicate with them. You must tell Fréron and Tallien and the others that I'm doing everything I can. They'll listen to you. I need money, to pay people. The money you gave me before won't last long.'

'Citizen Fréron would no doubt make the comment that the people you pay do little enough for the cause of the Republic. And from what I hear, most of your money goes on maintaining the Montpelliers' expensive household. Auguste and her brother should learn to live more frugally. They'll draw attention to themselves, living as they do in that big house in Kensington Gore. I cannot get you more gold. I have no more.'

Someone was trying the door of the shop; they could hear the handle being rattled. 'You must go,' commanded Perceval. 'And don't come here again.' He started towards the locked door, with his key in his hand; and Raultier picked up his hat and moved away from the counter just as Perceval opened the door wide and his latest customer came in, blinking at the relative darkness inside the shop.

Perceval nodded briskly to Raultier, still holding the door open. 'Good day to you, doctor,' he said. 'I'll let you know as soon as the spectacles you ordered are ready.'

Raultier went unsteadily out into the street, momentarily blinded by the late afternoon sunlight, and went to his horse, which he had paid a ragged boy to watch. He took the horse's bridle, but stood for a moment as if any further action was, for the time being, beyond him. He felt cold, in spite of the warmth of the sunshine.

Last summer, in the closing days of the Terror, when news came to London daily of the deaths of so many of the men who had led his country deeper into terrible bloodshed – Robespierre, St Just, Couthon, Hanriot – Raultier had hoped against hope that he would hear that Fréron had been amongst those executed. But Fréron survived, along with Tallien and Barras, to climb into a position of even more power in the government. The three of them were known as the jackals of the Republic, feeding on the leavings of men greater by far than they were, though none would dare to whisper it in Paris.

Raultier had first met Louis Fréron, the radical journalist who had risen to be one of the most feared members of the Convention, when he worked at the Hôtel Dieu, long ago, before the fall of the Bastille. Fréron, burning with idealism, had been writing for his paper, *L'Orateur du peuple*, about the Paris hospitals, and the terrible plight of the poor. Raultier – earnest, humanitarian, trusting – had admired Fréron's work, and counted the influential politician as his friend; so when Auguste was accused of treason, who else should Raultier turn to for help but his good comrade Citizen Fréron?

Fréron had helped him, yes, but at such a price. He told Raultier, in a voice quite chilling in its ruthlessness, that the Montpelliers would only be allowed to leave France alive if he, Raultier, promised to discover and send back vital information about the English war effort from London. A contact would be arranged for him. Fréron also told Raultier that if he failed, the penalty for treason would still be exacted, wherever they were, and Auguste would die.

Soon after their arrival in London, Raultier, still hoping that the nightmare would end, that Fréron's threats would vanish into empty air like the early morning mists that soon became so familiar to him in this place of exile, received a note from a spectacle-maker in Clerkenwell called Perceval Oates, telling him that the lenses he had ordered were ready for collection. Raultier had ordered no lenses, but he had gone regardless; and Perceval had let him know that he was to be his contact with his masters in Paris. Raultier had soon learnt that the gentle-looking spectacle-maker could be as ruthless as Fréron. *You are failing badly, Raultier . . .*

With Perceval's contemptuous words still ringing in his ears, Raultier pulled himself together and rode, not to his home, but down Chancery Lane to the bustling thoroughfare of the Strand, where he once more left his horse, this time outside a shop that stood on the corner of Carting Lane. He came out again shortly afterwards, holding an oblong leather box. He placed it with some care in the pocket of his coat; then he remounted and continued his journey.

An hour later, Auguste heard that Raultier had arrived at the house. She made her way swiftly downstairs to the study, where he was waiting for her. He drew a cloth bag fastened by a drawstring out of his coat pocket and handed it to her, saying, 'There is very little gold in here. Perceval has no more, and this is all I have left. Do you understand me? He has no more.'

Her eyes were full of scorn. 'So you've failed even in this? I thought your last letter was sent safely by the English astronomer.'

'No. It did not reach Paris in time, if at all. Haven't you heard that the Royalist landing has been successful?'

Clutching the gold, Auguste turned abruptly to go. Raultier reached out after her with despair etched on his face. 'Auguste.

Please. There is something else I must talk to you about.'

She waited, but still said nothing.

'I have something here,' he went on quickly, 'that you should perhaps keep with you. I don't think you will ever actually need it; but I still want you to have it.' He reached inside his long coat again, this time for the slim leather box he'd bought from the shop at the corner of Carting Lane. He held it out to her. She gazed at it, but did not move; and so he opened the case himself. In it was a small, brass-barrelled flintlock pistol, with a butt cap made of brass, in the form of a leopard's head.

'Are we in so much danger?' Auguste breathed. 'Can Fréron reach us even here?'

'It's a precaution, that's all,' said Raultier swiftly.

'A precaution . . .' She was shaking her head now in disbelief. 'You frighten me, Pierre. Dear God, how you frighten me.'

He put the open case swiftly down on a nearby table and moved towards her, as if to comfort her. But she backed away from him towards the door, and her hands were outstretched, to ward him off.

'You told us we would be safe here. You lied to us. You lied.'

XXXIX

Tis the great art of life to manage well
The restless mind. For ever on pursuit
Of knowledge bent, it starves the grosser powers;
Quite unemployed, against its own repose
It turns its fatal edge; and sharper pangs
Than what the body knows embitter life.

John Armstrong, 'Madness' (1744)

After his failed interview with John King, Jonathan was taken by Pollock to an obscure wing of the Treasury building where the Home Office had been granted extra space in order to accommodate the increase in clerical work that had been necessitated by the war. This was to be Jonathan's new place of work. The Chief Clerk assured him, without directly meeting his eyes, that he would still be dealing with crucial Home Office matters; his contribution was still vital. But Jonathan, too experienced a hand to be thus deceived, knew very well what all this meant. He was no longer trusted with confidential material. His career prospects were in ruins.

He was also told, as an afterthought, that Abraham Lucket would no longer be working for him. It was perhaps as well, thought Jonathan, for Lucket; but all the same he was surprised to discover how much he would miss his assistant, with his lively street chatter and his artless vanity.

Afterwards Pollock had departed almost with relief. No joy, thought Jonathan, for the older man to see one of his former protégés thus disgraced.

A junior clerk had been instructed to show Jonathan the minutiae of his new employment, which seemed to consist mainly of copying general Home Office briefings for the county deputies, and reading and filing seditious circulars; no escape from them, then. Jonathan sat in his new office, which was even smaller than the last, and started on some of the work which the clerk had handed over to him: the summarising of an interminable report from one of the colonial offi-cials, which required distribution, in duplicate, to the various depart-ments of state. In the midst of all this, Jonathan also sent some letters of his own.

At five o'clock he left Whitehall and walked along to Hungerford Stairs, where a man in his thirties, hollow-cheeked and with thin, straw-coloured hair, was slouched against some barrels that had been stacked up against the riverside wall. When he saw Jonathan he pulled himself up and said, as Jonathan drew close, 'It's been a long time, Mister Absey.'

It was indeed a long time – almost a year – since Jonathan had used this man, James Stimpson, self-styled informer and spy. Stimpson had once had more regular government work, reporting to the Home Office when Dundas was in charge there on the activities of the radical London Corresponding Society, to which he'd gained entry by feigning enthusiasm for its ideals; but eighteen months ago he'd given evidence for the government at the trial of two of its members who were being prosecuted for sedition, and ever since then, his identity too well known to the radicals for further work of that nature, he'd been employed only sporadically by the occasional London magistrate, and by people such as Jonathan. Stimpson never ceased to complain bitterly about this apparent injustice and the lack of reward for his oft-stated loyalty. As an informer, he mixed in a variety of circles, some of them fairly disreputable, but he had a useful nose for gossip, a knack for blending unnoticed into most types of company, and a constant need for money.

He listened keenly enough as Jonathan asked him, down there by the river with the noise of the boatmen and the cries of the gulls in their ears, to both observe and make discreet enquiries about the household and acquaintances of the *émigré* Montpelliers in Ken-sington Gore. Stimpson nodded. No need for him to write anything down; his memory, Jonathan recalled, was immaculate.

'Anyone in particular, Mister Absey?'

Jonathan hesitated. He had grounds to suspect – and dismiss – every single one of them. But he must have missed something, somewhere . . . 'A doctor called Raultier,' he said. 'Ralph Wallace, a manservant.

An ex-priest called Norland. A discharged Navy man who's a mute: William Carline. Any male servants who are English; but they must be literate, they must be well-read . . .' He was thinking of the proverb from Blake. 'Watch them all, for anything at all suspicious, anything they're trying to hide. Don't let anyone know what you're doing. And mention my name to nobody.'

Stimpson nodded. 'I'd assumed that,' he said, 'or you'd be doing it yourself.' Then he repeated the names, and haggled over his price. They arranged for another meeting in a week's time, and Stimpson sloped off, away from the river and up Brewer's Lane.

Jonathan headed the other way, to Adam Street off the Strand. He went into a tavern called the Three Tuns, and saw straight away, in the corner, the man he was to meet there: Tallis, a former Home Office colleague, and now a clerk at the Admiralty.

Tallis – older than Jonathan, stoop-shouldered, his whole physique seemingly worn down by lack of promotion, and resentment at the implacable Admiralty hierarchy – poured Jonathan some wine and said,

'I've done what you asked in your letter. Checked up on the records of an ex-Navy man called Carline. He was a purser on Crosby's ship, the *Heart of Oak*, but he was suspended two years ago on suspicion of milking the accounts.'

'No,' said Jonathan. 'That can't be right. He was dismissed a year ago. And flogged for it.'

'Two years. Most definitely.' Tallis drank his wine deeply. 'And a warrant officer wouldn't be flogged. This Carline was supposed to have falsified the ship's muster book, claiming wages and allowances for men who weren't there – it's a common enough purser's trick, though he protested his innocence throughout. And the case wasn't proved, so he was suspended; which was, I suppose, pretty much the same in outcome as the dismissal you spoke of. But flogged? No.'

Jonathan coughed. His throat still troubled him, especially in the smoky air of the tavern. 'What happened to him afterwards? Do you know?'

Tallis was searching in his pocket for a piece of paper. 'Here's an address in Portsmouth to which his Navy papers were sent. I copied it out for you. Otherwise there's nothing else in Admiralty records.' He handed the paper to Jonathan, who shoved it in his pocket unread, wearily acknowledging that here was yet another failure, yet another piece of information that had turned out to be misleading, if not utterly false. He coughed again, and Tallis leaned back in his chair, watching him curiously.

'Still looking for spies, then, Absey? Still investigating all those letters?'

'Letters,' said Jonathan, 'aren't my responsibility any more.'

'But you were good at your work.'

Jonathan was already standing up to go. 'I became too involved,' he said. 'They told me I was imagining things. Perhaps I was. Perhaps I still am.'

The town of Portsmouth was brought in disagreeable fashion to Jonathan's attention again the next morning when he arrived at his new desk to find a written order from the Chief Clerk telling him that he was to leave for that particular destination as soon as was practicable, to pursue the business of seditious literature that he had left unfinished. 'You will be pleased to deal with the matter in person this time; there will be no more sending of letters.'

Enclosed with the letter was a list of persons who had left the Portsmouth dockyard's employ without clear reason, at around the time the subversive leaflets had appeared. Pollock wanted him to interview the Port Commissioner and Clerk of the Cheque and to return with precise details concerning each individual on the list, in duplicate, for both the Home Office and the Navy Board.

Jonathan sat with his head in his hands, and estimated the days that this business would take: days of travel, of digging amongst a welter of official records and obscure muster rolls, with, no doubt, the officials concerned acting in the usual unforthcoming, belligerent fashion of those who suspected their standards of work might be found wanting by the officious Home Office. He would be away at least a week, maybe more. His daughter's killer would have yet more time to cover his tracks.

XL

Notwithstanding the terrible misery which prevails
among a numerous part of the people of Paris, the
rest of the metropolis wears an aspect of prosperity.
The fair sex are more lively than ever; and we see
spirited horses, with splendid harness and carriage
(though few in number, on the account of the dearness
of forage).

Letter to *The Massachusetts Magazine*, July 1795

Dying of cold, dying of hunger,
People robbed of your rights,
How quietly you murmur;
While the impudent rich,
Whom you spared once in kindness,
Loudly rejoice.

Sylvain Maréchal, 'Song of the
Faubourgs' (1795)

It was noon on the seventh of July, the same day on which Jonathan Absey had received his peremptory instructions to visit Portsmouth. Forty-six-year-old Pierre Simon de Laplace, former luminary of the Académie Royale des Sciences until its repression by the Revolutionary leaders for being élitist and unnecessary, was making his way purposefully along the rue de Richelieu. Every so often his fastidious nostrils twitched in distraction at the appetising midday scents from the elegant restaurants hereabouts, for it was in this area that the Deputies of the Republican Convention often chose to eat. A fine carriage was sweeping down the road, no doubt bearing another of the egalitarian leaders of the Republic to his repast; Laplace jumped out of the way, lest the wheels, splashing through a puddle left from yesterday's rain, should soil his suit. He hurried on.

Only the other day, a business errand had taken him, mercifully in a carriage himself, past one of the streets that led from the lowly Faubourg St Antoine. At the corner of the street he had seen a bread shop, where ragged men and women, children too, barefoot, queued for their meagre rations. Their faces were harrowed with hunger, and despair filled their eyes.

Laplace, as a man of science, found this situation vastly interesting because it seemed to him that, all in all, nothing had changed. There had been perturbations, admittedly, in the normal course of events during the years of revolution. He himself had been proscribed in the December of 1793, and had retreated in hasty exile to Melun; he had only dared to return once Robespierre was dead. All those deaths, all the power struggles; and what now?

The poor still starved. The men of power called themselves by the egalitarian name of Deputy, and claimed to be representatives of the people. But they were just as fat as the *aristos* had ever been.

He considered it all with care. 'First came the overthrow of the tyrannous monarchy,' he said to himself, 'and now we have the reaction against the Revolution, because it engendered its own tyrants in turn: Marat, Danton, Robespierre. What next, I wonder? There is disorder and hunger throughout the land. It is possible, yes, quite possible, under the laws of the universe, that shortly a new tyrant will emerge . . .'

Last year he had written and published a voluminous book called *La Théorie des satellites de Jupiter*, in which he demonstrated that the eccentricities and inclinations of the planetary orbits in relation to one another would always be small, constant and self-correcting. He had used this theory, with some satisfaction, to assert yet again his belief in the basic stability of the entire planetary system. He was convinced that he would be able to work out the probability of historical events too, if only all the facts were to hand, and were scientifically definable.

He was forced to step aside yet again, this time as an intimidating gang of *jeunesse dorée* spilled out of a restaurant just ahead of him. They were clearly drunk, and looking for trouble. Laplace, whose father was a humble cider-maker from Normandy, despised them, because these young men were rich, and thus avoided conscription to the Garde Nationale. Often they were the sons or nephews of deputies. They wore their own kind of uniform: square-skirted coats, tight trousers, low boots and high cravats. Their hair dangled in long locks over their ears, with the remainder plaited at the back of their heads. They carried either postboys' whips, or short sticks weighted with lead. Their normal prey were the poor, especially if they suspected them of being former Revolutionaries.

They set about their baiting now, by casting a red cap of liberty into the gutter and forcing passers-by to spit on it. When one elderly man refused, they tipped him head-first into a nearby horse trough and left him to struggle out, frightened and spluttering.

Laplace crossed the road, as many did, and hurried on. Mentally he was preparing more notes for his latest work, *Exposition du système du monde*.

'Every event,' he muttered to himself as his feet pattered along the pavement, 'is actually determined by the general laws of the universe, and is probable only relative to our knowledge . . .'

That old man, for instance. If he had known that the *jeunesse dorée* were just around the corner, he would never have ventured down the street. But once he was seen by them, the events that unfolded were inevitable. Laplace had once prepared a paper for the Académie, claiming that it would be possible to predict the outcome of a game of dice if one had precise knowledge of every factor, such as the weight of the die, the exact way in which the hand moved, the strength of that hand, and the force of each throw.

'It is our greater or lesser knowledge of constant factors,' he said aloud as he walked along, 'that constitutes their relative possibility. And this stability in the system of the world, which assures its duration, is one of the most notable among all phenomena. Just as Isaac Newton claimed. Yes, yes . . .'

Pleased with his thoughts, he vowed to write all this down as soon as he reached his home, where he would lunch with his wife Marie-Charlotte, who was twenty years younger than he was, and his six-year-old son.

But first, he had a rather interesting letter to deliver.

He had worked all that morning at the Bureau des Longitudes, which had been established by the Republican government only that year to administer all matters pertaining to navigation and astronomy. How very fortuitous that the Republic had at last acknowledged that it needed scientists – '*les charlatans modernes,*' in the words of the dead Marat – to provide its armies with ever more deadly weapons, and to guide its vessels of war through enemy-infested seas.

During the course of the morning, he'd received several letters. One of the many irritations of the war, in his opinion, was that his precious mail was often delayed by a matter of several days, even weeks. Look, for instance, at the missive he'd had this morning, from the amateur astronomer in London called Alexander Wilmot. For some time now, Wilmot and he had been holding a profitable correspondence regarding the orbits of the moons of Jupiter. But this particular letter had taken three weeks to reach him, instead of four days, as it ought to.

And, of course, there would be a further delay, because the letter was in English, and would have to be translated for him. He was taking the letter now, as he took all his English mail, to an Irishman called Nicholas Madgett, who worked for the French Admiralty as a translator of English documents and newspapers. Madgett was the ablest linguist Laplace knew, with considerable knowledge of the sciences also, which meant he could be relied upon to convey all the precise nuances of Wilmot's long-awaited letter.

Madgett looked harassed, and not at all pleased to see him when Laplace walked into his office, but Laplace didn't care.

'It might be a few days before I get round to it,' Madgett muttered.

Laplace looked at him coldly. 'Please see to it that the translation of this letter reaches my desk at the Bureau by nine o'clock tomorrow morning.' He turned to leave, but stopped suddenly. 'Oh, and this came inside the same packet. It's another of those Titius letters.'

He was surprised, and mildly interested, at the way Madgett seemed to go rather pale at the mention of the unknown Master Titius. There had been other letters to Titius in the past, and each time Madgett's response had been the same. Laplace moved nearer to the Irishman as Madgett opened the letter and spread it out on his desk. Laplace, seeing that it was a list of stars and their brightnesses, peered more closely at it.

'How strange,' Laplace said. 'Some of those numbers are quite wrong.'

Madgett nodded. He was still pale, but a feverish excitement seemed to have taken hold of him. He couldn't tear his eyes from the star list.

Laplace shrugged and started again towards the door. Irishmen – all eccentric and emotional. Everyone knew that the Irishmen in Paris – and they lived here in considerable numbers at the moment – were here because they detested William Pitt's English government. But the ones like Madgett were clever, and had their uses.

Laplace started to open the door. Then he turned back. 'You'll be quite sure to have that letter ready for me by tomorrow morning, at the Bureau?' he repeated. 'It's been delayed long enough already. It's most important.'

'Yes, yes,' said Madgett impatiently, still staring at the star list.

Laplace huffily made his way out, and closed the door with a bang.

The letter from Alexander Wilmot to Pierre Simon de Laplace, about Jupiter's moons, lay unheeded on Nicholas Madgett's desk, as the Irishman who worked on secret intelligence for the French government pulled from a drawer of his desk a small book called Lefèvre's *Mythologie*, and laid it eagerly beside the letter to Master Titius. Then he drew from his bookshelves an astronomer's guide to the magnitudes of the stars, and swiftly he began to make notes beside some of the star names on the letter. When that was done, he leafed intently through the *Mythologie*, running his finger down the pages; and on a fresh sheet of paper he began to write.

The Brittany expedition sails on . . . four thousand Royalist troops . . . Carnac.

'Too late,' he exclaimed bitterly, 'too late,' and pressed on.

Unverified reports . . . Tinténiac . . . Vilaine . . .

Ah.

He pushed it all aside to write a short note, which he folded and sealed. He went to open his door, and called brusquely for a messenger. 'Take this, now,' he instructed, 'to Louis Fréron.'

'But sir, the Convention will be sitting—'

'I don't care. I don't care if Fréron himself is speaking. Deliver it to him. *Quickly.*'

Part Four

10 July – 28 July 1795

XLI

Ye loyal inhabitants of Brittany, who have honoured me with your confidence, see now that it has not been betrayed. The English government, roused by your perseverance and misfortunes, has granted your request. An army comes to second your efforts, and I bring you all the succours you have demanded.

French officers and soldiers, who, like you, for these four years past have fought for their King, now hasten to join you, and your princes are soon to place themselves at the head of your invincible columns.

Joseph, Comte de Puisaye, Commander in Chief, Declaration to the Catholic Emigrant Army of Brittany, Carnac, July 1795

Over two hundred and fifty miles to the south-west of Paris, the spume-laden sea lashed the jagged rocks of the Brittany coast as the English convoy, buffeted by the wind ever since it left the shelter of Quiberon Bay, rounded with caution the headland of St Gildas de Rhuis and made for the relative calm of the inlet that enclosed the Vilaine estuary. On board the English ships were the Chevalier de Tinténiac and his army of three thousand native Breton troops, newly recruited at Carnac; and their spirits were high.

The Republican fleet was still penned into Lorient by Lord Bridport's ships. The Comte de Puisaye was secure on the Quiberon peninsula, twenty miles round the coast to the west, with his army of *émigré* Royalists continually swelled by thousands of Bretons flocking to join him. Already Puisaye had taken three forts; and the Chouan bands, his allies, held the crucial stronghold of Auray. Of the Republican army there was no sign; Hoche was rumoured to be far away, at Landévant, cowed, and waiting for reinforcements.

A swift, co-ordinated Royalist advance, spearheaded by Puisaye from the south, and this army of Tinténiac's from the east, could be expected to destroy Hoche's hesitant forces within a matter of days.

Even in the relative shelter of the bay, the sea was riven by currents, and still disturbed by the lingering remnants of those strong winds that had delayed the landing of the primary expedition at Carnac. Nevertheless, the English transport ships, in a superb display of seamanship, were soon standing by in the calmer waters beneath the headland; and the air was filled with the rumble of heavy anchor cables and the harsh issuing of orders as the English sailors, scornful of these foreign recruits, set to work on hoisting out the boats and getting the Bretons, many of them seasick after their journey, on to the shore of their native land.

At last the soldiers were all disembarked, looking stiff and uncomfortable in their English-made uniforms of scarlet coats and black, wide-brimmed hats. As they gathered on the beach, their officers, *émigré* Royalists all of them, clad in the white uniforms of the old Bourbon army, rode up and down their disordered lines, and by dint of much shouting and sword-waving, and the occasional blow, got their recruits at last into some semblance of military order, with the baggage carts and gun carriages drawn by more horses interspersed between the columns. By noon, Tinténiac's army, officially to be known as the *Compagnie Bretonne*, was ready to leave this windswept and muddy beach where the Vilaine opened out into the sea.

Noel-François Prigent, scout, intelligence officer and adviser to the expedition, rode his horse up on to a rocky bluff. He breathed in the sea air and looked down approvingly at the line of soldiers winding slowly up from the beach along the dirt track that the fishermen and farmers used. They were raw recruits, yes, but ardent nonetheless. They'd been trained, briefly, before their departure from Quiberon, in the rudiments of handling their English muskets, and many of them were still struggling to master them. But they'd told their officers, 'We can use the bayonets. And our fists. *Vive le Roi!*'

They were strong enough fellows, too, fit and tough; he saw they had already fallen into a steady rhythm behind their *fleur-de-lys* banners, even though the way lay uphill, and their packs were heavy. They carried on their backs six days' supply of food, sufficient to get them to within striking distance of Landévant, and Hoche, while hopefully rousing the whole countryside *en route*. Not a shot had been fired so far in resistance; not a single living soul had been seen, enemy soldier or peasant. There were a few lonely stone farmhouses scattered about, but they seemed deserted. Their inhabitants had presumably hidden, wary of any soldiers, on whichever side they fought.

A rider on a big black horse detached himself from the snaking line of soldiers and urged his mount up the hillside to join Prigent. This was the Chevalier de Tinténiac. Slender, fine-boned and with aristocratic features, he was a striking contrast in his white Bourbon uniform to Prigent, who wore a loose brown coat and whose long dark hair was blown about by the breeze. The two men were old comrades; they'd worked together as English agents for the intelligence network based in Jersey before Tinténiac, a soldier by training, rejoined the Royalist army under Puisaye.

Prigent nodded a greeting to his friend and gestured towards the long, steadily moving file of men below them. 'It's going well,' he said. 'All of Brittany will be ours soon. Within a month, who knows? We could be marching into Paris.'

Tinténiac smiled. 'With three thousand untrained men? Hardly.'

Prigent shook his head impatiently. Tinténiac was brave; no doubting that. But he was sometimes too cautious, too painstaking for Prigent's liking. 'Three thousand?' he objected. 'Just wait. The Breton resistance will come flocking. Charette's Vendéan army will join us. General Hoche – when, and if, he deigns to appear – will take one look at what faces him and flee eastwards as fast as he can.' Prigent watched approvingly as supply wagons rumbled by, laden with ammunition boxes covered with tarpaulin against the damp. Two heavy six-pounder guns in field carriages followed, accompanied by a dozen gunners from Rotalier's Artillery, survivors of the Flanders débâcle.

'Hoche is no coward,' said Tinténiac quietly.

'Neither are those men down there.' Prigent waved his hand expansively towards the marching column. 'And we're in our own country. Our homeland. Lead on, chevalier, to victory!'

Tinténiac smiled and bowed his head briefly in acknowledgement. 'Be sure that I will.' For a moment the two men's faces were lit with mutual fervour. Then Tinténiac spurred on his horse and cantered back down the grassy escarpment to take his place at the head of the leading column, a resplendent figure indeed in his white coat with its scarlet sash and ribbons.

Noel-François Prigent gazed back to where the English convoy was already making its way out to sea again, to rejoin Warren's fleet anchored in Quiberon Bay. Then he took a swig from the little bottle he carried with him, which contained the medicine prescribed by the good Doctor Raultier in London, and followed Tinténiac down the hill.

XLII

Let us trust to nothing but God and ourselves; for I
repeat it again and again, there is nothing else left
on which we can rely with safety.

Major Calvert, on the defeat of the British
army in Holland, 1795

It was evening, the 14th of July. Jonathan Absey stood on the
first-floor landing of the George Inn, in Portsmouth's bustling
High Street, and pointed almost despairingly to the room behind
him – *his* room, in which he'd resided unwillingly for six days now –
where the gathering twilight was scarcely relieved by the two almost-
expired candles that guttered fitfully on the table by the window.

'I need more candles,' said Jonathan. 'Candles, to write by.'

The elderly servant to whom he was speaking – Jonathan had already
deduced that he was more than a little deaf – stood scratching his
forehead beneath his grizzled wig. Then his bemused face suddenly
lit up. 'Candles,' he said. 'For writing. Just like the Navy men. The
minute they set foot on shore, there they are, busy with their pens and
papers. Orders, warrants, requests . . .' He shook his head in wonder.

'Yes,' said Jonathan. 'Look. I have reports I have to write, and letters
to send, by morning. Could you bring me candles and ink, straight away?'

'Candles and – ?'

'*Ink*,' said Jonathan. Driven to distraction, he pulled out some coins.
'Candles and *ink*.'

The servant took the money, quickly knuckled his forelock in a
gesture of obedience, and turned to go.

'Bring me a bottle of red wine as well,' ordered Jonathan. Then he
retreated to his little room with a sigh, closed the door, and sat at the
table. Propping his chin in his hands, he gazed out into the bustling
High Street, where the lamps had just been lit, illuminating a laden
coach from London that was noisily disgorging its passengers and
their luggage.

He'd travelled here himself on that same mail coach, in a state of despair at having to leave behind his quest for Ellie's killer, yet knowing that he had no option if he wanted to keep his job. Arriving in Portsmouth in the early evening, stiff from the long journey, his lungs filled with the stale air of the packed carriage, he'd arranged for a room here at the George, then gone down to the shingle beach and walked by the sea. The salt wind had whipped at his clothes, and the grey, choppy sea seemed to reflect the turbulent sky.

The last time Jonathan was here, just over a year ago, Lord Howe's fleet had been about to leave Spithead to tackle the French squadron in the Channel; and Jonathan could not forget the throng of sailors and dockyard workers, the tumult of preparation in the yards, the bustle of the senior officers and their entourages arriving at the gates, the desperate scurrying of the midshipmen and bosuns as they rousted the old hands out of the taverns and on to their ships.

But now the deep harbour was empty of ships. The desultory work continued as ever at the mast pond and the building slips; the air was still pungent with the smells of tar and rope; but without the great men-of-war anchored at Spithead, without the English sailors who were its lifeblood, the town of Portsmouth seemed leached of vitality; as if all that sustained it was far away, and this was a time of waiting, of suspended animation.

Afterwards Jonathan had gone walking round the town, his head bowed, till he found his way to a half-empty tavern in the Point and drank enough wine to enable him to get a fitful sort of sleep.

The morning after his arrival he'd braved the blustery wind and set off for the Port Admiral's office, which was, like the George, in the High Street. There he announced himself as a representative of the Home Office, and declared his business; only to be told that sedition in the dockyards was the concern of the resident commissioner, and he should make himself known at the yard itself. So he walked across the Hard, leaving Portsmouth Point behind him, and approached the two high gates that guarded the great naval base. He was escorted past the wharves and the mast pond, where the work of the ship-wrights and carpenters continued as ever, until he came to the

Commissioner's house. Here the elderly Sir Charles Saxton, representative of the Navy Board, welcomed him in a somewhat harassed
fashion, and grumbled for a while about the Port Admiral, and the
impossibility of simultaneously answering to the Admiralty, and the
Navy Office, and the yard officers, as he had been trying to do for
the last five years. Then he sent for his junior clerk to take Jonathan
round the yard and introduce him to the Clerk of the Survey, the
Master Storekeeper, and the three Master Attendants; after which
Jonathan was guided back to Commissioner Saxton's house, where he
asked for the Clerk of the Cheque.

'He's not here,' said Saxton regretfully.

'Then may I perhaps wait for him in his office?'

'I'm afraid you'd have to wait a long time. He's gone to Alum Bay
with one of his clerks to do a muster. There are several uncommis-
sioned vessels at anchor off the Isle of Wight, and it's his job to make
a record of their crews.'

Jonathan closed his eyes briefly. 'Could I ask when you expect him
back, sir?'

Saxton made a gesture of apology. 'Three days? Perhaps four, or
five?'

Jonathan was filled with fresh despair. The Clerk of the Cheque,
Davies, was one of the officials he specifically had to see, for it was
his job to keep the dockyard staff lists, and circulate reports of trouble-
makers to the clerks at the other yards. His absence meant that
Jonathan wouldn't be done with this business for a week, maybe longer.

His spirits leaden, he returned to the George and began a letter to
Stimpson in London. He'd already sent a note to the informer before
leaving for Portsmouth, to tell him that he couldn't make the meeting
they'd arranged; but now he wrote again, stipulating that Stimpson was
to write to him with news of everything he'd found out. He thought,
too, of Alexander; he was haunted by the fear that Alexander might
have tried to get in touch with him and found him gone from the
capital; so he wrote to him as well, his pen flying over the paper,
explaining where he was and exhorting his half-brother to find out, if
he had not already done so, if anyone other than the scarred coachman
accompanied Guy de Montpellier on his night-time journeys. He told
Alexander, and Stimpson too, to write to him at the George.

And then he had nothing to do except wait for Davies to return.

Commissioner Saxton was helpful enough, in that he found one of Davies's assistants to show him the dockyard musters, so he could begin a cursory check on the names he needed to look up; but Jonathan quickly realised that only Davies's expert knowledge could fill out the bare records for him. As an outward show of duty, Jonathan also asked around the town about the seditious leaflets, and visited the magistrates. Each time the London mail coach arrived he looked for letters from Stimpson and Alexander; but there were none.

In the meantime, in this time of waiting, he continued with a search of his own, for he still had a crumpled piece of paper in his pocket on which was written the address to which Carline's discharge papers had been sent. Tallis at the Admiralty had told him that Carline was dismissed not one year ago, but two; and that no officer was ever flogged. Another discrepancy, originating, perhaps, in some lie of Carline's, or merely in some fault of communication. Nevertheless, while he was here, he would find out more.

He made enquiries about the address Tallis had given him, and found his way one night, after several false starts, to a lodging house in Portsmouth Point, that jumble of mean lanes and alleys that lay between the High Street and the shingle beach. He asked the man who opened the door a mere inch or two if someone called Carline had lived there, and was told brusquely, 'For a while. Then he left.'

'When did he leave?'

'He disappeared about a year ago. Hadn't paid his rent, damn him.' The man was suspicious of Jonathan; he wanted to close the door.

'Did he have work in the town?' persisted Jonathan.

'At the dockyards. They'd tell you more there.' The door slammed, and Jonathan turned away in frustration. Who would tell him more?

Davies, the Clerk of the Cheque.

Again, Jonathan would have to wait.

On the morning of his eighth day here, Jonathan went as usual, more out of habit than in hope, to the dockyard; and he found that Davies had at last returned from his duties on the Isle of Wight. Commissioner Saxton had already told the senior clerk about Jonathan's business, and Davies seemed well prepared and obliging; in fact he'd already looked up the names of the suspects Jonathan had been ordered to investigate, and was able to give categorical assurances that none of them had been involved in any kind of trouble. He accounted for them all: one had left for family reasons; another, a carpenter, had left for Winchester to set up his own business; and so on.

'You'll find no treacherous talk among the men in the yard,' he assured Jonathan as they stood together in his office.

'Nevertheless, those leaflets were found here.'

Davies shrugged apologetically. 'I'm afraid that intruders – and troublemakers – do get in. The gates are well guarded, but in a huge place like this, with provisions and workmen constantly going in and out, there's always a danger of spies. But the men here are basically loyal. They know that the safety of England rests with our Navy.'

'Of course.' Jonathan gazed down at the notes he'd made. 'There was just one other person I wanted to ask you about. Carline. William Carline.'

'Carline,' repeated Davies, frowning. 'Yes, I remember him. Surely you don't suspect him of sedition?'

'Just a routine check, like the others. But he left suddenly, didn't he?'

'Yes. He was with us less than a year . . .' Davies broke off as a cart laden with timber rumbled past the office in the direction of the wharves, briefly drowning out conversation. Then he went on, 'He was in fact dismissed. Last summer.'

Jonathan's heart was beating unevenly. 'Dismissed?'

'Yes.' Davies lifted one of his heavy registers down from a shelf and opened it, carefully turning the pages. 'Let me see . . . It was actually on July the 11th that he was struck off. I wasn't here, unfortunately; I was away for most of June and July, visiting the other dockyards. Apparently he was caught pilfering copper, to be sold off in the town. Stupid of him. He was tried by our own dockyard commission, here.'

'Is that customary?'

'Yes, unless the case is considered important enough to go to the Assizes . . .' Davies was running his finger down one of the pages. 'Here it is. He was found guilty, and whipped. A rather sordid episode, for a man who had been a warrant officer.' Davies looked up at Jonathan. 'You perhaps already know that he was suspended from the Navy before he came to work here.'

'I heard that he was a purser, suspected of falsifying his ship's accounts,' said Jonathan. 'The Commissioner here must have known of his record; and yet he was taken on almost immediately, in a position of some responsibility. Isn't that unusual?'

Davies sighed and closed his heavy book. 'Not if you'd seen how desperate we were for clerical staff in the summer of two years ago. All the refitting of ships, the mustering of crews for the transports to the Low Countries; we were in dire need of capable clerks, and Carline was good. Clever. I used to leave him in charge of writing receipts for the ships' stores, checking contractors' deliveries and so on, and I never found any evidence of trickery.' He turned to face Jonathan. 'He always used to protest his innocence of the Navy charge – he said it was his superiors who'd falsified the accounts and tried to blame it on him. He was, after all, only suspended on suspicion of fraud, not convicted. I found him useful, and trustworthy; that was why I was so surprised to find out he'd done such a stupid thing as stealing copper. As I said, I'd been away for a few weeks around the time it happened; I only heard of it when I got back. By then it was all over, the conviction and the flogging. He left Portsmouth almost immediately.'

'He was taken ill,' said Jonathan, 'directly after the flogging. He lost the power of speech.'

Davies shook his head regretfully. 'Ah. No more philosophy, then.'

'Philosophy?'

'He was fond of it. He liked to quote some passages, especially those of a strange writer called Swedenborg. Carline knew a lot about the stars as well as philosophy, but of course that was to be expected, as he was a former Navy man –' He put his register back on the shelf almost regretfully. 'Is that all, then, Mr Absey? We'd let you know immediately, of course, if we found any more of those leaflets, or the men responsible; but in all sincerity, I think it unlikely. Petty theft can be a problem here, I'll admit, as at every dockyard; but treachery? I hope, I very much hope not.'

He glanced again at the leaflet Jonathan had given him, and smiled. 'German George. I remember these appearing amongst the men, but we laughed at them. They'd chosen the wrong target, because most of our labourers can't read.'

Jonathan thanked him, and turned back slowly to go through the gates and make his way up into the town.

So much for Carline: a sordid and petty story of a purser suspended on suspicion of fraud two years ago – not one, as Alexander, and presumably the Montpelliers, believed – and then, one year ago, charged with theft again, this time convicted, and flogged from the dockyard last July. He'd actually seen the evidence for himself, written in the yard's register. Ellie had been murdered in June, while Carline was still in Portsmouth. All he'd found out was that Carline was a well-read thief, who'd lost the power of speech. An odd, dishonest character; but there was nothing further here to help him in his quest.

Why had the matter been kept so quiet? Perhaps such secrecy was more common than was thought. Jonathan had heard rumours that some of the senior officers at the yards were themselves suspected of being involved in systematic thieving from the stores, and he wondered if something of this nature lay beneath Carline's disgrace; though Davies himself had seemed honest enough.

He paused outside the great gates, which clanged shut behind him, and looked out to sea, where a lonely vessel was heading into the harbour; perhaps bearing dispatches, Jonathan guessed, from the squadron that guarded the Channel. For a few moments he stood there and gazed out at the grey, encompassing ocean, at the indistinct horizon, and he thought of the British ships and the soldiers they'd carried to the far-off Breton coast.

Then he marched on up into the town. At the George, there was a letter waiting for him, from Alexander. The landlord handed it to him in the hallway, and Jonathan broke it open immediately.

'*Dear brother,*' Alexander had written. '*I am in receipt of your letter. I must assure you that I have not forgotten what you requested; but I cannot visit the Montpelliers until I have done as they asked and completed the calculations for the lost star. I hope your business in Portsmouth goes well.*'

Jonathan screwed the sheet up in his fist. 'That star. That star,' he muttered under his breath. 'He's obsessed. They are all obsessed . . .'

The landlord was watching him with interest. Jonathan pushed the letter in his pocket and said, 'Were there any more letters for me?'

'No, sir. That was it.'

Jonathan had expected news from Stimpson. He burned with frustration.

He went out again to the coach office down at the Point to book a seat on the Mail; only to be told that the coach was full for the next day, Saturday, and there would be none travelling on Sunday. Jonathan went back to his room, and sat and prepared his report for Pollock; and he wrote until almost all his candles had burned down again. Then he sat and stared out into the night, thinking of the Montpelliers, who sheltered his daughter's killer.

XLIII

I hate that drum's discordant sound,
Parading round, and round, and round;
To me it talks of ravaged plains,
And burning towns, and ruined swains.

John Scott, 'Ode' (1782)

Two hundred and fifty miles away, the Chevalier de Tinténiac and his column were leaving the Atlantic coast far behind them as they advanced into the Breton interior. So far they had met with little opposition, apart from the occasional skirmish with isolated bands of Republican soldiers, who were easily scattered. The Republican garrison of Vannes had not emerged, presumably preferring the security of the town walls to a battle in the open countryside surrounded by an ardently Royalist population. In fact the further Tinténiac's army had marched, the more local men had joined them, wearing ragged clothes and armed with ancient fowling pieces and hayforks. These newcomers had delayed their progress, but they'd also guided them to some useful sources from which to replenish their supplies, showing them abandoned farms with hidden stores, and caches of rations left by the fleeing Republicans.

By the sixth day of their march, they'd emerged from the wooded valleys of the hinterland to find themselves on bare upland; and when it was time to stop for their midday rations the soldiers found what respite they could from the hot sun by settling beside the sparse, shrubby trees and rocks that bordered this desolate road while they foraged in their packs for bread and cheese. Tinténiac and Prigent had drawn a little apart from the main force. The Chevalier had his maps spread out on the ground and was studying them intently, while Prigent, who had eaten well and drunk the best part of a bottle of wine he'd purloined from the farm where they'd slept the previous night, was lying peacefully on his back with his hat over his face.

'According to my reckoning,' said Tinténiac, frowning in concentration at his map, 'we're about four leagues north-east of Vannes and seven leagues east of Auray. If we start to head west when we come to this tributary of the Arz river, we could be within striking distance of Hoche's army in two days' time.'

Prigent said sleepily, 'Yes. Indeed.'

'Unless there's been a change of plan,' pondered Tinténiac, almost to himself. 'Puisaye said he'd get word to us if there was. It's so quiet, I could believe he's already advanced from Quiberon and driven Hoche eastwards—'

He broke off suddenly as the sound of distant hoofbeats pierced the still air. Springing to his feet, he shaded his eyes against the sun to scan the far-off track. Prigent got up in a more leisurely fashion and put his hands in his coat pockets.

'Perhaps it's news from Puisaye.' Tinténiac's voice was tense.

'As you say, it's probably a message to tell us that the entire west of the peninsula, from Vannes to Dinard, has fallen to the Royalists,' said Prigent confidently.

The rider was visible now, coming down the track from the north. He spoke to the sentries who stood on the crest of the hill, and they appeared to indicate the vantage point where Tinténiac stood with Prigent at his side. The rider urged his horse on towards his goal; and they saw, as he came close, that his face was harrowed with exhaustion.

'Chevalier de Tinténiac?' he gasped from his saddle. 'I have a message for you.'

He was fumbling deep into his coat pocket. Tinténiac took the slim packet he held out and asked eagerly, 'Is it from the Comte de Puisaye?'

The messenger looked puzzled. 'Not from Puisaye, chevalier. This message comes from Paris.'

Tinténiac looked up sharply. 'Paris?'

'Yes.' The messenger slid wearily from his horse. 'I have orders from the Royalist Agency. It took me five days to reach Rennes, because I had to make detours and ride by night to avoid the Republican guard. Then another day to reach Ploermel. Since then I've been riding around, asking these damned Chouans for news of you –'

Prigent offered the man his wine bottle, and he drank thirstily while Tinténiac read the letter. Then the Chevalier took Prigent's arm and drew him away a little. 'It's from the Comte d'Artois,' he informed his friend quietly. 'The letter tells us to march north. To St Brieuc.'

He handed Prigent the letter and turned back to the dust-covered messenger. 'How does the Comte d'Artois know our position? Why are orders being sent to us from Paris?'

The man lowered the bottle and wiped his lips. 'Monsieur, don't you realise? News has already reached Paris. The whole of the west has risen against the Republicans. Hoche is in retreat. If you march northwards now, you can cut off his escape. It seems Puisaye's messengers have all missed you; but thank God, I have not.'

Tinténiac anxiously eyed the messenger, who was drinking once more. 'What do you make of this?' he asked Prigent in a low voice.

Prigent was scanning the letter swiftly. 'The Agency controls virtually all the Royalist intelligence on the mainland,' he replied at last, turning back to Tinténiac. 'Its members are in contact with the English, with the exiled princes, with everyone; their knowledge of the present situation will be far, far greater than ours. You have to do what it says.'

Tinténiac stared into the distance. In the hot, still air around them, the murmur of the soldiers at rest rose like the hum of bees. Somewhere a horse whinnied restlessly. Tinténiac said quietly, 'Why hasn't Puisaye sent a messenger?'

'Perhaps it's as he says.' Prigent nodded towards the man from the Royalist Agency. 'The country ahead is in uproar. No one knows where to find us. At any rate, I can vouch for the signature. It's definitely that of the Comte d'Artois.'

Tinténiac didn't reply, but continued to gaze westwards. What lay there? Empty countryside? Was Puisaye harrying Hoche to the north, even as they idled here? Were they missing their chance of glory?

He made his decision.

While they had been talking, the youthful Breton officer Georges Cadoudal had come up to join them. Tinténiac, still unhappy, turned to him and said, 'There's been a change of orders. We're to head north, to St Brieuc.'

Cadoudal, who had been fighting with the Chouans for two years, said grimly, 'But sir. The men are starting to get tired, and we're almost out of supplies. Two, perhaps three days' marching westwards would take us to Quiberon, and Puisaye. But north? How are we going to eat?'

'We must forage,' said Tinténiac tiredly. 'I've had instructions, Cadoudal, from the Royalist Agency; and we have to obey them.'

The rain started the following day, soon after the Chevalier de Tinténiac's army began to struggle across Lanvaux Moor, a long, upland crest of rock-strewn heath that slowed the soldiers' pace to a weary trudge, and made progress for the supply carts and gun carriages almost impossible. Along with the rain, a stubborn summer mist had settled across this bare moorland; and the straggling trail of infantry and officers, red and white uniforms muddied and filthied so they appeared the same colour now, faces grey with fatigue, trailed with difficulty across the trackless terrain, trying to pick a path between peat bogs and scattered rocks. Now and then megaliths loomed like grey giants out of the mist.

They had lost their way. The Chevalier de Tinténiac, his white coat and scarlet sash stained and torn, his boots mired to the knee, was leading his horse now, his slender figure bowed with tiredness. A gun carriage slipped to one side and its wheels became embedded in a bog; he himself supervised its extraction, but he swore in despair when some ammunition cases slipped and fell into the murky water. Then he went to seek out Prigent.

'This place is cursed,' muttered Tinténiac to his friend in an undertone. 'The men have lost all their spirit. I'm afraid that they'll start to desert. I think I've seen some of them turning back already.'

Prigent said, 'They're superstitious fellows, and they don't like it here. It's these stones.' He gestured towards one of the vast prehistoric megaliths whose outline they could just discern to their right. 'They say this moor is haunted by the Akous.'

'For God's sake. Akous?'

'The Akous of Brittany,' Prigent answered. 'Spectral creatures from the hellish regions, who call out to those about to die. Don't worry, though, chevalier. They'll forget all this ghostly talk just as soon as they've got hot food in their bellies and wine in their throats. We should reach the outskirts of Ploermel by nightfall. All we need is a granary, and a few good fires with plump sheep roasting, and they'll be happy enough.'

Tinténiac looked around. 'I only hope you're right.'

'This has slowed us down a little. That's all.' With that, Prigent bade him adieu and marched on, whistling a cheerful Breton song. The Chevalier de Tinténiac stood momentarily alone in the mist, which curled its tendrils around him like silent wraiths.

And then came the unmistakable retort of a musket and the sound of a ball whistling somewhere close by.

Tinténiac ran forward to where Prigent had pulled up abruptly.

'It's just a sniper,' Prigent said. But already Tinténiac was turning back to his men with a look almost of despair on his face. 'Halt! Prepare your arms!' he cried.

He had seen what Prigent had not. For just one moment, after the sound of the shot, a breath of wind had lifted the swirling mist and he had glimpsed something that turned his blood cold with horror.

About two hundred yards away stood a body of troops facing them, muskets levelled; and beyond them were more, stretching away into the mist. They wore blue coats with white linings and lapels; scarlet collars and cuffs, and black hats with red plumes. The Garde Nationale, the Republican infantry, in their thousands. That first shot must have been a stray. Tinténiac yelled hoarsely to the men behind him, 'Muskets – make ready!'

But there was no time for his men to respond, and he knew it. They had walked straight into a trap. Even as he called out his orders, the rattle of enemy fire drowned out his words. He glimpsed them briefly again, the battalions of enemy infantry, like a vision from hell; then they vanished into the mist and the haze of smoke from their musket fire.

And then came the scream of injured men, Tinténiac's men, Chouans and officers, and the neighing of terrified horses. Up there on the bare hillside, men splashed and floundered blindly in the boggy ground. Prigent clung to Tinténiac's side, gasping, 'If we could get a six-pounder set up, we'd send them running –'

'No,' said Tinténiac bitterly, 'no, it would take a dozen six-pounders and half a battalion of gunners to make any impact on such a force.' Some of his officers were already trying to roll a gun into place over the rough terrain; others were running amongst the Chouans, exhorting them to show courage, screaming at them to load their muskets and fire. But their weapons, like the powder for the guns, were damp.

Another roll of musket fire rumbled through the mist from the Republican army. The odour of choking smoke and of burnt cartridges filled the air. Behind Prigent a man screamed and fell, struck by a musket ball in the stomach; he writhed in agony in the mud. Some of the Chouans were already turning away; crouching low, they started to flee back up towards the menhirs in the mist.

Tinténiac and Prigent ran to help the gunners from Rotalier's regiment, who had somehow managed to get the six-pounder into place. Another officer close by was reaching for the gunpowder cartridges when something hit a nearby rock with an earth-shattering crash and passed on with a roar. The officer fell back, his face a mask of blood: the rock had been struck by a cannon ball, and splinters of stone had slashed open his cheeks and eyes.

'Cannon,' breathed Prigent, 'they've got cannon.'

The mist was lifting now. When the dense, whitish-grey clouds of the cannon fire subsided at last, they could see a hostile battery at the forefront of the ranks of the bluecoats. Another cannon boomed and a ball ploughed directly into the main body of the Royalists. Men were thrown aside; limbs, fragments of weapons and of flesh were flung into the air. More Bretons were starting to turn and run back up the hill whence they had come, to the shelter of the mist that still clung to the higher ground. Prigent and the Royalist officers chased despairingly after them, using the flat of their swords to admonish them. 'Turn, men of Brittany! For your God, your king, stand together! Defend yourselves . . .'

The Blues were advancing. Their drums rolled like thunder. At a single barked command from one of their officers, they stopped and prepared their muskets again. Behind them, more columns of Republican soldiers could be seen moving into place.

Tinténiac fell at the next volley. Prigent knelt swiftly beside him, and saw that a bullet had gone through his chest. The blood flowed bright crimson against the muddied cream of his uniform. The Republican battery boomed again. The remnants of Tinténiac's army turned and fled, struggling uphill in wild disorder through the peaty mud, some crowding behind the menhirs for cover from the deadly hail of musket balls and grape. The stench of gunpowder filled the air; the drums rattled menacingly once more, and the Blues advanced steadily, in line, bayonets at the ready. Wounded Chouans lay where they had fallen, moaning in fear and pain.

Prigent was on his knees, cradling Tinténiac's body; but he knew that the chevalier was dead. Less than a hundred yards away, on the flank of the advancing line of soldiers, he saw a Republican gun crew hard at work as they loaded, rammed and fired; so close, that he saw the ball leave the muzzle. Betrayed.

He turned and ran too, up into the mist, sobbing for breath.

At Quiberon, General Lazare Hoche was not in retreat, nor had Puisaye advanced to the east. Instead, at the Republican base of Landévant, Hoche had ordered his army, freshly reinforced by troops from the Spanish war, to retake Auray; then he proceeded to drive Puisaye and his Royalist venturers back down the narrow ridge of the isthmus to the peninsula. And there the Royalists waited, trapped, for Tinténiac's relief force to arrive.

XLIV

*Like a man walking alone in the dark, I resolved to
go so slowly, and use so much circumspection in all
matters, as to be secured against falling, even if I
made very little progress.*

René Descartes, *Discourse on the Method of
Rightly Directing One's Reason, and of Seeking
Truth in the Sciences*, Part II (1637)

The government offices of Whitehall hummed with the
continued news of the success of the Brittany landing. The
dispatches, which took on average a week to ten days to make
the journey from Quiberon Bay, came in regularly, filled with accounts
of how the Chouans had joined Puisaye's Royalist force in their thousands. The talk, both in the great offices of state and the humbler
rooms of lowly secretaries and clerks, was jubilant, congratulatory. It
seemed that the crisis of England's failure in this war was over at last.

Jonathan Absey, meanwhile, had finally returned from Portsmouth
on the 19th July. The next day, having handed in his report, he'd
reinstated himself in the half-forgotten corner of Whitehall to which
he'd been demoted, and continued with the routine matters that
awaited him. He also listened with care to the latest news from
Brittany; he read every report, and last night he'd studied an article
in *The Times* with particular attention.

*On the 10th inst, M. de Tinténiac, at the head of three thousand men,
was landed at the Vilaine estuary, from whence he has proceeded inland
to penetrate the country northwards, marching against Muzillac, and
into the environs of Vannes.*

*M. de Tinténiac has fought six different actions with the enemy, in
every one of which he has been victorious. He has found also the means
of forming a junction with several bands of Chouans from the interior.*

Jonathan had folded the news sheet up carefully. Confirmation, indeed, that the Chevalier de Tinténiac's diversionary force had not been betrayed; there had been no Republican force waiting for them.

He had been so sure, two weeks ago when he accosted King, that Raultier was a Republican spy who had betrayed both Puisaye and Tinténiac; just as he had been sure that in uncovering the spying ring, he could expose the killer of his daughter. He'd been wrong in the first assumption – of the second he was still sure.

The next day Jonathan left his office at noon and went to track down Stimpson, who told him that he had watched the house in Kensington Gore and its inhabitants on several occasions, but he had nothing new to add to what Jonathan knew already. Ralph Wallace, the manservant, had once been accused of assaulting his wife, but the magistrates had dismissed the case on the grounds of her provocative behaviour. Matthew Norland, the ex-priest, visited the Montpelliers frequently, though he had a small house of his own, at Hockley in the Hole; and he attended Mass at the Sardinian chapel in Lincoln's Inn Fields, where he sometimes conducted Bible classes for the Catholic *émigrés* nearby.

'Find out more about him,' Jonathan said wearily. He'd dismissed Norland almost from the beginning. A former priest who was over-fond of brandy seemed the least likely of them all as a murder suspect; but he had to try everything.

And Carline, flogged from the dockyard for theft? Stimpson confirmed that Carline was a mute, and Auguste de Montpellier's lover. The French lady clung to him, said Stimpson with his hollow-cheeked leer, every hour, every minute of the day.

After his meeting with Stimpson, Jonathan went to the Navy Office in the Strand, on the pretext of checking some minor detail concerning the report he'd just prepared on the Portsmouth dockyard. He asked there for details of Carline's dismissal – which ought to have been forwarded here from the yard, as should be all such disciplinary matters – but was told there was nothing. He wondered if it was just another example of the incompetence that Commissioner Saxton had complained of so bitterly.

He thought briefly of going on to the Piazza, because he wanted to find Rose Brennan, to check that she was safe; but he didn't, because he remembered too vividly his guilt after their coupling, and the scorn in her eyes. Rose would have to look after herself. Besides, he knew that if he was to hold on to even his present lowly employment, he must attend to his duty, and to Pollock's warning, and not be seen consorting with prostitutes.

So he returned to Whitehall and bent his mind, for the moment, to his work, poring over his papers till late and resolving to himself that soon – tomorrow night, if possible – he would pay a call on his brother Alexander.

The following morning he was given the task of copying out and registering some Home Office dispatches that detailed the supplies for the troops in the West Indies. From what he had heard, these supplies took so long to cross the Atlantic, and were so depleted by the climate, and the distance, and the open thievery at the other end, that it was hardly worth the trouble of sending them. But he set about the work and kept his silence; and when the copies were completed he prepared to take them himself to the other departments of government: lowly work indeed.

It was late afternoon by the time he'd delivered the final copy to the Admiralty. He was on his way back to the Treasury when he saw Richard Crawford standing by the entrance to Montague House, in company with a man dressed in a dark green coat, with fine brass buttons that Lucket, he thought with sudden nostalgia, would have envied. This man was younger than Crawford and striking in appearance: tall, with long fair hair.

Jonathan had no intention of stopping to speak to Crawford. He'd no particular desire to endure the little Scotsman's solicitude over his demotion; and besides, he still wondered if it might have been Crawford who reported him for his frequent absences.

But the thoroughfare was too congested to allow a wide berth, and besides, Crawford had seen him now. Jonathan braced himself for the encounter.

'Your servant, Master Absey,' said Crawford.

'And yours,' Jonathan responded tersely, and went on his way. But he was aware of Crawford and his companion watching him.

Jonathan's next port of call was the Paymaster-General's office. He took his time walking there; and once, as he glanced round, he thought he saw a tall, fair-haired man some way behind him, slipping into a recess between two buildings just as he turned. It was Crawford's companion.

Jonathan frowned, uneasy. The crowds of departing Whitehall staff, of porters on errands, and food vendors, and chair-men shouting for business, pushed past in a noisy mêlée. He moved back into the shadows that lurked beside the imposing Treasury doorway, and waited. After some moments, he saw the blond man coming through the crowds, passing him and steadily making his way up Whitehall Place in the direction of the Strand.

Jonathan watched him warily. Who was he? And what was his business with Crawford? There was something vaguely familiar about him; Jonathan felt sure he had seen him before, but perhaps in another context, another setting. Why had he been following Jonathan? Was he another of those who had dogged his footsteps ever since he started to ask questions about the Montpelliers?

Whatever his business, the blond man was moving quickly now. He was young and fit; Jonathan wasn't. Jonathan, hurrying after him, was starting to breathe heavily. The man strode up St Martin's Lane, then turned right. Somewhere in the labyrinth of alleyways between Bedford Street and Long Acre, Jonathan lost him.

Jonathan pulled up, his heart thumping with exertion, and looked around the unpromising place in which he found himself. It seemed almost dark here, because so much of the sunlight was cut off by the dank walls of the high tenements. Lines of threadbare washing were strung between broken windows; ragged children played half-heartedly in the gutter that ran down the middle of this narrow alley. A baby squalled in some upstairs room.

Then, at the opening to a dark lane, he thought he saw the man with fair hair, moving quickly: Jonathan hurried up the lane, and found himself at the back of a coachmaker's workplace. The smell of sawdust and varnish filled the air, and from the yard beyond the wall he could hear the rasp of metal against wood, and the chatter of apprentices. To one side of him was the wall; to the other was a high timber warehouse with steps to the first and second floors, and at the top a windlass, for shifting the heavy raw materials of the coachmaker's trade.

He heard the creak of a chain, from high above him. He looked up sharply and leapt aside in the same second.

Half a ton of timber planking, bound in rope, was swinging down rapidly towards him, at the end of a long chain attached to the windlass. It crashed to the ground inches from where he had been standing.

Jonathan pressed himself back against the wall. He was shaking.

"Ware timber!' someone called belatedly from the yawning door above.

No one else around seemed to have noticed his narrow escape. The apprentice boys, still chattering, came to unfasten the planks of timber and heave them, one by one, into the coachmaker's yard. Jonathan, breathing hard and deep, turned and made his way swiftly down Bedford Street to the wide thoroughfare of the Strand, which now seemed heartwarmingly safe to him, in spite of the assorted rogues and thieves at every street corner.

Jonathan started to walk slowly home, with the letter he'd been supposed to deliver to the Paymaster-General's office still crumpled in his pocket. An accident, he told himself shakily, an accident; though the stealing of his Dover letter had not been an accident, the torturing of his son had not been an accident.

That evening he was to meet James Stimpson outside a gaming house in King Street where the informer spent much of his time. He went to the rendezvous with little expectation of anything, except the loss of more money spent on payments that he could ill afford. But he was to be surprised: firstly by the fact that the hollow-cheeked, sparse-haired informer was already waiting for him; and secondly, that he had some news.

'The priest,' Stimpson said. 'Norland. There are records of him. From Paris.'

Jonathan felt a leaping at his heart. 'How do you know?'

'I learnt it from the French informer, Valdené.'

'I know him,' nodded Jonathan. Before the Revolution, Valdené had been assistant to the French king's chief of police in Paris. Exiled by the Committee, an ardent monarchist, Valdené had managed to smuggle out some of the old police records, and he was now in London, helping the English government in its efforts to root out traitors by supplying information about suspect *émigrés*. 'What did he tell you?'

'He didn't tell me much,' shrugged Stimpson. 'He was suspicious – went on about how he usually only gives his information to official Home Office employees. I'd have done better if I could have mentioned your name—'

'But you didn't?'

'Oh, no. But I did find out that the priest was arrested in Paris in the summer of 1792. And he was thrown into prison.'

'What for?'

Stimpson's pale eyes glowed with salacious pleasure. 'Valdené obliged me with the exact phrase, Mister Absey. Norland was accused of *une agression sexuelle*. A sexual offence.'

Fiercely Jonathan gripped the man's shoulders. 'What did he do?'

'That, Valdené didn't tell me.'

'Then you must find out more . . .'

Stimpson was raising his eyebrows enquiringly. Jonathan fumbled in his pocket for money, and Stimpson loped off in the direction of the gaming house. Jonathan stood there in a mixture of disbelief and shock. A sexual crime. Norland. Norland, the former priest . . .

XLV

Tonight the sky cleared and I saw Jupiter roaming godlike through Capricorn. Later I gazed on Antares, ten degrees below the emerging moon; while Capella lurked in the north, low in the summer haze.

Sometimes I long to soar with the stars. There must be music up there in the clear air, the sound of stars singing.

You remember the legend? Brave Hercules fought the crab that was sent by Juno to destroy him; he grappled with the poisoned claws that tore and burned at his body's soft flesh. But even as Hercules thought himself the victor, one of his enemy's claws pierced his skin, and the slow-acting poison sank secretly in.

The sea-crab was later raised by a grateful, jealous Juno to the bright heavens.

I looked for you tonight, but I could not find you. All I have left is my quest for the lost star. Let me find it before it is too late . . .

It was later that same evening, and Auguste was reading the letter she had found in her brother's room. Carline came up behind her, so she put it swiftly down on her desk, her hands trembling as she did so. Carline, placing his hands on her shoulders, kissed the nape of her neck, and his lips lingered over the narrow ribbon of red silk that she wore as adornment.

She turned to him, and they faced one another silently. Her eyes were bright with unshed tears. She ran her fingers down his back, feeling the warm, ridged scars beneath the smooth fabric of his shirt. 'Oh, where have you been?' she breathed. 'No matter . . . How I have missed you.'

He took her hand, and held it. She pressed his fingers to her lips and whispered, 'Time is running out for my brother. Why does Wilmot take so long?'

Carline reached for a blank sheet of paper on Guy's desk and picked up a pen. 'Perhaps,' he wrote, 'you would like your little English mouse to stay with us for a while?'

She nodded. 'If Wilmot was here,' she said, 'he would surely make quicker progress in the work we have asked him to do.'

'Very well. I will see to it,' he wrote.

He kissed her then, and they made love all through the brief hours of darkness, pausing only to gaze through the open window from their tumbled bed as Venus rose in the east, just before the sun.

Carline hurt her sometimes as he loved her. She could not be sure how much he comprehended what he did; for he muffled her cries with his kisses, so that even in the extremity of her passion, she seemed, after all, as silent as he.

After some sleep, little enough, she was woken by the morning sun pouring through open curtains. Carline was already dressed, and seated at the desk. She went to see what he had written.

'Your mouse, your little monsieur mouse, has a brother rat. Did you know?'

Auguste read sleepily, her bruised lips moving round the words. She was tantalised, and pleaded to know more, but he kissed her and refused to write again.

XLVI

*Many a night have I been practising to see, and it
would be strange if one did not acquire a certain
dexterity by such constant practice.*

William Herschel, Letter to William Watson,
7 January 1782

I n the leafy suburb of Clerkenwell, where the trees shaded the
pleasant little houses by the Green, and the fields and hay meadows
were but a stone's throw away; where the gentle hum of the workshops of the many jewellers and locksmiths was often the only indication of the proximity of the great city, Alexander Wilmot was busy.
Had it not been for his necessary attendance to his duties at the church,
and the routine which Daniel endeavoured to impose by bringing him
his meals, and reminding him when the nightwatchman had cried one
of the clock in the street outside that it was perhaps time for him to
rest, he would scarcely have been aware of the passage of the days and
the nights.

He was working on Guy's calculations, with the candles always lit
at his desk. Day after day, hour after hour, he pored over the figures
until his good eye ached, trying to fit parabolas that would reconcile
Guy's observations with his own and create a pattern of orbit for the
lost star.

He had no music pupils now, but that was a loss that faded into
insignificance compared to the knowledge that his new friends, the
Montpelliers and Doctor Raultier, needed him. As for Jonathan,
Alexander had heard nothing more from him since receiving an odd
and scarcely legible letter from Portsmouth. He assumed his brother
was still absent from London; and he found himself fervently hoping
that Jonathan's official duties at the port would distract him from his
disordered, ill-defined suspicions of the Montpelliers and their friends.
To Alexander it seemed that his brother had been almost on the verge
of dementia on his last visit, with his delusions about murder, and

Selene, and red-haired girls; almost as moonstruck, in fact, as poor Guy.

Every few days, Alexander interrupted his work to visit the clerk at the Royal Society, to enquire if there was any acknowledgement yet of the package to Laplace which had contained Raultier's letter to Master Titius. The answers continued to be negative, which was another source of anxiety to him, but at least there was some benefit from these fruitless walks; for one day, on his way home from Somerset House, on an afternoon when the summer rain enveloped London in a grey pall, the idea came to him that he would try reducing his calculations to a minimum, as he had when studying the orbit of Herschel's Georgian planet. He would cut the Gordian knot, in effect, by assuming that Selene moved in a circle, not an ellipse. The result would be over-simple; but at least it might help him to form some kind of conjectural path, from which he could then move on to more sophisticated calculations.

And so, on reaching his home at last, his clothes and shoes saturated with rain, he went straight to his study, lit more candles, and sharpened his pen afresh. Daniel came in, and insisted that he should change his shoes and his wet cotton stockings, and Alexander permitted him to light a fire for him; but further interruptions he would not tolerate. Eagerly he reached for fresh paper and tried circles of different radii, as he had with Herschel's planet; and he found that, yes, there was some link; yes, he was able to fit together the figures that marked the points of its journey into one conjectural orbit . . .

He sharpened his pens, he called to Daniel for more paper; and he worked on feverishly, using his meagre figures to the utmost of his ability, this time to ascertain the mean distance of the object's orbit from the sun. A headache was beginning to throb warningly at his temples, but he was only vaguely aware of the discomfort. Daniel came in to ask if he wanted anything, and tiptoed out again even more quietly when there was no reply.

Alexander covered sheet after sheet with his calculations; until, with bated breath, he found himself at last writing down:

'*Selene travels at a distance of 2.8 times the Earth's orbit from the Sun . . .*'

On a fresh piece of paper, with a hand that was scarcely steady, he inscribed Titius's famous table of planetary distances:

Mercury	0.4	(x10)	4	(-4)	0
Venus	0.7		7		3
Earth	1.0		10		6
Mars	1.6		16		12
—	–		–		–
Jupiter	5.2		52		48
Saturn	10.0		100		96
Herschel's Georgian	19.6		196		192

And then he wrote in: *Selene. 2.8 times 10 = 28. 28 − 4 = 24.*

The orbit of Selene − the object seen by himself and Guy − fitted the sequence exactly. Midway between Mars and Jupiter, at the precise place predicted by Titius.

Alexander leaned back in his chair and rubbed his eyes. His headache was worse, but he hardly noticed it. He started work again, checking and re-checking his calculations, until his last candle sputtered and died. And always he arrived at the same miraculous figure. *2.8* . . .

He realised that the star should be visible now, tonight, low in Sagittarius, just to the left of Scorpius and the red giant Antares. He stood up at last in the darkness, and went to the window. It had stopped raining.

He went out on to the roof. The sky, washed clear of impurities by the day's rain, was dazzlingly clear, like a stupendous, unasked-for gift. With shaking hands, he set up his telescope and looked with his good eye at that region of the sky where he had calculated that the planet should be.

At first he could see nothing but the familiar stars of Sagittarius: the naked-eye double Zeta Sagittarii, and third magnitude Eta and Phi, and all the different nebulae of the constellation. His disappointment bruised him with its intensity. He had never lamented the loss of his good telescope, and the uncertainty of his eyesight, as much as he did now.

Perhaps, even with the Montpelliers' wonderful telescope, he would not be able to see it, he thought. Perhaps he was entirely wrong in his calculations. He gazed longingly at Sagittarius. There were rich Milky Way star fields here, together with numerous clusters and nebulae. But he would not be distracted from his task. With almost painful absorption he made the minute adjustments necessary to move his telescope carefully to and fro in an attempt to search for the lost star in every fraction of that precious area of the heavens.

And then he was blessed with a brief instant of clarity, a sudden pathway through the infinite sky, and he saw it perfectly, as he had seen it two years ago but been so afraid to believe; as Guy had seen it, more often, more recently, and had refused *not* to believe. It was close to Beta Sagittarii and he knew straight away that the eighth magnitude object at which he gazed was not a star, scintillating uncertainly, but some celestial body with a sharp, fracturing light, even with the hint of a disc, exactly where his calculations had predicted.

The sighting, perhaps, of a planet.

And then, the vision was gone. The moment of clarity had been an elusive gift, and turbulence in the atmosphere had robbed him of it. But he was convinced of the significance of what he had seen. Surely now he could offer Guy de Montpellier hope that his search might be close to its end.

Alexander rested his good left eye and sat back, breathless, dazed.

XLVII

My good stars, that were my former guides,
Have empty left their orbs, and shot their fires
Into the abysm of Hell.

Shakespeare, *Antony and Cleopatra*, III: xiii

Half a mile away, Pierre Raultier paused in the darkness of the city's low streets and he too gazed up at the sky. The moon hung over the rooftops, a slender crescent. He could see Capella in Auriga low in the north, and the giant red Antares due south; but the lesser stars were invisible, for here amongst the crowded tenements and shabby taverns of Holborn the high rooftops obscured the horizon, and the light of the yellow oil lamps outside the shops and alehouses dimmed the clarity of the sky.

He went on his way homewards, aware of the beggars and wastrels and all the rest of London's putrefying life around him. For many days now he had been searching the streets for more information to send to Paris, haunting the places where his fellow French exiles gathered, and the taverns used by soldiers, and even the lowly drinking dens where the disaffected of the city met together to whisper against the government and talk in low voices of their own discontent. But he learnt nothing at all that would release him from the terrible burden of failure. Indeed, all he seemed to hear everywhere was talk of the Royalist victory in Brittany.

He got back to his lodgings at last, weary and soul-sick and as sober as he'd ever been in his life, to find a man waiting for him in the darkness outside his door in Eagle Street. Raultier, instantly alert, felt alarm racing through his veins; and then he looked at the man again and recognised him as Alexander Wilmot, the plump little English astronomer. Wilmot looked hot and shabby, and his round face with its milky white eye was quite red with excitement. Raultier thought at once of the vital letter he'd so foolishly entrusted to this man; he wondered if Wilmot had come to tell him that he'd never sent it. All his frustration, all his bitter sense of failure, threatened to overwhelm him; he stepped forward and demanded harshly, in the darkness of the doorway,

'You have news for me? Something to say, about the letter?'

The tone of his voice was such that Alexander stepped back, stricken. 'There's no news of it yet,' he stammered out at last. 'In fact there might even have been a slight delay—'

'A delay?'

'Yes. They told me that the mailing of letters to Paris was running late by a week or so, because of some formality. I'm sorry, Doctor Raultier. But your letter to Master Titius should most certainly have reached Paris by now. Have you another you would like me to send?'

The little astronomer looked so overwrought, so pitiful, that Raultier could not bring himself to admonish him further. There was, after all, no point. His letter had been delayed, critically so. He drew a deep, steadying breath and put the agony of his failure to one side. It was something of which he would have to count the cost, in full, very soon.

'There will be no more letters,' he said quietly. 'Why have you come to visit me?'

He noticed then that the little astronomer looked painfully excited. The papers he was clutching shook in his plump hands. 'I've come,' Alexander whispered, 'because I've found her again.'

It took Raultier some time to realise that he was talking about Selene.

At first Alexander was worried that he had timed his visit badly, for the doctor seemed quite distracted; but slowly Raultier became warmer in manner, even if he seemed to achieve this with something of an effort. He invited Alexander upstairs to his gloomy but tidy rooms, where at last he took the papers that Alexander was waiting with such eagerness to hand over to him. Laying them carefully on the table by the window, Raultier lit some candles, then poured a glass of madeira for them both and invited his guest to sit. Alexander did so, and sipped a little, and strove to present an air of calmness despite his fast-beating heart.

Seating himself at the table, Raultier bent over Alexander's papers and assessed them intently by the light of the candles. Then he looked up at his visitor and said quietly, 'You have found its orbit.'

'Yes. Yes, I have . . .' Alexander made a huge effort to steady himself. He put down his glass and moved over to join Raultier in his scrutiny. 'I've been trying to estimate its path by fitting parabolas to both mine and Guy's recorded observations. You will see, if you look here, and here, that its orbit is almost circular. Guy has made one clear sighting, and I two; together, they were just enough to give me sufficient material for my calculations . . . This object's path fits with no other known body; it must be something of more significance than a comet. Tonight I searched amongst the bright stars of Sagittarius, as my calculations predicted . . .'

'And?'

Alexander's face was still flushed as he gazed at Raultier. 'I saw it,' he said.

Raultier sat up, his eyes never leaving Alexander's face.

'I used a telescope with a secondary mirror to limit diffraction,' Alexander went on hurriedly, 'as I do when viewing the Georgian planet. The image was blurred at first by the turbulence in the atmosphere; there was some scintillation, and I thought for a moment that I must be wrong, and that it was a star and not a planet. These brief hours of darkness give us so little chance to read the skies, and there is no time for error . . . But I was fortunate. There were some moments, a few precious seconds, when darkness was complete, and the atmosphere was uniform along my line of sight, and I saw it, oh so clearly, in that brief instant of calm . . .' He bowed his head, suddenly overwhelmed by the immensity of what he was claiming. 'Of course, my eyesight is not good, and my telescope's powers are limited. Others, with more expertise than me and better instruments, may think differently . . .'

He let his voice trail away, feeling that he had said too much, had been betrayed by his own foolish excitement. But Raultier was once more gazing with an intent expression at the papers Alexander had given to him. He looked up at last, his strong face quite steady, and said,

'Forgive me if I've seemed slow in absorbing all this. As you know, I've had my doubts about this object's existence; but it seems to me that your evidence is formidable.'

Alexander nodded eagerly. 'Guy must know of it as soon as possible.'

'Of course. But we must be careful that the excitement of this discovery doesn't adversely affect his health . . .' He paused a moment, thinking. 'Auguste and Guy are expecting me tonight at their home. I will go to them immediately, and explain what you've seen. Then I'm sure that they'll want you to tell them about it yourself. For Guy, this will be the best, the very best of news.'

'Indeed, I hope so,' breathed Alexander. 'How is he, Doctor Raultier?'

Raultier had put down his glass now, and his big hands were clenched tensely against his thighs, belying the calmness in his voice. 'He has a cancerous tumour, that lies close to the base of the cranial cavity. Some days he seems well. At other times the sickness has him utterly in its grasp.' He hesitated. 'The pain I can do something for, but I fear that he suffers much in his mind.'

A falling star, burning out as it plunges to the ground. Alexander, sitting there in that warm, candlelit room, with the raucous night sounds of London's summer streets rising to the open first-floor window and the doctor's rows of medicine bottles exuding the sanitised smells of death and sickness all around him, felt such emptiness that he could hardly move.

He said at last, 'How cruel, to die in a foreign land.'

Raultier didn't reply, but remained with his head bowed. Alexander hesitated, then got to his feet. He cleared his throat. 'I think I had better go,' he said uncertainly. 'I've taken enough of your time.'

Still Raultier didn't move. Alexander gestured towards his papers, which lay spread out on the table. 'I'll leave these copies of my figures here for you, shall I, doctor?'

Raultier stood up slowly at last, like one arousing himself from a dream. 'Your figures,' he said. 'Yes. I will see that Guy gets them.'

Alexander let himself out. He hurried swiftly down the stairs, into the darkness of the dimly lit Holborn street and began his long walk home.

XLVIII

I have overthrown some of you, as God overthrew Sodom
and Gomorrah,
and ye were as a firebrand plucked out of the burning;
yet have ye not returned unto me, saith the Lord.

Amos 4:11

It was as Alexander was tramping along narrow Milton Lane that he slowly became aware that an unfamiliar smell of acrid smoke was overlaying the more usual odour of the Clerkenwell distillery. He thought, at first, that it must be the tile kilns across the fields at Bagnigge Wells; the stench must be drifting this way, though he had not been aware of any wind, and in fact the July night seemed close and still.

But then his thoughts began to ramble without sense, like a ship's compass distracted by some unknown base metal, as he saw the people gathering in the darkness at the edge of the Green, with faces lit by a strange, glowing light that was the light neither of moon nor stars. He followed their gaze down the little alley, and saw bright flames leaping from his home, saw a trail of bitter smoke rising from charred window frames and crumbling roof; he saw old Hannah sitting on the ground nearby in her stinking petticoats with tawdry bags of possessions by her side, lamenting, while her thin spinster daughter ran to and fro in the garish glow. 'Help us. Please help us.'

The crowd murmured, faceless, indifferent. There was no pity in their eyes; why should there be? – for life was hard, and ever had been. To be sure, some conscientious souls had searched for a fire-mark somewhere about the building in case it was insured with a private company, which could then have been instructed to send its trucks and leather-hatted firemen carrying hoses and grappling irons to deal with the inferno. But Alexander's wood-and-plaster home was not insured, so the only source of help was the parish fire-fighting engine.

And no one knew where it was. Someone had called at the Clerkenwell Watch House, but the part-time constable, who might have known, was absent, at a cockfight in Long Lane. At last, sullenly, as if realising their entertainment had to be paid for in some way, the onlookers found buckets, and started to work the water pump on the Green, and to carry the buckets, hand over hand, in a line, to Alexander's charred house, which was already in ruins. They did it to stop the blaze spreading to their own dwellings, thus proving that the most distilled selfishness breeds neighbourliness, of a kind.

Meanwhile Alexander, his lungs scorched by the heat, his shabby clothes holed and charred irredeemably by flying sparks from the crumbling timbers, ran for the stairs of his house, only to realise that of course they were not there. He was choking, and his eyes were streaming as he called out, in an agony of despair, 'Daniel! Daniel!'

He ran away from the Green, further down Jerusalem Alley, in hopes that Daniel might have taken refuge beside the tavern. The smoke still stung his eyes, but the flames were not so bright here and there was darkness between the doorways, in the narrow courts that closed up on him; a lack of light as profound as any blackness described by Laplace when he wrote of the possibility of there being a star so dense that it could pull all light back into itself; and indeed, he thought, this had to be some such horror, an epitome of negation, for he saw a cluster of men – were they men, or were they creatures spawned of darkness? – just as he heard Daniel's muffled cries of distress coming from their midst.

He saw with his good eye, which he now cursed, that they held Daniel spreadeagled, face down over a tipped-up barrel from the distillery. They had pulled his threadbare breeches from his hips, and one of them, his face hot with bestial humours, was forcing himself on the boy vilely. Daniel struggled, but the others held him down, grinning, their teeth white in the darkness.

Daniel was sobbing, for the man's gross desire was hurting him. Alexander called the boy's name and ran towards him, but the other men, faceless, ragged – there were more of them now, for some of the fire-watchers had sloped along to watch the fun – turned to seize Alexander, and held him cruelly, pinioning his arms. When he tried to cry out, they gagged him with a greasy rag that choked him; but they did not blindfold him, oh, no, they made sure, very sure, that he saw everything, wrenching back his head painfully each time he shut his eyes. They whispered like the devil in his ear: 'Look, look, you fool. Can't you see how the little whore is enjoying it?'

Another of them took his turn with Daniel. The men who were holding Alexander laughed anew at the boy's fresh agitations, and dragged their prisoner nearer, so they could be closer to the sport. At least this brought release of a sort, for now they let Alexander close his eyes.

He tried not to listen, and endeavoured to force his mind far, far away. He remembered the effulgent beauty of the Magellanic clouds, and how he used to watch them, making crude measurements night after night with his simple, cross-haired telescope, scribbling his observations down almost wildly to save his sanity during the bestialities of a sea-calmed crossing of the southern oceans; when the decks crawled with slimy things, and the phosphorescent nights whispered of more evil than he had ever thought to see again, until now.

They left Daniel bruised and barely conscious. They laughed at his limp, half-clothed body and threw him back to Alexander. The boy's soft skin was besmeared with sweat and the grime of men.

Alexander reclothed Daniel with care, and bathed his face with water from the pump by the Green. Then he sat on the steps of the charred shell of his home and held Daniel in his arms, soothing him with low meaningless words as the stars wheeled overhead and the crescent moon rose above the steeple of St John's church. The air was acrid with the stench of smoke. He wondered if the men who had done this thing to Daniel had also set fire to his house. He had noticed the sidelong looks he had been given lately by his neighbours; he had sensed the growing unfriendliness of those who were once kind to him.

He had no home now. Smelly Hannah was allowed to sleep on the straw in the Watch House cell, with her daughter at her side, but she, like Alexander, did not sleep; Alexander knew, because the noise of her lamentations came through the narrow bars of the tiny window all night long, and rose to the stars, rebuking them.

Venus appeared before dawn, five times brighter than Sirius, only to fade as the sun came up slowly over the marshes to the east of the city. In the harsh early morning light, a big carriage came slowly to the house, driven by Ralph.

'I have been told to take you to them,' Ralph said. 'Are you ready?'

'Yes,' Alexander replied quietly. 'I'm ready.'

It was late afternoon, and Jonathan was delivering another batch of colonial documents to the various departments of Whitehall; but his mind was far away from the papers he carried, and the places he delivered them to, because less than an hour ago he had received a note from the lean informer Stimpson. *'I have news. I'll call on you at six.'*

It was two days since Stimpson had told him what he'd discovered about the ex-priest Norland; two days in which Jonathan had to force himself into waiting, because Stimpson would have access to places now closed to him. *Norland*, he kept thinking. Norland, an ex-priest, a sexual offender; surely a former man of the cloth couldn't be a killer – but *who else*? Jonathan, remembering the strange words her attacker had uttered to Rose, had been trying to find out more about William Blake, and had discovered that the poet had a loathing of organised religion, and hated priests. Could that be the reaction also of a man who had once been a priest, and was disgraced? Jonathan had searched for the poem Morrow had told him about, and he'd found in it another line which he could not forget:

'Prisons are built with stones of Law; Brothels with bricks of Religion.'

As he waited for Stimpson, he felt almost sick with tension.

It was nearly four o'clock. He was walking back slowly towards the Treasury, his deliveries finished and two hours to go before the meeting, when he heard his name spoken. He turned and caught sight of Abraham Lucket, leaning nonchalantly against the wall with his hands in his pockets. It was nearly three weeks since Jonathan had seen him.

Lucket tipped his wide-brimmed hat back a little from his face, looked all around, and sauntered across to Jonathan.

'I've just heard,' he said. 'There was a fire in Clerkenwell last night. Nothing much, but it sounds as though it was close to where your brother lives.'

Jonathan felt cold. 'How do you know?'

Lucket shrugged. 'There are watchers posted in Clerkenwell. I hear these things.'

Of course he did. Once he used to report them to Jonathan. Jonathan reached automatically into his pocket for a coin, then stopped, and said slowly, 'You didn't need to tell me this. You don't work for me any more.'

Lucket nodded and gave a sly grin. 'So they tell me.'

Jonathan gave him the money. 'Thank you,' he said. 'I'll go there directly.'

When Jonathan saw his brother's house burned to the ground, and smelled the reek of acrid smoke, he was gripped by a presentiment of evil. I should have visited him as soon as I got back from Portsmouth, he rebuked himself silently, before this business with the priest distracted me. I should have warned him . . .

But against what? Against whom?

He suddenly realised that an old woman, dishevelled and filthy, was shuffling towards him. Recognising the half-crazed old crone who lived in the rooms below Alexander's, he started to move instinctively away, but she clutched at his arm with her dirty fingers.

'*Then the fire of the Lord fell,*' she quavered, '*and consumed the burnt sacrifice, and the wood, and the stones, and the dust.*' She gripped his arm tighter, her toothless mouth still working. 'It was a punishment, you know. Punishment.'

Jonathan felt trapped. With relief he saw that the woman's daughter had followed her and was already detaching her mother's gnarled hand from Jonathan's coat sleeve.

'I beg your pardon, sir,' she said to him. Her greasy, pinned-up hair was slipping to her thin cheeks; there were dark rings beneath her eyes. 'My mother is distressed. That was our home.'

'I know,' said Jonathan. 'I'm sorry. Do you know if your neighbour, Alexander Wilmot, is safe? He's my brother.'

Hannah pushed herself forward again eagerly. 'I saw him. Last night.'

'My brother Alexander?'

'He came with a flaming brand,' she said in a low, confiding voice, 'to light the sacrifice to the Lord; to punish the sodomites who dwelt in this place, the servants of Baal . . .'

Hannah's daughter said swiftly to Jonathan, 'My mother thinks she saw someone, last night, setting fire to the house. She imagines things. She doesn't know what she's saying.'

But Jonathan was stooping to catch the old woman's words. 'Hannah?' he said. 'Tell me again; you saw someone?'

She looked up at him with bright, beady eyes. 'He was a servant of the Lord. An angel. He was young; his face was calm, and his hair was long and fair. He did what had to be done. *Take the prophets of Baal, and let not one of them escape . . .*'

Jonathan stepped back. Young. Calm. Long fair hair. Could it be the man he'd seen with Crawford?

He reminded himself shakily that he was jumping too quickly to conclusions; he was listening to the rantings of an old, demented woman. Even her own daughter didn't believe her. Why should he? House fires were common enough amongst these old timber build-ings; all it took was an accident with a candle or an oil lamp, or some live coals spilling from the grate . . .

Alexander.

Hannah's daughter said quickly, 'A carriage came for your brother this morning. He's gone to his friends, to watch the stars.'

Jonathan gazed where she pointed, as if the carriage could still be seen taking Alexander westwards, to Kensington. So Alexander had gone at last to the Montpelliers, just as he'd been urging him, and Jonathan was afraid for him.

He turned his back on the ruined building and walked slowly away. At Gray's Inn Lane he hired a cab to take him to Whitehall. People were staring, and he realised that his coat and his hands were smeared with soot where Hannah had clutched at him.

As he was crossing the courtyard to his office he saw Ellis, the clerk who'd found him sleeping at his desk. Jonathan didn't expect Ellis to speak to him, but in fact the clerk seemed to be heading purposefully in his direction. Jonathan waited warily.

'Absey,' Ellis said. 'I was sorry to hear about your demotion.' He looked round swiftly and said in a lower voice, 'I wouldn't be at all surprised if Crawford had something to do with it. I think you should know that he's been spreading gossip about you. If you ask me, he's bitter about his own lack of promotion, so he tries to pull others down too. Watch him.'

With that, Ellis nodded and hurried on.

Jonathan stood there, conscious of the stink of burning timber that still clung to his clothes. He was thinking: Crawford told Pollock I was searching through the files in Middle Scotland Yard. No one else could have known. Perhaps it was Crawford who reported my absence to King, on the day the foreign mails were taken from me . . .

All acts of minor mischief, committed, perhaps, in revenge for Jonathan's rejection of the Scotsman's repeated offers of friendship. But Crawford, on that day in Middle Scotland Yard, had warned Jonathan about the Company of Titius. Why warn him, if Crawford was determined, in his own petty way, to drag Jonathan down?

He went on to his office to finish his business there, then he went to meet Stimpson, who had, by methods Jonathan didn't care to investigate, gained access to the papers of the French former police officer Valdené; and Stimpson told Jonathan, with a leer, that the priest Norland was arrested in Paris three summers ago for sexual misdemeanours involving young boys.

'Someone complained,' explained Stimpson. 'Someone whose altarboy son had fallen into Norland's clutches. Norland was stupid; he should have gone quietly to the kind of Paris brothel that specialised in such things and paid for what he wanted.'

'There was no violence? No hint of assault?'

'Oh, no. Nothing like that at all, sir. In fact according to the evidence, the boy in question was rather disappointed when the whole business was stopped. Norland paid him well, apparently. There was no damage. Just a nice bit of pederasty.'

Jonathan kneaded his aching forehead with his clenched hand. 'And those dates I gave you?'

'The priest was busy at those times, sir – at least as far as I could tell. He holds a Bible class at the Catholic chapel in Lincoln's Inn Fields, where he spends a lot of his evenings; there are witnesses to say he was there each night you mentioned: the 8th, the 12th and the 20th of June.'

'Until late?'

'Till very late. He's a busy man. I've written out the exact times, and the people who saw him. Here you are.'

Jonathan took the scrap of paper. It had always been a slim chance that it was Norland; and besides, he was used by now to disappointment. He said bitterly, 'I wonder how he finds his entertainment nowadays. These Bible classes. Do children attend them? Boys?'

Stimpson's pale eyes widened. 'I don't know, sir. But I could find out.'

Jonathan paid him, and said curtly, 'Don't bother.'

When Jonathan got home that night, he found a letter waiting for him. In it Mary told him that she was leaving Chelsea, with Thomas. She was going to stay with relatives, she said, far away, in the North Country. She wouldn't tell him where, for that was the only way, she felt, that she could be sure that Thomas would be safe.

He crumpled the sheet in his hand and bit his lip against the sudden shaft of pain that tore through him. He stared out of the window, at the bright early evening sky; and he thought of his son Thomas, who towered over him and clung to him with love, and liked him to make paper boats that floated at the river's edge. He thought of his daughter. At least once he'd been able to hope for revenge for what she'd been made to suffer. But now, as his failures clustered around him, it seemed that even that frail hope was being taken away from him.

Late that night, unable to sleep, he went out again, and walked the four miles to Chelsea, past the five ponds and Jenny Whim's tavern, along the footpath that led through straggling fields. He went, not to the cottage, which was deserted now, but to the river, to the pebbled beach where he used to bring Thomas and Ellie.

He sat on the half-ruined jetty as the sun started to sink. He threw skimming stones into the water, until darkness veiled the sky, and the first stars came out.

He looked up at the stars almost with hatred.

XLIX

But when the planets
In evil mixture to disorder wander,
What plagues and what portents! what mutiny!
What raging of the sea! shaking of earth!
Commotion in the winds! frights, changes, horrors,
Divert and crack, rend and deracinate
The unity and married calm of states
Quite from their fixture!

Shakespeare, *Troilus and Cressida*, I: iii

right stars wheeled over the coast of France. The crescent moon and the constellations of summer – Cygnus, Lyra, Aquila – illuminated the cliffs and beaches of the Quiberon peninsula. In London news of the final triumph was eagerly awaited: news that the *émigré* Royalist army, reinforced by numerous Chouan bands, were sweeping the last of the Republicans from their Breton strongholds.

But the clouds were gathering. Even as the dispatches continued to make their way slowly seawards to England, full of ten-day-old reports of *émigré* triumphs and Hoche's despair, a storm was beginning, far out in the Atlantic, to roll its way towards the Breton coast. And Puisaye, far from sweeping all before him, was penned in on the Quiberon peninsula. His only hope rested on a desperate action to break free, an all-out assault on the enemy lines that enclosed him; and, though he had no way, now, of sending messages to the Chevalier de Tinténiac, he was about to stake the entire success of his plan on the conviction that his ally was encamped in the wooded hills beyond Auray, waiting only for the sound of battle to march down and deal a crucial blow to Hoche's unprotected rear.

Day broke calmly enough, on the morning Puisaye had designated for the attack on the encircling Republican troops; and the grey light of early morning revealed the combined army of Royalists and Chouans filing northwards along the narrow ridge of shingle that linked the

331

peninsula to the mainland, towards General Hoche's army. At first, in spite of their lesser numbers, the advantage seemed to belong to Puisaye's men; the sun was barely up before his combined Royalist forces – Hector's Royal Marines, d'Hervilly's White Cockade regiment, Dresnay's Breton Legion, and the Loyal Emigrant battalions – rushed on the first of the enemy's trenches near the hamlet of Ste Barbe and swept the unprepared Republican forces aside. The *fleur-de-lys* banners were hoisted high, and the old Bourbon battle cries resounded along the coast, mingling with the clash of sabres and the rattle of musket fire. Puisaye himself, drawing briefly aside from the mêlée, trained his telescope on the wooded hills behind Auray, willing the Chevalier de Tinténiac and his army to appear out of the morning mists and fall on Hoche's men from behind.

But no relief force emerged. Instead Hoche's reinforcements poured out of Auray and retook their trenches. As the outnumbered *émigrés* fell back, the Republican general gave the order for concealed batteries of guns on each wing to open up, so that the Royalists were raked with a terrible fire that scythed through their retreating ranks. Hoche's cavalry rode forth to cut down the stragglers, and Puisaye's surviving troops fell back in exhaustion to Fort Penthièvre on the isthmus. From there they watched the Republican batteries being dragged closer, ready to annihilate them the next day. All hope of Tinténiac's troops arriving was abandoned.

At least the sea was their friend, they thought, for the English ships that were anchored in the Bay of Quiberon had drawn close, ready to protect them with the might of their guns. But then came the night of the storm, and the stars were extinguished in their thousands by the wind and rain that swept across the Breton peninsula. Unseen now, Hoche's blue-coated Republicans advanced in the darkness along the isthmus to the fort, where waiting traitors, former prisoners of war in England who had gained their freedom by swearing loyalty to the Royalist cause, opened the gates to let them in. The defenders, roused too late, were cut down; the tricolour was hoisted; and as the grey dawn broke, Hoche's triumphant Republicans swept southwards, driving their quarry remorselessly through the storm-swept Breton villages of Kergroix and St Julien, and Quiberon itself, down to the Pointe du Conguel. The Royalists fought valiantly at every stage, but they were hopelessly outnumbered, and hampered by the hundreds of camp followers who fled with them. There, on the southern tip of the peninsula, the Royalists were caught like rats in a trap with the raging sea on three sides and their enemy on the fourth.

The survivors of Puisaye's army formed ranks on the beach at Port-Haliguen, and, in the continuing storm, prepared to stand firm while the guns of the English ships attempted to cow the advancing enemy. But then Puisaye himself turned and fled, in a small, storm-tossed boat that took him out to the waiting ships. Others followed as best they could, Royalists and Chouans, fighting their way out in similar craft or trying to swim through immense waves and hostile currents. Many drowned or were shot; while those who chose to make a stand stood and fought with increasing despair as Hoche's men drew closer. Some still hoped for Tinténiac's relief force to appear from behind the drifting smokescreen of battle; but they hoped in vain. Many of them died at the sea's edge with their swords in their hands, calling out the name of their king, who was dead, and their God, who had been forbidden to them, as they spilled their blood on the rocky shores of their homeland. The survivors, a little over seven hundred of them, were marched off to captivity in Auray, while the British frigate *Anjou*, carrying grave dispatches, set sail through heavy seas for the coast of England.

L

I have tortured them with powers, flattered them with
attendance to find out the critical moments when they
would act, tried them with specula of short or long
focus, a large aperture or a narrow one; it would be
hard if they had not been kind to me at last.

William Herschel, 'On Telescopes' (1785)

'Can you see it yet, Alexander?'

It was night-time, and Guy de Montpellier leaned forward in yearning eagerness from where he sat in the corner of the rooftop observatory. His almost savage beauty, now honed by illness, was thrown into clear relief by the light of the stars that burned overhead.

Alexander turned from the precious telescope to face him. Guy wore black, as usual; the colour of poets, of death. His cravat was crumpled carelessly at his throat, his drawn-back hair was greasy and lustreless with fatigue; his skin was white with tension at the corners of his mouth; and yet his beauty was still compelling. Alexander thought of what Raultier had said. '*The pain I can do something for, but I fear that he suffers much in his mind.*'

Alexander said quietly, 'No. Not yet,' and Guy sat back with a little sigh. The only others who were with them up here, Auguste, and Matthew Norland – who was silent and sober for once – drew breath too, as if taking some respite from their painful concentration.

No Raultier. No Ralph. No Carline. Without her lover at her side, Auguste was as subdued as Alexander had ever seen her. She wore a close-fitting gown of some soft, blue-grey material that seemed to melt into the shadows that surrounded them. She had powdered her cropped hair, robbing it of its vibrant hue; and her face, too, was drained of colour.

Daniel was downstairs, asleep. He'd been given a small chamber of his own, at the back of the house. He would not visit Alexander in his room; indeed, he had hardly spoken to him, and had not smiled, either, since they came here three days ago. He still seemed to be afraid.

'You're safe here,' Alexander had urged him. They were all good to him; who could have been kinder to the boy than Raultier, who had tended his burns, and Auguste, who had brought him dainty dishes to eat? And yet Daniel seemed to look even at Alexander now with fear and mistrust. It was as though he blamed him for what had happened on the night of the fire; and Alexander's heart was sore.

It was exceptionally hot and airless, even for July. There had been a threat of thunder all day, and the heavy purple clouds had built up to the west, hovering over the distant reed-lined marshes of the lonely Thames. All morning, Alexander had worked in his room on his figures for the lost planet. But later, in the absolute stillness of the humid afternoon, he'd gone outside to explore the gardens, alone.

The heat was oppressive. Slowly, seeking out the shade, he made his way down overgrown paths. In a walled rose garden, filled with overripe blooms that drooped in the heat; he came upon a ruined pergola, half buried beneath canopies of rank greenery; he felt spied upon by crumbling lichen-covered statues that seemed to gaze at him with malevolent eyes from their forgotten bowers. He had gone back inside, not soothed but somehow disturbed by this neglected abundance.

The clouds vanished as nightfall came, leaving the skies clear, but there was still a heaviness in the air, a sultry menace. All around the big, half-empty Kensington mansion the ancient trees shut in and enfolded the dusty heat, as did the overarching sky, moody, oppressive, pierced from time to time with almost painful clarity by the constellations of the turning of the year. Hercules was sinking now from its midsummer zenith; gradually the shortening days would pull the bright constellation down, down to the Lernaean marshes, till even red Alpha was dimmed at its very heart. Jupiter, still luminous to the south-east, was also distancing itself slowly, as the nights circled by and July's heat prepared the way for August's heavy ripening.

Alexander's mind ached with weariness as he adjusted the lenses yet again, and moved the guider, and scanned the dark rifts of the Milky Way. They were all watching him, but he was too busy to realise how rapt was their attention; even if he had known of it, it was doubtful whether it would have made him happy, as it once would have done.

Working with the big telescope, his left eye ached as it had not ached since his time at sea, when the brilliant noonday sun glaring on tropical waters had threatened to blind him completely. He had no fear of tonight's sightings blinding him, for Selene was elusive.

Every day since his arrival here, he had worked on his calculations, checking and re-checking each line of figures. He knew it was a miracle, of sorts, that he had taken copies of his papers to Raultier's home on the night of the fire; for if he had not, all his work would have been lost in the stinking ashes of his home. He felt guilty that he was not inclined to be more grateful to Providence for that, at least.

Each night, during the all too brief hours of darkness, he had come up to the rooftop and longed for the distant obscurities to clear, for some miraculous sighting to fight its way towards him through the glittering, ever-shifting texture of the constellations that studded the dark night sky. And yet it had not happened. He worried that his figures were wrong. Each night he saw in Guy's face how the young man's hopes had been raised almost too painfully.

'You must take your turn,' Alexander said quietly at last to Guy. 'Your eyes will see more than mine ever can.' He tried hard to hide the anxiety in his voice. Even if his figures were correct, he knew from the ellipses he had so carefully drawn that the bright object he believed he had seen was moving nearer and nearer to the sun's rays, and within days would be lost to them until the time of its return, which would, as Raultier had already told him, be too late.

He went to sit at the little desk on which the papers had been laid, but he didn't light the lamp: even its dim glow could be enough to adversely affect the astronomers' seeing powers on such a crucial night as this. Instead he moved the paperweights and straightened the goose-quill pens, and touched the little flask of ink that was as black as the overhead sky. He gazed into the darkness, trying to recapture the moment that he had seen the star, the star he too now thought of as Selene. He tried to recall the way it had filled him with an acute, an almost astonishing sense of joy – the kind of joy that he thought, perhaps, he would never find again. His head throbbed with the intensity of his concentration, and the silence hung over the rooftop like a pall.

Norland was beside him now, pouring him wine in the darkness. Tonight the former priest's fleshy body made Alexander recoil. Norland had been kind enough to Alexander and to Daniel; he had spoken to the boy with solicitude, and suggested to Alexander that perhaps Daniel's wish for solitariness was his way of coping with the ordeal of the fire. Alexander knew he should be grateful for the ex-priest's concern. But all he could think now was that Norland's clothing smelled of perspiration, and his forehead was oily with sweat.

'Madame misses her young riding master, I think,' Norland whispered lazily to Alexander, gesturing towards Auguste. 'Half of her wants to watch the stars, while the other half looks down the London road for Carline.'

Alexander shifted hotly in his seat, no longer wanting to hear Norland's salacious gossip about Auguste, or Carline, or Guy: hadn't he already heard and seen so much more than he should have done in this house? He was here to find the lost star, for Guy; it had become his sole purpose, almost his redemption, just as it was the young Frenchman's. Yet the ex-priest, determined to continue with his chosen topic of conversation, appeared oblivious to his mood. He reached comfortably for more wine and went on, 'I've often wondered, you know, if Carline's frequent absences are all a carefully calculated part of his strategy. Auguste is quite distracted while he is away.' He fixed his bloodshot eyes on Alexander and grinned. 'Perhaps you should practise the same tricks on your boy Daniel. You have spoiled him, I think, Master Wilmot. You should teach him to be grateful, you know.'

Alexander was horrified that Norland was once more probing his secret. Who else guessed? Did Auguste? Did Guy? Did that explain the curious, almost pitying way in which he'd seen Norland look at Daniel? For a second he felt sick with a nameless dread, but then the moment passed, obliterated from his thoughts, because Guy was turning round to him, his face transformed.

'*It is there*,' was all Guy said. It was all he needed to say. His dark eyes, with the shadows so prominent beneath them, blazed with joy; his unkempt hair fell about his fever-etched face. Such beauty, thought Alexander, entranced. Such beauty . . .

Alexander hastened to move his own clumsy bulk towards the telescope. The others gathered round him; the very air seemed brittle with excitement. He gazed through the ocular, scarcely daring to breathe, and he saw a clear pathway up to the eighth magnitude star that he had seen four days ago; only it was not a star, but had moved along its own ellipse, exactly the one he had predicted, and it gazed back at him with a clear, pale light . . .

Selene.

He turned to the others, his heart beating painfully fast. 'It is there, where it should be.' He found their intense expectation almost too much to bear. 'But it could be a comet . . .'

'No,' said Guy rapturously, 'it cannot be a comet; its outline is too clear; nor is it a star. Look again, Alexander. It has a still light, a pure light; it does not scintillate, as a star would . . .'

'We need more sightings,' said Alexander, 'we need to magnify its image; we cannot be sure of anything yet,' but his hands were shaking with the enormity of what he had seen, and he knew that Guy had to be right, that this was neither a comet nor a star. He moved aside, to let Auguste take her turn at the telescope; he turned back to his papers, and lit the tiny lamp and leafed through them hurriedly; and yet he didn't really need to check his figures. Already he knew that his calculations were right, and this object did indeed lie where Titius had said it would, between Mars and Jupiter.

After some moments Auguste stepped back from the telescope and turned to her brother. Her face was unnaturally pale beneath her powdered hair. 'Oh, Guy. My love, we have found it . . . My little monsieur mouse has found it.'

Guy looked almost as if he would back away from her. But Auguste touched Guy's face with her hand, and reached to kiss his lips. For a moment they clung to one another, oblivious; and then Auguste rested her cheek against her brother's shoulder. She looked insubstantial, as if his arms were all that held her there.

Alexander tore his gaze away from them and turned back to the telescope. He looked once more, but saw nothing. Some nebular disturbance in the vast expanse of universe that lay between him and this star had caused it to vanish. He stepped back from the telescope, stricken.

'What is it?' Guy asked, breaking away from Auguste.

'I can no longer see it.'

Guy's face still shone with excitement. 'But tomorrow we'll find it again. After all, we have its orbit now.'

Alexander briefly pressed his palm to his good eye, which was strained from peering into space for so long. 'Perhaps,' he said. 'Perhaps.'

'You hesitate. Why?'

Alexander gestured towards the telescope. 'There's something wrong with the object lens. We need to get it checked before we look for the star again.' Only tonight he had noticed a fault in the crown glass, perhaps caused during its manufacture by some debris from the furnace, or incomplete polishing. It was the tiniest of imperfections, yet it could still jeopardise their next, crucial observation.

'But we haven't time.' Guy was beginning to look agitated. 'We must search for the star again tomorrow . . .'

'I have a friend who will help us,' said Alexander quickly. 'He has a shop in Clerkenwell. Doctor Raultier knows him. He will polish it for me.'

'Yes,' Guy said with fervour. 'Perceval Oates. I have heard of him. And then tomorrow, after one more sighting, we can tell the whole world what we have found.'

He looked round at them all, his face alight with hope; and suddenly they all began to talk, in hushed but joyful voices, of what they had seen. More lamps were lit, and wine was brought to refresh them; though Alexander made it his first duty to carefully cover the telescope and all its parts against the ruinous dew. When he had finished he stood there gazing out at the blackness of the sky. Fatigue overwhelmed him. Did Herschel feel like this, he wondered, when he first dared to contemplate the thought that he had found a new planet?

Then Norland brought him red wine, and said to him, 'Drink.' Alexander took it but recoiled anew from the big priest, whose suspected knowledge about Daniel and himself glittered in his dissipated eyes. Suddenly Alexander saw the flaccid lechery in his lips, in his tongue that lapped the stray wine drops greedily. The wine fumes went to Alexander's head as he sipped, for he had not eaten; he looked up at the sky, his elation quite gone.

It was not Norland's presence alone that affected his mood. Something had been amiss in his all too brief sighting of the star. But what? If it truly was the object he had seen four days ago, then it had moved along a path that was precisely as he had predicted. Even so, his uncertainty lingered.

Shaking his head, he drank more wine. After that he remembered little more of the next hour, except for Norland clapping him on the back so that he almost choked on his drink, and Guy talking intoxicatedly of Selene, his eyes glittering as if they burned either with stars, or with the disease that was destroying his brain; while Auguste clung to her brother, nestling close as if she would never let him go. Alexander tried to preach caution, to remind them that they needed another, clearer sighting before their figures would be complete enough to convince others; but they were not really listening.

When midnight came they went below to the music room, where Guy, still exhilarated, gathered his slim body into an excess of passion and struck sparks of celestial harmony from the worn keys of the harpsichord. Norland leaned back in the most comfortable chair, glass in hand, and hummed; while Alexander listened, quite entranced, his uncertainties for the moment suppressed. Auguste gazed silently, obsessively, at her brother's face.

Down below the big door opened and slammed shut again. Someone was coming up the stairs, and they looked at each other like conspirators. It was Raultier; he came in, and looked at the wine glasses and then at Guy; he absorbed the young man's white face, his taut body, and he said, his voice almost shaking with scarcely restrained emotion,

'It is past midnight. What madness is this?'

Guy looked up, once, then started scornfully to play again. Alexander, seeing that the doctor looked exhausted and was covered with dust from his journey, stumbled to his feet and made an effort at apology. 'We did not realise it was so late.'

Norland had arisen also, his bulky frame filling the room anew with the pungent smell of stale perspiration. He said, with an emphasis that was almost mocking, 'Good doctor. A small celebration is warranted, surely, on the night that Selene is found?'

'It isn't definite yet,' Alexander broke in anxiously. 'The object was too fleeting for complete certainty. We need more predictions, more sightings—'

But Norland interrupted him decisively. 'Master Wilmot is as self-deprecating as ever. But there can be little doubt. If you had been here earlier, Raultier, you might have seen it for yourself.'

'I was busy.' Raultier seemed almost too weary to speak; long lines of exhaustion furrowed his cheeks. 'So Selene is found at last,' he went on. 'But Guy, Guy, you should not be drinking wine. You were so sick, only yesterday. Let me take you to your room.'

Guy stopped playing and swung round to confront him. 'We have found Selene, Raultier. And there is nothing left to keep us here. Nothing. When can we leave this place? When can we go home, to our own country?'

Raultier hesitated. 'Soon. I promise . . .'

'Soon it will be too late.' Guy's face was very pale. 'And I can see in your eyes that there is no hope. You were never very good at lying, were you, Raultier?'

Raultier seemed unable to reply; and it was Norland who moved next, Norland who got up and went over to Guy. 'Come,' he said. 'I will take you to your room. It's late. We are all over-tired.'

Guy started to rise slowly, as if now every limb was weighted with lead. He turned to Alexander and said with an effort, 'You'll remember that tomorrow we must take the telescope lens to that good friend of yours in Clerkenwell?'

Raultier looked up sharply. 'Clerkenwell?'

'There's a fault in the object lens,' Alexander explained quickly. 'Something very minor. I thought Perceval could help us.'

'Yes,' broke in Guy, his face once more alight with eagerness, 'and then we shall have another night of star-watching. We will see Selene again . . .'

He faltered visibly. Auguste moved swiftly to take his arm, but Guy shook himself free, and turned on her. Alexander saw that his face was white as he whispered to his sister in an anguished voice, 'Leave me alone, damn you, leave me; will you never stop tormenting me?'

Alexander thought, He's ill, he doesn't recognise her, he doesn't know what he's saying; though Auguste had stepped back as if he'd struck her. Then she hurried out, head held high, spots of colour burning on her cheeks, as Norland helped Guy from the room.

Raultier and Alexander were the only ones left. Alexander would have turned to leave, feeling himself to be nothing but an intruder, but then he remembered that there was something he had to say.

'I received a letter today, Doctor Raultier,' he began hesitantly. 'From the Royal Society.'

Raultier said slowly, 'A letter?'

341

'Yes. It was from Pierre de Laplace. In it he said that your message arrived safely and he passed it on to the appropriate person.'

Raultier nodded, but it was as if the news meant nothing to him. 'Yes,' he said. 'Thank you.'

'I'm sorry it took so long to reach Paris.'

'I've told you. It really doesn't matter now.'

Alexander left the doctor then. Slowly he went up the stairs to his solitary bed. On the way he looked into Daniel's room, and saw him sleeping there, like an innocent child in the throes of some dream; but there were traces of tears on his silken lashes.

Alexander told himself that he had some consolation in that the boy was still with him; but reason told him that it was only because he had nowhere else to go. Alexander went to his bed, and lay down, and his heart was so sore that he thought he would never sleep again.

Auguste sat alone in her bedroom until the house was silent. Her maid had come to her, but she had dismissed her. Slowly, at last, she got up and undressed herself. She put on a soft peignoir of creamy silk, that fastened with a sash round her waist. Then she picked up a candle-stick and slowly made her way to another bedchamber, a smaller one, at the back of the house.

Daniel was not asleep. He sat on his bed, silent and heavy-eyed, watching her.

She gazed down at him. 'You have been waiting for me?'

'Yes,' said the boy.

She put her candlestick on the window ledge. A draught caught the flame, and long shadows leapt across the walls. She went to sit beside him on the bed, and took his hand in hers, stroking his fingers one by one. 'Ah, *mon pauvre*,' she whispered. 'We are both exiles in a foreign land, are we not? I come only to offer you comfort. You do not mind my visits?'

He shook his head. Auguste whispered, 'We all want you to be happy here. So happy . . .'

Letting her silk robe fall from her shoulders, she took Daniel's face in her hands, and slowly kissed him.

LI

'Tis all in pieces, all coherence gone,
All just supply and all Relation.

John Donne, 'Anatomie of the
World', from *The First
Anniversarie* (1611)

It was the next morning, the 28th of July, and Jonathan was pacing his tiny office, while a long, obscure report that he was supposed to be copying for the benefit of a minor government official in the West Indies lay unheeded on his desk.

Sometimes he felt that he was being given these mundane and mind-numbing tasks to stop him having the time to ask any more questions. He had no proof of this; just as he had no proof of the growing conviction that he was still being watched. He'd got into the habit now, as he walked to his home, or went to some lowly place in the evening to dine, of stopping every so often and looking behind him. He could never be sure of what, if anything, he saw to confirm his suspicion. Just, perhaps, some swift movement of shadows in an alleyway twenty or thirty yards distant; or the awareness off, someone slipping off into a crowd; or a feeling that he could not shake off that eyes were following him.

Four days had passed since he had visited the scene of the fire. Alexander was now beyond his reach, and Jonathan was afraid for his brother, but there was little he could do; he guessed that Alexander's allegiance would now be firmly with his new friends, and any approaches by Jonathan would not only draw attention to his continuing investigation, but would most likely be rebuffed anyway by Alexander.

In his efforts to obtain further information about the Montpellier circle, he now had only Stimpson to rely on; and the lean informer's efforts seemed to have ground to a halt. All Jonathan knew was that Raultier had an alibi for the attack on Rose; Guy and Ralph had been seen, both of them, getting into the carriage at the moment when Rose was assaulted; Carline, though he had a criminal record for theft, was mute, and was, moreover, in Portsmouth at the time of Ellie's murder; and Norland, despite an even shadier background, had been seen at the Catholic Chapel on each of the nights when the girls were attacked.

He'd just sat down at his desk again and drawn pen and paper towards him when there was a knock at his door and Lucket sidled in.

'Thought you'd like to know your brother's in town, Master Absey.'

Jonathan said, 'You shouldn't be here. You'll get yourself into trouble for doing these things for me.'

Lucket shrugged and made his usual futile attempt to smooth down his stubborn, sandy hair. 'It's dull, what I do now. I'd rather work for you.'

Jonathan pushed his papers to one side. 'Where is my brother?'

'He's visiting the spectacle-maker, Perceval Oates, in Townsend Lane. He's been there for some time. Was still there when I left, waiting for a lens to be ground, or something. Got a Frenchman with him; not the doctor, but another one, a younger one, looks pretty sick to me.'

Guy de Montpellier, thought Jonathan. Aloud, he said, 'Did they come in their own carriage?'

'No. It was a hired one. There were three of them came into town in it: the Frenchman, your brother, and someone else; someone older than the Frenchman, but still quite young. He was tall, with long fair hair . . .'

Jonathan rose slowly to his feet. 'A servant?'

Lucket shook his head decisively. 'No. He was too well dressed for a servant. He wore tasselled boots, and a fine coat. Dark green it was, with big brass buttons.'

Long fair hair, a green coat – the exact description of the man with Crawford. Jonathan was gripping the edge of the desk.

'I noted him especially,' Lucket went on, 'because I've seen him before. He was the man at the Angel, the one who brought the doctor the message that made them both rush off.'

So this man was Raultier's nameless companion on the night that Priss of the Blue Bell died. Jonathan felt dizzy. Oh, if only he'd known before. If only he'd been able to set Lucket to watch the Montpellier house, and not Stimpson. If only he himself had seen this man's face more clearly that night at the Angel . . . He felt sick with apprehension. 'Do you know who he is?'

'I guessed you'd be interested, so I asked some questions. His name's William Carline.'

Jonathan sat down again. Carline. Auguste's lover; a petty criminal. He said, with an effort at calmness, 'Is the carriage that brought them to Clerkenwell still waiting for them?'

'No, sir. It set off back towards the city when they'd paid the driver. No doubt they'll be hiring another at the end of Turnmill Street when they're ready.'

Jonathan was digging in his pocket, searching for coins. 'I want you to go back there quickly. Choose a driver for them and pay him to make sure there's a small accident to the carriage – something that will delay them for a while – just past the Halfway House on the Kensington Road. Do you understand me?'

Lucket had done this kind of thing for him before. He said, 'Oh, yes. I understand.'

Jonathan gave him the money, and he departed; and then Jonathan sat there thinking: this Carline was at Portsmouth in June last year when my daughter was killed. And he cannot speak. Everyone – Alexander, Stimpson, now Lucket – has told me so. But he sounds so very much like the man I saw with Crawford: and didn't I see the two of them *talking*?

What did it mean, if Carline wasn't a mute after all? What bearing could it have on his investigation, when Carline wasn't even in London at the time of the first murder? Everything? Nothing?

Pulling on his coat, Jonathan left Whitehall and walked swiftly through Charing Cross and along the Strand to Covent Garden. He asked for Rose Brennan at the Piazza, and was told that she had indeed been seen there earlier that day. But it took him some time to track her down, and he was beginning to face the prospect of failure when he found her at last, standing in the scanty shade of one of the numerous tavern-shacks. The midday sun was beating down from a steely sky. When she saw him, her face seemed, briefly, to open up in some kind of hope. He wondered what it was she expected of him. Whatever it was, he suspected he would fail her.

'Mister Absey,' she said. 'Now, what brings you here?'

'Rose, there's something I want you to do.' He was trying not to look at where the tawdry lace barely covered her young, almost childish breasts. 'I want you to come with me, to see if you can point out the Frenchman who gave you the gold.'

Her face was closed to him again. 'Jesu, mister. I don't want any dealings with that madman again.' She shook her head. 'Anyway, I've told you often enough that it wasn't the Frenchman who tried to kill me.'

Jonathan said, very carefully, 'I know. But there's someone else I want you to see. And I think he might be with the Frenchman now.'

She said warningly, 'It wasn't that scarred coachman either. I told you that.'

'No. Not the coachman.'

He saw her small face become set in obstinacy. Jonathan said desperately, 'If you come with me, you needn't go near him. He won't even know you're there.'

She said, turning her face aside, 'I don't want to see him. I told you. And I'm tired of your questions. If you're not going to give me any money, then leave me alone, will you?'

He gripped her suddenly, heedless of the crowds who thronged the Piazza, of the stifling smells of fruit and rotting vegetables and stale beer from the drinking dens. Her body was slight and insubstantial; she gazed up at him through the red-gold curls that tumbled round her face and he said to her urgently, 'There are things beside money, Rose. Perhaps I can help you in other ways . . .'

But her mouth twisted with weariness and she said bitterly, 'What else is there besides money, mister? How can anyone help me without it? All I want is money, enough money to get me away from all this, and luck enough not to catch the pox in the meantime; what did you expect me to ask for?' She pulled herself away from him. 'That I want someone to *love* me?'

'Rose,' he said, catching her arm before she should leave him. 'Oh, Rose.' Some mummers capered past, bringing with them more crowds, and noise. He took her into the darkness between the shacks, and he knew that it was madness, that he was over-tired, but suddenly he was burbling like a lovesick lad, Bedlam-bound; the words poured out, more words than he had spoken for a long time, for a lifetime. 'Rose,' he said, 'you shall come away from all this. I will find you somewhere safe. A little cottage, quiet and peaceful, near to green fields, and I'll come back to you, every night . . .'

She laughed openly at him. 'What,' she mocked, 'and me a whore?'

'How old are you, Rose?'

She shrugged. 'Dunno. Seventeen? Eighteen?'

Ellie was eighteen when she died. He said desperately, 'It's not too late,' but her eyes, older than his, told him that it was, and that he was making an inordinate fool of himself.

'Well. Come on,' she said. 'Get your end away. Jesus Christ, that's all you really want, isn't it? And then you can take me to find this man you're after, if it makes you feel better about your sly hungering to be up my skirts again.'

'No,' he said, shaking his head as she began to unlace her bodice, 'no, I have not come for that.'

'Haven't you?' she said: and she was already baring her breasts for him in a weary manner.

He struggled to steady his ragged breathing, and clenched his hands at his sides, but she laughed at his torment and cupped her small breasts in her hands, lifting them to taunt him.

'There, now. Don't ramble to me again of cottages in the country. And if you're set on taking me to see the Frenchman, it will cost you double.'

LII

All Bodies whatsoever that are put into a direct and simple Motion will so continue to move forward in a straight line, till they are by some other effectual Powers deflected and bent into a Motion, describing a Circle, Ellipsis, or some other more compounded curve.

Robert Hooke, *Attempt to Prove the Motion of the Earth* (1674)

Guy de Montpellier gazed out of the window of the hired carriage as it headed westwards to Kensington. 'It looks as if it will rain,' he said.

Alexander, warm and uncomfortable on the seat opposite him, knew Guy was afraid that they might not be able to look tonight for the lost star. He struggled to balance himself as the heavy carriage lurched along the rutted road, and replied earnestly, 'It may rain, yes, but the skies could clear by nightfall.' Yet despite his encouraging words, the lowering clouds in the west filled him with foreboding.

They'd had to hire a carriage for their journey to London, because Ralph had gone missing. Carline had ridden to get one for them at the Knightsbridge turnpike; and as Guy and Alexander were getting in, to Alexander's surprise and unease Auguste told them that Carline would accompany them in the carriage, in case Guy was taken ill.

So they'd gone, all three of them, to Townsend Lane, where Alexander asked Perceval to check and repolish the object glass from the Montpelliers' telescope. They had to wait some time in the little shop that smelled of snuff and slightly stale linen as Perceval examined Alexander's specifications, then scrutinised and repolished the lens, and checked it again. After he'd finished, Perceval took Alexander to one side and gave him something for Raultier: a portable telescope securely wrapped inside a cloth pouch with a drawstring neck. Alexander was surprised. Raultier hadn't mentioned to him that he'd ordered it, and he was even more surprised by its unexpected weight.

'Please give it to the good doctor yourself,' Perceval said earnestly.

At last their business there was finished. Carline had remained out in the street, seemingly in a world of his own; now they joined him, and all three were then forced to wait an inordinately long time outside Perceval's shop for the carriage to take them home. The link-boy they had sent to nearby Turnmill Street for one did his errand sluggishly, and so Guy, Alexander and Carline stood in the dusty heat of Townsend Lane while Perceval busied himself clearing his shelves of goods and closing up his shop behind them.

Alexander watched in surprise as the spectacle-maker started locking up his shutters. 'You're closing early, Perceval,' he said.

'I'm going away,' replied Perceval tersely. 'For some time.'

At first Alexander could not absorb it. He had planned, when all this was over, to return to new lodgings in Clerkenwell; he had hoped that things would be exactly as they were. 'When are you coming back?' he asked anxiously. 'Will we be able to play music together again?'

Perceval stopped what he was doing. 'I will be back. But I don't know when.' Seeing Alexander's face, he added, 'I'm sorry.'

The carriage arrived at last, manned by a surly driver. As they passed Southampton Row, Carline opened the door and jumped out, slamming the door behind him. Alexander, perplexed, looked out of the window after him, but Carline had already disappeared amongst the crowds. Guy just shrugged. 'He's always done what he wants,' he said.

And now, at long last, they had left London behind them. The heat increased as they moved slowly along the Kensington Road, past the fields and lanes and market gardens of the village of Brompton. The trees on either side shimmered with dust and to the west the sky had turned to pewter.

Alexander saw that Guy looked mortally tired. There were shadows beneath his eyes, and his fine-textured skin was drawn tightly over his cheekbones. The young Frenchman had been animated, eager even during the business of the lens; but now, as he leaned back against the shabby velvet cushions of the jolting carriage, his slim body seemed heavy with fatigue; and Alexander guessed that he was in pain, because his hands were clenched against his thighs as he braced himself silently against the rocking of the coach.

They were almost at the Halfway House, a ramshackle inn set askew like a bone in the throat of the Kensington Road. It was a place of ill repute, where even in daylight footpads were said to lurk; and in the gathering darkness of the approaching storm, with the trees breathless and the birds silent, it looked forbidding indeed, with its dark windows set deep in its rambling gables, and a grimy forecourt bounded by tumbledown sheds and pigsties.

There were a few London-bound coaches standing before it, their horses being tended by ostlers as the travellers took refreshment inside. A bunch of wagoners up from the West Country, dressed in grimy smocks against the dust of the road, lounged on a bench by the inn door, ale-pots in their hands. They stared pugnaciously as the carriage went by, and Alexander withdrew his gaze, anxious to be past the place.

But just as they were almost clear there was a sudden jolt that knocked the breath from Alexander's body. The coach bumped and lurched on a little way further, but it was leaning heavily over; and now Alexander could hear the grinding of an axle against the rough surface of the road. Both Alexander and Guy were flung off balance as the coach tilted so sharply that it seemed as if a wheel had come off, and settled its bulk lopsidedly to the left, where the door had swung open with the force of the impact. There was a fierce creaking of metal and wood, as the frame of the heavy vehicle adjusted to the strain; and Alexander, almost thrown to the floor, could hear the whinnying of the frightened horses, accompanied by the coachman's loud curses.

Guy was pulling himself up against the steep angle of the seat, his eyes dark with pain in the whiteness of his face.

'The lens,' he said urgently. 'You have it safe?'

'Yes,' said Alexander, panting for breath after the shock of the impact, 'yes, I have it safe, here in my pocket.' His hand fastened round the little package of chamois just as the coachman, coarse-faced, reeking of gin, came to the half-open door and said sourly,

'You'll have to get out. The horses can't pull us free with you two inside.'

Alexander wondered if the man's drinking was the reason for this calamity. He said, as assertively as he was able as he scrambled awkwardly out through the wildly sloping door, 'How did it happen?'

'How d'you think?' muttered the man rudely, almost turning his back on him. 'Hole in the damned road, what else?'

Alexander, gazing back at the lopsided vehicle, saw that the carriage had gone into a deep rut, well to the left of the crown of the road; and he knew then that there was no good reason for it, except carelessness. They had the whole road to themselves.

He would have protested more, but he knew from experience that in the face of his complaints the coachman's rudeness would only increase, exposing Alexander's ineptitude in such dealings in front of Guy. So he turned quickly, to see if his companion needed help, but Guy was quick-moving in spite of his vile illness, and he let himself down from the wildly tilting carriage to stand aloof while the surly coachman went round to the horses' heads to begin the work of heaving the carriage back to the crown of the road.

They were in full view of the courtyard of the inn. The skies overhead were leaden now, the heat overwhelming. Alexander, feeling the sweat prickle at the nape of his neck, was aware of faces turning to stare; of fingers pointing. The bearded wagoners were sneering openly at the fate of their carriage.

There was a shiver of wind and the first heavy drops of rain began to fall. Alexander glanced anxiously at Guy, who stood at a distance with his back to him; then he looked around in growing concern for some kind of shelter for his sick companion.

And then everything was forgotten, because with a sensation of utmost disquiet, even of fear, he saw his half-brother coming hurriedly towards him from amongst those who were gathered in the courtyard of the inn. Alexander was shocked by Jonathan's appearance. His eyes were red-rimmed, as if he hadn't been sleeping; his face was haggard, and he looked fraught with anxiety.

'I have to talk to you, Alexander,' he said. He nodded swiftly in the direction of Guy, in the distance. 'Is that man Guy de Montpellier?'

'Yes,' said Alexander. 'Yes, he is.' He moved instinctively to block Jonathan's view of Guy, as if to protect the sick young Frenchman. 'What do you want? How did you know we would be here?'

Jonathan ignored his question, and instead glanced agitatedly at the empty carriage, then back at Alexander, as if there was something he could not understand. 'But where's the other one? Where's Carline?'

Alexander felt cold. 'Carline left us earlier.'

Jonathan was wiping the rain from his cheeks, his eyelids. He said, almost desperately, 'Listen to me, Alexander. I have to warn you. The Montpelliers and their friends are involved in dangerous business. I beg you, don't go back to them; come away, now, with me –'

The rain was coming down heavily now, making speech difficult. Alexander answered, his voice shaking with agitation, 'I think you forget, brother, that it was you who told me to get close to them. And this I have done.'

Jonathan stepped forward. 'Alexander. Please listen –'

Alexander was shaking his head vehemently. 'We have achieved great things together. Great things. You cannot tell me now that I must leave them—'

He was forced to break off, because his words were drowned by the cacophony of creaking harness as the horses, their great sinews straining under the crack of the driver's whip, succeeded at last in pulling the carriage out of the rut into which it had settled. Now the vehicle rocked on its great iron springs, safely back on the road. The rain sluiced down, and in the distance thunder rumbled.

Jonathan put his hand on Alexander's arm. Raindrops were streaming down his face. 'Alexander. I beg you to listen to me. I was wrong, so wrong, to send you there in the first place; I wish to God I never had. You must believe me when I tell you that the Montpelliers are no friends of yours.'

Alexander stared at him, his wig askew, his clothing soaked in the pouring rain. 'You would try to take this from me as well? The friendship that I've earned? They offered me shelter. I had nowhere else to go.'

'They are dangerous people. They are not what they seem—'

'My God, my God,' said Alexander, pulling his arm away, 'you would see me robbed of everything. How you have stored up your hate for me.'

'*Alexander . . .*'

'Leave me alone,' said Alexander.

He turned away from Jonathan and walked unsteadily back to the carriage, where Guy was already climbing in. Alexander followed him, and saw on Guy's face an expression of utter weariness. 'We can rest here,' Alexander said, 'for a while, if the journey is too much for you,' but Guy merely gestured for them to go quickly, so Alexander shouted up to the coachman and the carriage lurched off, proceeding with almost painful slowness because the lonely road was fast becoming a quagmire in the heavy rain.

Guy had closed his eyes. Alexander settled himself by the window, feeling sick at heart.

It was only after some time that it occurred to Alexander to check for the items that Perceval had given him, and he realised with dismay that although he had the object glass, he no longer had the heavy telescope. He tried frantically to think what might have happened to it, but all he could remember was that he had laid it, in its cloth pouch, on the seat beside him. When the coach had tilted sideways and the door had swung violently open the telescope must have rolled along the sloping seat and fallen out. It would still be lying there, in the mud at the side of the road. His heart sank still further, because he would have to go back for it. But first he had to get Guy safely home.

He saw Guy watching him with those bright, pain-ridden eyes. 'Is everything all right?' Guy asked him sharply. 'Do you still have the lens?'

And Alexander drew a deep breath, saying, 'I still have the lens. Everything is well. Yes, everything is well.'

Guy looked out of the window. 'The clouds are lifting to the north,' he said. 'The sky will be clear tonight.'

Jonathan, careless of the rain that poured down on him, watched until his brother's carriage was out of sight. He was just turning to go when he saw something lying in the mud, close to the place where Alexander's carriage had lurched to a standstill. He picked it up. It was a long cloth bag, containing something solid and heavy; and when he opened it up, he saw that it was a telescope.

Tiredly he put it into the deep inside pocket of his greatcoat, then he tramped back through the rain to the courtyard of the inn, where Rose Brennan sat in the hired carriage, clenching the folds of her tawdry print gown in her fingers. She feigned nonchalance as Jonathan climbed in to join her, but not before he'd seen that for a moment she'd looked anxious, almost frightened. Jonathan called to the driver to move on, then he sat beside her and closed the door, aware of the rain dripping from his coat and his boots on to the straw at their feet.

A double failure. Carline had not been there after all, for Rose –

and himself – to identify. And, far from warning his brother, Jonathan had succeeded only in further alienating Alexander, who had gone back to the Montpelliers in an outburst of renewed loyalty.

Jonathan leaned back against the musty leather upholstery, and the carriage started on its long journey back to London.

'That was him,' said Rose suddenly. 'Standing over beyond the carriage, in all that rain. The Frenchman who rambled of stars, and talked of a lady called Selene. It was him who gave me all the gold.'

'Yes,' said Jonathan. 'I know.' He realised she was trembling violently. Trying to forget his own searing disappointment, he put his hand over hers, in an effort to calm her.

'He left,' she went on. 'After he'd paid me.' She shuddered. 'He climbed into the carriage with the big, scarred man that I told you of, who was up in the driver's seat. I was watching them go off down the street when I felt the rope go round my neck—'

'Yes,' said Jonathan. 'Yes. There was someone else, that I hoped would be here. Someone else I wanted you to see. But I was mistaken. I will take you home now.'

She pulled her hand away from his and stared blankly out of the window, biting her fingernail. Jonathan tried to speak some meaningless words of comfort to her, but she made no acknowledgement of him or his words, and her cheeks were still pale.

He ordered the driver to take them as close as the carriage could get to her shabby lodging house in Grape Street. He got out first, and helped her down. 'Be careful,' he said. 'Don't go out on the streets again tonight.'

She looked at him with something of the old, mocking challenge. 'You'd have me starve?'

'I'll come for you later,' he said desperately. 'We'll go somewhere to eat and we'll talk about the other things you could do; you don't have to live like this . . .'

'Jesus,' she said wearily. 'You're going to start talking about cottages in the country again.'

'No—'

She pushed his hand away as he reached out to her. 'You're like those church men who come out on to the streets ranting to girls like me about our sins, and can't wait to get up our skirts. So someone tried to kill me; it's a hazard of the trade. No need to use it for an excuse, mister, every time you feel that itching at your groin. I can see it in your eyes now – you'd have me here, now, up against the wall, wouldn't you? Wouldn't you? You could at least be honest about what you want.'

Jonathan said raggedly, 'I'll call for you at eight.'

He climbed back into the carriage, and the driver whipped his horses on. Long after she'd gone, the scent of her cheap perfume continued to haunt him. She thought him a fool; and doubtless she was right. So far he'd been wrong about everything, it seemed. So far he had failed, at everything.

Jonathan told the driver of the carriage to take him to Whitehall. It was late in the afternoon, and the hot July sun had burned through the clouds, drying all traces of the recent heavy rain from the city's streets. He trudged from where the carriage dropped him to his office, his clothes and his boots still wet. Once there, he slung his greatcoat over the back of his chair and looked to see what tasks awaited him.

A sealed dog eared letter lay on his desk. It was addressed to Jonathan Absey at the Home Office, with pencilled notes indicating that it had gone first to Montague House, then, in error, to the Board of Trade, before finally catching up with him here. Jonathan broke the seal, and found it was from Robert Davies in Portsmouth.

Dear Mr Absey

Since your visit two weeks ago, I have been asking more questions about William Carline. I have uncovered some matters of which I think you ought to be aware.

Carline was indeed suspended from the Navy for suspected theft in the summer of 1793, as you had been informed. But he always declared his innocence; and in the matters of the Yard with which he dealt I found him a meticulous worker, and clever too, with his books and his learning. A valuable man in these times of trouble; almost indispensable, and certainly not a spreader of seditious literature.

All this I told you. But I have since found there was something else.

Last summer, at a time when, as I explained to you, I was away for some weeks on other business, Carline assaulted and almost killed a girl who used to come daily to sell bread to our men. He lured her to a deserted shed down by one of the wharves, where he raped her and tried to choke her to death. He insisted afterwards that she was a whore, who had unfairly rejected him.

As you will know, we have our own disciplinary body here in the yard, in the interests of security; but if cases are severe enough they are sent to the Winchester Assizes. I would have thought that Carline's crime merited trial and a prison sentence at the least; I can only guess that the Commissioner made the decision to keep it all as quiet as possible because the public airing of such a crime could easily have ignited trouble between the dockyard and the town. Thus, with the knowledge of only the most senior officers here, Carline was flogged, in private, and dismissed.

I would appreciate it if you, as a senior official, would handle this information with discretion. I should have stayed silent, perhaps; but I heard also, on making enquiries in the town, that the girl died soon after the attack. Unable to bear any longer the memory of what happened to her, she drowned herself.

I feel that some crimes should be punished as they deserve. I have a daughter, you see.

Jonathan sat back, the letter clutched in his hand. It must, after all, be as he'd thought; he'd not been wrong. His heart was racing. Carline must be the killer. July, June: the slight discrepancy over dates must be an error, or perhaps a deliberate falsification of the records even, on the part of those who protected the sinister group of astronomers . . .

He stood up. His first task was to find Carline for himself.

He walked quickly to a tavern by Charing Cross where Lucket and his cronies sometimes lurked; of Lucket there was no sign, but there were other faces that he knew. He paid an old hand at this kind of game to set watchers at the Knightsbridge turnpike, to look out for the tall blond man in the green coat; and then he went back to Whitehall to find the Chief Magistrate, Richard Ford, because he wanted to lay a private prosecution for murder.

LIII

The charm dissolves; the aerial music's past;
The banquet ceases, and the vision flies.

William Shenstone, 'Elegy XI' (1764)

The storm had moved on and the skies were growing lighter by the time Alexander and Guy's carriage reached its destination at last. As Guy got out, Alexander explained to him that he had a further errand, then he instructed the surly coachman who had so nearly brought them to disaster that he wished to return to the Halfway House. And so Alexander retraced his route, back to the ramshackle inn on the Kensington Road, to look for the lost telescope.

The stretch of the road where the accident had taken place was furrowed now with mud, thanks to the rain and the passing of many carriage wheels. Alexander searched up and down, but he knew already that his task was hopeless. The telescope, if it had indeed fallen here, would have been stolen, or ground into the mire by now. He walked across to the inn to ask if the package had been handed in there, but he received a curtly negative reply.

With a heavy heart, he told the driver to take him back to the Montpelliers' house. And as he entered the hallway he met Raultier, in his hat and coat, just about to leave.

Raultier greeted him civilly. 'I hear you've been to get the object glass polished.'

Alexander said, 'Yes. We've been to Perceval's shop.'

Raultier was nodding. 'The sky is clearing at last. Tonight you'll be able to look for Selene again.'

He was about to move on, but Alexander barred his way. 'Doctor Raultier. There's something I must tell you. Perceval gave me a telescope to deliver to you. He said you were expecting it. But on our way back we had an accident and I'm afraid it's lost.'

The change in Raultier was so dramatic that Alexander was almost frightened. The doctor stepped forward, and caught Alexander by the arm. 'A telescope? From Perceval Oates?'

'Yes. I'm so sorry. I've been back to look, but there was no sign of it.'

Raultier seemed to speak with difficulty. 'What kind of telescope was it?'

'I didn't see it; it was wrapped up. But I imagine it was some kind of portable reflector, with a mahogany case, because it was very heavy.'

'Heavy?' whispered Raultier.

'Yes. Unusually so—'

'Ah . . .' Raultier seemed to have gone quite white. He stepped back, his hands hanging limply at his sides.

Alexander, feeling sick at heart, said, 'Of course I'll recompense you for your loss. It was all my fault; I should have taken better care of it.'

Raultier was clearly making a huge effort to restore himself to normality. But his voice was bleak as he replied, 'No. It wasn't your fault. Guy told me about the coach almost overturning. How could you be blamed for that?' He seemed to be thinking hard. At last he said, 'I was going back to London anyway. I'll call at Perceval's shop, and discuss the matter with him myself—'

'No,' broke in Alexander, 'Perceval has left London.'

'Left London?'

'Yes. He was shutting up his shop even as we left. He said he had to go away. He didn't know when he'd be back.'

And this time indeed, Raultier seemed utterly stricken. He gazed at Alexander with something beyond despair; and then, slowly, he went towards the door and let himself out.

Alexander stood in the empty hall, burdened with the knowledge that once more he had let Doctor Raultier down. Slowly he climbed the stairs, intending to go to his room; but on his way there he decided to visit Daniel, because this morning the boy had spoken, briefly, of feeling unwell. He made his way towards Daniel's bedchamber at the back of the house and opened the door quietly, anxious not to disturb him if he slept.

And then indeed Alexander felt that his world was slowly tumbling into pieces around him, for as he stepped in, he saw that Daniel was on his bed, not asleep but naked, and hideously entwined in the brawny arms of the big ex-priest, Matthew Norland.

Norland was more than half disrobed. His haggard face glistened with sweat in the musty heat of the little chamber, and his long, iron-grey hair hung loose. He moved ardently, sighing aloud gross words of affection, and Daniel was silent, obedient; was he not always?

Neither of them had heard Alexander come in; neither of them saw him. So Alexander turned, drawing the door shut again behind him, and stumbled up the stairs to his own room, and retched his heart out into the stale pot beneath his bed, emptying his guts again and again, thinking, *Why didn't I see it? Why didn't I realise what was happening?*

By the time he came downstairs again, it was late afternoon. Through the windows he could see that the skies had cleared, and the July sun shone with renewed resplendency on the overgrown lawns and lush trees that surrounded the house, but he didn't notice any of it.

With a great effort of will, he went to Daniel's room first. He pushed the door open with shaking hands, because he was afraid that the vile ex-priest would still be there. The bedchamber was empty, but the sweat-scent of Norland lingered; and as he stood there, Alexander felt he was at his own aphelion. In spite of the splendour of the dying afternoon, this, surely, was the abode of darkness, where lost souls bewailed the absence of God, the absence of goodness itself.

He wandered blindly round the big house that was not his home, discovering no one, until at last he found Daniel sitting hunched in a chair in the music room, gazing at the harpsichord. Alexander wondered if the instrument reminded him of their lost home, their lost life in Clerkenwell, and he could hardly speak for the emotion that welled in his breast.

He walked up to the boy at last and Daniel did not look at him, but continued to rock silently in his chair.

At last Alexander said, '*Why, Daniel?*' and Daniel turned to him then, and said,

'Because he told me to.'

'Who? Norland?'

'No. The other one. The other one . . .'

He had started to tremble, and Alexander thought wildly, who can he mean if not Norland? Who can he mean? But he couldn't question him any more, for the boy had wrapped his arms around himself and was rocking obsessively.

Alexander, unable to bear his distress, tried to put his arms round Daniel to comfort him. 'It's all right,' he said quickly. 'We will leave this place. We will find another home, together—'

Daniel pushed him away.

Alexander went to search for the man who had done this to him.

He made his way out into the overgrown garden, which was hot and sleepy in that faltering time just before late afternoon sinks into early evening. The bees, their memory of the heavy rain quite vanished, hummed over the tangled honeysuckle as Alexander pushed his way down paths that were almost covered with thyme. In archways and crevices of greenery stood statues that were mottled with age, and in one terraced nook he saw a little waterfall sparkling amongst the fronds of fern. The beauty of this place seemed to mock him.

He found the big ex-priest at last, sitting alone on one of the terraces, drinking wine and idly toying with the pieces on a lacquered chessboard that lay on the table before him. Next to the chessboard sat an almost empty bottle. Alexander, coming up to him, swept the bottle aside. It shattered on the paving stones, and the silence after it was like an abyss.

'When?' said Alexander. 'When did it start?'

Norland shrugged, and Alexander saw that he was drunk. He wondered how he could ever have trusted that dissipated face.

'Answer me,' Alexander said, 'damn you,' and he gripped the seated man's shoulders, and shook and shook, as those men had shaken Daniel, outside his burning house.

Norland said surlily, 'Let me go.' He shrugged off Alexander's hands and adjusted his coat. 'It wasn't me who started it all. You've only yourself to blame. Why did you bring him here?'

Alexander gazed, stupefied, as the insects hummed busily over the lavender beds. The scent of the flowers was like dung in his nostrils.

Norland, bitter with drink, went on, 'So you saw me with him. You really think I was the first here to enjoy him? Poor Daniel.' He laughed shortly. 'He assumed, I think, that you brought him here as some kind of payment for your sojourn with the Montpelliers.'

Alexander shook his head. 'No. No.'

'Didn't you see the way that Auguste looked at him, that first night? She saw immediately that here was a novel, delectable morsel; it was she, you may recall, who tended him, who bathed him and saw to his injuries. That was the start of it. The very next day, during the long, hot afternoon, while you worked on your calculations, she and Carline fed him strong wine, and grapes dipped in honey, while Auguste whispered her sweet words of vice to him. After that he knew what was expected of him. He believed it was what you wanted.'

'*No.*'

'Where were you, master mouse, master astronomer?' Norland got to his feet heavily. 'Oh, you were too obsessed with your search for Selene, with your craving for fame and glory, just like the rest of them. They hurt him, you know, Auguste and her silent satyr Carline. Auguste is capable of deeds that would make a strong man flinch, and she urged on her lover to teach your boy the pleasure that can be found in pain, though I would guess that perhaps he knew it already . . . My God, Wilmot, and you come out here to blame *me* for it all? While you were busy with your stargazing, they summoned me to take my turn, and the boy knew what to do, oh, he knew what to do, with all of us, one by one . . .'

Alexander was beyond speech, beyond sense almost, as Norland went on scornfully, 'Dear Christ, if you had any thought at all for the boy, you'd never have brought him to this place of all places. Never.'

Alexander turned blindly from him and stumbled back into the coolness of the house, for the brightness of the sun threatened to overwhelm him. 'Daniel, Daniel!' he cried out.

But Daniel had gone. His room was empty. He had taken his clothes and few possessions with him.

Alexander became aware then that Norland was following him. He turned, hating him. 'Did Guy know anything about this?'

'No. Nor Raultier either.' Norland laughed tersely. 'Guy can think of nothing but the redheaded bitch he once loved; he believes that by finding this star, this planet or whatever it is you hunt after, he will be able to lay her ghost to rest. And Raultier, as you know, is lost in his hopeless love of Auguste, indeed, has sold his soul to the devil for her. I told you, I warned you at the beginning of it all, that this place is the abode of the damned.'

Alexander pushed past him and sought refuge in his room, but of course there was no solace there. He would have to leave, for surely, he could not stay in this house a day, an hour, a minute longer. Soon he would encounter Auguste, and her acolyte Carline; how could he bear now to even be near them? Norland had been right in one matter at least: Auguste was rapacious, and her lust contaminated the house. He remembered what he had witnessed in that candlelit room – so long ago, now, it seemed – when Auguste had drawn her brother into her arms and he had thought her actions then to be a selfless outpouring of consolation for the sick, deluded Guy.

As he began to get his things together, as pitiful in their meagreness as Daniel's, there was a knock at his door and Guy came in, Guy with his eyes laudanum-bright, and his face furrowed with pain, and hope. He didn't even notice that Alexander was preparing to leave, but came up to him, and said eagerly,

'Will you be ready tonight, to look for Selene? The skies are quite clear. We only need to see it once more, to be quite sure of its path; isn't that what you said?'

Alexander, his heart aching for the sick young man, knew that he couldn't leave him now, not when he was at the very point of achieving the only thing in his life that still held any meaning for him.

'I will be ready,' he said. Afterwards he would leave this place. He didn't know where he would go, or what he would do; it didn't really matter.

For Alexander, darkness had already fallen.

LIV

Without dimension, where length, breadth and height,
And time and place are lost; where eldest Night
And Chaos, ancestors of Nature, hold
Eternal anarchy.

John Milton, *Paradise Lost* (1667), Book II

Ralph the coachman lay blindfolded in the dank cellar that had been his prison for a length of time that seemed endless. His pain-racked body was curled up in straw that was fouled with his own excrement. When he heard the door opening, and the men coming in once more, he trembled and cowered against the wall.

At first, when they had seized him, he had tried to fight. But there had been too many of them, and he'd been quickly pinioned and borne off to this hell, where they had locked him without a word, and left him to hammer his fists against the stone walls until they were raw and bleeding. Then they came down to him again, and chained him to the wall, and blindfolded him; and someone almost tenderly dislocated his finger joints one by one.

He knew that it was the man he feared most who led the way, because of the faint but hateful scent of the snuff he used. Blindfolded Ralph heard this man exhale sharply at the stench of his fear-drenched body, and heard his delicate fingers lift a pinch of snuff from a tiny box which snapped shut again before he said,

'Well, Ralph. You are a murderer, are you not?'

Ralph sobbed, his voice husky with suffering. 'I tried to kill my wife. Yes, I meant to kill my wife . . .'

'You succeeded in killing the others,' said the man softly in his Scottish lilt. 'First the girl from the tavern, with her long red hair; and then the pretty little songbird.'

'No. No, I swear I did not kill them—'

He sensed the movement of air as the man leaned forward and whispered, 'You took your pleasure first, of both of them. Then you strangled them.'

'*Jesu, I killed nobody . . .*'

There was a silence then, far more frightening than any sound, a silence broken at last by the whisper of more men coming towards him; and he cowered, whimpering like a dog. One held his hand. The other pulled carefully, and manipulated the tendons of his swollen knuckles with all the delicacy of a fiddle player tuning a precious instrument. Ralph screamed aloud.

'And then,' went on the man with the snuff, as if nothing had interrupted him, 'you tried to kill the girl with the flowers. But someone raised the alarm, and so you ran.'

'*No* . . .' Ralph broke off, conscious of the sweat pouring down his cheeks as his tormentors prepared for a fresh assault. The stench of his body, of his suffering, was unendurable. 'Yes,' he whispered suddenly. 'Sweet Jesu, yes, I did it.'

For had he not tried to kill his own wife with his big hands, with these fingers that were now so brutally maimed? Dear God, had he not tried to choke the life from her, even though he loved her more than his own life? Perhaps this softly spoken man was right. Perhaps in some moment of lunatic rage he'd tried to kill again, and this time succeeded; for, heaven knew, he realised how it was done, knew what it felt like to squeeze the life from something so delicate, so tender; to see the flailing of the body, the panic-stricken eyes . . .

Tears rolled down his scarred face, soaking the ragged blindfold. The quiet-voiced man said,

'Good. Very good. You will go free now, Ralph.'

Ralph gazed towards the sound of his voice stupidly, the pain from his wounded joints addling his brain. 'Free?'

'You expect to be punished for your crimes, don't you?'

'Yes. Yes, of course . . .'

'Punishment will come. But let me tell you, before it does, that I am giving you one last chance to atone for your wickedness.'

'What do you mean?' whispered Ralph.

'You will be set free, soon, but there are conditions. You must not go back to the house in Kensington, do you understand? You must not speak with those people, none of them, not even the doctor.'

'Then where will I go? Where will I go?' Blind Ralph rocked himself, like a bereft child.

'You will be given money,' the man said quietly, 'to find yourself lodgings in London. You must not leave London. The constables are after you, Ralph. They will ask you more questions, about the murdered girls. And you will not lie to them, as you tried to lie, at first, to me. If you lie, or try to run, Auguste will die.'

'No. No . . .'

'So,' went on the man in his soft Scottish voice, 'will you tell these people what you told me?'

Ralph whispered, 'I will hang for it, then.'

'Perhaps.' The man shrugged. 'Is that not preferable to the torment you endure daily?'

Ralph heard the man's clothes rustling, and the clank of the tin vessel full of brackish water that was the only refreshment he had been offered. He felt its rim pressed carefully against his lip; he lapped at it desperately, inhumanly, like a dog.

'After all,' the man went on, 'it's what your wife would have wanted, isn't it? That you should suffer, as she did?'

'Yes,' nodded Ralph, his scarred face dark with anguish. 'Yes.'

He heard the sound of further movement, was aware of the flickering shadows of the candle against his blindfolded eyelids. Another voice came out of the silence. 'Is he ready?'

It was the voice of the man who had tortured his hands.

'Yes,' said Ralph's interrogator, 'he is ready. Give him some coins and let him go.'

The blindfold was pulled from Ralph's eyes, and Ralph was pushed, still half blind, in the direction of the door, but he did not go through it, not yet. Instead, as his eyes adjusted to the gloom, which was relieved only by a single candle, he stared in horror at the second man – the one who had so carefully broken his fingers. Their eyes met and the man smiled and said quietly, 'No one will believe you, you know.'

They unlocked his shackles then and hauled him up the steps by his shoulders, while his hands hung twisted and useless at his sides. He stood in the doorway and they pushed him towards freedom.

Ralph staggered blindly out into the bright London afternoon. Why had they let him go, only to tell him that he would have to confess it to others? He knew that if he confessed, he would surely die.

Whimpering under his breath, half mad with pain, Ralph wandered aimlessly, not knowing where he went, not caring. For they had told him that he must never go home, neither could he run from the cruel streets of the city where his tormentors lurked; or Auguste, whom he loved, would die.

Never to go home. Indeed, he was beginning to think that all his memories of that old life were an illusion. Perhaps he had killed, and forgotten. Perhaps he was truly mad, just as they had told him.

Lucket, bored after doing what Jonathan had told him to do, was roaming the mean streets that edged Leicester Fields, looking idly for a game of dice in one of the gambling dens there to while away the early evening time. He bought cherries from a stall, eyeing with rapacious lust the almost naked bosom of the girl who sold them until he got closer and saw how the smallpox had pitted her skin like diseased fruit; then he entertained himself by spitting the stones at a mangy dog asleep in the gutter and watching the crowds mill by.

He drew himself slowly to attention when he saw the big, scarred man in the shabby coat drifting along with them, his body slow and heavy as if he was suffering, and his eyes looking as if the hounds of hell were after him.

Lucket remembered him. He was the one who'd driven the French doctor and Alexander Wilmot from Clerkenwell to Kensington, on the night when Lucket had visited the Bull's Head.

He spat out the last stone with some force, and it stung the dog's muzzle. The dog jumped away, howling. His hands in his coat pockets, Lucket sauntered after the man, mingling with the crowds. The man turned off down a narrow alley, and Lucket followed at a distance, wary because of the scarred man's size. Just then the man turned, and saw that he was being followed, and a look of terror crossed his face. He began to run in the direction of Soho, along Broadwick Street; and Lucket, frowning, hurried after him. At last the man ran into a blind lane off Ryder's Court, where he turned like an animal at bay; and Lucket was just reaching in some trepidation for the knife in his pocket, wondering what to do next, when the man sank to his knees and started to whimper brokenly, 'Yes. I did it. I killed them, all of them.'

He was holding up his fists to hide the tear-ridden ugliness of his face; and Lucket saw, with horror, that his hands were horribly mutilated. It had been done recently; the joints were swollen and immobile, and several fingers stood out at crazy angles, like a scare-crow's.

'All right, mate. All right, now,' Lucket said soothingly, and went slowly towards him.

'He talked,' Ralph was whispering, almost to himself, his voice shaking with fear. 'I didn't know that he could talk . . .'

LV

*If we indulge a fanciful imagination and build
worlds of our own, we must not wonder at our going
wide from the path of truth and nature; but these
will vanish like the Cartesian vortices, that soon
gave way when better theories were offered. On the
other hand, if we add observation to observation,
without attempting to draw not only certain conclusions, but also conjectural views from them, we
offend against the very end for which only observations ought to be made.*

   *I will endeavour to keep a proper medium; but if
I should deviate from that, I could wish not to fall
into the latter error.*

William Herschel, *Letters* (1785)

C arline. Jonathan was back in his office, reading and re-reading
the letter from Davies, which he'd taken with him across
Whitehall to the office of the Chief Magistrate Richard Ford;
but he'd been warned, outside Ford's door, that the magistrate was in
conference with Under-Secretary King. So he had gone away; and,
sitting once more in his room, he reconsidered the wisdom of going
to the authorities. The Montpellier group was being protected still;
had he any grounds for thinking he might be believed, in the matter
of the murders, any more this time than he had been in the past? And
so he waited for the message he was expecting from the watchers he'd
set on the Knightsbridge turnpike and all roads leading to it, because
it seemed to him that his only option now was to go after Carline
himself.

A mute man who spoke; a brutal rapist; the killer of his daughter.
His quest was almost over.

He thought suddenly, in this time of waiting, of the telescope that
had been dropped on the Kensington Road.

It was deep in the pocket of his greatcoat, which he'd slung over the back of a chair to dry out after the downpour. He pulled the package out, and began to peel off the damp wrapping, wondering if it was worth trying to save it, or if it was already ruined. He wondered again if telescopes were usually so heavy. Rummaging in the drawers of his desk for a paper knife, he prised the lens away with some difficulty.

And he found, packed away inside the mahogany tube so snugly that it might have been made for them, two dozen golden French coins: *louis d'or*, with the king's head on one side, and an angel on the other.

Republican gold: the kind of gold Rose was given. No one had believed him when he claimed that Raultier and his circle were working not for the British, but for the Republicans; and were being protected by a man who killed to steal back the gold. His allegations had been so flatly dismissed that he'd given up believing them himself.

Suddenly he remembered Richard Crawford's expression, when Jonathan came across him talking to the blond-haired, blue-eyed man in the green coat who Jonathan was now sure was William Carline. Crawford had warned Jonathan from the beginning against investigating the Company of Titius. Crawford had, with his destructive gossip, perhaps ensured that the one person on Raultier's trail would not be believed. *Why?*

He reminded himself shakily that the Brittany expedition was a success; that he had been wrong before. But there were things he had to know; questions he had to ask. He stood up and replaced the coins in the telescope then put it back carefully in his coat pocket. He walked to Montague House, and climbed the stairs to Crawford's room. He knocked; no answer. He tried the door but it was locked.

Jonathan, bitterly regretting Lucket's absence, hurried down again to the porter's office and informed the man on duty that there was a problem with the lock on the door of his room in the colonial department. He insisted that it needed dealing with immediately; and the porter went off into the yard, grumbling under his breath, leaving the sets of spare keys that were on the board behind him unguarded. Jonathan quickly identified the bunch of keys for the upper rooms and climbed the stairs again.

He tried all the keys in Crawford's door. At last he found one that fitted. Letting himself in, he closed the door. Then he started to search through the drawers of Crawford's desk.

They were all unlocked and as he worked through them he found nothing but pay lists, letters to ordnance suppliers, and all the routine paperwork to be expected in Crawford's dreary job. Jonathan closed them and gazed round the room, which smelled of snuff.

He noticed a bookcase by the window, crammed with dry-looking volumes. Jonathan went over and scanned them: there were legal books, political essays, a hand-bound history of London's churches.

And then, squeezed tightly between them all, he saw another, smaller book. The lettering on its spine was so faded as to be scarcely noticeable. Jonathan drew it out and gazed at its cover.

Lefèvre's *Mythologie*.

This copy was bound in dark green leather; his and Raultier's were black, and Raultier's contained a lock of red hair, but otherwise they were identical. With unsteady hands he turned the pages till he came to Selene. Once more he gazed at the familiar picture.

Was Crawford paid in French gold too?

He put the book back. He let himself out swiftly and relocked the door, then went downstairs to the lobby again.

He just had time to replace the keys before the porter returned. The porter was looking displeased. 'I couldn't find anything at all wrong with that lock, Mr Absey. Perhaps you need to get your key checked over.'

'I'll do that,' said Jonathan. 'Thank you anyway for your trouble.'

He went outside and stood in the early evening sunshine, struggling to come to terms with the possibility that it was Crawford who gave Carline his orders; Crawford who had told the blond Englishman that those girls, the first of them his daughter, should be killed to safeguard Raultier's treacherous occupation.

He was trying to think where he would find Crawford now. What sweet revenge the little Scotsman was getting on the masters who'd left him behind.

He heard someone speaking his name. Whirling round, he saw Lucket, almost bursting with excitement.

'Sir, sir. I have him, sir!'

'Who?' He was still thinking about Crawford, and Carline.

'The scarred coachman you once asked me to look out for!' announced Lucket triumphantly. 'Ralph Wallace is his name. He confessed to me, blubbered like a child even though he's so big. He said that he did the murders, all of them. So I took him along to the Great Marlborough Street Watch House, gentle as a lamb, he was, sobbing all the way. The constable has him there now, in a cell –'

He went on, happily embellishing his tale.

But Jonathan, leaning back against the wall, he was thinking, No. This isn't right. It can't be Ralph. Rose saw him driving away . . .

In a state of bewilderment and anger, he set off with Lucket for the Great Marlborough Street Watch House, the place where Ellie's body had been taken over a year ago.

Richard Crawford, who had been seeing to certain items of business also, was at that very moment knocking with some urgency at the rear door of a building in Whitehall Place, a private dwelling which was known also as Cadogan House. A footman who clearly knew him escorted him to the usual room on the first floor then left, closing the door firmly.

Crawford took off his hat, panting from the climb. 'I need to talk to you, sir,' he said. 'It's about Absey.'

The man behind the desk regarded him coldly. 'I thought I told you to deal with him some time ago.'

'I did,' said Crawford quickly, 'in exactly the way you suggested. He has been thoroughly discredited, sir. No one will ever listen to anything he says again.'

'Then it sounds as if you've been successful.'

Crawford hesitated. 'To an extent, yes, sir. But Absey is stubborn. He's still asking questions.'

'He has no actual proof of anything, though? You've taken care of that?'

'He has blundered dangerously close to the truth on more than one occasion. But I think I've dealt with almost everything . . .'

The man leaned forward, his eyes narrowed. 'Almost?'

'There is a girl, a flower seller. She is a crucial witness.'

A silence.

Then the man said, 'Deal with her.'

LVI

*Pale Death with impartial foot knocks at the doors
of poor men's hovels and of kings' palaces.*

Horace, *Odes,* I.iv (23 BC)

Rose Brennan busied herself about her dingy little room,
choosing ribbons for her bonnet. In the narrow street below
her window, the fruit sellers and ballad singers of St Giles
were fervent in their cries, and a gang of ragged street urchins noisily
played some game with sticks against the churchyard wall, in an effort
to forget the hunger that pinched their stomachs.

Rose liked the noise. It was better to her by far than the silence of
the rainswept country road she'd travelled along that afternoon, and
the desolation of the half-ruined inn to which Jonathan Absey had
insisted on taking her, to look at the Frenchman. She shivered and
touched her neck, resurrecting the memory of pain.

And then she turned, distracted, because someone was knocking
down below at the door that opened out directly into the busy street.
Mother Gardiner, whose lodging house this was, must have gone to
answer it, because a moment later she called shrilly up the narrow
stairs that led to so many other little rooms like hers,

'Rose! Hurry now, girl. There's a gentleman here for you.'

Rose feigned irritation, but smiled as well. She'd told him not to
bother, but he'd called all the same. She still thought he was mad, this
Master Absey, with his tired eyes and tired face, who asked her again
and again about coins and stars. But Jesu, no one else had helped her
after the man had tried to kill her; and if Master Absey had a fancy
to ask questions before spending his good silver coins on her, then
why shouldn't she let him? She'd be wise to make the most of it all
while it lasted; life had taught her that much, at least.

So Rose crammed on her beribboned bonnet and primped her red
curls in the mirror, and realised, from the sound of St Giles's church
bell striking above the hubbub of the streets, that though he'd said

eight, it was only seven. She was amused by his eagerness. Master Absey seemed to fancy himself half in love with her, even if he was more than twice her age. Well, at least he didn't give her any reason to fear him.

But still she couldn't help but despise him for being a man; and herself, for earning her living from men.

She sauntered down the twisting stairs. Mother Gardiner stood in the hall, her arms folded across her ample bosom, and grinned at her. Rose went to the open doorway and stopped.

It wasn't Master Absey. It was a man she hadn't seen before, or she'd surely have remembered him, because he was young and tall and as handsome as could be. His clothes were plain, but good: he wore a dark green coat and kersey breeches, with new cotton stockings and brightly buckled shoes. His long fair hair looked as if the sun had bleached it.

He said nothing at first, just looked at her with his dark blue eyes, as if reminding himself of something. Rose felt a shiver travel down her spine in spite of the heat and she said, confused, 'You're sure it's me you want, sir? I was expecting Master Absey.'

He spoke then. His voice was slow and well modulated. He said, 'You are Rose, aren't you? I've come to take you to him.'

She hesitated, and then her eyes widened as she saw the carriage he pointed to, down at the far end of the alley where it widened out into St Giles High Street. It was a hired carriage, but of the better kind, with two good horses and a liveried driver. The urchins, chased by a yapping dog, were running around it, excited.

'Did he send that carriage for me?' she asked.

'Indeed. He's eager to see you again.'

She shrugged, then let the door close behind her and followed him, her feet trip-tripping over the dirt-smeared cobbles in her new, pretty shoes. The dog was cocking its leg against the wheel of the fine carriage and the man booted it aside sharply. She was upset for a moment by the creature's whines of pain, but then she forgot about it, for the man was helping her into the vehicle as if she were a lady. He said something to the coachman and got in beside her.

The carriage moved off eastwards. Rose leaned back against the cushions. The man didn't say anything else, and Rose found that a little odd, though she didn't mind too much, because she was enjoying looking out of the window. Jesu, how different these low, filthy streets seemed from this fine perch. Two carriage rides in one day: it was good to be a lady, if only for a while. Perhaps she should play along with Master Absey's whimsical little games after all, and not laugh at him so when he rambled on of cottages and green fields.

But soon the man's silence began to unnerve her. They were travelling along High Holborn now, and just as they were passing Leather Lane she turned to him suddenly and said, 'Where's Master Absey? Do we have to go much further?'

'You'll find out soon enough,' he said.

Rose went still. His voice. She suddenly realised that she'd heard that voice before. Coldness crept through her veins, as if her blood was turning to ice. 'Where are you taking me?' she repeated stubbornly, though she could feel herself starting to shake. 'If you don't tell me, I'm going to stop this carriage and get out, right now, I swear I am—'

'I'm telling you nothing, Rose,' said the man softly, 'because, you see, you already know too much.'

She knew him now, oh, yes; she'd not seen his face, but she knew his voice, because she'd heard him speaking, that night when he tried to choke her to death, and took the coins off her.

She flung herself towards the door, but she couldn't open it; and even as she struggled with the handle, the man leant over her and threw something round her neck. She tried to cry out through the closed window for help, but the cry died in her throat as his strong hands tightened the ligature cruelly.

The carriage rolled onwards into darker, lonelier streets. Rose's hands clawed the air and her feet drummed the floor as if in the throes of some dark passion. Her eyes stared from their sockets, her tongue choked her mouth and a yellow stream of urine soiled the fine petticoat and stockings that she had put on for Jonathan Absey. She heard the fair-haired man whisper, almost with triumph, '*A dead body revenges not injuries,*' and she died slowly enough, thinking in her agony of green fields.

LVII

It was just past seven of the clock, and Jonathan was still at the Great Marlborough Street Watch House, whither Lucket had directed him in such haste; though there was no hurry now, because Ralph was dead, hanged by his own hand, using his own knotted clothing secured to the high barred window of the dirty cell the constable had locked him in.

Lucket was stunned by the man's death. He rubbed his hand in perplexity through his bristled hair and said, again and again, 'But I thought this was the best place for him, sir. He came with me, meek as a lamb; he wanted to give himself up, I swear it. He told me he killed them all . . .'

Jonathan was angry, and dismayed. After he'd finished berating the constable for leaving Ralph unwatched, he sent to an undertaker's to arrange for the body, with its scarred, discoloured face and bulging eyes, so grotesque in death, to be taken away. The undertaker took his time, though, to arrive, and Jonathan waited for him, pacing the floor of the Watch House.

He turned suddenly on the constable, who must have been heartily sick of his questions but didn't have the courage to defy him.

'Did you feel that the man knew what he was saying when he confessed? Did you think he was in his right mind?'

The constable looked defensive. 'He wasn't happy, sir. No one confessing to a bunch of murders would be, now, would they? But he seemed sure enough about it. And so did the two men who came to hear his confession.'

The constable had already told Jonathan that two official-looking men with orders from the Chief Magistrate had come here almost immediately after Ralph's arrival to question him.

Jonathan had said, 'Did you send for them yourself?'

'No, sir. They just came. Somebody must have told them he was here.'

Who had told them? Who had told the Chief Magistrate? Surely nobody else had known, yet, that Ralph was here, except himself and Lucket. Jonathan had already guessed he was being watched. Was Lucket being watched too?

He said harshly, 'So they got his confession down in writing?'

'Oh, yes. They'll be glad they did now, as the fellow's topped himself.' The constable gestured at Ralph. 'At least he's saved the hangman a job.'

Jonathan was looking again at Ralph's big body, ungainly, even more so, in death; at his scarred blue face, at his hideously protruding tongue and bulging dead eyes; and, ugliest of all, his brutally maimed hands. It must have taken more strength in the face of pain than Jonathan would have thought possible for the man to knot his own clothing and slip it round his own neck with such recently tortured fingers.

Poor Ralph. He had served the Montpelliers and their friends loyally, even in the manner of his death, by confessing to crimes that he did not commit; and by then ensuring that no further questions could be asked of him.

Jonathan continued to pace the Watch House, thinking of Ralph's last hours, waiting only for the undertaker to arrive before going to check if news had come in yet that Carline had been found. The bells of St George's church were chiming nearby, as if tolling for Ralph's death. Once more he was facing defeat, because Ralph had confessed; and there was no one to argue with that confession.

Except for one person . . .

With an exclamation, Jonathan pulled out his watch: it was half-past eight. He strode to the door and flung it open, leaving the constable and Lucket staring after him. He started to run as fast as he was able along crowded Marlborough Street and past Soho Square, to Sutton Street and the crowded tenements of St Giles. It was a good half-mile, and he was panting heavily by the time he knocked on the door of the seedy lodging house just off the High Street. The door was opened to him by a hard-faced landlady who folded her arms and looked him up and down.

'I've come for Rose,' he said breathlessly. 'I told her I would call earlier, at eight, but I've been delayed—'

She glared at him suspiciously. 'But Rose has gone. A man with a coach came for her.'

'Christ, no,' he said, his heart racing so fast he could hardly breathe. 'What time did she go? When did this man come for her?'

'At about seven,' she said, shrugging.

'What did he look like?'

'Are you from the Watch or something, mister? We don't want no trouble here.'

He thrust some coins at her. She examined them, then said, 'He was younger than you. Tall, fair-haired, handsome. She was happy enough to go off with him.'

Carline. He turned and ran almost blindly southwards past Long Acre and James Street to the Piazza, pushing his way through the evening crowds of merrymakers and thieves and charlatans who were gathered there. It was like looking for Ellie. So many bright, painted faces as he floundered along, looking, looking . . . Feverishly he scoured one grimy all-night alehouse after another, raking the scavenging prostitutes with tiredness-rimmed eyes.

Dawn was breaking by the time Lucket found him at last. Lucket was almost as hot and breathless as his master, what with running all around the town to find him and the excitement of the news he'd picked up on his way. 'Sir, sir,' he gasped. 'Another girl found strangled, sir, in Robin Yard, off Leather Lane; a red-haired strumpet. They're saying it's the one who was a flower seller, the one he tried to kill before; her name's Rose. Strangled with a cord like the others, and dumped on a dunghill.'

As daylight crept over the city, Jonathan went to the mortuary beside St Bartholomew's Hospital at Smithfield, where they'd taken Rose. With her frail, broken body, she looked scarcely more than a child.

He was aware that if he'd left her alone, if he hadn't questioned her time and time again in an effort to identify the man who had tried to kill her, she might not have had to die.

As the morning bells struck eight, he left her and took a hackney to Whitehall. There were things he had to do, people he had to see; he needed to make quite sure that there would be no failure this time when he set about the final business of dealing with Carline the murderer.

But it appeared that nothing could be done by anyone yet, because he arrived to find that there was a summons, for all Home Office clerks, to attend the Chief Clerk's office immediately.

News had been received from Brittany.

LVIII

'*From Sir John Warren, HMS* Pomone, *Quiberon Bay: –*
'*Gentlemen. I am extremely sorry to inform you that the fort and peninsula of Quiberon was taken by assault, owing to treacherous measures. In addition to the misfortune of the place having been surprised by treason, the fact of the night being remarkably dark, with a hard gale of wind at the north-west, rendered it impossible for our gun-vessels to work up close to shore.*

'*I sent my own boats, as well as those of the men-of-war, inshore, and commenced a heavy fire upon the different columns of the enemy who were pressing down on the remainder of the Royalist army. I have been able to save about one thousand troops, with all the generals and staff, the greater part of the Corps of Artillery, and nine of the Engineers, with 1,400 Chouans, and several regimental colours.*

'*I have every satisfaction that no blame whatsoever can attach to the officers and men of the English navy in this disastrous affair, as every effort and support was made use of by them in putting the place in a proper state of defence. As soon as I have things in order I intend to take possession of the islands of Hedic and Houat, unless I receive orders to the contrary . . .*'

The Chief Clerk finished reading aloud the copy of the letter which had been sent to all government departments at first light, and looked round the table in the long room where the anxious staff of the Home Office were gathered.

'I thought you ought to be told as soon as possible,' he said. 'Soon the whole country will know. Captain Durham from the *Anjou* arrived at the Admiralty at dawn with these dispatches.'

The clerk sitting next to Jonathan seemed stunned. He spoke with an effort. 'Can anything be done for the prisoners?'

'No,' said Pollock tersely. 'It's too late. The National Convention sent swift orders that they were all to be executed. Tallien and Fréron in particular amongst the Republican leaders were adamant that Puisaye's men should die as traitors, because they were in possession of English weapons, and dressed in English uniforms. Over seven hundred men were shot, at Auray, and Vannes, and Quiberon. Captain

Durham's other letters confirm all this . . . Excuse me . . . I find this almost impossible to talk about . . .' Pollock found his handkerchief in his pocket and blew his nose. He looked tired, ill, almost. 'It has been a difficult morning.'

'But the news was good,' said another clerk in disbelief. 'Up till now, the talk has been of nothing but victory.'

Pollock rubbed his forehead. 'The initial landing was successful, yes. But Hoche received massive reinforcements. And Puisaye, in order to make any real advance inland, needed the support of the Chevalier de Tinténiac, whose men were supposed to march from the interior and take Hoche by surprise on the day of the crucial battle.' He looked round at them all. 'Tinténiac failed to arrive. And Captain Durham says that just as he was about to leave Quiberon Bay, news was being brought in that the Chevalier has in fact been killed, and his column scattered. There were some survivors, who reported that he'd been diverted by a false message. He and his men marched straight into a heavily armed force of ten thousand National Guards.'

'Who sent this false message?' someone asked.

'The survivors claimed that it came from the Royalist Agency, and was signed by Artois himself. But Artois strenuously denies it, and as he was actually in England at the time of its sending, it must have been a forgery.' Pollock shifted the papers on his desk; he still seemed dazed. 'Tinténiac is dead, and most of his men are dead too, or scattered around the Breton countryside where they fled after the ambush; so we shall probably never know. Whatever happened, it's clear that the Republicans knew every detail of the strategy in advance, and the forged letter had the desired effect. Puisaye's army stood no chance at all without Tinténiac's men.'

'Spies,' breathed one of the clerks, thumping his fist on the table. 'Damned spies. They are all around us.'

'It could have been the Spaniards who let the plans out,' argued another clerk, shaking his head. 'Wasn't the government in Madrid given information about this expedition in advance, in the hope of keeping its army in the war?'

'That is so,' said Pollock. 'But the strategy failed. The Spanish have already sued for peace with the French.'

There was a long, stunned silence. Someone said at last, 'Spain, to leave the war? That means we're quite isolated now. The rest of Europe has given up the fight.'

Pollock lifted his grey head. 'It seems like it, yes. But we must not abandon hope yet, gentlemen.'

Another clerk said quietly, 'What do Pitt and his ministers have to say about all this, sir?'

Pollock clasped his hands together. 'The Chief Minister is very much shaken. He had high hopes of the Comte de Puisaye's expedition. But he believes that we must continue to support the Royalists. There is talk that there may even be another attempt at landing troops on French soil, under the Earl of Moira.'

'What does the Minister for War think?' put in someone else.

Pollock hesitated. 'Dundas is of a different persuasion to Pitt. He thinks that now we should concentrate our armed forces against other, more achievable targets in a region where we command the seas: namely, the French colonies.'

Jonathan took no part in the general debate that followed. He sat there silently, thinking of those young soldiers trapped like rats on the rocky Breton shore, with the wild sea roaring at their backs, and the Republicans' muskets aiming at their chests. Were they still hoping, even then, that Tinténiac and his betrayed army would come to their rescue?

He had noted earlier that there was only one absentee from this gathering: Richard Crawford. Jonathan got up and left the room, the din of his fellow clerks' debate receding as he set off swiftly along the corridor towards the stairs. But he was forced to stop when a messenger barred his way.

'Master Absey,' said the messenger. 'The Under-Secretary wants to see you in his office.'

Jonathan stared at him in surprise. 'Now?'

'Yes, sir.'

Jonathan followed him, his mind in a frenzy. He had to find Crawford, but there was no denying the Under-Secretary's demand. He wondered if this peremptory summons had some bearing on what he'd discovered. Perhaps the Under-Secretary had remembered what Jonathan had been trying to tell him about Republican spies. It was even possible that he might have decided to believe him – now that it was too late.

John King was sitting behind his desk, grim-faced. 'Absey,' he said. 'What have you to say for yourself?'

Jonathan took a step back in surprise. 'I'm sorry?'

King's face was dark with anger. He got up from his chair and glared at Jonathan.

'I think you know what I mean,' he said. 'I called you here to explain *this*.'

He pushed forward a document that had been lying on his desk. It was marked Most Secret. Jonathan, bewildered, picked it up and looked at it; it seemed to him to be nothing but a report from one of the county deputies, containing a list of suspected but minor trouble-makers. Jonathan said, 'What do you wish me to explain, sir?'

'Enough of this charade!' snapped the Under-Secretary. 'It was found this morning on your desk, Absey. The contents don't matter a great deal; they're actually of little importance. What does matter is that this is a Most Secret file. And it isn't the first time this kind of thing has occurred. I'm sure I don't need to remind you about the Vere Street incident.'

Jonathan realised at last what was happening. He said, 'I have never seen this document in my life. Who found it? Who was looking through my papers? Am I under some kind of surveillance?'

King shook his head in impatience. 'Far from it. Don't add an imaginary sense of persecution to your list of faults, Absey. It was found purely by chance, by a diligent member of staff who considered it his proper duty, quite rightly, to inform me.'

Crawford? Jonathan said bitterly, 'I deny this absolutely. I tried to tell you the last time we spoke, sir, that someone had gone through my desk: only on that occasion something was stolen, not planted. Someone's trying to discredit me . . .'

'Someone?' queried King heavily.

Jonathan took a deep breath. 'I think you should be asking Richard Crawford about this, sir.'

King looked scornful. 'Are you going to blame the incident of the Vere Street papers on Richard Crawford also? Are you going to deny that you took those papers? Enough!' The Under-Secretary slammed a sheaf of papers angrily down on his desk. 'Enough of your excuses, and your putting the blame on others, and your rambling nonsense about spies, and messages, and missing letters. When I first came here,

William Pollock told me you were one of the soundest of his men. He would certainly be hard put to describe you in that way now.'

Jonathan bowed his head, silent.

'I think it would be best,' went on the Under-Secretary curtly, 'if you gathered your things together and left your office as soon as possible, Absey. There are grounds for prosecution, as you must surely realise; the misappropriation of Most Secret files is a serious offence. I think that we can spare you, and ourselves, the ignominy. But if there's any more trouble, anything else at all, then believe me, I will not be so lenient.' He lifted his finger warningly. 'Your arrears of pay will be calculated accordingly. Consider yourself dismissed.'

LIX

*If we had confined ourselves to the sending of regular
and substantial Supplies, which was at all times in
the Reach and within the Means of this Country,
we would have acted a wise and efficient part.
Instead, we have constantly amused ourselves and
trifled away the time in forming Fancies about
Splendid Expeditions.*

Henry Dundas to William Windham,
March 1796

So Jonathan went into his office for the last time, to cursorily
sort his papers and gather together his few personal possessions:
a pen-sharpener, a brass paperweight, an old snuff box that he
had never used, a small book of tinted maps of the British West Indian
islands, and the carved ivory paper knife that his daughter had given
him long ago.

Then he made his way back to Montague House, and climbed the
stairs to Crawford's office; this time it was unlocked and he threw
open the door almost violently, but there was no one in. Jonathan
stood there a moment, breathing deeply to steady himself. The scent
of Crawford's snuff lingered malodorously in the air.

Forcing himself into a semblance of calm, he left the building
and walked slowly past the Admiralty to the Paymaster-General's
office to collect the last of his wages. There were many people around
that he knew, hurrying about their everyday business from one
department to another, but it seemed to him that they pretended
not to see him. People who didn't know him stared at him curiously, because his eyes were red-rimmed with lack of sleep, and he
was unshaved.

The Paymaster-General's clerks were all busy, so he waited his turn
in the queue. Those who were before him were talking about the
Quiberon disaster and it seemed to Jonathan that already the initial

horror elicited by the morning's news was giving way to weary cynicism.

'The venture could never have succeeded anyway with those two hot-headed Royalist generals in charge,' one young clerk was saying. 'Puisaye and d'Hervilly. Look at them. Squabbling like schoolboys from the moment they landed. How much English money has been wasted on backing them?'

Another nodded. 'Some people think it's just as well the disaster came so early. At least the expedition has foundered before any English troops were sent across. Imagine the cost of setting up a full-scale English campaign on the mainland of France . . .'

It was Jonathan's turn to see the clerk about his pay. He muttered, 'My name is Absey. There should be some money for me.'

The clerk looked at him narrowly and counted out the wages owing to him. Jonathan signed for the money and went out.

He stood there alone in the courtyard, thinking of the betrayed soldiers, and of Ellie, and Rose. He thought of Henry Dundas, Minister of War, who Jonathan knew had always been reluctant to give explicit English support to the French Royalist landing. He'd heard Pollock talking, and King, of how Dundas had protested vehemently in a Cabinet meeting that such a venture was partisan warfare best left to the Royalists and Republicans to fight out one against the other; that English forces should never become involved in a civil war in mainland France . . .

He felt suddenly as if he was looking into some bottomless void.

No, he said aloud. No. His mind still reeling, he went back down Whitehall to Montague House. Once more he climbed the stairs to Richard Crawford's room. He took a deep breath and knocked, and heard the command to enter. This time Crawford was in.

'Absey,' he said, jumping nervously to his feet. 'I was sorry to hear your news.'

Jonathan said, 'Yes. But it was my own fault, in many ways. I've made mistakes.'

Crawford moistened his lips and waited, still tense.

'I've been stupid and confused,' Jonathan went on, 'chasing phantoms. Now I need to find some other post. There must be something I can do, in some lowly office somewhere. I was wondering if you could put in a word for me.'

'Why, yes. Yes, of course.'

'Perhaps we could meet later to discuss it? This evening, when you have finished work?'

'Certainly,' said Crawford after a little hesitation. He still looked surprised but there was undoubtedly relief, too, written across his features, that Jonathan was in control of his emotions. He pushed his spectacles up from the end of his nose. 'Shall we say, at six o'clock?'

Jonathan nodded agreement. 'We could meet at the Cross Keys. It's that place I told you about, in the Strand.'

'Yes,' said Crawford. 'Yes, indeed.'

Jonathan, as he turned to leave, noticed that the book had disappeared from Crawford's shelves.

Jonathan went home after that. He washed, and shaved, and had just finished changing his clothes when he heard someone knock at the door. When he went to open it, he saw that it was his landlady.

'I'm sorry, sir,' she said. 'I know this will be inconvenient. But I need your room.'

Jonathan frowned in bewilderment. 'Why? I'll pay you more, if you want.'

She seemed distressed now. 'It's not that, sir. Not that at all.'

He realised, then, that she had been told to evict him. He said, 'I'll get my things together immediately.'

'Oh, but you can have till the end of the week—'

'They told you that, did they?'

He could see fear in her eyes. He said, 'It's all right. Really, it doesn't matter.'

She hurried off in confusion. Quietly he shut the door again and began to pack his belongings.

He was finished by five o'clock. Everything was ready. He locked up his desk, then put on his coat and walked back to Whitehall. He settled himself on a low wall, in a shadowed recess by the Royal Chapel, just down from Whitehall Yard, and watched the clerks and secretaries leaving one by one in the afternoon sunshine. In the distance he saw Richard Crawford coming out from Montague House. His fussy, bustling walk was unmistakable. From time to time he dabbed his nose with his handkerchief, and looked round furtively, as if to check that he wasn't being watched.

Jonathan got up. He waited until Crawford was almost out of sight. Then he started to follow him.

It turned out that it was not a long way to Crawford's final destination, though Crawford did his best to conceal the fact. The route the Scotsman took was tortuous, all the way up to the King's Mews by Charing Cross, where Jonathan lost him for a few moments amongst the milling crowd of pedestrians. But then Jonathan saw that his quarry was in fact retracing his steps, forcing Jonathan to sidestep swiftly into the shelter of a doorway until he'd gone past. Crawford turned into Whitehall Place, scarcely two hundred yards from his original starting point; and Jonathan, who had kept him just within his sight all the time, stepped back into the shadows and waited. The houses here were tall and imposing. Crawford knocked at the door of the second house, and it opened almost immediately. Looking round one last time, Crawford hurried in.

The house was the private residence of Evan Nepean, former Under-Secretary to the Home Office and the War Office, and, since spring, First Secretary to the Admiralty; the man who, it was said, was the mastermind behind English intelligence for Dundas, in his days at the Home Office, then the War Office. Nepean had a reputation for being clever, shrewd and secretive.

How often, wondered Jonathan, had Crawford visited that house before?

He settled down to wait.

Crawford came out at last, looking anxiously all around him. Leaving Whitehall Place, he turned down Great Scotland Yard in the direction of Northumberland Street. After a few moments, Jonathan quickened his pace, and overtook him.

He took Crawford by surprise. The man looked ill when he saw him. 'Jonathan,' he said. 'I thought I was meeting you at the Cross Keys at six.'

'It's almost time. We'll walk there together,' said Jonathan.

Crawford managed a sickly smile, but it was clearly an effort. 'Of course.'

Northumberland Street was crowded. The early evening sunshine had drawn out vendors and pickpockets and mangy beggars to mingle with the homeward-bound workers. Jonathan suggested a back way to the Strand, along Craven Street, away from the crowds, he said. Crawford hesitated at first, but Jonathan was insistent, and led the way briskly through the rookery of ramshackle buildings and dingy courts. Crawford had difficulty keeping up with Jonathan's longer stride; soon his face beneath his warm wig was pink and perspiring, and his spindly little legs looked as if they wouldn't carry him much further.

'Jonathan,' he gasped at last, 'I think you've taken a wrong turning. This way surely leads to Hungerford Wharf, and not to the Strand at all.'

Jonathan pressed on as if Crawford hadn't spoken. A moment afterwards, as they passed a narrow, high-walled alley, Jonathan suddenly stopped and pointed at it. 'This is the way,' he said decisively, and turned into the dark opening. Crawford, close on his heels, took a few hesitant steps then stopped. 'No,' he said, looking round, 'this cannot be right . . .'

But before he could even think of making his way out again, Jonathan had moved on him swiftly and hauled him up by his shoulders against the damp-stained wall.

'Now, tell me, Master Crawford,' he said, 'tell me exactly what's going on, will you? You think I'm a fool, and yes, perhaps I am, in many ways, but not so much a fool that I think a dead man can commit murder.'

Crawford, smaller and weaker than Jonathan, was panting with fright. 'I don't know what you mean!' His breath was sour in Jonathan's face as he struggled ineffectually to escape.

'Oh, I'm quite sure that you do.' Jonathan, his heart overflowing with rage, tightened his grip on the other man's shoulders. 'Ralph Wallace confessed at the Watch House to the murders of Priss and Georgiana, as he was told to – wasn't he? – wasn't he? – but Ralph couldn't have killed Rose, because by then he himself was dead. It was Carline who killed Rose, just as he killed the others.'

Crawford said scornfully, 'Carline? Never heard of him. You're talking nonsense.'

Jonathan shook him hard. '*I saw you talking to him.*'

This time Crawford blanched. Jonathan went on relentlessly, 'Carline was the murderer. Wasn't he? He strangled those poor girls, to get back the French gold Guy de Montpellier had given them. And it was you who gave him his orders, to silence them by whatever means were necessary . . .'

Crawford was trembling now, but still he said nothing. Jonathan shook him harder, so his head slammed back against the wall with a sickening thud. Crawford's wig slipped over his forehead; he began to moan, and his lip bled where he had bitten it. Jonathan hauled him up against the wall again. 'Admit it, damn you.'

Crawford licked his lips. 'He wasn't meant to kill them,' he whispered. 'He was just meant to get the gold back. That was all. But he said, afterwards, that killing them was the only way to silence them. No one realised, at first, how much he enjoyed it . . .'

Jonathan clutched at Crawford's shoulders in a fresh burst of rage; Crawford whimpered, '*It wasn't my fault.* I did try to warn you. I tried to tell you at the beginning to stay away from them all . . .'

'Dear God.' Jonathan wiped his perspiring forehead with his cuff. Crawford seized the chance to try to wriggle free, but Jonathan swiftly pinned him against the wall again. 'How long has this madman Carline been in British pay?'

Crawford looked around fearfully. 'I can't tell you. I can't tell you anything else, because I don't know—'

Jonathan hauled him away from the wall and made as if to throw him against it.

'Stop,' moaned Crawford. 'You'll kill me—'

'Yes. I will. Answer me, damn you. How long?'

'Almost two years,' groaned Crawford.

'Two years?' echoed Jonathan in disbelief.

'Yes. So I was told . . . After he was suspended from the Navy, he got a job at the Portsmouth dockyard. Apparently he volunteered as an informer, and sent reports to the Navy Office about all the shady practices there; he was good at his work . . .'

'All that time,' whispered Jonathan. 'All that time.'

'But then, a year ago, he was flogged for theft—'

'He was flogged for rape,' broke in Jonathan raggedly. 'He assaulted and raped an innocent girl.'

'No!'

'It's true. Later she took her own life. Carline should have died for it but his masters in London saw to it that he was protected; they knew what kind of scum he was, and still they employed him . . .'

Crawford was trembling again. 'I didn't know, I swear. I just obeyed orders. I was told last summer to get him to London, to install him with the Montpelliers; he was meant to protect them; that was the first time I met him. All I knew was that he was clever, and was an expert on stars and telescopes, and he was willing to work for us . . .'

A pulse of rage was beating anew in Jonathan's temple. 'So you set a murderer free in London.'

'I tell you, I didn't know at first! And anyway, those women, they were little better than whores; they knew the risk they ran in what they did . . .'

Jonathan drew back his fist and hit him in the mouth. 'One of them was my daughter.'

Crawford sagged in horror; the blood flowed freshly from his lip. '*No . . .*'

'It was last summer. She was the first.'

'But – I thought your daughter died in June . . .'

'Are you trying to pretend that Carline didn't kill her?' Jonathan had his fist raised again. 'Are you trying to protect a vile murderer still?'

'No, no,' whispered Crawford. 'But it was early July when Carline came to London.'

'You're a damned liar. It was June, I tell you. Afterwards there were five more killed. Five more innocent girls. And all the time, Carline was protected, by men like you.'

Crawford was shaking violently. 'I didn't know. I swear I didn't know what he was doing, not until the girl from the Blue Bell died; I thought she was the first. And then it was too late to stop him, too late to expose him –'

Jonathan was still gripping him by the collar. 'Yes. Too late, because the Brittany expedition was underway. You and those you work for wanted Raultier to betray it to the Republicans – didn't you? – and so Carline had to be protected, and Raultier had to be allowed to work on, in blind ignorance of his double betrayal . . . Tell me, Crawford. Who was behind all this?'

At first Crawford didn't reply. Jonathan shook him again. 'It was the English who wanted the expedition to fail, wasn't it? The English. Answer me. I want to hear you say it. *The English . . .*'

Crawford's face was smeared with sweat and blood; his powdered wig hung askew; but even so his eyes gleamed with a strange fervour as he gazed up at Jonathan. 'They are people with England's true interests etched on their hearts,' he whispered at last. 'Wise people, Jonathan, much wiser than someone like you could ever understand, with your drinking, and your miserable family, and your scorn for people like me—'

Jonathan stopped him by putting his hands round his throat. 'Damn you, Crawford, damn you to hell, and those who gave you your orders. Thousands are dead because of them. And my daughter –' His voice broke. At last he said, 'You should die for this.'

Crawford was struggling in his grip, and gasping. 'I can't breathe, please, I'm choking . . .'

Jonathan realised how easy it would be to kill him. 'You will know, then, what it felt like for those girls as Carline pulled the cord around their necks. Who gave you your orders? Who? I want to hear you say it.'

He released him a little. Crawford coughed and wheezed as he filled his lungs with air. Jonathan watched him and said slowly, 'It was Nepean, wasn't it? Did he arrange all this on his own or did Dundas know as well?'

Crawford's face was grey as Jonathan's hands tightened on his shoulders; and yet he glanced up at him with malevolent eyes. 'I think you've asked too many questions, Jonathan.'

'*Answer me.*'

But this time Crawford's lips were tightly sealed; he was showing, at last, a flicker of obstinate courage.

'In that case I'll take your silence as a yes,' breathed Jonathan. 'And I shall have to decide what next to do with you.'

Crawford trembled again. He licked his lips and looked swiftly all around. 'Have a care, Absey,' he said urgently. His breath was sour, rank. 'Think where your loyalties lie.'

'My loyalties? My daughter died!'

Crawford's lip curled in faint but unmistakable contempt. Jonathan punched him hard in the stomach and Crawford doubled up, retching.

Jonathan hauled him roughly to his feet. 'One last question, damn you. How did Raultier's messages get through?'

'Haven't you guessed?' Crawford was still struggling for breath; but his question had in it a spark of defiance.

'Guessed what?'

'It was your brother, Absey. He was the courier.'

It was Jonathan's turn now to feel cold with fear. 'Surely you're not telling me that Alexander knew all about this – this treachery?'

Crawford threw him a bitter look. 'Ah, how sweet if that were true . . . No. Your brother is too stupid for such subtlety. He didn't have any idea what he was doing. The fool.'

Jonathan shook Crawford so hard that his head was jolted back against the wall again. Crawford gasped with pain.

'Tell me about my brother,' ordered Jonathan.

'Your brother,' faltered Crawford, 'he writes regularly to the Bureau des Longitudes in Paris – didn't you know that?'

Indeed, he did not know. But dear God, he should have done. 'Go on.'

'Jesus, you're hurting me, Absey . . . Your brother agreed to send Raultier's message to the Bureau, along with his own. He's as blameworthy in this as any of them.'

'But *he didn't know what he was doing* . . .'

'Do you think that will save him? From either side?'

Jonathan said, 'You will not get away with this, I swear.'

'Neither will your brother. And neither will you, Absey—' He broke off suddenly to bend over, coughing and spewing bile again, and Jonathan stepped back in revulsion.

He realised his mistake too late. Two burly men stood at the entrance to the narrow yard, with their shoulders and fists braced for action. Jonathan guessed with a sinking heart that they had probably been waiting, on Crawford's orders, at the Cross Keys. When Crawford failed to turn up, they'd come searching for him. Jonathan realised, also, that their orders would be to kill him.

Crawford had straightened himself up, to gesture with authority to the two men. 'This is Absey. Take him.'

Jonathan looked round swiftly but the walls of the yard were high and blank and afforded no possible grip. There was nowhere to run except past the men, who were already starting to move in. There was a flash of metal as they produced knives; Jonathan backed slowly up against the furthest wall, while Crawford watched eagerly, licking his blood-flecked lips.

And then Crawford let out a yelp of surprise. One of the two men had turned on him suddenly, and pinioned his puny arms behind his back. Crawford started to scream, but already the other man was towering over him. With his knife he struck Crawford hard in the chest again and again; and the little Scotsman crumpled to the ground, his mouth bubbling blood, his face fixed in an expression of surprise, and horror.

Jonathan was running, dodging through the narrow gap between the men and the alley wall. One of the attackers caught hold of his coat, but Jonathan, with the force of desperation, lashed out at him, catching his face with the back of his fist; and the man staggered, losing his balance. Jonathan skidded right, his feet pounding along a narrow, filthy lane that led into Villiers Street; he thought he could hear their heavy footsteps behind him, but temporary respite was at hand, because in Villiers Street he came across the evening crowds again. His chest heaved, he gasped for breath, but still he ran on, darting and weaving among the throng of people, knocking some of them aside, crashing into a street vendor's stall, tripping over a fruit barrow as he headed towards the Strand. At last, and only because he could run no more, he pulled up at the entrance to an alleyway and looked all around, sobbing for breath; but he could see no sign of his pursuers.

He'd been lucky. The two men had been sent to kill Crawford because Crawford had known too much. But now, so did he. He had no doubt that the two killers would be after him still.

He set off back towards Brewer Street, trying to keep to the busier thoroughfares where he could be lost in the crowds. Occasionally he stopped in some sheltered place, a corner or a doorway, still breathing hard. He waited and watched, but there seemed to be no pursuers.

Not yet.

He reached his lodgings and hurried up the stairs to his room. They would follow him here, he knew, but he should have just a little time before they came. When he was ready he looked round at everything that was so familiar to him; then he went over to the window and, standing carefully in the shadows by the wall, glanced out into the street.

Two figures were lurking on the pavement opposite. One of them was idly leafing through a newspaper, and the other was leaning back against the wall with his arms folded. Watching this house.

Jonathan drew swiftly back, cursing under his breath, and prepared to wait them out. As the room grew darker, he lit no candles, but sat there in the gathering gloom. Occasionally he heard impatient knocking at the door below, that led out into the street. Once his landlady came up the stairs, her footsteps swift; she tapped at the door to his rooms, and called out anxiously, 'Mr Absey. Are you there, sir? There's people here, asking for you . . .'

He didn't reply. She tried the handle, and left; he heard her talking to someone in the hallway below.

He started to pace the room, counting the minutes as they went by. Time was running out for him, if he was ever going to catch the killer of his daughter. And he was also very much afraid that time was running out for Alexander.

LX

*W*e have seen them all, now, move along their appointed paths.
The summer is past its zenith. Mercury, swift messenger, already
gallops eastwards away from the sun, and Venus is almost hidden
from view, even to those who wait until the dawn to see her. Corona Borealis
crowns the sky at midnight like a rich semi-circlet of jewels: proud Ariadne's
treasure, with bright Alphecca at its heart. But surely the greatest treasure
of them all is Selene herself; and yet, even though she is found at last, I am
afraid; for does this mean that there is nothing now to keep me here?

Last night, I dreamed that she came to me. But her beauty was a mask,
and afterwards I dreamed of death.

It is the waiting that I cannot bear.

Guy de Montpellier put down his pen and stared into the blackness
outside his window.

Surely, the waiting was nearly over.

It was the final night for star-watching. There had been some clouds
earlier, but by evening they had cleared and the darkness brought its
own serene beauty; though Alexander found no joy in it.

Last night, after Daniel's disappearance, the sky had proved after all
too disturbed from the thunderstorm for star-watching. Guy, stricken
with disappointment, seemed consoled only by his trust that Alexander
would be there the next night to help him once more; and so Alexander
was held a captive here, in spite of the rage burning in his heart, for
he knew that Guy was innocent; Guy had no knowledge of what his
sister and her lover and the ex-priest had done to Daniel.

And, as if they knew he would have left instantly if he had
encountered one of them again, Alexander had seen none of them –
neither Auguste, Carline, nor Norland – since yesterday. Nor had Ralph
or Raultier returned to the house. The mausoleum stillness of the great
mansion was completed by the departure of the servants, who had

been dismissed earlier that day. Alexander had watched them carrying their few belongings down the carriage way to the turnpike. There was no one he could ask who had dismissed them, or why, except for Guy: and so Alexander's questions went unvoiced, because it seemed to him that the young man was hardly conscious of their leaving; or, indeed, of anything.

Alexander, thinking always of Daniel, had been on the point of departing himself, several times. But he had only to look at Guy for his intention to be postponed. The young man's sickness was consuming him; and Alexander was afraid for him, lest he died alone. So Alexander stayed on. But a little before dusk he had gone to his room and repacked his few possessions.

An hour ago he had eaten his solitary evening meal. The servants, before leaving, had left a joint of cold mutton in the dining room, but the flies that buzzed around it had more appetite for it than Alexander did and he had pushed his plate to one side after only a minute or two. Guy had appeared briefly, but had eaten nothing. Instead, he spoke of Selene, but his moments of burning lucidity were clouded by a recurring confusion. Sometimes he seemed to forget that Alexander was there, and once he even appeared to be talking to someone else, in a low, agitated voice. As his illness burned in his fever-bright eyes, he reminded Alexander of a star in some bright autumn constellation, shining with a lucidity that seemed unquenchable until all of a sudden a chilling mist fatally occluded its brilliance.

The time drew nearer. For the first hour after sunset Alexander knew there would be turbulence caused by the disparity in temperature between the sun-warmed building and the cool night air; but now he judged that the heat would have dispersed, and the atmosphere around them should be calm. Everything was ready. He felt his skin prickling with apprehension.

Earlier he'd laid out all that they needed. The great Dollond telescope, with its freshly-polished object lens, stood firmly on its tripod base, challenging the sky to yield up its secrets. Alexander had all his precious papers, too, settled beneath big brass paperweights; each sheet was filled with the orbital calculations he had made for Selene, his projections that fulfilled a set of radii of almost three times the earth's distance from the sun, just as Titius predicted. His words echoed over and over again in Alexander's mind: '*But should the Lord Architect have left this space empty? Never!'*

There was something in the Mars–Jupiter gap – but what? Was it really a planet? Was it perhaps a moon, or some other celestial body?

Looking at the figures anew, Alexander was tense, distracted. He had to wipe his palms free of perspiration on his crumpled linen hand-kerchief before checking the telescope again and adjusting it to the correct quartile. Guy sat nearby in silence, his chair drawn close to the observatory wall, one arm resting on the parapet. He had discarded his coat in the late evening heat, throwing it on to the little couch in the corner. His billowing silk shirt gleamed in the faint light of the lantern that was their only illumination other than the bright stars overhead.

It was then that Auguste came up the stairs and out on to the roof, with her lover following behind. Alexander felt an almost physical shock at the sight of them. Auguste's cropped hair gleamed redly in the low lamplight, unpowdered, as he had seen it only on that night when he intruded on Guy and Auguste in the secret, candlelit room. Once more she wore the scarlet ribbon round her neck, and its colour was garish against the whiteness of her skin.

Alexander stared at them, motionless apart from his hands, which were clenching and unclenching at his sides. Hatred and fear boiled in his heart in equal measure.

'The telescope,' Guy said. Alexander forced himself back to attention. Now was the time. He lowered his head to the eyepiece, but his heart was still hammering. All that he loved had been destroyed; and even as he prepared himself for this last, vital seeing, Daniel's anguished answer to his own anguished question seemed to ring in his ears.

> *'Why, Daniel?'*
> *'Because he told me to.'*
> *'Who? Norland?'*
> *'No. The other one . . .'*

Had the boy meant Carline?

There was nothing visible in the darkness of space. He turned away, and forced himself to look at Auguste and her lover. Carline was writing something now at the little desk, with its quill and ink and dish of sand all set out in precise array beneath the cold stars. Auguste was leaning over his shoulder, watching. How could Daniel have meant

Carline, when Auguste's lover did not speak? Just at that moment Auguste put her hand to her mouth as if suppressing a smile at what she read, then she draped her arms round Carline's neck. Her white, apple-firm breasts in their low-draped silk gown rose and fell rapidly.

Alexander thought she must be drunk, to come up here so openly with Carline when she surely realised that Alexander knew what they had done to Daniel. Didn't she know he was likely to abandon Guy the moment he saw her?

Guy himself was staring at his sister as if he hardly recognised her; he seemed bewildered, vulnerable. With a heavy heart, Alexander acknowledged that he would have to endure the presence of Auguste and Carline for Guy's sake. He wondered if the two lovers had counted on this.

He wiped his hands again on his handkerchief and then he started, with infinitesimal movements of his fingers, to adjust the turning screws to their final position. Auguste had seated herself on the low couch in the corner, and was leaning forward, watching him. Carline stood at her side. They were both silent now.

'It is time,' said Guy fervently at his shoulder. 'She is near . . .'

And at last, for Alexander, the urgency of what he was doing produced in him a state of single-minded purpose. He looked through the ocular with his good eye, his hands quite steady now on the turning screws, waiting, waiting for that clear pathway through to the heavens. The object lens revealed with fresh clarity the shimmering lightness of the Swan nebula with its sprinkling of faint stars along one side; the naked-eye double star, Beta Sagittarii; and the Milky Way starfields in which the constellation was so rich. There it was. An object of the eighth magnitude, in the appointed place . . .

Yet Alexander didn't call to Guy, for he sensed that somehow it was not as it should be. He felt the intensity of Guy's gaze burning into him.

'Do you see it?' Guy was asking at his shoulder. 'Is it there?'

Alexander straightened, and moved back at last from the telescope. 'Yes. It's there.'

Guy took his place. For several moments he gazed through the eyepiece; then he moved away again, his skin bleached of colour, his eyes dazed, as if in a trance. He breathed, '*We have found it.*'

Auguste stood up and came towards them. Alexander stepped

forward to bar her way: this was Guy's moment, not hers, and besides, he'd already guessed she'd been drinking, and he was afraid she would knock the telescope out of alignment.

But he was too late. She had reached the telescope, and had taken her brother's place there.

She was so close now that underneath the scent of her perfume Alexander could smell the feral heat of her body. He thought of what she had done to Daniel, and the bile rose in his throat. He saw how she touched the viewing piece of the telescope almost with reverence, and lowered her head to gaze through the ocular. She let out a little sigh, then turned to beckon to Carline; he came forward, and as she moved aside he bent to look also, his face impassive.

And Auguste turned to Alexander at last. She reached out to touch his arm, but he flung her hand aside as if her fingers burned him. She drew back a little. 'Ah, monsieur mouse. You are angry with me.'

'Stop,' cried Alexander hoarsely, lifting his hand; whether to strike her or to prevent further words he himself didn't know. 'For God's sake. Haven't you said, and done, enough?'

'Perhaps,' she replied in a quiet voice. 'I am truly sorry.'

Alexander shook his head. 'I'm going now. There's nothing to keep me here.' He turned towards the stairs to descend to his room, where the valise with his few possessions awaited him.

'Very well.' Her voice followed him. 'But before you go, there's something I want to tell you. About Selene.'

Alexander stopped and, despite himself, slowly turned back to her. Guy was standing close by, but with his back to them all, oblivious, gazing at the night sky. Auguste placed her hand possessively on her brother's shoulder and said quietly to Alexander, 'Didn't you ever guess, poor Monsieur Wilmot, that I was Guy's Selene?'

Alexander shook his head in disbelief. Was this another attempt to mock him? 'But Selene died in Paris . . .'

'Only in spirit,' replied Auguste. 'But her body lived on.' Slowly she spread out her hands. 'This body you see in front of you.'

And then Alexander remembered the golden dance of shadows he had seen, so long ago, it seemed, in the secret room of this very house; he remembered how he had been so entranced by the beauty of brother and sister in each other's arms.

'*Your hair,*' Guy had whispered to her, '*Oh, your beautiful hair . . .*'

Alexander closed his eyes. It had been in front of him all along. Guy sought Selene amongst the stars; but all the time she was here, encamped in this woman's vile body. Guy's love for her had destroyed his health and his sanity.

Then there was no time for anything else, because Guy turned and stumbled towards them, calling out his sister's name. His face was a terrible void, and in his eyes was only blackness. With one hand he clutched the back of his head as if he would tear away the tumour that pressed against his brain; and then he began to scream.

LXI

Oh, dark, dark, dark, amid the blaze of noon,
Irrecoverably dark, total eclipse
Without all hope of day.

John Milton, *Samson Agonistes*
(1671)

As darkness fell that evening, Pierre Raultier made his way on foot to Clare Market, where the shops of the moneylenders and pawnbrokers stood cheek by jowl with squalid taverns, and the half-ruined tenements that were the homes of the poor. With him he had his big leather bag, which contained not medicines, but some of his precious doctor's instruments, and his medical books.

He sold them one by one for silver. And then, as night engulfed these lowly dwellings, he hurried to a lodging house at the back of Leicester Fields, which was home to an old printer who was skilled in the forging of documents.

Raultier used some of his silver to purchase the papers needed for the Montpelliers and himself to travel; though he wondered, as he waited in a fever of impatience for the man to carefully inscribe the false names, how far they could go, with Guy in the throes of his terrible illness. They should have left London weeks ago. Perceval had known that it was more than time to leave. How Raultier cursed the search for the lost planet that had trapped them here.

As he walked swiftly back to Holborn, the sticky night heat seeped into his skin and strong smells of beer and tobacco that issued from the rough taverns clustered at this end of Eagle Street assaulted his senses. Typhus fever raged again in such parts of London this summer. Looking up at the sky to where Jupiter shone steadfastly over the rooftops to the south, he remembered how the ancients believed that disease was caused by the triple conjunction of Saturn, Jupiter and Mars. Now it was known that many diseases were caused by poverty, and filth, and overcrowding; and yet, thought Raultier, men of medicine like himself were in reality no closer to curing such scourges than the ancients had been.

The sound of a nearby street organ jangled discordantly in his ears. Reaching his house at last, he began to climb the steps to his room; then, remembering that his supplies of laudanum were badly depleted, he turned and went out once more, down Dean Street to the apothecary's shop, past the broadsheet vendor at the corner who was crying out the latest news; and indeed, as he entered the apothecary's shop, setting the doorbell jangling, he saw that the apothecary himself was busy reading through a news sheet on which the print had scarcely dried; he was clicking his tongue, and running his finger down each line, pausing every now and then to adjust his pince-nez on his sharp nose. When he saw Raultier standing there in the shadows, he lifted his head companionably and said,

'This is a bad business, my French friend, a bad business.'

Raultier, thinking of the typhus outbreak in the Field Lane area, said, 'Yes. It is as bad as I have known.'

'Indeed. So many of those poor soldiers dead . . .'

Raultier looked up sharply. 'Soldiers? What do you mean? Of whom do you talk?'

'Why, those lads they landed at Quiberon. Your brave lads, the Frenchies. Haven't you heard the news yet?'

'I've not seen anyone. I've not heard anything—'

The apothecary was shaking his head so vehemently that his pince-nez were almost dislodged. 'Nearly all killed, they were. They expected more soldiers to turn up and help them, so it says here, but they never came . . .'

Raultier whispered, '*Let me see.*'

The apothecary handed over the sheet. Raultier held it with trembling hands, and the words danced before his eyes.

'*. . . Of all the various events which have marked the progress of the present war, the most afflicting to humanity, and the most disastrous in its consequences, is that which we have to lay before the Public this day. Six or seven thousand victims to a most just cause, fighting for the religion of their forefathers, and for the re-establishment of the Throne of their lawful Monarch, against a band of ferocious usurpers; fighting, in short, to rescue their relatives remaining in France from* *the yoke of Tyranny, have fallen a sacrifice to their barbarous enemies. Some were killed by the sword, and thus have terminated their miserable career; others have surrendered themselves to their cannibal persecutors, and seem to have avoided death on the field of battle, only to suffer it in a more frightful and ignominious shape, according to the horrid forms of the revolutionary Tribunal . . . It appears that the Republican General Hoche, having received very considerable reinforcements, to the number, as is supposed, of 40,000 men, attacked the Royalists on the Peninsula. The Emigrants were never in that force they were stated to be, being in all only four thousand men, besides four thousand Chouans. The circumstances of this disastrous business are so little known that we can only speak of them from report; but there is a rumour that expected reinforcements from the interior were diverted by treachery . . .'*

'A disaster,' said the apothecary. 'To take those lads there, in English ships, and leave them there to die. What a price to pay.'

Raultier pushed the sheet back into the apothecary's hand, and he thought: *the gold.* The gold in the telescope that Alexander Wilmot had lost. It was payment. They had received his letter after all; and they had made use, with devastating effect, of what it contained . . .

He took the laudanum, paid for it, and went unsteadily out into the dark street, where the organ was still playing. His final obligation was paid; but at such a price.

Once in his room, he locked his door and burned all his papers in the grate, until the stink of scorched paper seared his nostrils. He also burnt Lefèvre's *Mythologie*, tearing the pages from the little book and casting them on the fire until all were consumed. Only then did he notice that the lock of red hair had fallen to the floor. He stooped to pick it up and held it tenderly in his hand as if all his experience of happiness was enclosed there; and just for a moment he even felt something like hope fill his burdened heart, because he had done what he was meant to do, and in return he had been promised freedom, for himself, and Guy, and Auguste . . .

His hand closed round the lock of hair, crushing it. How long, he reprimanded himself as he stood there in the darkening room; how long, you fool, will you go on deluding yourself? Auguste's vision of freedom would have no place in it for him. And, gazing at his big, clenched fist, he wondered when he had first started to realise that the love that had consumed him for so long was dying.

He threw the lock of Auguste's hair on the fire, then watched it shrivel and turn white in the dying embers. Ashes, like everything else.

At the same time his mind, now empty of hope, began to resonate with a tumult of unanswered questions. The first cold fingers of fear were starting to creep through his veins, and a dark suspicion was casting its shadow. In these last, tense weeks he had been too preoccupied with the matter of getting his letters to their crucial destination to waste precious time in doubt, or reflection; but now he was thinking that if the information he had given his English contacts at the time of the Chauvelin affair had been so very valuable, why had they not used him, or even approached him once during the two years that followed?

Could it be that they suspected him all along of working for the Republicans?

The fire in the grate glimmered still, but he had gone cold. Closing his eyes, he remembered his relief when, instead of his expected denunciation as a spy at the inn off Tyburn Lane, Crawford had instead given him government employment. How easy it had been to get exactly what he wanted from the loquacious Prigent. Anyone, anyone at all could have told Crawford that Prigent was loyal. But he, Raultier, had been brought in for the task instead. *Why?* He drew his hand shakily across his forehead. Was it because Crawford knew that Raultier would send the intelligence he gleaned from Prigent straight to his masters in Paris?

Was it because the British wanted the expedition to fail?

A fever possessed him now. He packed his leather-bound chest with what remained of his books and his instruments, his charts and his medicines, as swiftly as he could; but even so, by the time he'd finished, it was after eleven. He blew out his candles, locked his door, and walked quickly down Eagle Street, in the dim glow of the street lamps, to the stables at the back of the White Boar inn. He imagined he was being followed. He wondered if he would always hear pursuers, now.

The man who tended the horses was still there, finishing off his tasks by the light of a lantern. 'Going out at this hour, Monsieur Raultier?' he enquired cheerfully, leaning on the handle of the rake with which he'd been gathering up the scattered straw. 'You doctors are always on duty.' Putting his rake aside, he led Raultier's mare out into the yard and harnessed it. Without replying, the grim-faced Raultier gave him a coin and swung himself up into the saddle; and as if in some dark dream from which he could not awake he rode along the familiar streets of the city, along the Oxford Road, and down Tyburn Lane past the empty, night-engulfed expanse of Hyde Park. Somewhere to his left, beyond the market gardens and the barracks, was the tavern where he had been taken to meet Richard Crawford. Yes, he had been duped. The blood of thousands of Frenchmen was on his hands. He rode on, turning westwards at the lodge as he had done so often, guiding his horse out into the country along the turnpike road. There, where there were no houses, and the stars burned down on him, mocking him, he stopped, and gazed up at the sky, and he wished he was dead, like all those soldiers on the beaches of Brittany.

He heard the sudden thunder of approaching hooves and pulled his horse in to the side of the road as the night mail coach scraped by with scarcely inches to spare. Its driver yelled curses at him for being a half-witted fool; and the coach rumbled onwards. The reins were slack in Raultier's hands as he stared into the darkness. His horse started to pull at the roadside grass.

The English, and Crawford, had known he worked for the Republicans all along; they had used their secret knowledge to play another, deeper game in which he was a pawn, in which he and others were expendable. Gathering up his reins, he urged his weary mount on, to the Montpelliers' house, because Raultier had promised them their safety, and, whatever the truth of all this, one certainty remained: Guy and Auguste were not safe now. And neither was he.

He left his horse by the front steps and went in swiftly through the front door, which was unlocked and unattended. As he started to climb the staircase, he heard the sound echoing through the house of a man screaming in unendurable pain.

LXII

*What am I to say now, when I am supposing that
there is some all-powerful and malignant Deceiver,
who has taken care to delude me about everything
as much as he can?*

René Descartes, *Meditations on
First Philosophy* (1641)

William Carline had carried Guy across to the couch in the corner of the rooftop, and laid him there with sure hands; but all the time the sick man struggled, in such physical or mental pain – did it matter which? – that it was not to be borne. Auguste lit more lamps, and tried to place cushions beneath her brother's head, and crouched on the floor beside him, bending her burnished head over his dark one; while Alexander Wilmot, so distressed for Guy that he could not think what else to do, tended the abandoned telescopes, covering the lenses so they would not be hurt by the night air, and placing paperweights on the sheaves of paper on the table with trembling hands.

Then there were footsteps on the stairs, and Raultier was there.

The doctor had a bottle of laudanum with him. He hurried across to the couch, and trickled some of it gently between Guy's lips. Guy, who was lapsing into intermittent unconsciousness, was so white, so frail-looking that he seemed dead already. Auguste was weeping, and saying, 'Pierre. Please. You must help him, there must be more you can do, to free him from his pain.'

Raultier replied, his voice hoarse, 'I have given him as much as I dare, Auguste.'

Carline was just watching, his exquisite face as sombre as death itself.

Auguste flung her arm across her brother's chest, where the perspiration freely soaked his white shirt. She loosened his neck cloth and caressed his hollow cheek, murmuring words of enduring love. 'Guy.

Guy, my dearest. We can go home. We can go back to the Midi, where the skies are so pure, so clear, that you will be able to watch the stars for ever, and you will be well again . . .'

Guy was struggling to raise himself. He gazed unseeing into the darkness, his eyes pain-bright. 'I have found her,' he whispered. 'At last.'

Auguste smoothed his damp hair from his forehead. 'Yes,' she breathed. 'Oh, my love.'

Guy sank back against the pillows, his eyes closing again. Raultier felt the weak pulse in the sick man's wrist, then he stood up slowly, almost despairingly. Auguste, rising too, clutched at Raultier's arm and gazed up at him with fear in her eyes. 'Pierre. We can take him home, can't we?'

He looked at her dazedly. 'It's too late. He's dying, Auguste. The tumour is pressing on the cranial nerves. He cannot be moved.'

'No,' she whispered, white-lipped, 'no, you are wrong,' and then Guy stirred, and with his eyes still closed and his face bedewed with sweat, he began to scream again thinly. Auguste gripped Raultier harder and almost shook him, saying, 'If there is really no hope, no hope at all, then you must end it for him. Dear God, I cannot bear this any longer.'

'I cannot do that,' said Raultier, harrowed. 'You know I cannot.'

Guy arched on the couch, the sharp perspiration pouring from his skin, his fingers opening and closing in a paroxysm of agony. Carline moved then. He crossed to the couch to hold the sick man down, as he struggled in the last torment of his battle for life. The lantern's flame flickered, sending ghostly shadows leaping about the walls.

Raultier said, 'I will go downstairs for more laudanum.'

'Laudanum is not enough, and you know it.' Auguste's voice was low, agonised. 'For God's sake, Pierre, forget your damnable oath and help my brother to end it. I beg you to do this last thing for him . . .'

Raultier turned to go quickly down the stairs. Alexander stood in the shadows at the edge of the rooftop balcony, hardly able to endure it as Guy screamed again, the high-pitched, terrible scream of an animal wounded to death. Auguste covered her face with her hands and whispered, 'Someone must help him. Someone must free him from this agony . . .'

And Carline, who had been kneeling at Guy's side all this time, turned to her. He said calmly,

'I will help him, even if the doctor will not.'

Auguste stepped back with a low cry of fear and horror. As Guy spasmed again, Carline drew a silk ligature from his pocket. Turning back to Guy, he looped it about his neck and tightened it with a terrible, sure strength around the straining tendons of his throat. For a few moments Auguste and Alexander were immobile with shock, scarcely able to take in what was happening, although already Guy's violent movements were growing weak. Carline's face was fixed in a grimace as the ligature clamped off Guy's larynx, starving him of air. Then the pressure forced the tumour at the base of the sick man's skull to intrude on the vital area of the brain stem, with immediate and deadly effect; Guy spasmed once more, and lay still.

Carline stood up with the ligature in his hand, his face expressionless again. Auguste rushed past him and threw herself on the couch, where she cradled Guy's body in her arms. For a few moments she lay there sobbing incoherently, then she lifted her head to gaze at Carline, her face ravaged by tears. 'You can speak,' she whispered. '*Who are you?*'

'I'm here to protect you,' Carline replied flatly. His chill blue eyes showed no flicker of emotion. 'I'm working for the only people who can save you now.'

'What do you mean?'

'Raultier has made mistakes.' As he spoke, Carline was meticulously rolling up the ligature. 'Someone has been watching him.'

Auguste shook her head. 'Why should I believe anything about you? All this time you could speak . . .'

Slowly Carline pointed at Alexander. 'Ask your little mouse here if you don't believe me. He has been watching everything, and telling his half-brother, who is a government spy, all about us.' He took a step towards Alexander, the coiled ligature still in his hand. 'Haven't you, mouse?' Tauntingly he flicked the ligature against Alexander's face.

Alexander recoiled, pressing his hand to his stinging cheek. 'No! I came here to help Guy find his star! That was all, I swear!'

Carline watched him, a thin smile on his lips. 'Do you know, I almost believe you. Perhaps you really didn't know what was going on. Otherwise you wouldn't have sent Raultier's letter to Paris.'

Alexander stared at him, bewildered. 'It was only a letter about the stars—'

'Oh, no. Not a star letter, mouse. It was a coded message, to the enemy, in Paris.'

'No,' Alexander whispered, stepping back, 'no . . .'

There were footsteps on the stairs and Raultier himself reappeared, with a medicine bottle in his hand, ready to hurry across the balcony to the couch; but he stopped, pale with shock, when he saw Guy's dead body, with his sister kneeling at his side. 'What has happened?' he breathed.

Carline turned to face him. 'I've simply done what needed to be done,' he said.

'My God,' Raultier said, beginning to tremble, 'you can speak.'

'Yes,' replied Carline. 'The little charade is over. There was never a time when I couldn't. Now you know why your ministrations didn't work on me, doctor.' He jerked his head at Guy's body. 'As for him, I've merely done to him what I've had to do every time he escaped to the city. Only this time it was his turn to die, instead of those redheaded whores he made such a fool of himself over.'

Raultier still looked dazed. 'You killed those girls in London?'

'Someone had to. People were asking questions about French gold. You've made a lot of stupid mistakes, Raultier. You didn't realise you were being manipulated; that you were working for the British all along. That there are powerful people in London who never wanted the Quiberon expedition to succeed—'

With a low, hoarse cry, Raultier plunged towards him, fists raised. Carline threw down the ligature and fumbled in his pocket for something; but by then Raultier was on him. The two men, locked together, stumbled back towards the edge of the balcony, where for a moment they swayed before the low wall with the blackness beckoning below. Physically they were well matched, but Raultier was older, slower than Carline. The younger man broke free with a grim smile on his face, and now he had a knife with a six-inch blade in his hand. Raultier, seeing it, backed away, closer to the roof edge, his hands outspread. He was breathing hard.

Carline feinted with the knife. Suddenly he flung himself at the doctor, and with terrible force he drove the blade of the knife deep into the doctor's chest. Raultier staggered back against the low wall, one hand clasped to the blade, and the blood from his wound spilled over his fingers as he struggled for balance.

Alexander lurched towards him, trying to catch him before he fell, but Carline brutally shouldered him aside to pull his knife from Raultier's chest and with his free hand he pushed the doctor over the balustrade, out into the empty air. Raultier screamed, but the sound was cut short as his body crashed to the ground far below.

Alexander backed away in shock and terror. But it was on him that Carline next turned, the bloodstained knife still in his hand. 'So, Monsieur Mouse,' he said softly. 'The crow could not fly. I wonder, can you?'

Alexander tried to jump to one side as Carline's glistening knife flashed close. Carline feinted another sweeping blow; and then as Alexander jumped again to avoid that terrible blade he clubbed Alexander on the side of the head with the hilt. Alexander dropped to the ground, stunned; and Carline, swooping swiftly to snatch up the fallen ligature, wrenched his wrists behind his back and bound them tightly together. Alexander moaned with pain and fought like a trussed animal, expecting any moment to feel Carline's blade piercing his body. But he realised suddenly that Carline was no longer watching him. Instead he had straightened up and was turning to face Auguste, who moved slowly towards him, her eyes brilliant in the whiteness of her face.

'You've killed Pierre,' she said.

She was holding a small brass-barrelled pistol. Alexander wondered where she'd concealed it; somewhere in her gown, perhaps. It was as if she had been expecting a moment like this. The gun was pointed at Carline.

Carline moistened his lips. 'Where did you get that gun?'

'Pierre gave it to me in case our enemies found us. But I never thought the enemy would be you.'

'Put it down, Auguste,' he said. 'You must trust me. I'll keep you safe.'

For a moment, her hand holding the pistol wavered. But then she lifted it again and whispered, 'How can I trust you, when everything about you is a lie?'

Carline said urgently, 'It was my masters who made me keep silent. Now, it's all over, we can go away together, you and I; anywhere you want . . .'

She hesitated, her eyes flickering uncertainly over him. 'Even to the Midi?'

'Yes, even to France! I have the papers ready, I have gold; I did all this for you, Auguste . . .' He was moving slowly towards her. Auguste gave a low, shuddering sigh; then she turned and looked at Guy, and a little sob escaped from her throat.

'I will take you home,' Carline said softly, holding out his hand to her.

Slowly Auguste began to lower the pistol. Carline moved closer, then took her in his arms and kissed her. Closing her eyes, she gave herself up to his embrace. Her arms dropped to her sides, and the pistol dangled loosely from her fingers. Carline lowered his head to kiss the curve of her white throat; and his hands moved round to the nape of her neck, caressing her there, toying with the knot of her red ribbon. She murmured something to him, and he smiled and kissed her cheek.

Alexander, lying dazed with pain from the blow Carline had inflicted, cried out in warning, for Carline had twisted his fingers in the ribbon at the back of her neck. Suddenly Carline pushed his whole hand through the ribbon and pulled at it with such violence that Auguste started to choke wildly. Her eyes grew wide with horror, and her hands jerked upwards; the pistol flew from her grip and over the balcony. Carline pulled harder. She was struggling, but already she was weakening.

Alexander, half sobbing in anguish, his hands bound, tried to stagger to his feet; but already he could hear Auguste's cries turning into terrible gasps; already he could hear the sound of her feet drumming against the floor as Carline all but lifted her from the ground. She hung like a marionette, twisting slightly. Spittle ran from her mouth, and her eyes were wide and staring.

'The last Selene,' Carline said softly. He held her there for a few moments more, then let her body fall heavily to the floor. '*Full of abominations and filthiness of her fornication.* An inconstant bitch, like the rest of her kind.'

'You have killed them all,' whispered Alexander. 'Guy, Raultier, Auguste . . .'

'All of them,' agreed Carline. There was still no flicker of emotion on his beautiful face. 'Now it's your turn, master mouse. Killing you would be a pleasure. Perhaps you should follow Raultier. But no doubt I can think of something better.'

Carline was coming closer. Alexander had managed to get to his knees, but his arms were still pinioned behind him. Desperately he tried to get to his feet but Carline pushed him back hard against the stone floor of the balcony. Kneeling on Alexander's chest, he pulled something out of his pocket, and Alexander saw that it was the little phial of pure spirit that he carried with him everywhere, to clean the lenses of the telescopes. He opened the stoppered phial swiftly, his weight pinning Alexander to the ground. Leaning over him, he looked intently into his eyes, and it was then that Alexander realised what he meant to do.

Alexander kicked out, and turned his head frantically from side to side as Carline brought the bottle near. But Carline cuffed him hard with his free hand, half stunning him again; and then he swiftly tipped the pure spirit over Alexander's good eye. At the last moment Alexander squeezed his eyes tightly shut, but that was no protection, and he knew it; already the harsh liquid was seeping between his lids, and was searing his tender retina with excruciating pain.

He screamed. He would have clawed at his face with his fingers, but his hands were bound. Through his cries he heard Carline whisper, 'Now you're a blind mouse. I would have liked to stay and see how you run before you die, but I cannot; you see, I have to burn this house and everything in it . . .' He paused and added almost regretfully, 'You must burn too.'

'No . . .' Alexander screamed; but in the silence that followed his despairing cry he heard Carline's footsteps, already retreating down the stairs; he heard his calm, cold voice, fading into the distance:

'Thou shalt make the whore desolate and naked, and shall burn her with fire . . .'.

Carline laughed; and then there was silence.

Alexander stumbled to his feet, and with faltering sideways steps he tried, with his tethered hands, to feel for the gap in the wall where the staircase was. But with the loss of his sight his balance seemed to have gone also, and he was afraid, so afraid of that long fall down into the blackness. Carline would be below by now, setting the curtains and other combustible fittings of the house alight; Alexander thought he could already feel the fire, like the fire in his eyes. His knees collided with a fallen chair that Raultier and Carline had knocked over in their struggle. His legs buckled beneath him, and he fell down sobbing, his eye burning with fresh agony.

For the moment the floor beneath his face was still cool. He laid his cheek against it, knowing that soon he would have to decide between the blackness and the flames.

LXIII

Apollo, Cynthia and the ceaseless lamps
That gently look'd upon this loathsome earth,
Shine downwards now no more . . .

Christopher Marlowe, *Tamburlaine the*
Great, Part 2 (1590)

As darkness fell, it seemed to Jonathan Absey that the watchers in Brewer Street had at last despaired of his return there, for after one final bout of knocking at the door below, they had turned to go. Jonathan, watching till they were out of sight, abandoned his unlit rooms and hurried down the stairs; only to be confronted by his landlady, coming out of her own room. He pulled up short.

'I knew you were there, sir,' she said quietly. 'All the time.' She pointed in the direction of the street. 'I thought it would be best to keep them waiting until it was dark. Then I told them I'd just caught sight of you in the distance, coming towards the house from the corner of Compton Street. I told them I saw you take one look, then run off.'

'Thank you,' said Jonathan.

And now he was riding westwards, desperately urging on the bony nag he had hired from a lowly mews stable off the Mall as slowly, all too slowly, London's dark streets gave way to the fields and sleeping hamlets of the countryside. He passed the Halfway House, with its ramshackle cluster of stables and pigsties; he passed great mansions slumbering within their high-walled gardens; and all the while the summer stars shone overhead, incandescent in the blackness of the sky.

His horse was growing tired. From time to time he stopped to rest it; and then, as he approached the stretch of road where he judged the Montpelliers' house to lie, he stopped again, because the night sky in that direction was bright, too bright, and a heavy orange pall eclipsed the stars. The warm July breeze shifted suddenly and came to him from the west; he smelled the smouldering stench of fire, and he remembered Alexander's charred house in Clerkenwell. The fear rose anew in his throat.

He rode on, kicking his hired nag, cursing it for its slowness. He reached the gateway of the house and galloped down the driveway that twisted between thickets of trees. The smoke seared his nostrils, and he saw, as the trees parted, that the house was indeed on fire. The conflagration had not reached every part, but most of the ground floor was ablaze, and flames leapt out from the lower windows. His horse reared and whinnied in terror. Jonathan scrambled from the saddle, and the animal broke free and galloped back along the drive.

Jonathan stood there, panting, on the lawn in front of the burning house. The air was filled with the acrid reek of smoke; charred fragments drifted around him to settle on his clothes, his skin. He thought, with a sick heart: surely no one can be left alive in there? But as he looked up to the line of the sky he thought he saw some movement against the stark ridge of the eastern roof where the flames had not yet reached.

He ran round to the only side of the house which was still free from fire. Something caught his eye; something gleaming on the grass in front of him. He crouched swiftly and found that the reflected light came from the brass barrel of a small-calibre pistol, with a butt cap also of brass, shaped like a leopard's head. Frowning, he picked it up and instinctively drew back the hammer, cocking it.

Then he looked up again sharply because a man had appeared round the corner of the mansion. The man stopped, and stood very still when he saw Jonathan. He was carrying a flambeau that underlit the angelic beauty of his face and made his long blond hair appear almost white. Carline. The man he'd seen with Crawford. Old Hannah's avenging angel. His daughter's killer.

Carline's moment of uncertainty was brief enough. Jonathan barely had time to absorb the shock of his appearance when Carline was once more striding purposefully towards him across the grass. In his left hand was the blazing flambeau; in his right a knife.

'Mr Absey,' he said, his face an expressionless mask. And Jonathan, his heart beating hard, learnt what he had already suspected: that Carline's muteness had been another ruse to deceive those who sheltered him. He raised the pistol slowly. Carline stopped; and Jonathan saw the sudden uncertainty in the man's dark blue eyes.

'You killed them all, didn't you, Carline?' he said. 'All the girls.'

Carline didn't answer. He licked his lips, like some beast of prey, his calculating gaze never leaving the gun. The rage continued to build up in Jonathan's heart, and he said, 'Did you know that the first one was my daughter?' He aimed the cocked gun at Carline's heart; and at last those chilling blue eyes met his.

'The first one?' repeated Carline. 'The first of the redheaded whores?'

Jonathan's hand shook; he fought to steady it. 'You killed her last June. You strangled her.'

Carline's eyes gleamed almost in mockery. He said, very slowly, 'But I was still in Portsmouth then.'

'You're lying,' said Jonathan. He kept the gun pointing at Carline's heart. 'You must be lying. My daughter was the first to die.'

'I know one of the sluts died in June,' said Carline softly. 'But it was Auguste de Montpellier who killed her. Not me.'

'*No!*'

'Yes.' Carline smiled slowly. 'Guy had gone into the town, driven by his usual obsession; only this time he'd taken some of Raultier's gold with him. Auguste realised the danger, so she followed him. She was too late to stop her foolish brother giving away the tell-tale gold, so she strangled the bitch herself and took it all back.'

'Auguste,' repeated Jonathan dazedly. 'I don't believe you—'

Carline shrugged. 'You have to remember that she'd learnt much, during that last year of danger in Paris. It was Raultier who taught her how to defend herself in case anything happened to him. How to kill quickly and silently, using one of his silk ligatures. He also taught her how to shoot. That's her pistol you're holding; he gave it to her. She was quite ruthless, in her love first for herself, and then for her brother.' He held the flambeau higher; it cast long, sinister shadows across the grass. 'She told me what had happened, when I went to live with them, and she said that if Guy should endanger them again in the same way I was to do as she had done.' He gave a cold smile. 'She didn't know that for me the killing would be a pleasure. And now I've killed her. You see, she was a whore too – the worst of them all.'

Jonathan stepped forward, his gun held ready. 'Where are the others? Raultier, Guy . . .'

'All dead, except your brother. He's up there on the roof.' He jerked his head upwards and involuntarily Jonathan's gaze was drawn to the ridge of the house where he'd thought he'd seen some movement a few moments before. It was all the time Carline needed. He reversed his knife into a throwing position and hurled it at Jonathan.

His aim was true. The weapon cartwheeled through the air and would have struck Jonathan in the chest had he not already raised his pistol hand as he whirled back to face his enemy. He took the blade full on the knuckles, in a scything blow that slashed at his skin and made him gasp out in pain. His finger tightened instinctively on the trigger; an explosion deafened him, and the gun recoiled in his hands. The smoke of the discharge cleared. Carline stood there, in the same place as he'd been before, apparently untouched by the shot.

Jonathan stood there panting, waiting for the man's next move, as the blood welled from the cut on his hand. And then he saw the neat red bullet hole in the centre of Carline's forehead; and at the same instant the blond man's eyes rolled up in their sockets, his knees crumpled, and he slumped to the ground, the flambeau sizzling beside him on the dewy grass.

From behind him, deep within the blazing building, came the sound of crashing masonry.

Jonathan threw down the pistol. He bound his wounded hand with his handkerchief and ran on round the side of the building. Ahead of him he saw an outer staircase built of stone that seemed to lead up the side of the house to the roof. He climbed it as fast as he was able, but the swirling smoke caught at his lungs and he was sobbing for breath by the time he reached the top. Looking down, he saw flames leaping from the windows in the main part of the house and heard roof tiles cracking in the heat. A cloud of smoke engulfed him. He choked and coughed and called out, 'Alexander!'

He thought he heard something, and turned swiftly. The smoke lifted, and he saw a young man lying on a couch at the corner of the balcony. It was Guy de Montpellier, motionless, his face cruelly mottled by the manner of his dying. At his feet lay the body of a woman, with cropped red hair, strangled also. He guessed she must be Auguste, his daughter's killer. Could it be true? Yes. Ellie was not strong, and this older woman, coming on her from behind, could have overpowered her. The smoke shifted again, and at last he saw his brother, on his knees. Jonathan ran towards him, calling out his name; and he saw that Alexander's wrists were tied behind his back. His mouth was bleeding, and his eyes looked red and raw. Jonathan breathed, 'Your eyes. What has happened to your eyes?'

Alexander lifted his head. His face was smeared with dust and blood. 'Carline poured pure spirit in them,' he whispered. 'He has blinded me.' He broke off, choking on the smoke.

Jonathan swore viciously and vehemently as he swiftly unfastened the cord that bound his brother's wrists. Then he pulled Alexander's arm round his shoulders and said, as steadily as he could,

'It's time to get out of here, Alexander. Hold me tightly.'

Together, they stumbled with painful slowness down the stairs. The heat of the fire spread out from the core of the building like a furnace, and Jonathan was afraid that the blaze might already be sweeping up the lower reaches of the staircase. He could hear the terrible noise of the inferno within: the roaring of greedy flames, the creaking of timbers being devoured. When they were only halfway down Alexander stumbled to his knees, and Jonathan had to grip him hard to save him from falling.

Alexander fought to regain his breath. 'You go on. Please. I'm putting you in danger. I'll follow . . .'

But Jonathan waited till he was ready, then lifted his brother's arm round his shoulder again. 'Save your breath,' he said gently. 'We're almost there. There isn't far to go.'

He was afraid for both of them, because the flames were leaping outwards from the windows at every level now, and above them the masonry was starting to crumble in the fierce heat. The smoke swirled thickly around, choking them, blinding them. Jonathan was almost ready to despair, when he realised that there were no more steps; they had reached the ground. Grasping his brother's arm even more tightly, whispering fierce words of encouragement, he dragged Alexander away from the house.

'Hurry,' he pleaded, 'please hurry.'

They were just in time. Above them there was a muffled roar, and Jonathan, pausing to look back, saw that a chimney stack was slowly toppling to the ground, crashing through the roof and strewing a deadly avalanche of masonry over the stairs that had brought them to safety. The flames were leaping all along the roof now; the Montpelliers' observatory was no more. A vicious current of air engulfed the house, throwing out whirling cinders and ashes.

Jonathan led his brother on, deep into the overgrown garden. Close to the house some of the trees were badly scorched; their leaves had curled and turned black in the heat. But further out the air was cool and though he knew it was only an illusion, the darkness seemed to offer protection.

Jonathan heard the sound of running water. He looked around and saw an ornamental stream, glittering blackly between fern-lined banks. He said swiftly, 'There's water here, Alexander. Perhaps if you bathe your eye, it might help. As soon as we can, we'll find a doctor to examine it for you.' He led Alexander to the stream and helped him kneel, so that his brother could cup his hands and sluice his eye with the cool water. 'Is that better?'

'Yes,' said Alexander. 'Thank you.'

'Can you see anything?'

Alexander turned to him. 'Perhaps a little.'

But Jonathan knew that Alexander was lying, and that his brother's good eye was damaged for ever. He sat by the stream while Alexander bathed his face, and gazed back at the burning house, and his own heart was filled with despair.

The fire was doing its work voraciously now, transforming the Montpelliers' mansion into a gaunt skeleton of stone and brick. Alexander had turned towards the house too, as if he could sense the glow of the blaze.

'Carline's dead,' Jonathan said at last. 'I shot him.'

'I'm glad,' Alexander replied. 'Was it he who killed the girls?'

Jonathan hesitated. 'Yes.'

'He hated all women.'

Jonathan bowed his head. 'Yes. What happened to Raultier?'

'Carline killed him too. Raultier was a spy, but you knew that, didn't you? That was why you asked me to come here.'

Jonathan rested his face briefly in his hands. 'Not at first. At first it was about Ellie. The spying only came later . . . Oh, Alexander. Can you ever forgive me? If only I'd known what I was getting you into.'

But Alexander, his foolish, fat older brother Alexander, turned to him with his blind face full of compassion, and put his hand over his, and said, 'How could you have known? You mustn't reproach yourself, Jonathan. You wanted to stop a killer; you wanted to stop Raultier spying, but there were people who didn't want him stopped . . .' Alexander paused then went on, almost wonderingly, 'Poor Raultier. He was devastated to learn how he'd been used by both sides. It must have been forced on him, the treachery, for by nature he was a good and gentle man. His one fault was that he loved Auguste, so much . . .'

'He was paid in gold,' said Jonathan. 'There were gold coins in a telescope. I found it at the Halfway House, close to where your carriage had been.'

'The telescope Perceval gave me,' Alexander whispered.

'It was you, then?' exclaimed Jonathan. 'You were carrying it? I thought it was Guy.'

'Perceval gave it to me, to give to Raultier. So he was a part of it all too. Perceval. I thought he was my friend . . .'

There was a moment's silence. Jonathan said at last, 'I have the gold with me, here. It's yours, Alexander.'

'I don't think I want it,' replied Alexander quietly.

He turned and gazed in the direction of the house. After a while he said, 'Is the house still burning?'

'Yes. All of it is burning now.'

'*Ah* . . .'

Jonathan guessed that he was thinking of Guy. He touched his brother's hand to let him know he was there, and Alexander held it tightly.

Jonathan said, 'Does your eye give you much pain?'

'Not now. The water helped.'

They sat in silence for a while. A night bird called out, somewhere in the darkness. Once Jonathan, gazing round, thought that he saw a woman's face, pale and wraithlike amongst the trees; but he quickly realised that it was a statue, clad in smooth drapery that was mottled with lichen. He thought of Selene, goddess of the moon and sister of the sun. '*When Endymion, her lover, lay sunk in eternal sleep in a cave on Mount Latmos, he was visited nightly by Selene . . .*'

The breeze stirred sharply, bringing to them the sour stink of burning timber. The fire was dying now, exhausted by its own virulence. All was silent. As far as Jonathan could tell, no one had come to this isolated place to investigate the blaze. The great house, charred and smoke-blackened, reared its frame starkly into the sky.

Alexander said at last, 'I was able to show Guy his star, you know. Just before the end.'

Jonathan turned to him. 'The one they called Selene?'

Alexander smiled. 'Yes. He died thinking he had found it.'

'Only *thinking* he had found it?' said Jonathan slowly. 'You mean he hadn't?'

Alexander nodded. 'It had all the motions and the orbit of a planet, but I saw that it had no disc, and it was so small, Jonathan, even smaller than our moon. It may be a fragment of some larger planet that broke up long ago. But I said nothing of this to Guy. I let him die thinking that he had found Selene.'

So even the star had been an illusion; a hollow redemption; just as Jonathan had been finally, irrevocably thwarted in his quest to find his daughter's killer. What would he have done to Auguste, if he had found her in time? What could he have done?

Jonathan still held his brother's hand tightly. He said with an effort, because his throat ached so, 'There will be people looking for us. We must head for the country well before daybreak.'

'I will not know when it is daybreak.'

Jonathan wiped some tears from his cheek with the back of his hand. Dear God, he was a child again, and no more use to his brother than he had been to Ellie, and Thomas, and Mary, and Rose. He said, 'You will, because I will tell you. In fact I think I can already see a lightening in the sky, far away, to the east . . .' He paused. 'Alexander, there's a wonderful star up there. A single bright star, just above the horizon.'

'To the east? Then it's not a star, but a planet. It's Saturn,' said Alexander, smiling gently. 'If you could look through a telescope, you would see its rings. It was Cassini, you know, who first realised that the rings were not solid; they could not be, of course, for they would be disrupted by the gravitational pull of Saturn. There is a unique transparency in the outer band. Some day you must look for it.'

'Yes,' said Jonathan, 'yes, one day I will. And there's something else close by; a wonderful yellow star, surrounded by others, by thousands, it seems . . .'

'You're looking at Capella,' said Alexander with reverence. 'Capella, in Auriga, is one of the most brilliant of stars; it's circumpolar, but at times it almost grazes the horizon. Auriga, the constellation to which it belongs, is crossed by the Milky Way, and there are rich starfields close by where even the smallest of telescopes can discover great treasures. Look back now, towards Saturn; midway you will see another bright star.'

'Yes. Yes, I can see it . . .'

'That is Algol. It will be fading now, with the approach of dawn, but Algol can still be one of the brightest objects in the sky, though it varies, so much, sometimes even as you watch it. Some call it the Demon Star, others the Gorgon's Head. Watch, and it will wink at you.' He smiled to himself. 'I studied it when I sailed the oceans, and I learnt its moods. The Arabs thought of it as evil, but I think no stars are evil, only people. Next, you must look for the five linked stars of Cassiopeia . . .'

Jonathan sat beside his brother in the dew-damp grass, and they both turned their backs on the shell of the charred house, where sparks still fluttered in the night breeze.

With a kind of calm joy, Alexander lifted his bright, blind face to the sky, and talked to his brother about the stars.

Postscript

This is a work of fiction. However, the following notes may be of interest.

After the defeat in Holland in the spring of 1795, the possibility of an invasion by the victorious forces of the French Republic caused very real concern to the British government. Rumours of spying activity were rife, and French *émigrés* in London came particularly under suspicion.

The Brittany landings, and the massacre of the British-backed Royalist army, took place in the summer of 1795. The Chevalier de Tinténiac's force was crucially diverted by a message purportedly from the Royalist Agency, which the Agency denied all knowledge of.

From the moment the news of the disaster broke, there were accusations that the expedition had been deliberately betrayed by a faction in the British government, in order to destroy any possibility of a heavy British commitment of troops in mainland France. The leaders of the Royalist cause were bitter in their claims of treachery; but the question of responsibility for the Quiberon disaster was also raised in parliament, by Fox and Sheridan. Responsibility for the disaster has been laid at various times on the possible duplicity of Spain, whose government was about to sign a peace treaty with France; on the inefficiency of the staff of the Admiralty, who gave conflicting orders to Puisaye and to d'Hervilly, and on the Royalist Agency, which always denied the authorship of the letter, and which was indeed unlikely to wish to cause the deaths of so many French officers, many of them of noble blood.

One of my chief sources for this story was John Ehrman's book *The Younger Pitt* (Volume 2), published by Constable in 1983. Ehrman discusses the various allegations of deliberate betrayal, and states that the whole matter was never successfully resolved but has been a subject of contention for historians 'from that day to this'.

Astronomy in the late eighteenth century

Since the time of Kepler, there had been serious conjecture about the possibility of a missing planet in the solar system. In the eighteenth century the mathematical theory of Titius, giving a numerical ratio for the distances of the planets from the sun which was developed and publicised by Bode in 1772, gave further impetus to the search for this planet.

Herschel's new planet at the outer limit of the solar system, which was discovered in 1781 and known as the Georgian planet until its name was officially confirmed in 1850 as Uranus, fitted into Titius's sequence of figures almost exactly. An international group of astronomers known as the 'Celestial Police' was established, in a renewed effort to find the planet that would fit into the tantalising gap between Mars and Jupiter; but none of these astronomers got as far as Guy and Alexander, in my story, until 1801, when an Italian monk, Piazzi, discovered Ceres, and found it was orbiting according to Titius's predictions.

Disappointingly, Ceres turned out to be too small to be ranked with the other planets; and soon other, similar bodies were found, also orbiting between Mars and Jupiter. William Herschel gave them the name of 'asteroid', or minor planet. For some time, these asteroids were thought to be the remains of a major planet, long since broken up; so Titius's celebrated prediction of the lost planet lying between Mars and Jupiter did appear, for a while, to be true.

But a further blow to the Titius–Bode law was struck when Neptune and Pluto were discovered, because their orbits failed to fit the theory. Whether the relationship between the other planets, described so accurately by the law, is anything other than coincidence is not known, but the matter continues to exert fascination amongst those interested in the history of astronomy.